KICK-ASS

KICK-ASS: THE NEW GIRL, VOL. 3. First printing. DECEMBER 2019. Published by Image Comics, Inc. Office of publication: 2701 NW Vaughn St., Suite 780, Portland, OR 97210. Copyright © 2010, 2011, 2012, 2013, and 2019 Dave and Eggsy Ltd. and John S. Romita. All rights reserved. Contains material originally published in single magazine form as KICK-ASS #13-18. "KICK-ASS", the KICK-ASS logos, and the likenesses of all characters and institutions herein are trademarks of Dave and Eggsy Ltd. and John S. Romita, unless otherwise noted. "Image" and the Image Comics logos are registered trademarks of Image Comics, Inc. No part of this publication may be reproduced or transmitted, in any form or by any means (except for short excerpts for journalistic or review purposes), without the express written permission of Dave and Eggsy Ltd. and John S. Romita, or Image Comics, Inc. All names, characters, events, and locales in this publication are entirely fictional. Any resemblance to actual persons (living or dead), events, or places, without satirical intent, is coincidental. Printed in the USA. For information regarding the CPSIA on this printed material call: 203-595-3636. For international rights, contact: lucy@markmillarltd.com ISBN: 978-1-5343-1349-1.

Fountaindale Public Library
Bolingbrook, IL
(630) 759-2102

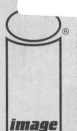

IMAGE COMICS, INC.
Robert Kirkman — Chief Operating Officer
Erik Larsen — Chief Financial Officer
Todd McFarlane — President
Marc Silvestri — Chief Executive Officer
Jim Valentino — Vice President
Eric Stephenson — Publisher / Chief Creative Officer
Jeff Boison — Director of Publishing Planning
                    & Book Trade Sales
Chris Ross — Director of Digital Sales
Jeff Stang — Director of Direct Market Sales
Kat Salazar — Director of PR & Marketing
Drew Gill — Cover Editor
Heather Doornink — Production Director
Nicole Lapalme — Controller

IMAGECOMICS.COM

STEVE NILES
WRITER

MARCELO FRUSIN
ARTIST

SUNNY GHO
COLORIST

JOHN WORKMAN
LETTERER

MELINA MIKULIC
DESIGN AND PRODUCTION

RACHAEL FULTON
EDITOR

COLLECTION COVER ARTISTS:
CHRISTIAN WARD
AMY REEDER

HIT-GIRL and **KICK-ASS** created by
MARK MILLAR and **JOHN ROMITA JR**.

ONE

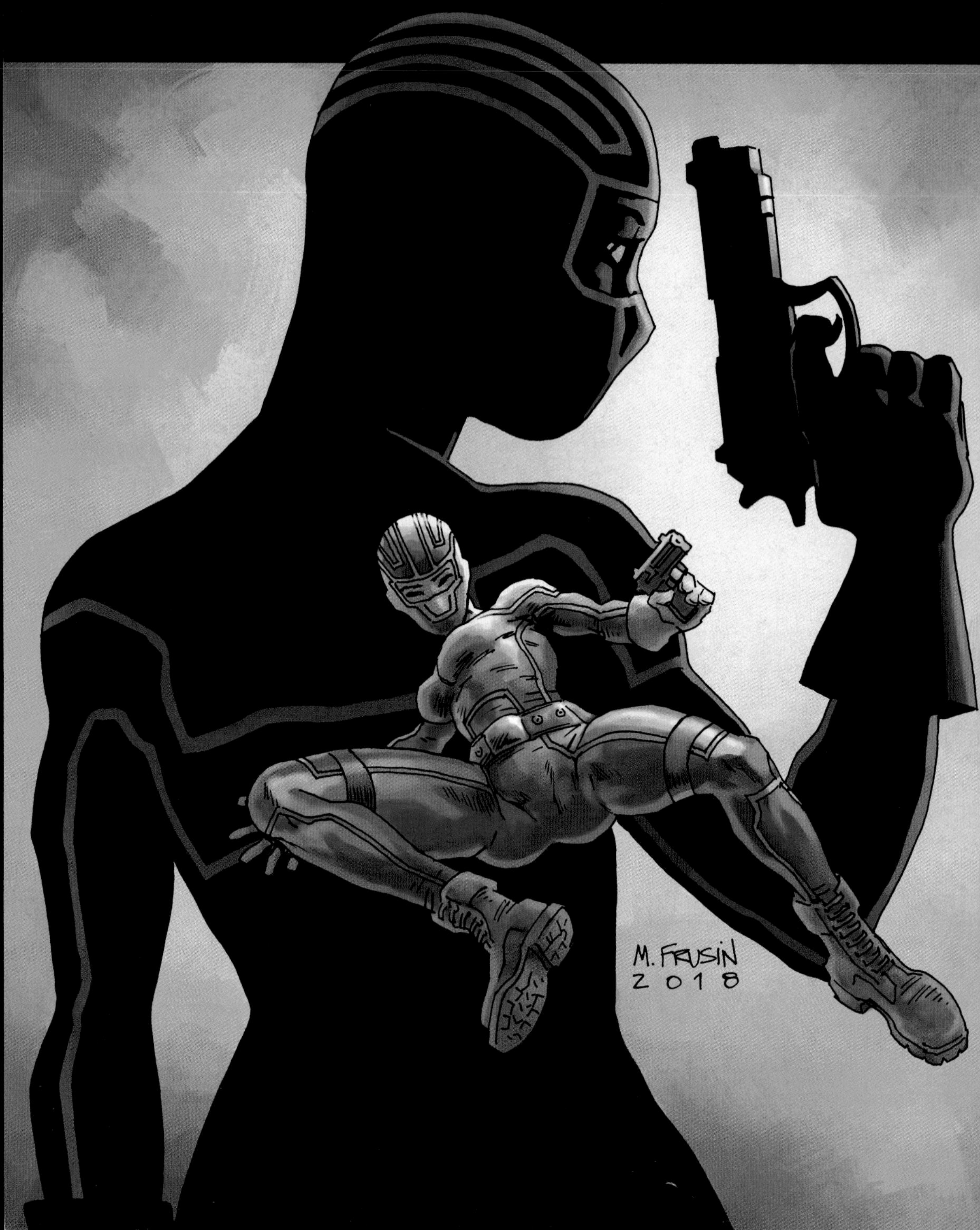
M. FRUSIN
2018

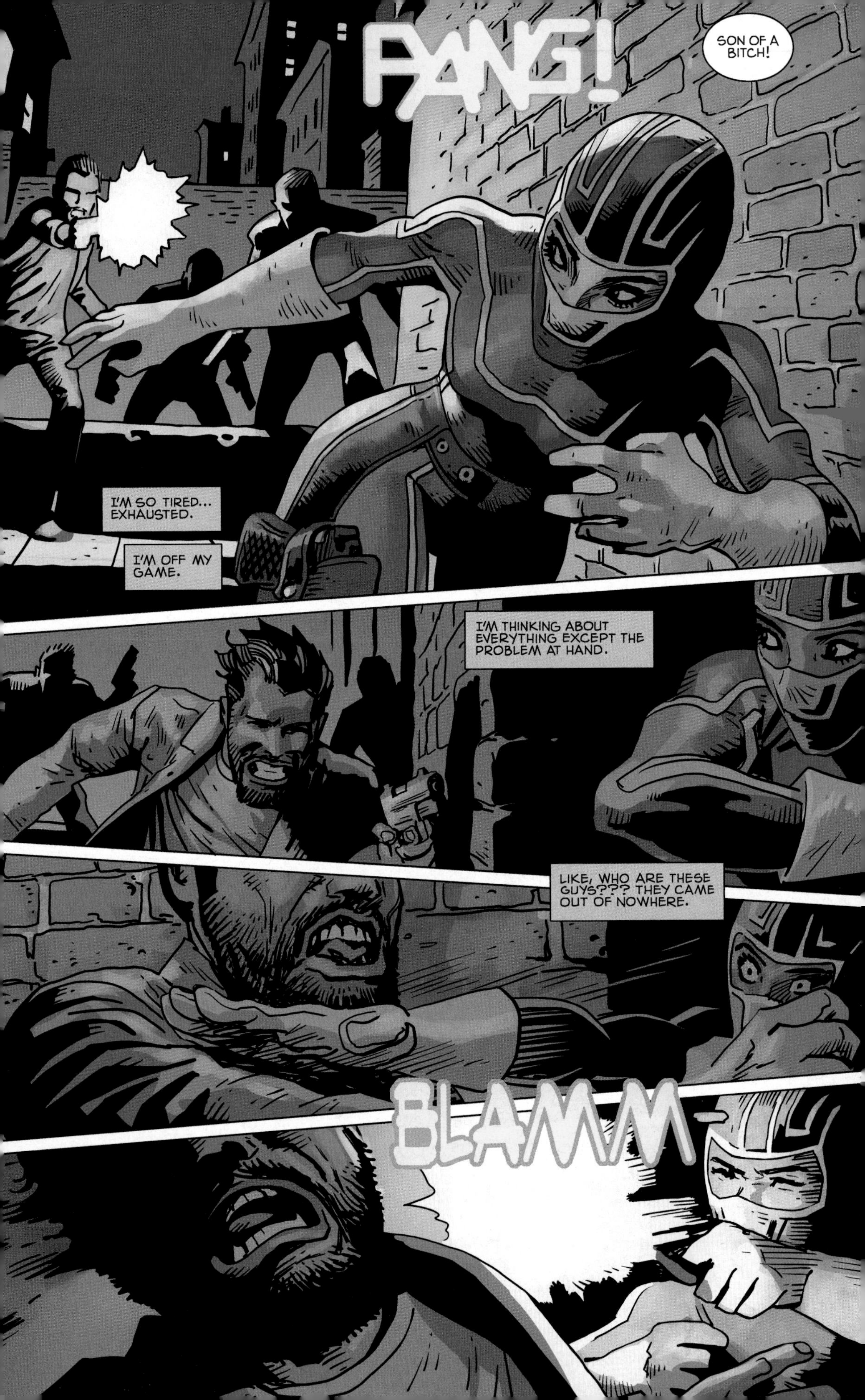
PANG!
SON OF A BITCH!
I'M SO TIRED... EXHAUSTED.
I'M OFF MY GAME.
I'M THINKING ABOUT EVERYTHING EXCEPT THE PROBLEM AT HAND.
LIKE, WHO ARE THESE GUYS??? THEY CAME OUT OF NOWHERE.
BLAMM

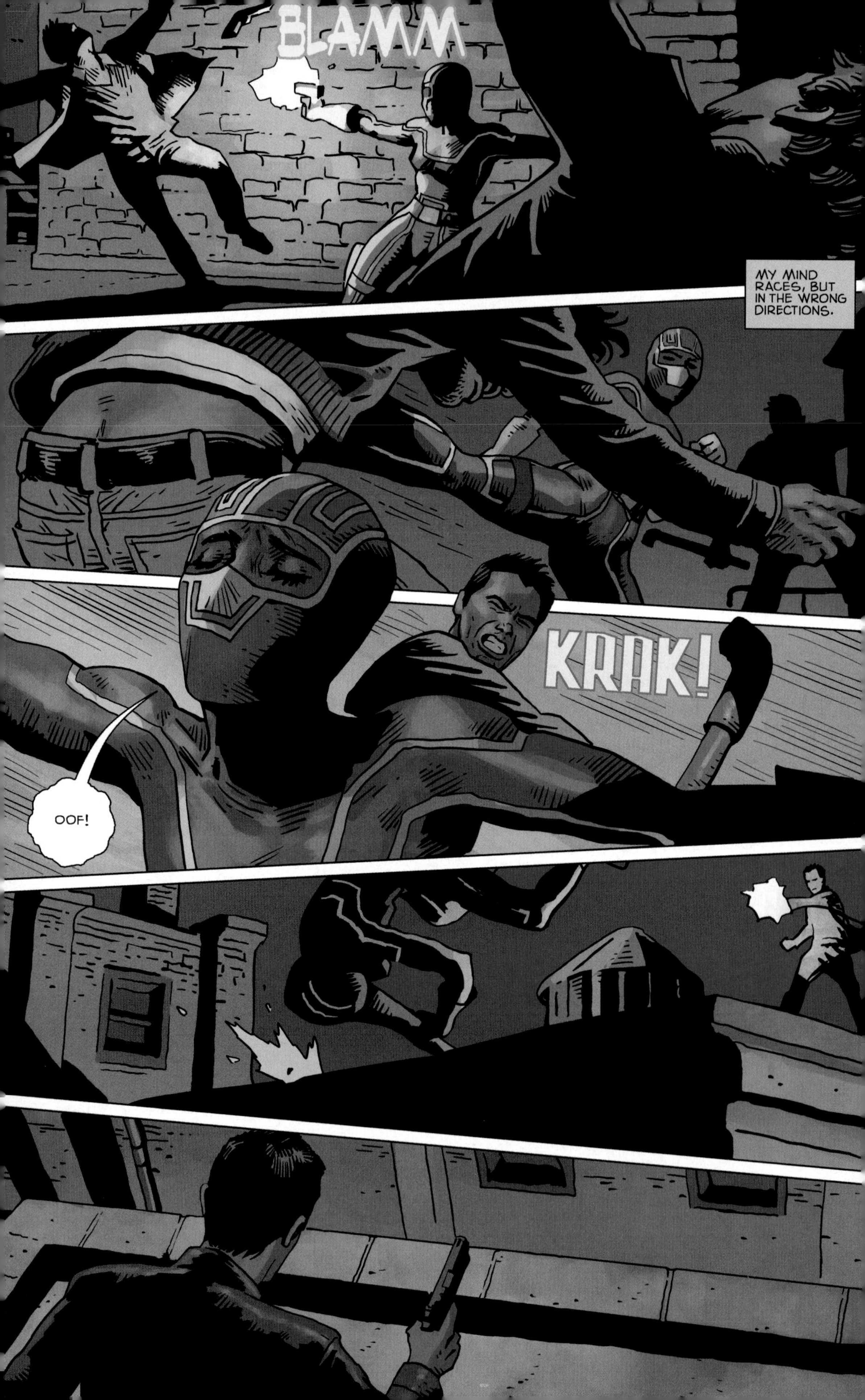
BLAMM
MY MIND RACES, BUT IN THE WRONG DIRECTIONS.
KRAK!
OOF!

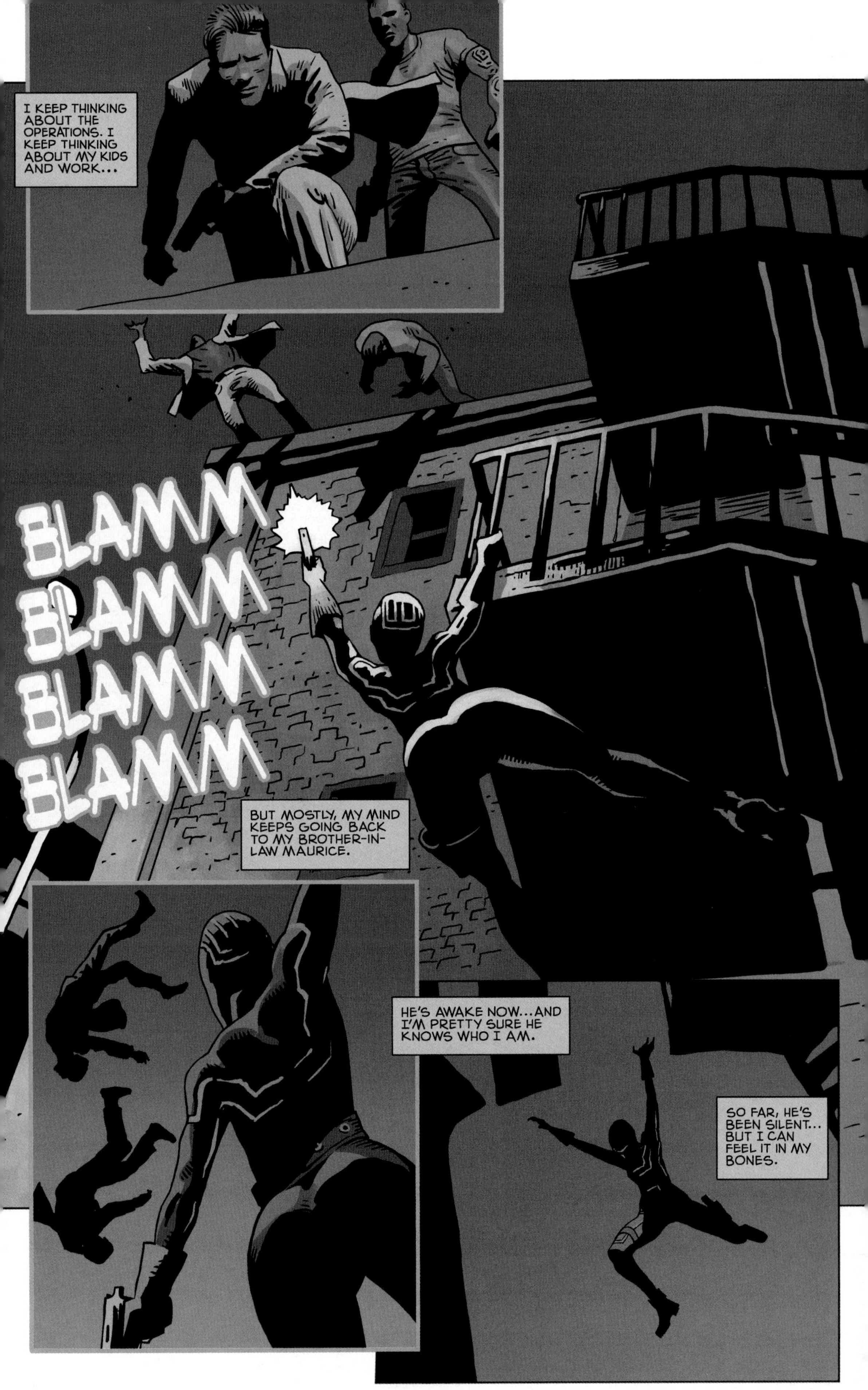
I KEEP THINKING ABOUT THE OPERATIONS. I KEEP THINKING ABOUT MY KIDS AND WORK...
BLAMM BLAMM BLAMM BLAMM
BUT MOSTLY, MY MIND KEEPS GOING BACK TO MY BROTHER-IN-LAW MAURICE.
HE'S AWAKE NOW...AND I'M PRETTY SURE HE KNOWS WHO I AM.
SO FAR, HE'S BEEN SILENT... BUT I CAN FEEL IT IN MY BONES.

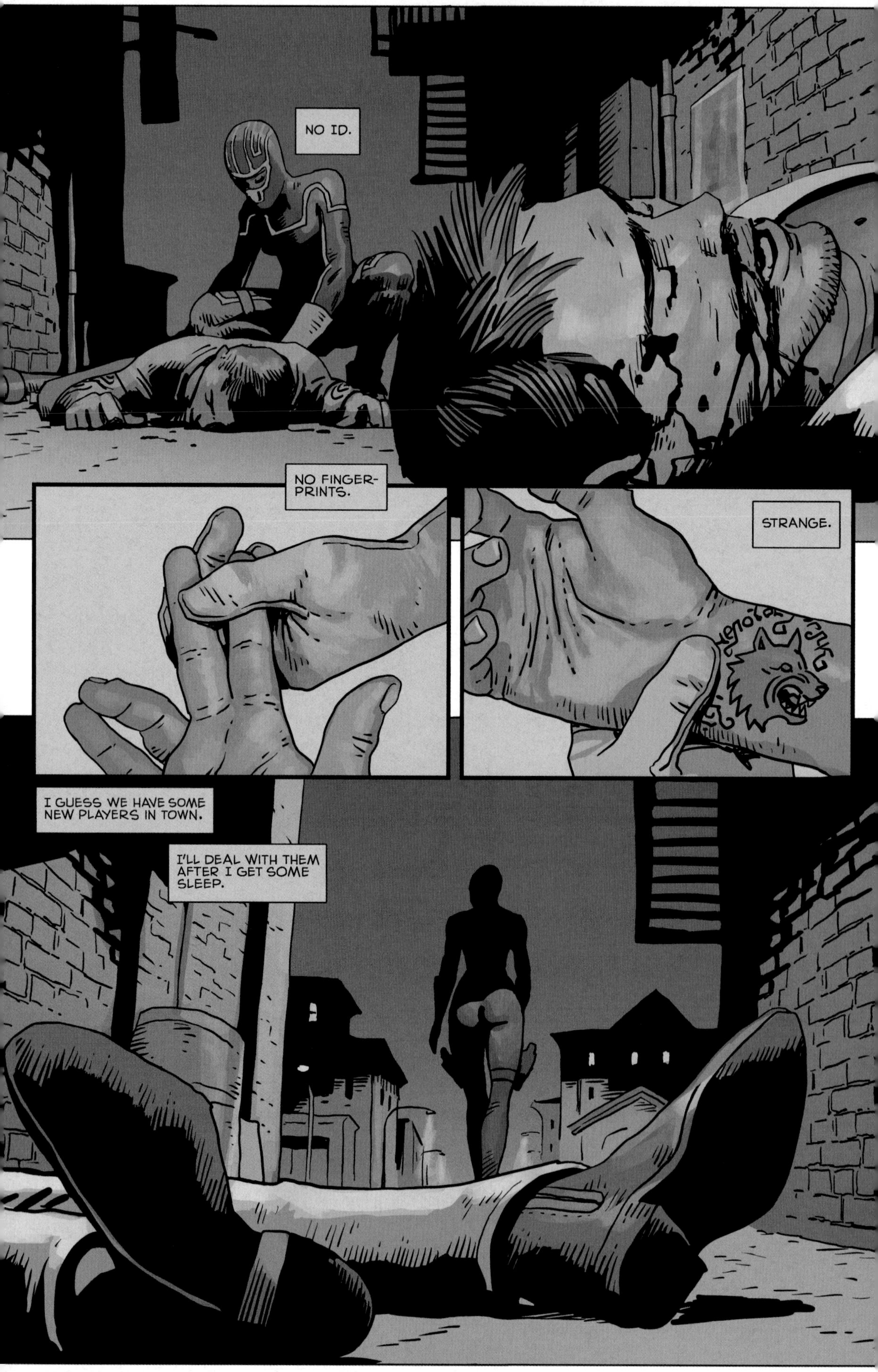
NO ID.
NO FINGER-PRINTS.
STRANGE.
I GUESS WE HAVE SOME NEW PLAYERS IN TOWN.
I'LL DEAL WITH THEM AFTER I GET SOME SLEEP.

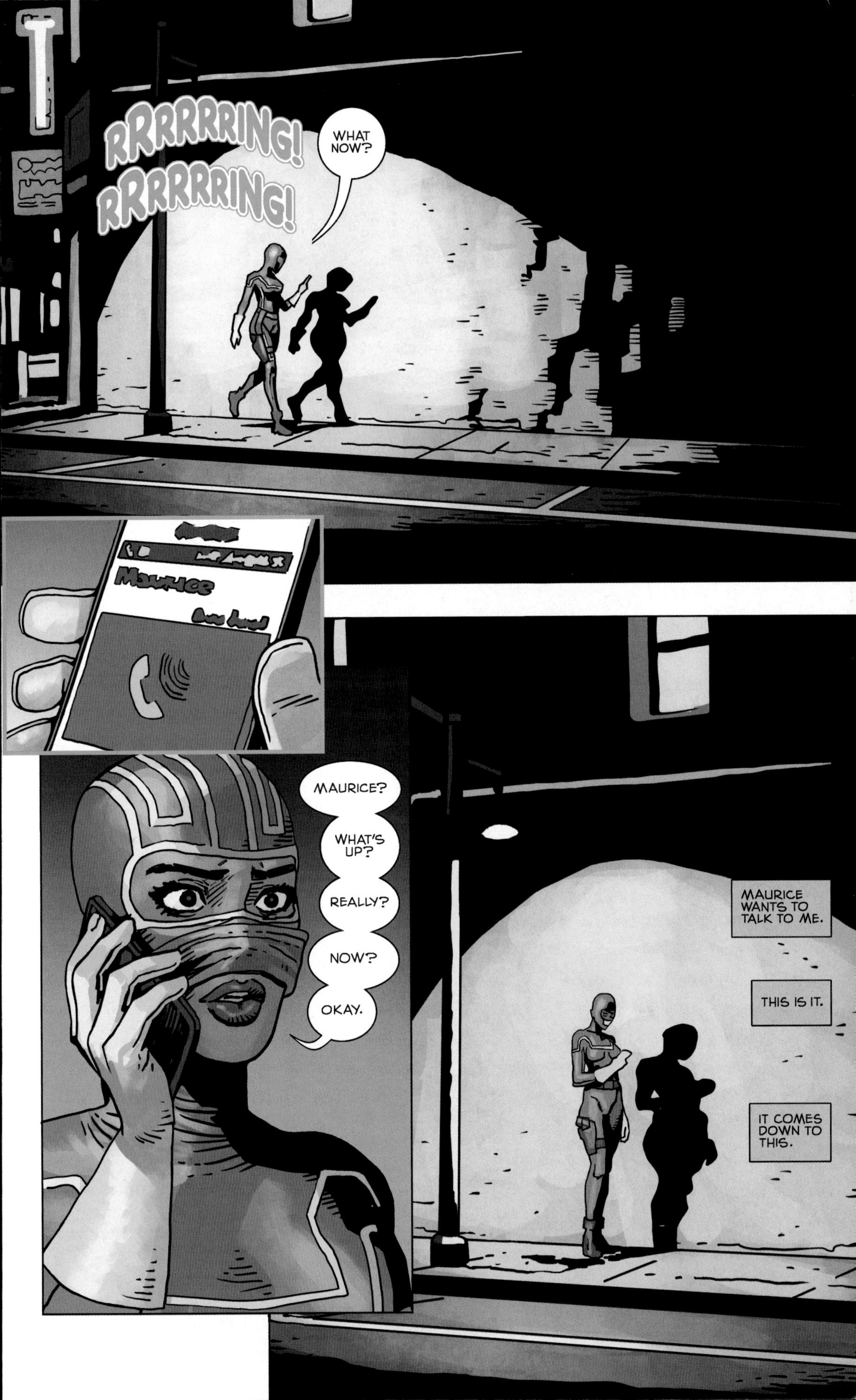
RRRRRRING!
RRRRRRING!
WHAT NOW?
Maurice
MAURICE?
WHAT'S UP?
REALLY?
NOW?
OKAY.
MAURICE WANTS TO TALK TO ME.
THIS IS IT.
IT COMES DOWN TO THIS.

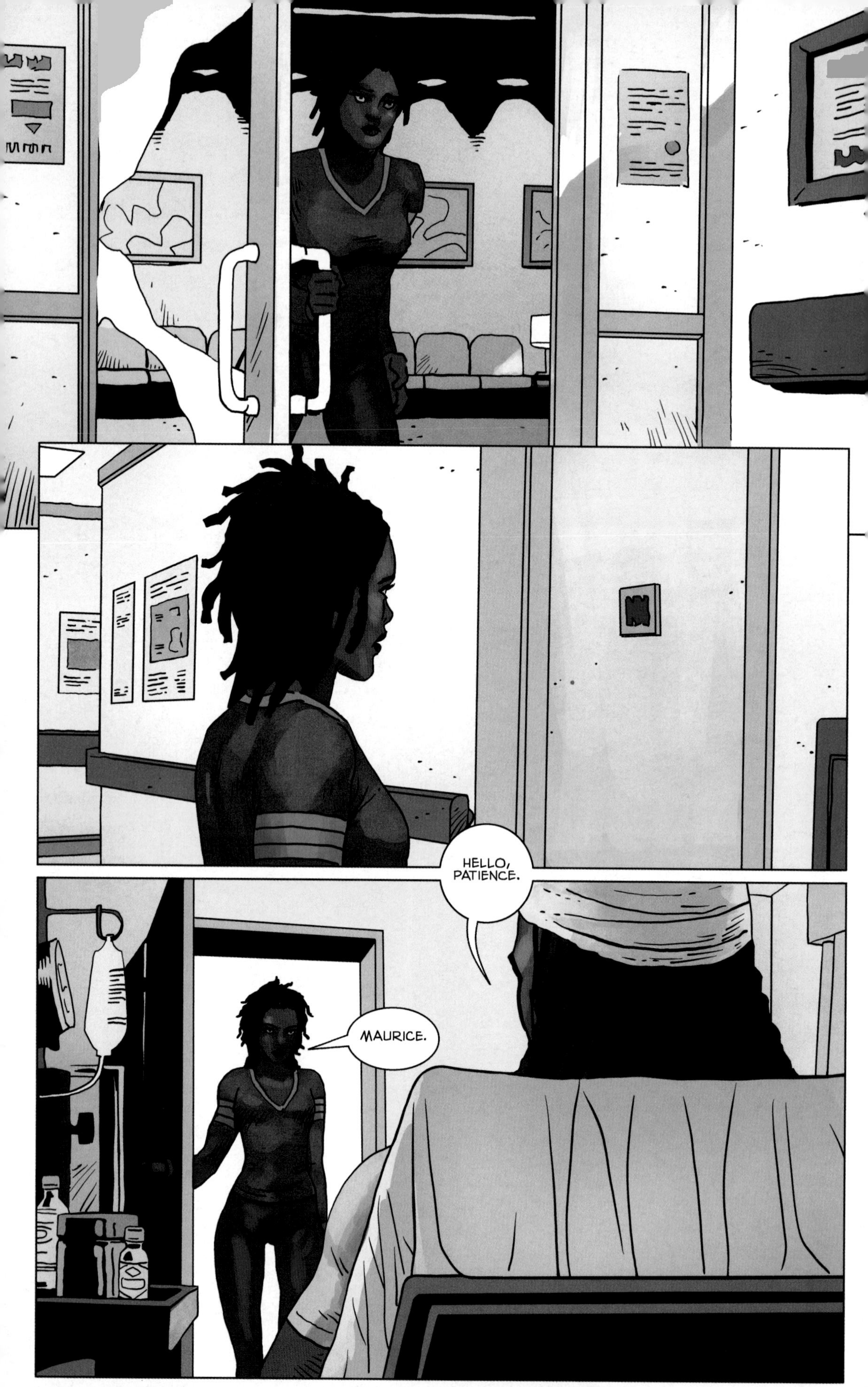
HELLO, PATIENCE.
MAURICE.

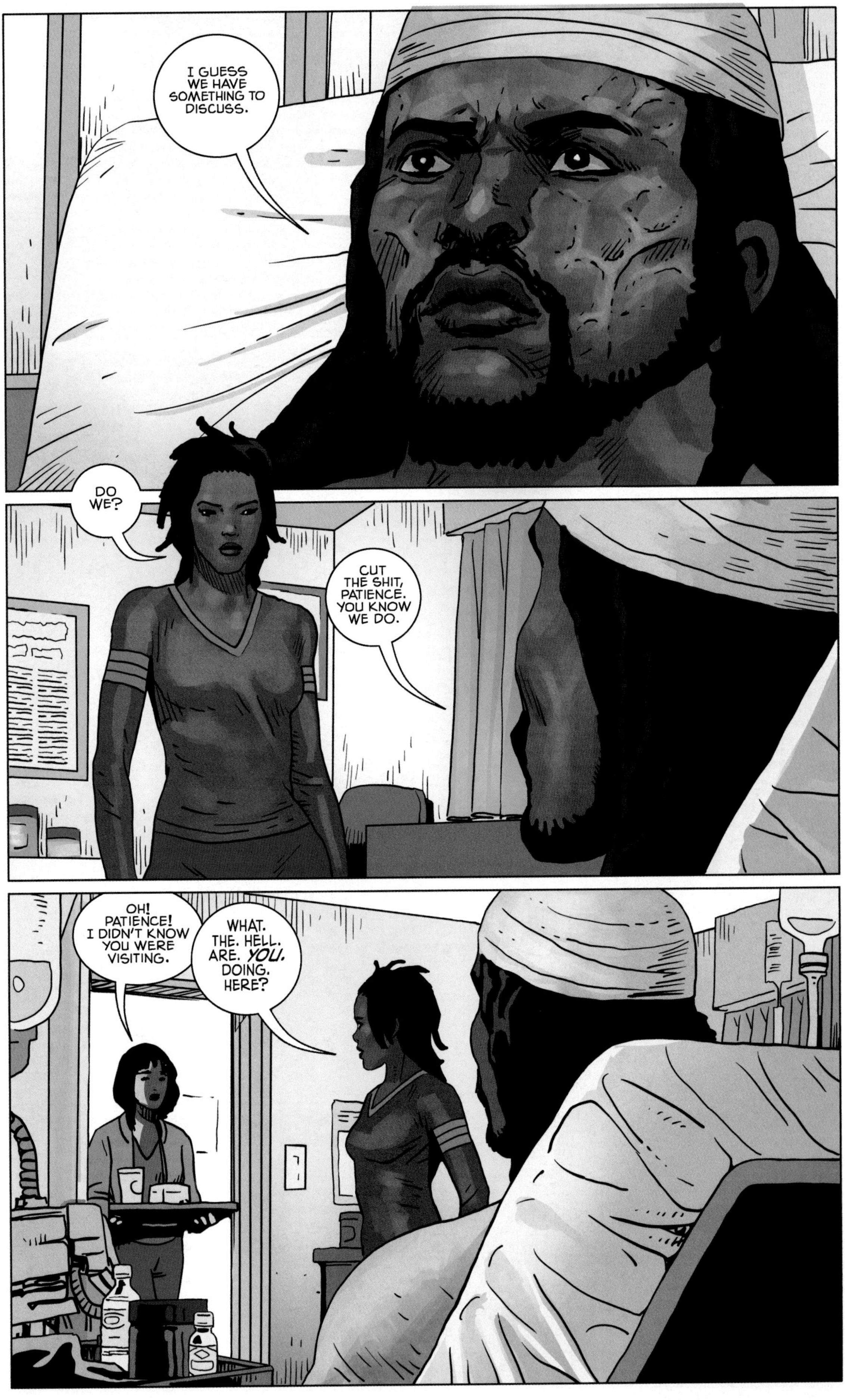
I GUESS WE HAVE SOMETHING TO DISCUSS.
DO WE?
CUT THE SHIT, PATIENCE. YOU KNOW WE DO.
OH! PATIENCE! I DIDN'T KNOW YOU WERE VISITING.
WHAT. THE. HELL. ARE. *YOU.* DOING. HERE?

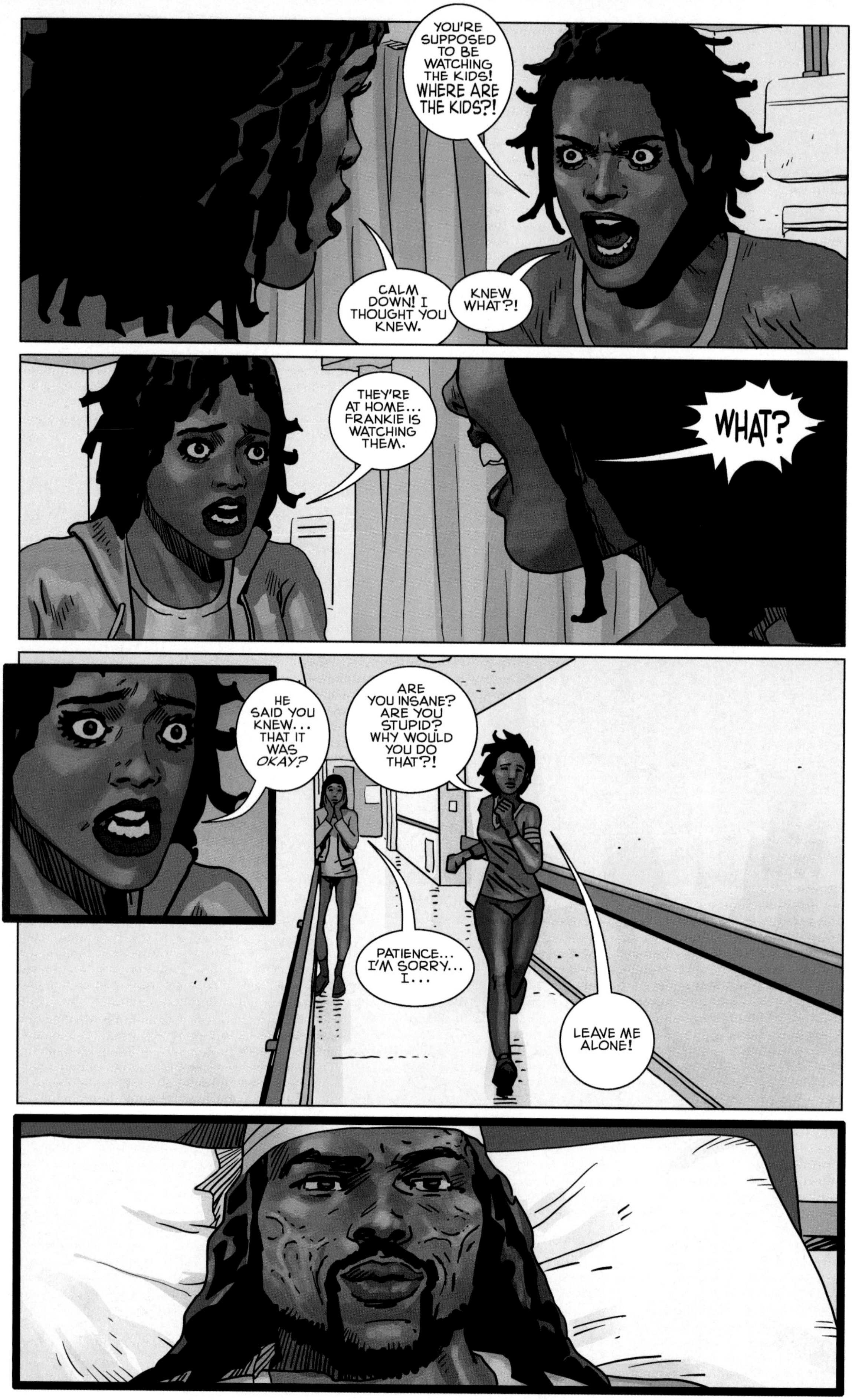
YOU'RE SUPPOSED TO BE WATCHING THE KIDS! WHERE ARE THE KIDS?!
CALM DOWN! I THOUGHT YOU KNEW.
KNEW WHAT?!
THEY'RE AT HOME... FRANKIE IS WATCHING THEM.
WHAT?
HE SAID YOU KNEW... THAT IT WAS *OKAY?*
ARE YOU INSANE? ARE YOU STUPID? WHY WOULD YOU DO THAT?!
PATIENCE... I'M SORRY... I...
LEAVE ME ALONE!

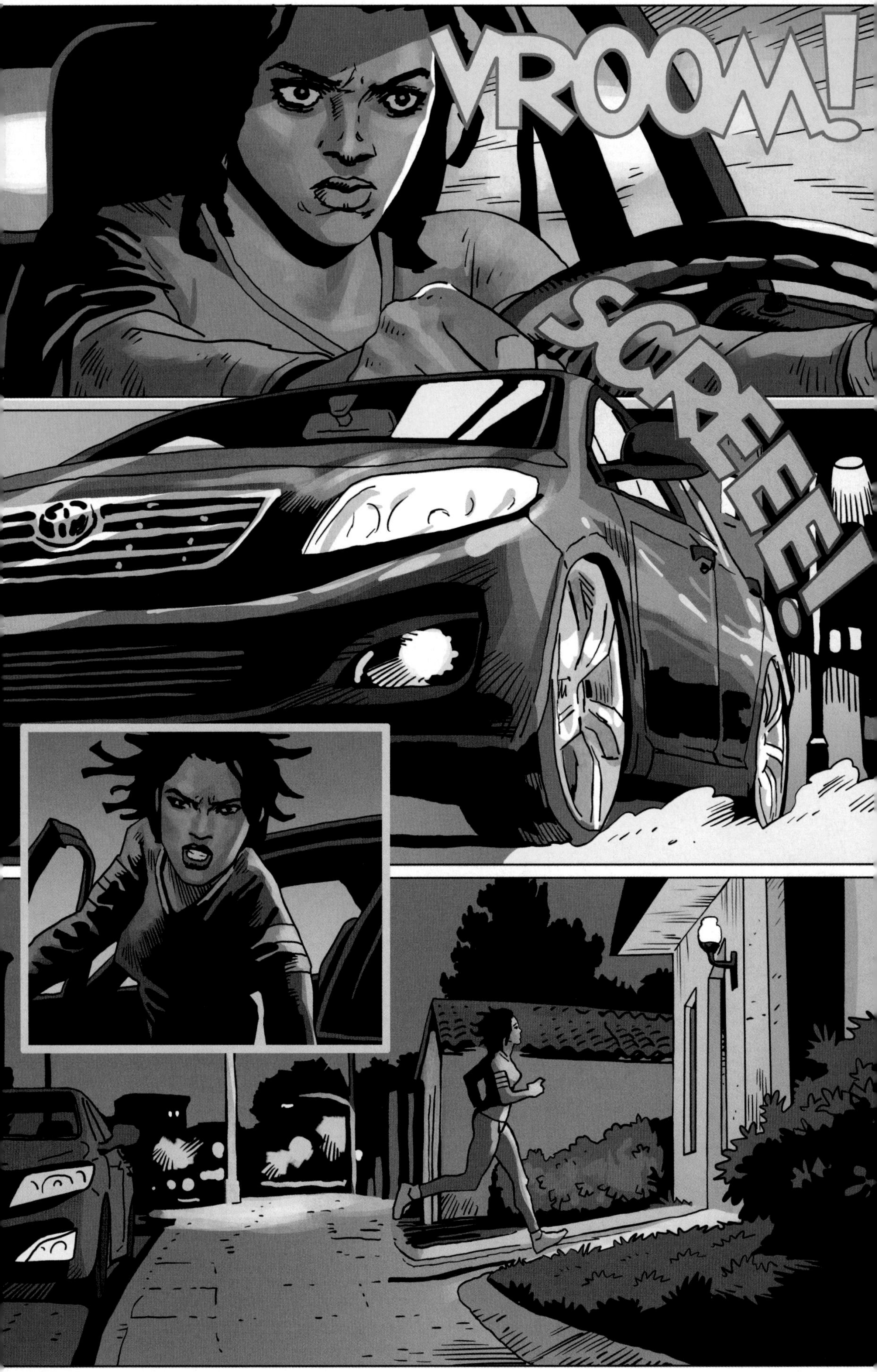
VROOM!
SCREEE!

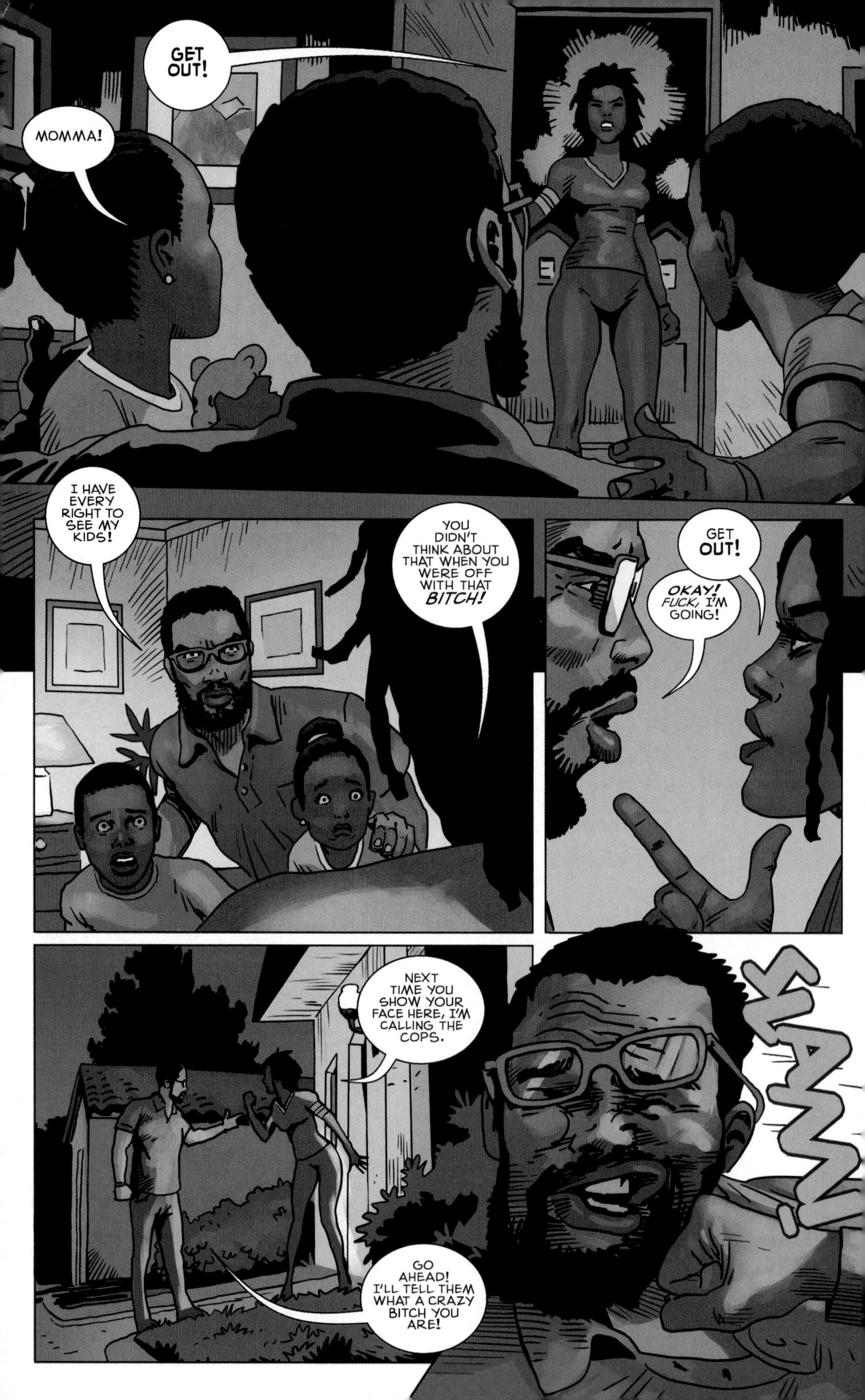
GET OUT!
MOMMA!
I HAVE EVERY RIGHT TO SEE MY KIDS!
YOU DIDN'T THINK ABOUT THAT WHEN YOU WERE OFF WITH THAT *BITCH!*
GET **OUT!**
OKAY! FUCK, I'M GOING!
NEXT TIME YOU SHOW YOUR FACE HERE, I'M CALLING THE COPS.
GO AHEAD! I'LL TELL THEM WHAT A CRAZY BITCH YOU ARE!
SLAM

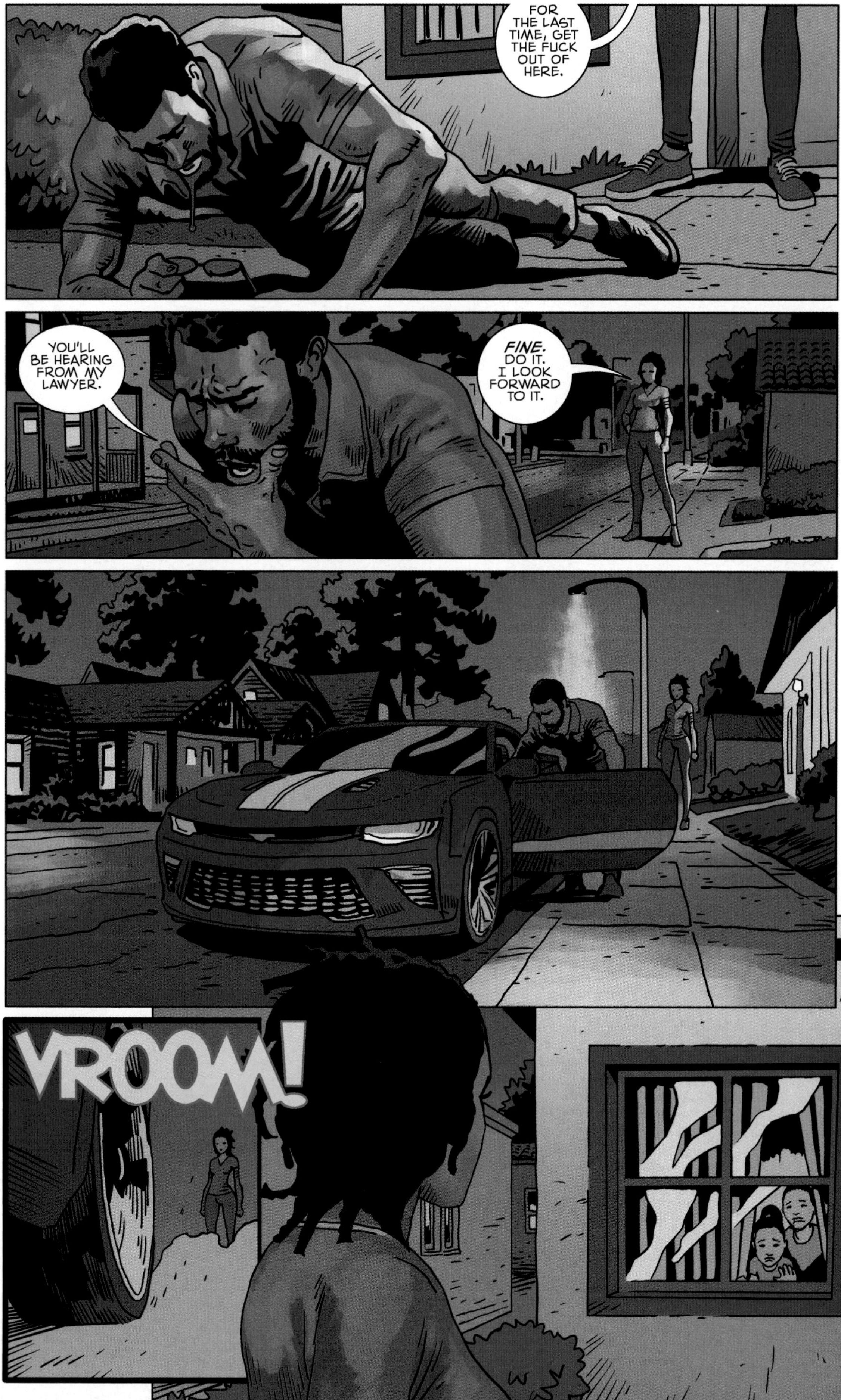
FOR THE LAST TIME, GET THE FUCK OUT OF HERE.
YOU'LL BE HEARING FROM MY LAWYER.
FINE. DO IT. I LOOK FORWARD TO IT.
VROOM!

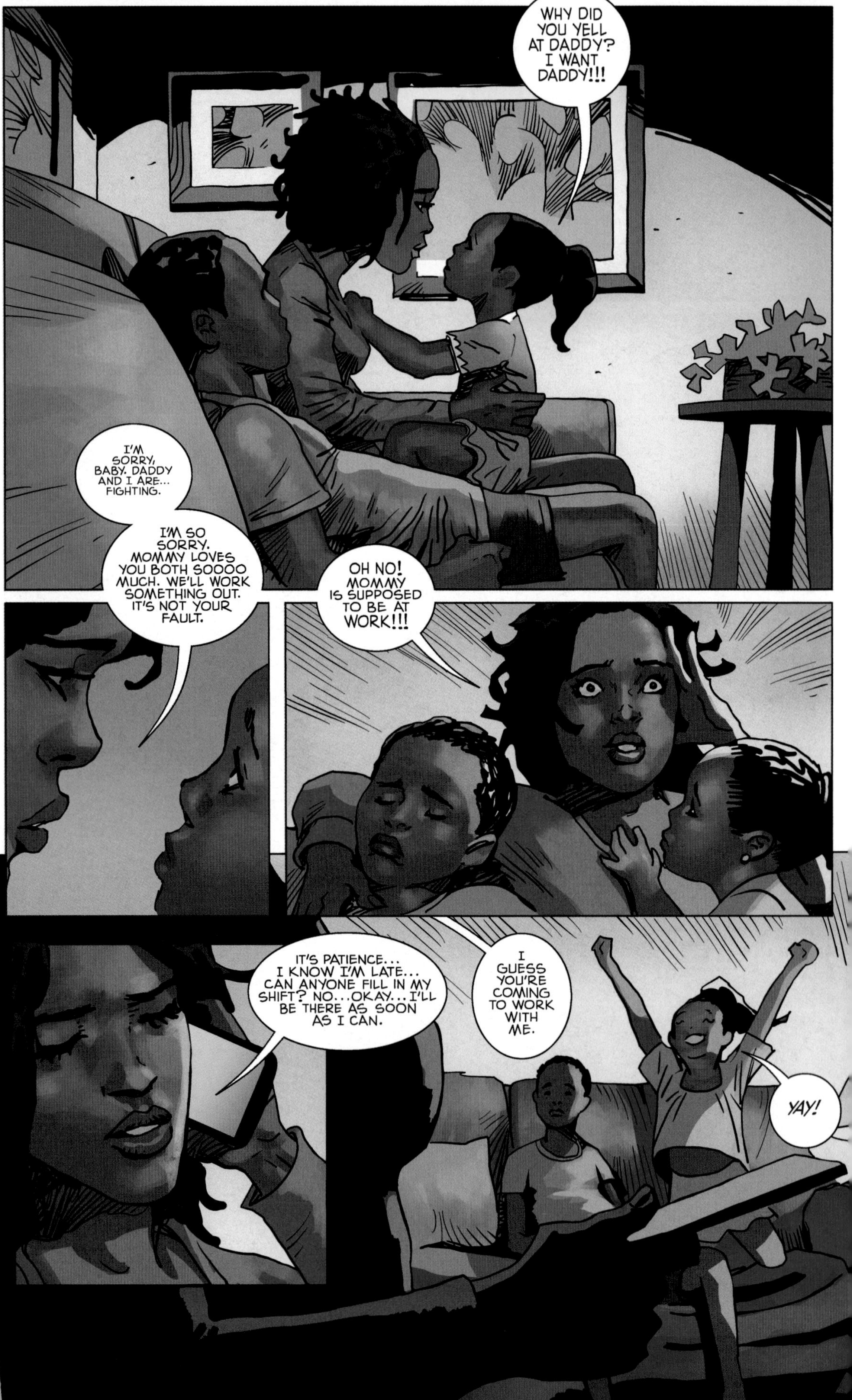
WHY DID YOU YELL AT DADDY? I WANT DADDY!!!
I'M SORRY, BABY. DADDY AND I ARE... FIGHTING.
I'M SO SORRY. MOMMY LOVES YOU BOTH SOOOO MUCH. WE'LL WORK SOMETHING OUT. IT'S NOT YOUR FAULT.
OH NO! MOMMY IS SUPPOSED TO BE AT WORK!!!
IT'S PATIENCE... I KNOW I'M LATE... CAN ANYONE FILL IN MY SHIFT? NO...OKAY... I'LL BE THERE AS SOON AS I CAN.
I GUESS YOU'RE COMING TO WORK WITH ME.
YAY!

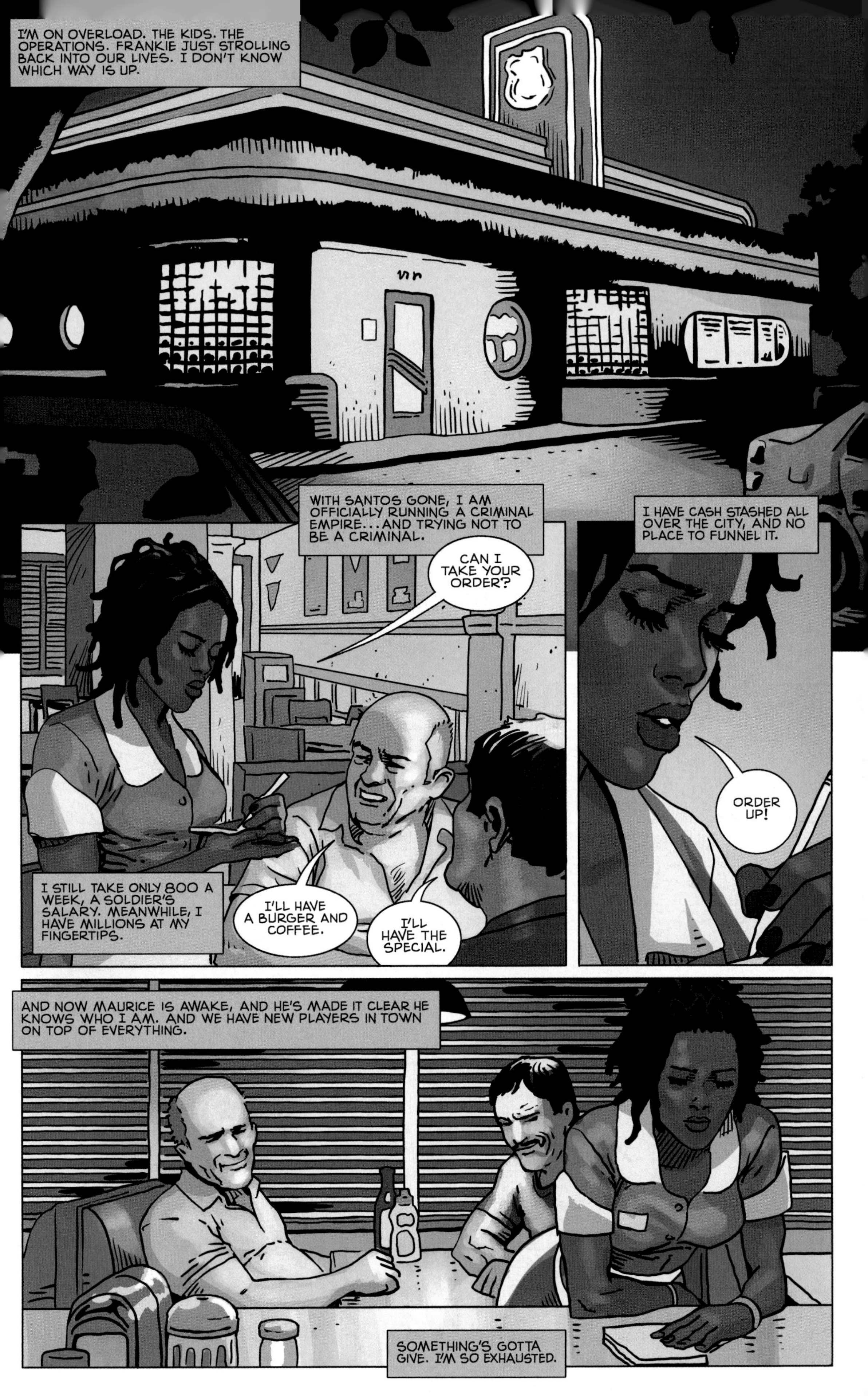
I'M ON OVERLOAD. THE KIDS. THE OPERATIONS. FRANKIE JUST STROLLING BACK INTO OUR LIVES. I DON'T KNOW WHICH WAY IS UP.
WITH SANTOS GONE, I AM OFFICIALLY RUNNING A CRIMINAL EMPIRE...AND TRYING NOT TO BE A CRIMINAL.
CAN I TAKE YOUR ORDER?
I STILL TAKE ONLY 800 A WEEK, A SOLDIER'S SALARY. MEANWHILE, I HAVE MILLIONS AT MY FINGERTIPS.
I'LL HAVE A BURGER AND COFFEE.
I'LL HAVE THE SPECIAL.
I HAVE CASH STASHED ALL OVER THE CITY, AND NO PLACE TO FUNNEL IT.
ORDER UP!
AND NOW MAURICE IS AWAKE, AND HE'S MADE IT CLEAR HE KNOWS WHO I AM. AND WE HAVE NEW PLAYERS IN TOWN ON TOP OF EVERYTHING.
SOMETHING'S GOTTA GIVE. I'M SO EXHAUSTED.

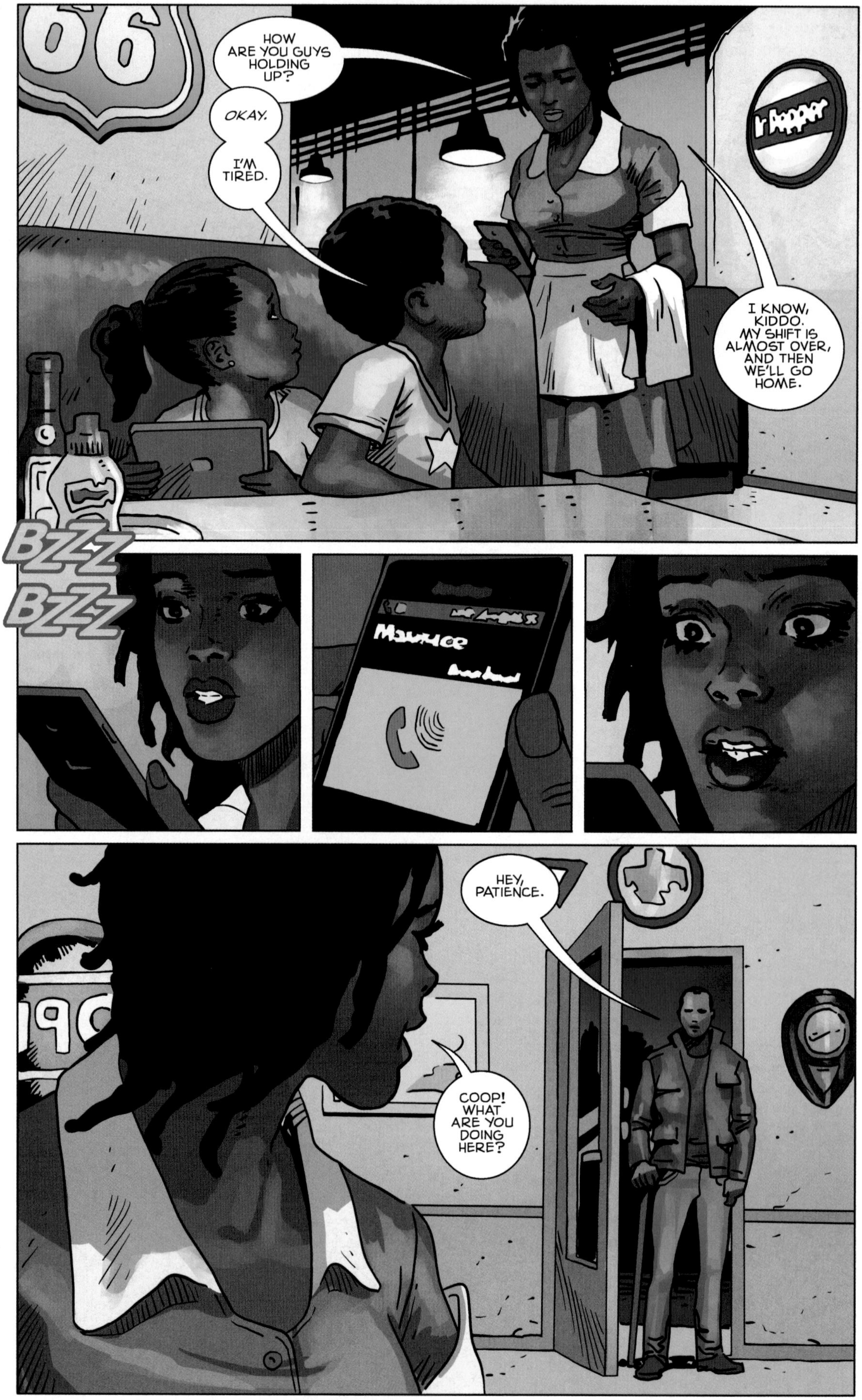

HOW ARE YOU GUYS HOLDING UP?
OKAY.
I'M TIRED.
I KNOW, KIDDO. MY SHIFT IS ALMOST OVER, AND THEN WE'LL GO HOME.
BZZZ BZZZ
HEY, PATIENCE.
COOP! WHAT ARE YOU DOING HERE?

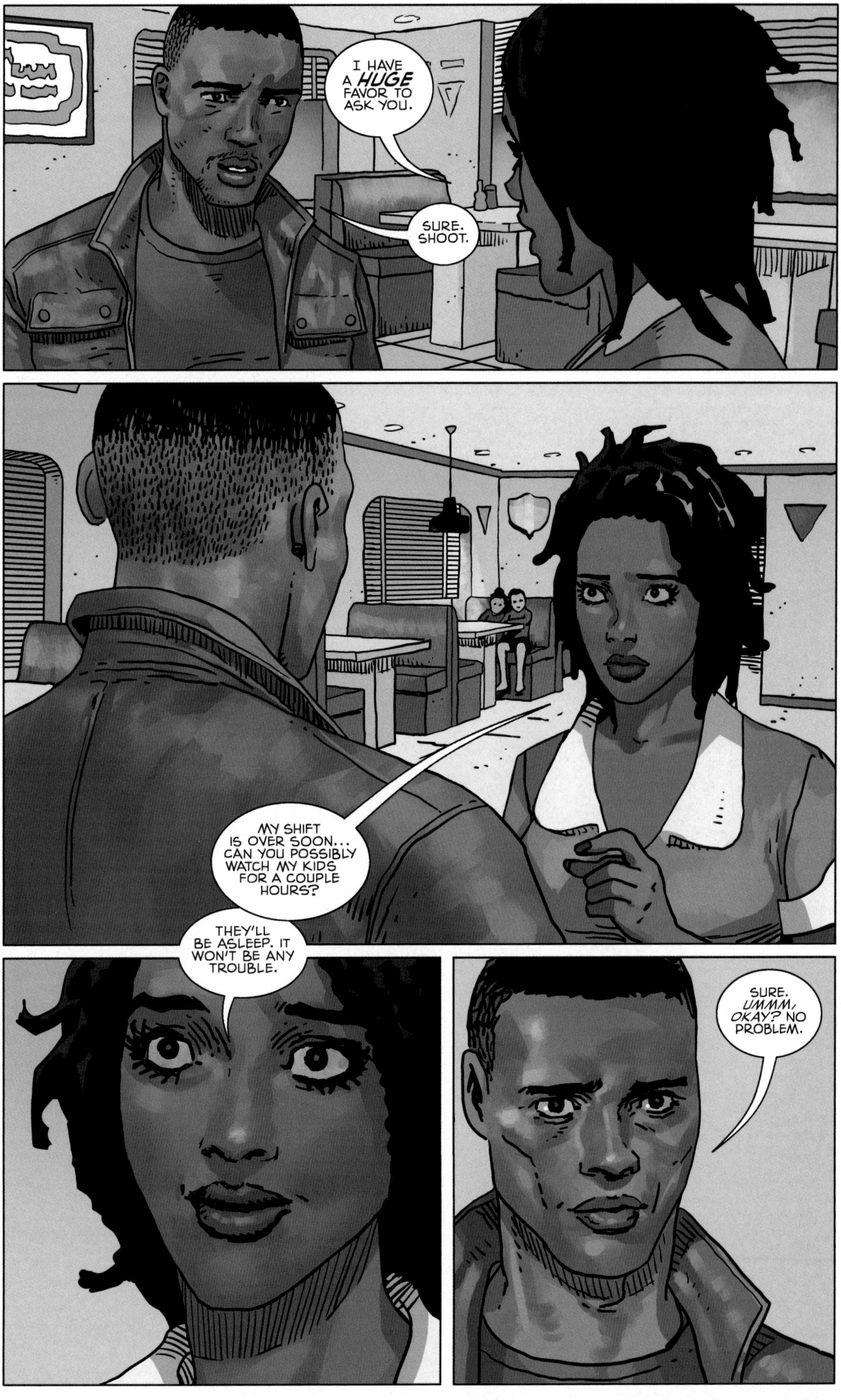
I HAVE A *HUGE* FAVOR TO ASK YOU.
SURE. SHOOT.
MY SHIFT IS OVER SOON... CAN YOU POSSIBLY WATCH MY KIDS FOR A COUPLE HOURS?
THEY'LL BE ASLEEP. IT WON'T BE ANY TROUBLE.
SURE. *UMMM, OKAY?* NO PROBLEM.

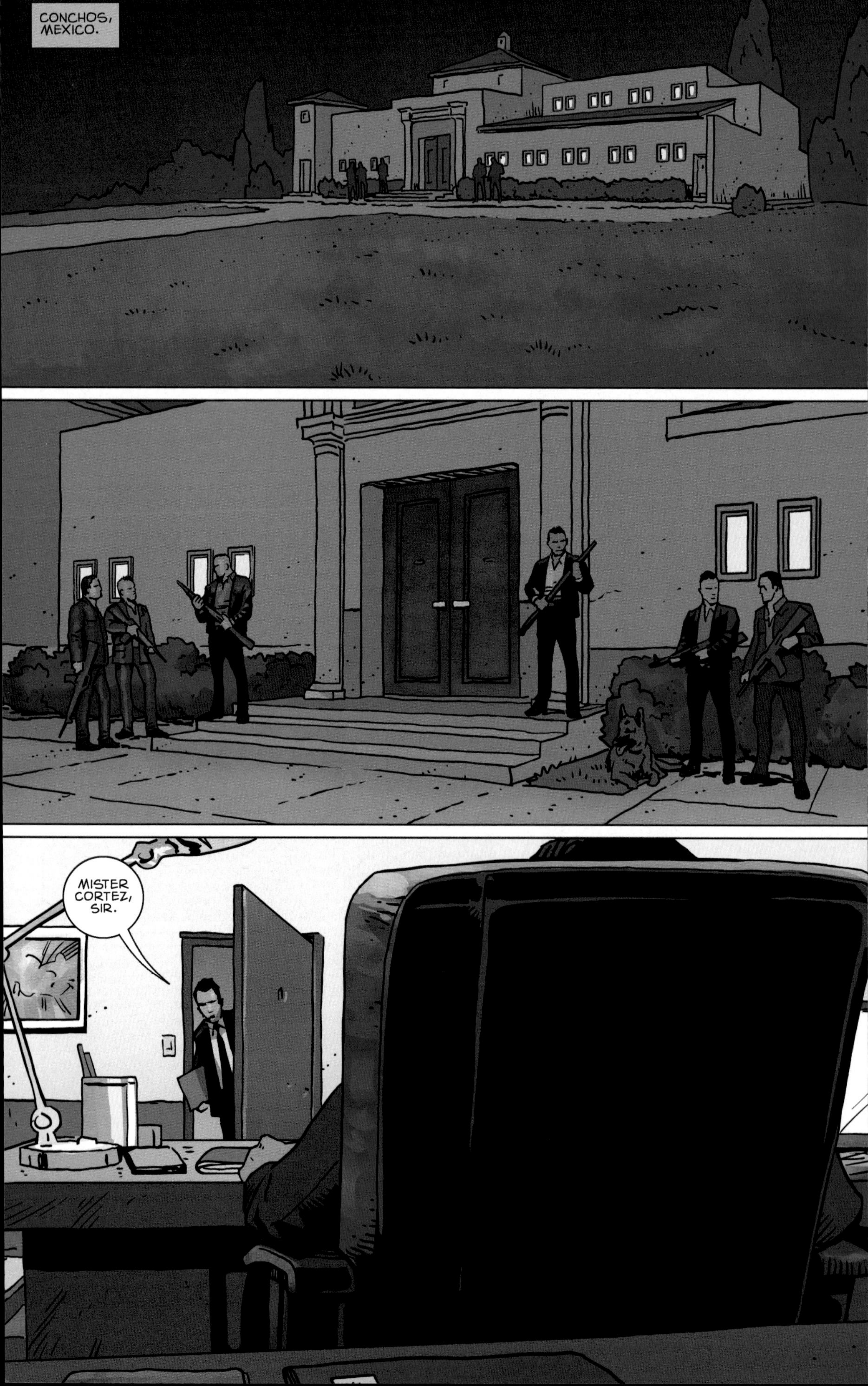
CONCHOS, MEXICO.
MISTER CORTEZ, SIR.

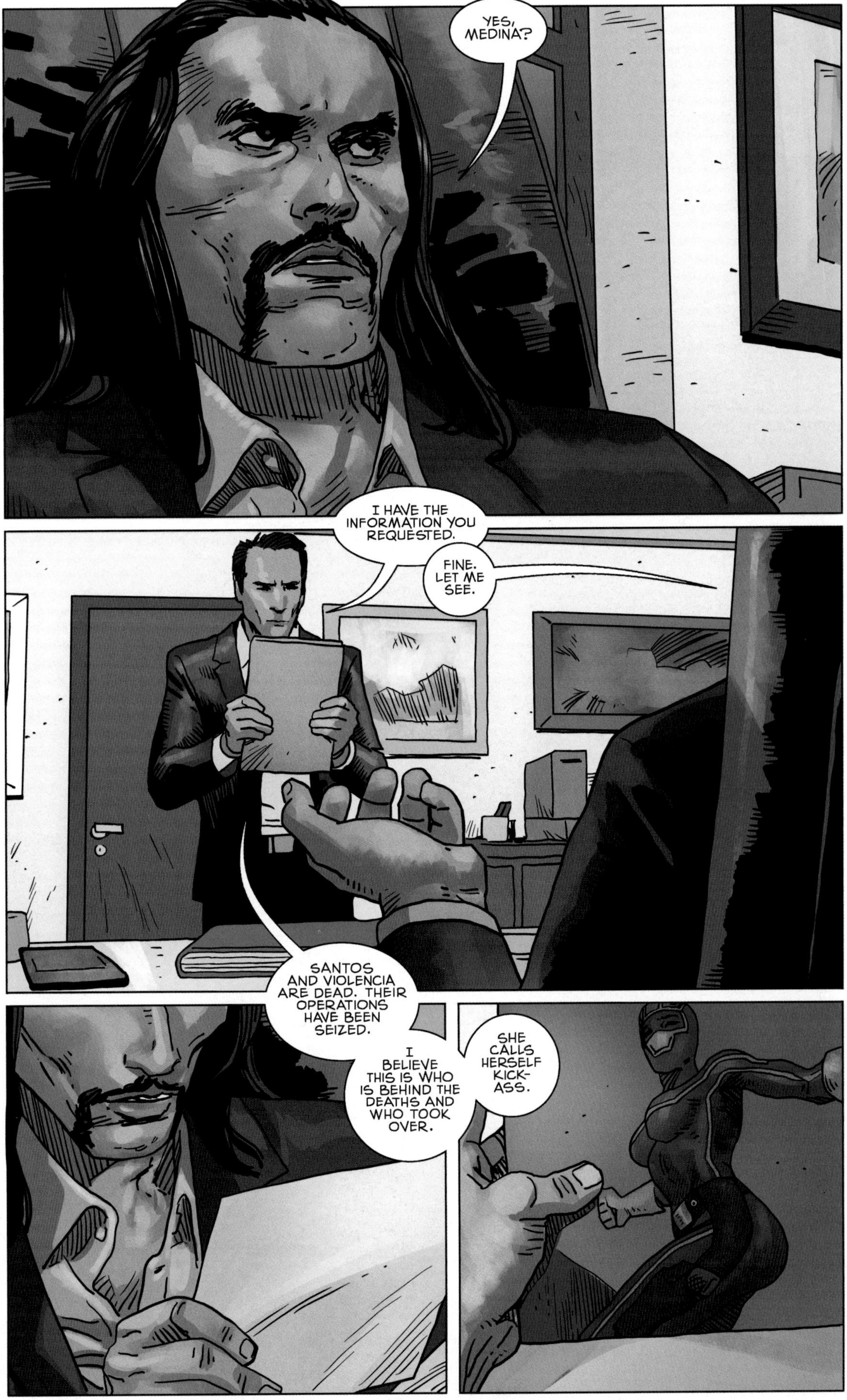
YES, MEDINA?
I HAVE THE INFORMATION YOU REQUESTED.
FINE. LET ME SEE.
SANTOS AND VIOLENCIA ARE DEAD. THEIR OPERATIONS HAVE BEEN SEIZED.
I BELIEVE THIS IS WHO IS BEHIND THE DEATHS AND WHO TOOK OVER.
SHE CALLS HERSELF KICK-ASS.

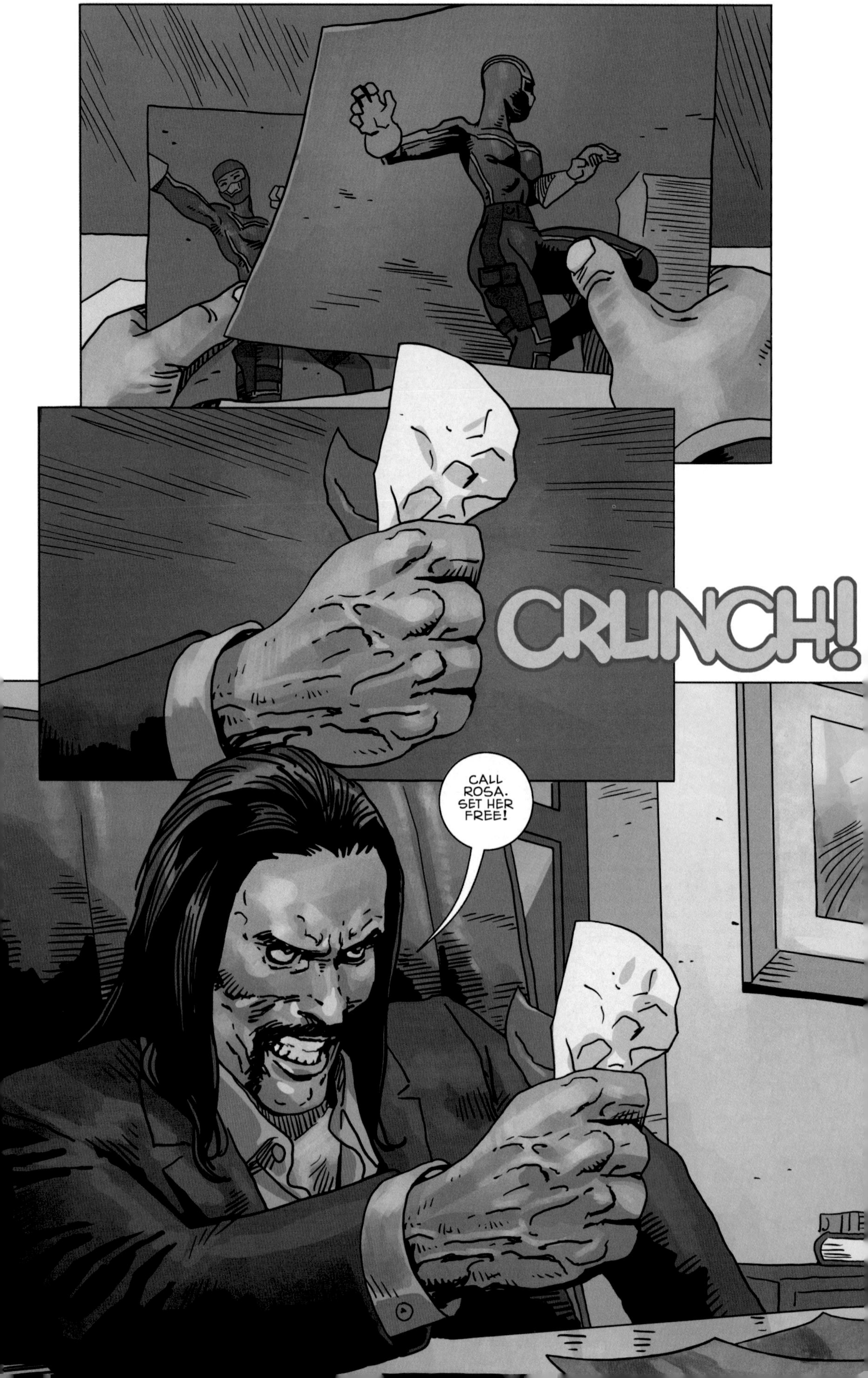
CRUNCH!
CALL ROSA. SET HER FREE!

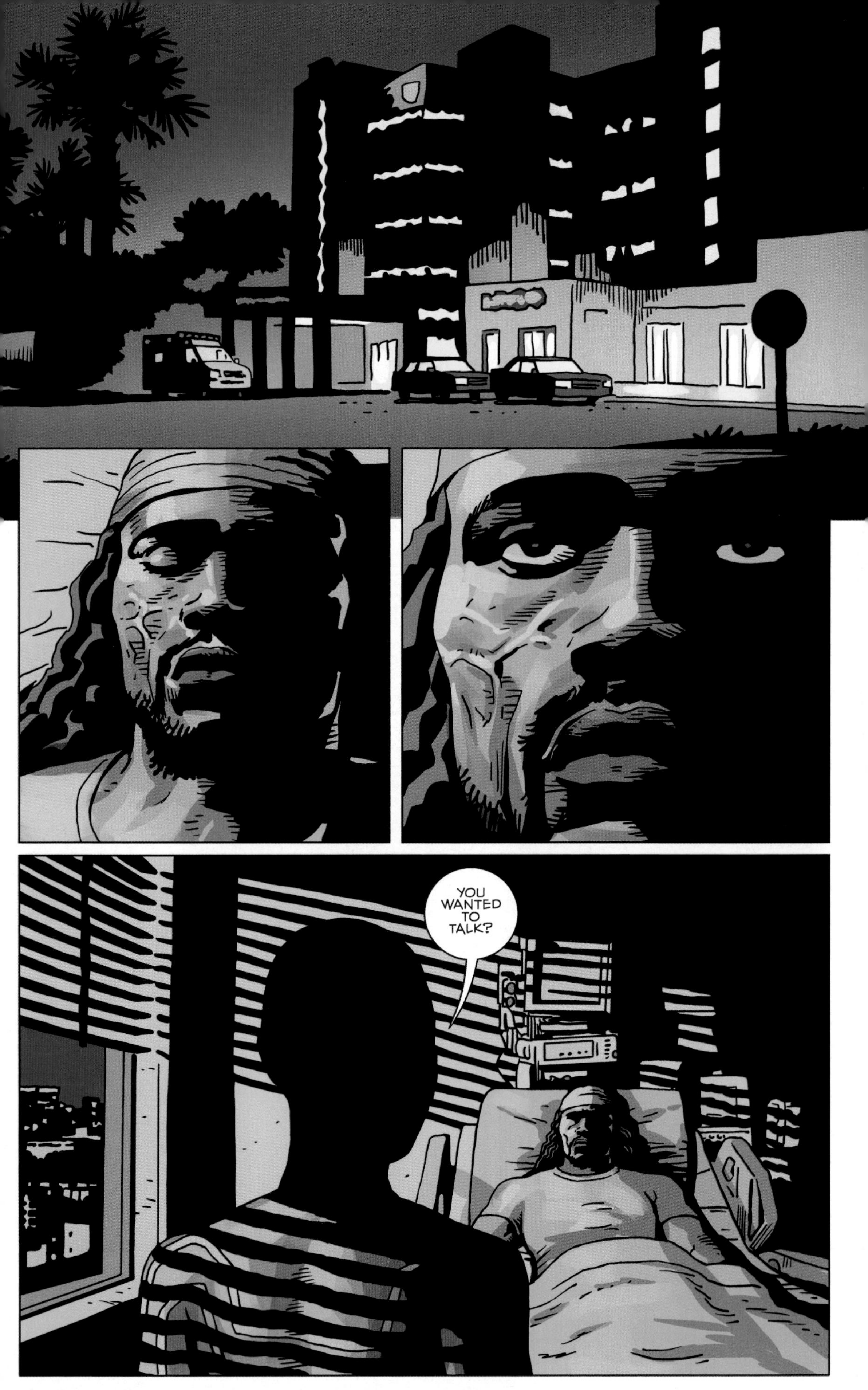
YOU WANTED TO TALK?

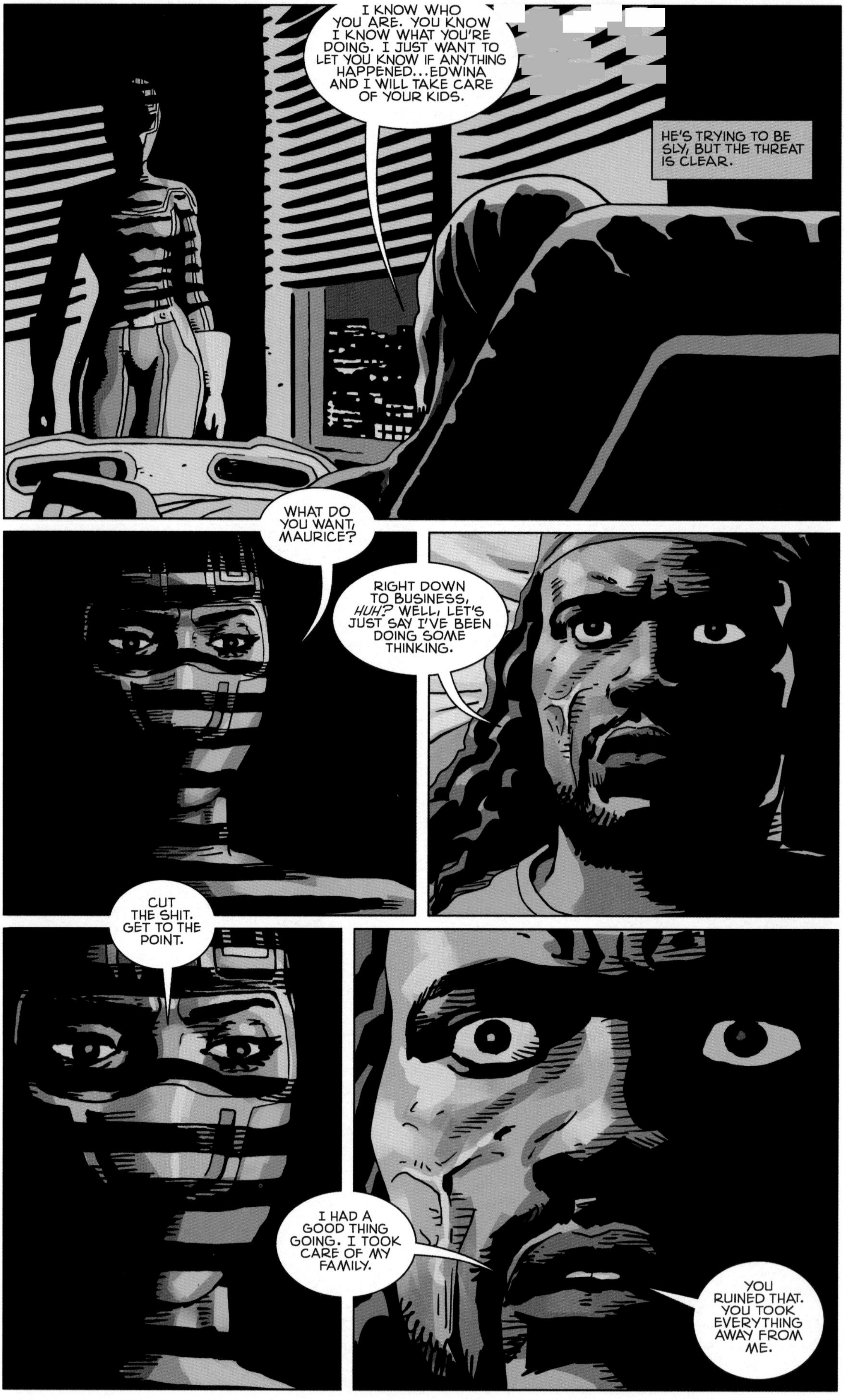
I KNOW WHO YOU ARE. YOU KNOW I KNOW WHAT YOU'RE DOING. I JUST WANT TO LET YOU KNOW IF ANYTHING HAPPENED...EDWINA AND I WILL TAKE CARE OF YOUR KIDS.
HE'S TRYING TO BE SLY, BUT THE THREAT IS CLEAR.
WHAT DO YOU WANT, MAURICE?
RIGHT DOWN TO BUSINESS, *HUH?* WELL, LET'S JUST SAY I'VE BEEN DOING SOME THINKING.
CUT THE SHIT. GET TO THE POINT.
I HAD A GOOD THING GOING. I TOOK CARE OF MY FAMILY.
YOU RUINED THAT. YOU TOOK EVERYTHING AWAY FROM ME.

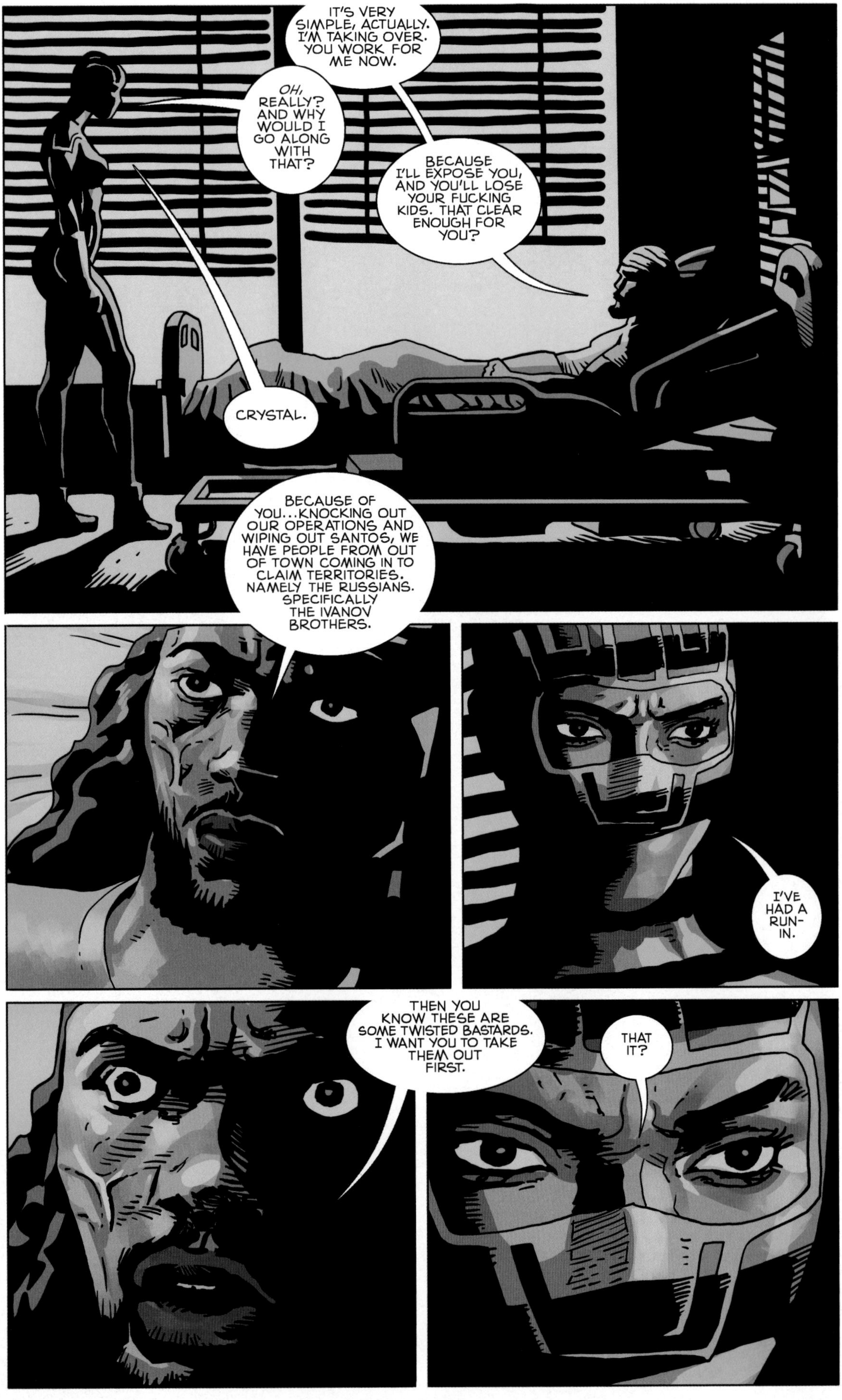
IT'S VERY SIMPLE, ACTUALLY. I'M TAKING OVER. YOU WORK FOR ME NOW.
OH, REALLY? AND WHY WOULD I GO ALONG WITH THAT?
BECAUSE I'LL EXPOSE YOU, AND YOU'LL LOSE YOUR FUCKING KIDS. THAT CLEAR ENOUGH FOR YOU?
CRYSTAL.
BECAUSE OF YOU...KNOCKING OUT OUR OPERATIONS AND WIPING OUT SANTOS, WE HAVE PEOPLE FROM OUT OF TOWN COMING IN TO CLAIM TERRITORIES. NAMELY THE RUSSIANS. SPECIFICALLY THE IVANOV BROTHERS.
I'VE HAD A RUN-IN.
THEN YOU KNOW THESE ARE SOME TWISTED BASTARDS. I WANT YOU TO TAKE THEM OUT FIRST.
THAT IT?

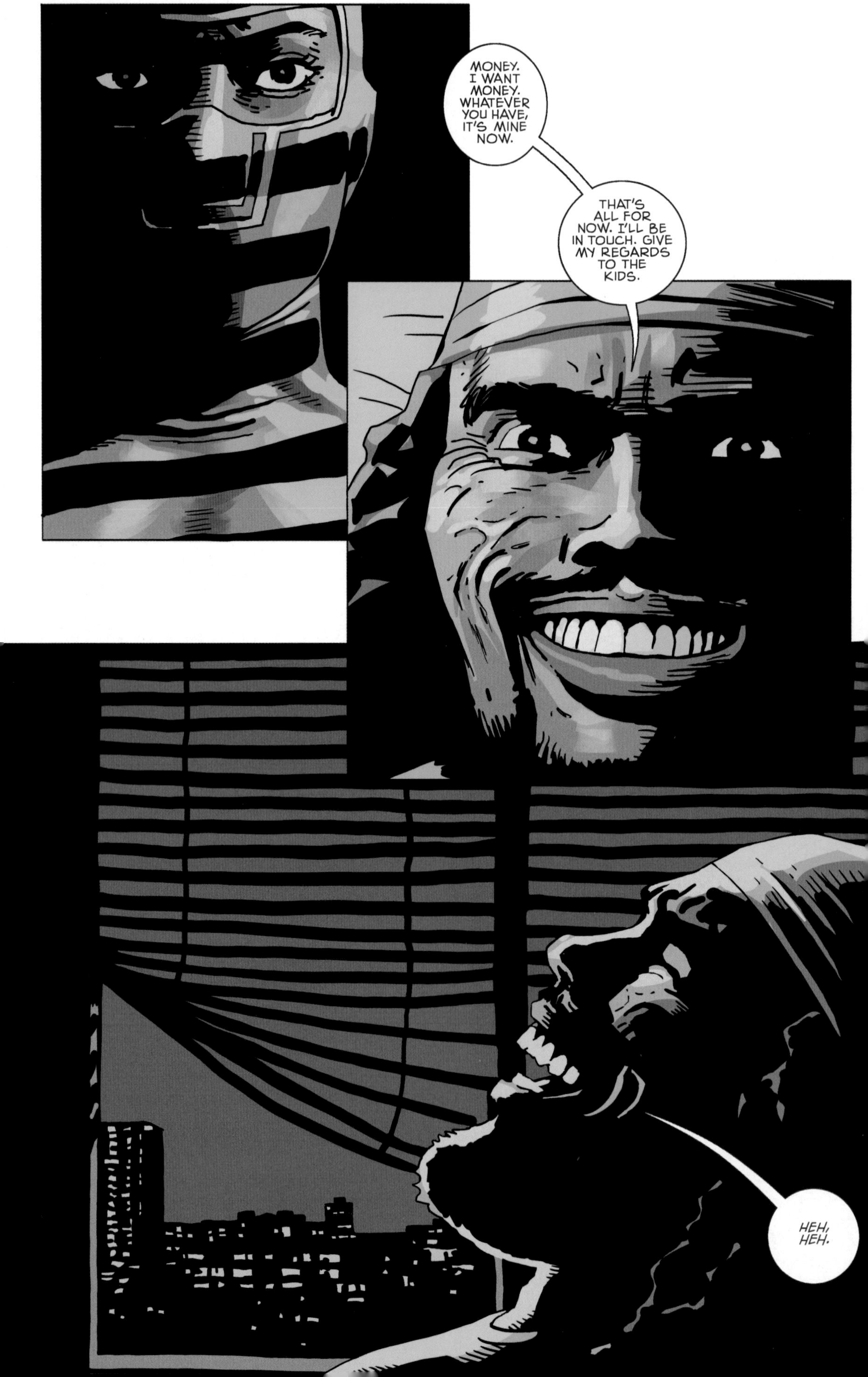
MONEY. I WANT MONEY. WHATEVER YOU HAVE, IT'S MINE NOW.
THAT'S ALL FOR NOW. I'LL BE IN TOUCH. GIVE MY REGARDS TO THE KIDS.
HEH, HEH.

TWO

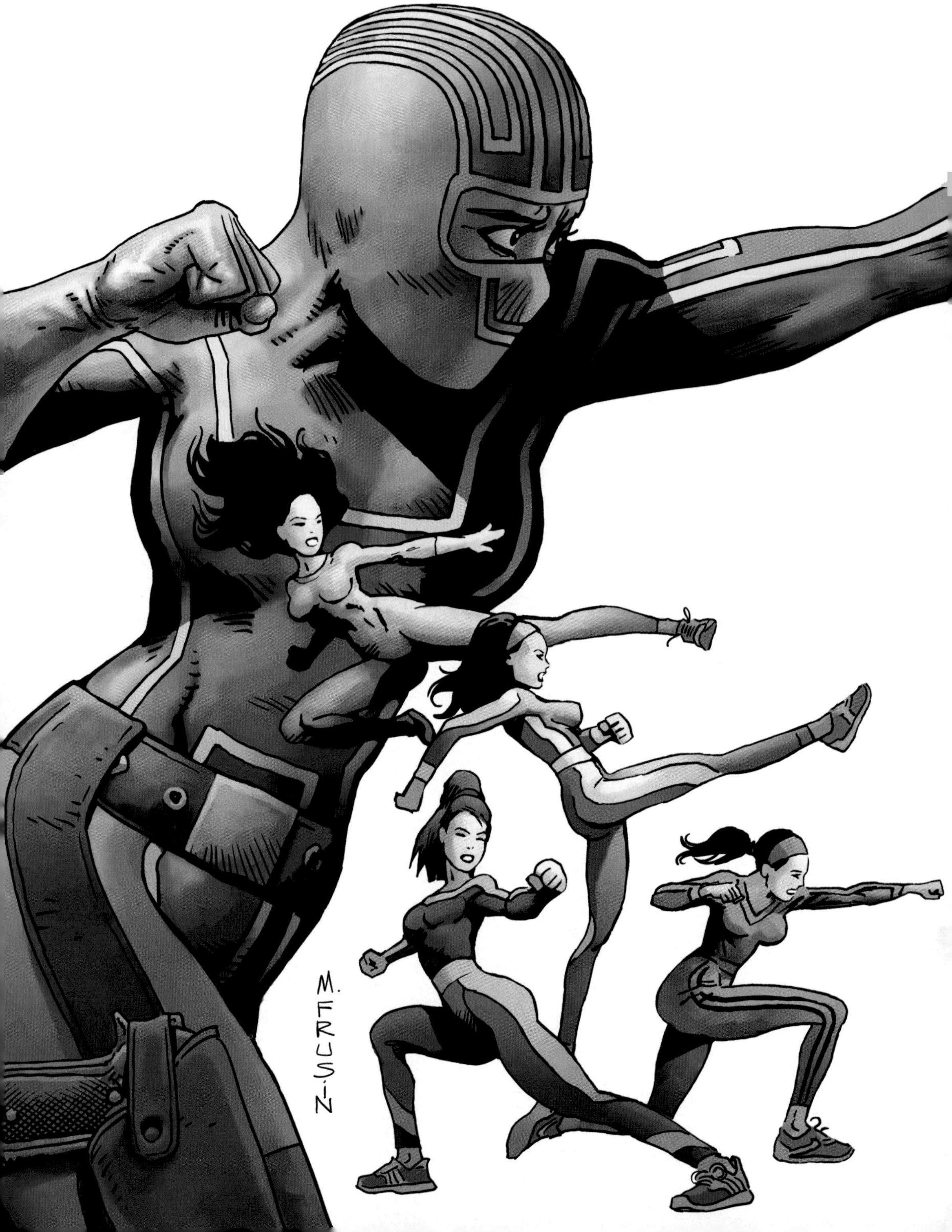
M. FRUSIN

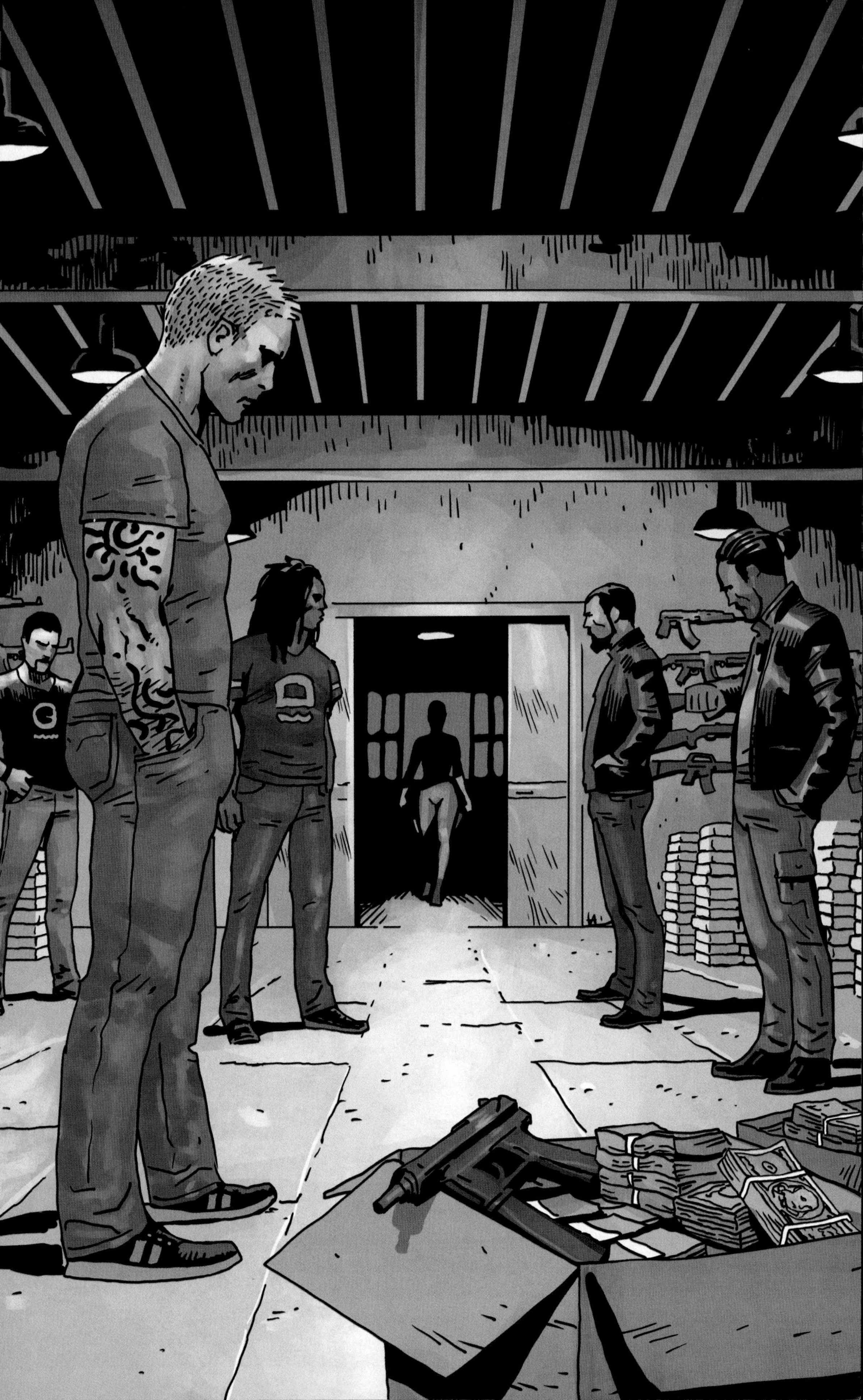

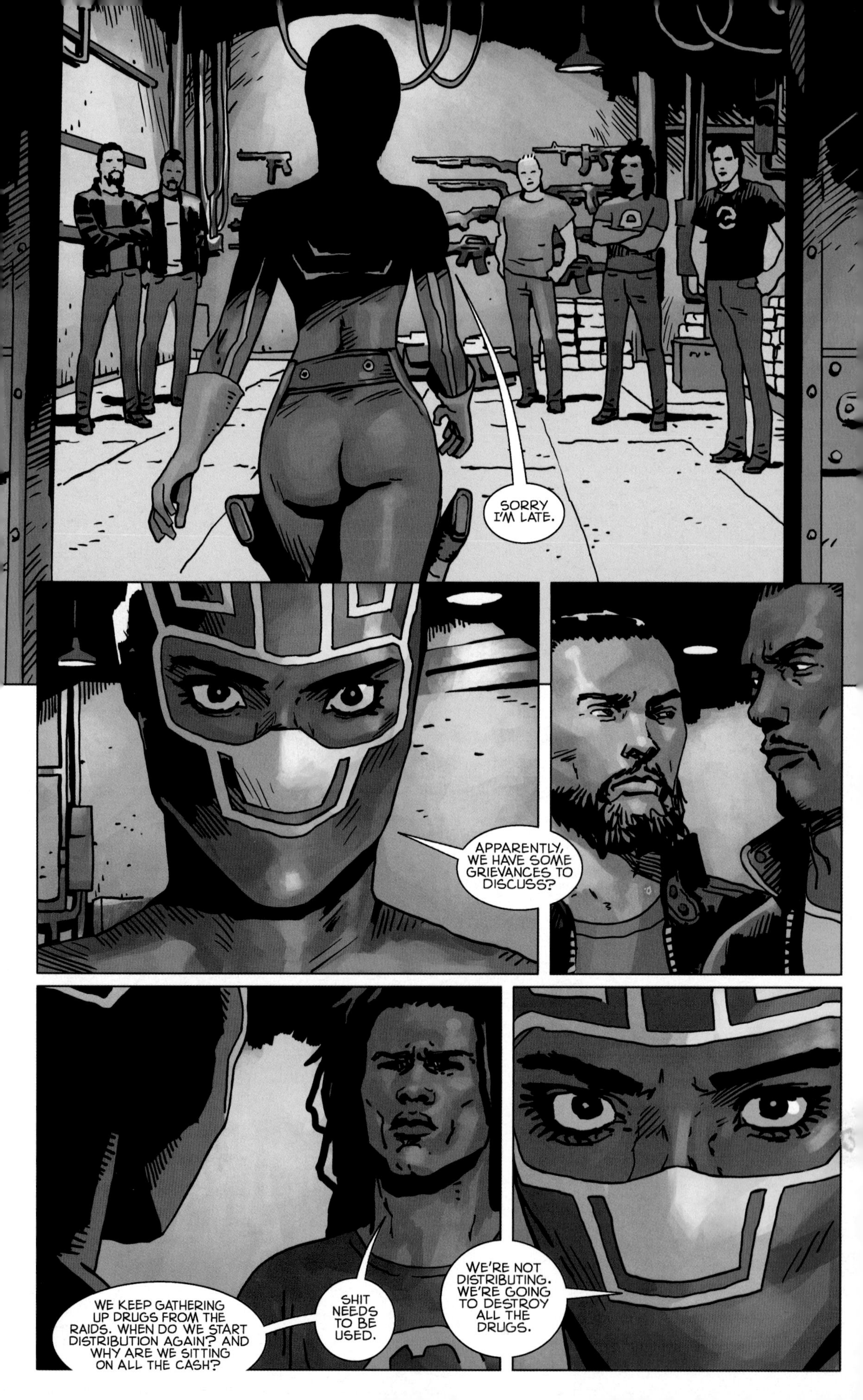
SORRY I'M LATE.
APPARENTLY, WE HAVE SOME GRIEVANCES TO DISCUSS?
WE KEEP GATHERING UP DRUGS FROM THE RAIDS. WHEN DO WE START DISTRIBUTION AGAIN? AND WHY ARE WE SITTING ON ALL THE CASH?
SHIT NEEDS TO BE USED.
WE'RE NOT DISTRIBUTING. WE'RE GOING TO DESTROY ALL THE DRUGS.

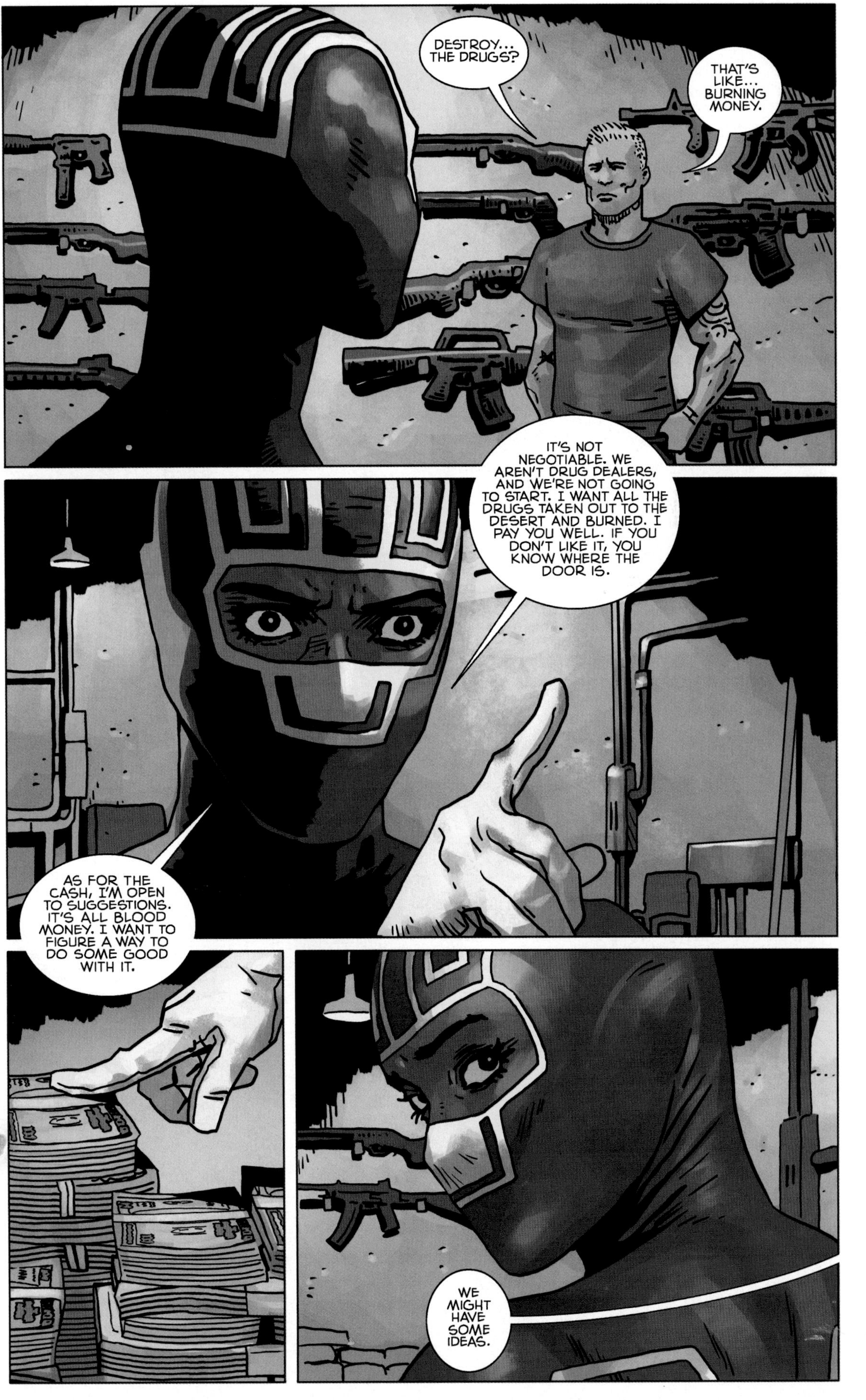
DESTROY... THE DRUGS?
THAT'S LIKE... BURNING MONEY.
IT'S NOT NEGOTIABLE. WE AREN'T DRUG DEALERS, AND WE'RE NOT GOING TO START. I WANT ALL THE DRUGS TAKEN OUT TO THE DESERT AND BURNED. I PAY YOU WELL. IF YOU DON'T LIKE IT, YOU KNOW WHERE THE DOOR IS.
AS FOR THE CASH, I'M OPEN TO SUGGESTIONS. IT'S ALL BLOOD MONEY. I WANT TO FIGURE A WAY TO DO SOME GOOD WITH IT.
WE MIGHT HAVE SOME IDEAS.

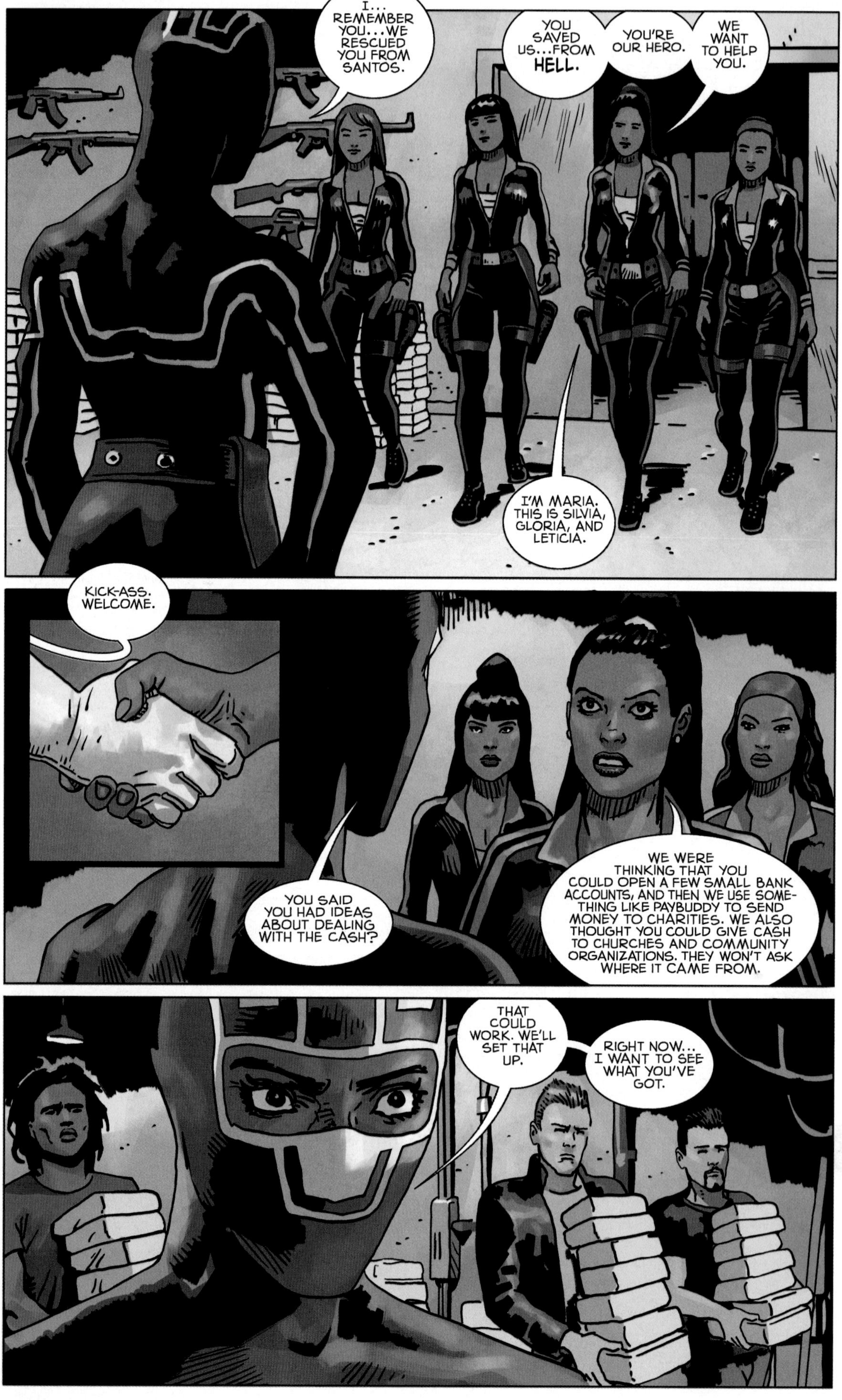
I... REMEMBER YOU...WE RESCUED YOU FROM SANTOS.
YOU SAVED US...FROM HELL.
YOU'RE OUR HERO.
WE WANT TO HELP YOU.
I'M MARIA. THIS IS SILVIA, GLORIA, AND LETICIA.
KICK-ASS. WELCOME.
YOU SAID YOU HAD IDEAS ABOUT DEALING WITH THE CASH?
WE WERE THINKING THAT YOU COULD OPEN A FEW SMALL BANK ACCOUNTS, AND THEN WE USE SOME-THING LIKE PAYBUDDY TO SEND MONEY TO CHARITIES. WE ALSO THOUGHT YOU COULD GIVE CASH TO CHURCHES AND COMMUNITY ORGANIZATIONS. THEY WON'T ASK WHERE IT CAME FROM.
THAT COULD WORK. WE'LL SET THAT UP.
RIGHT NOW... I WANT TO SEE WHAT YOU'VE GOT.

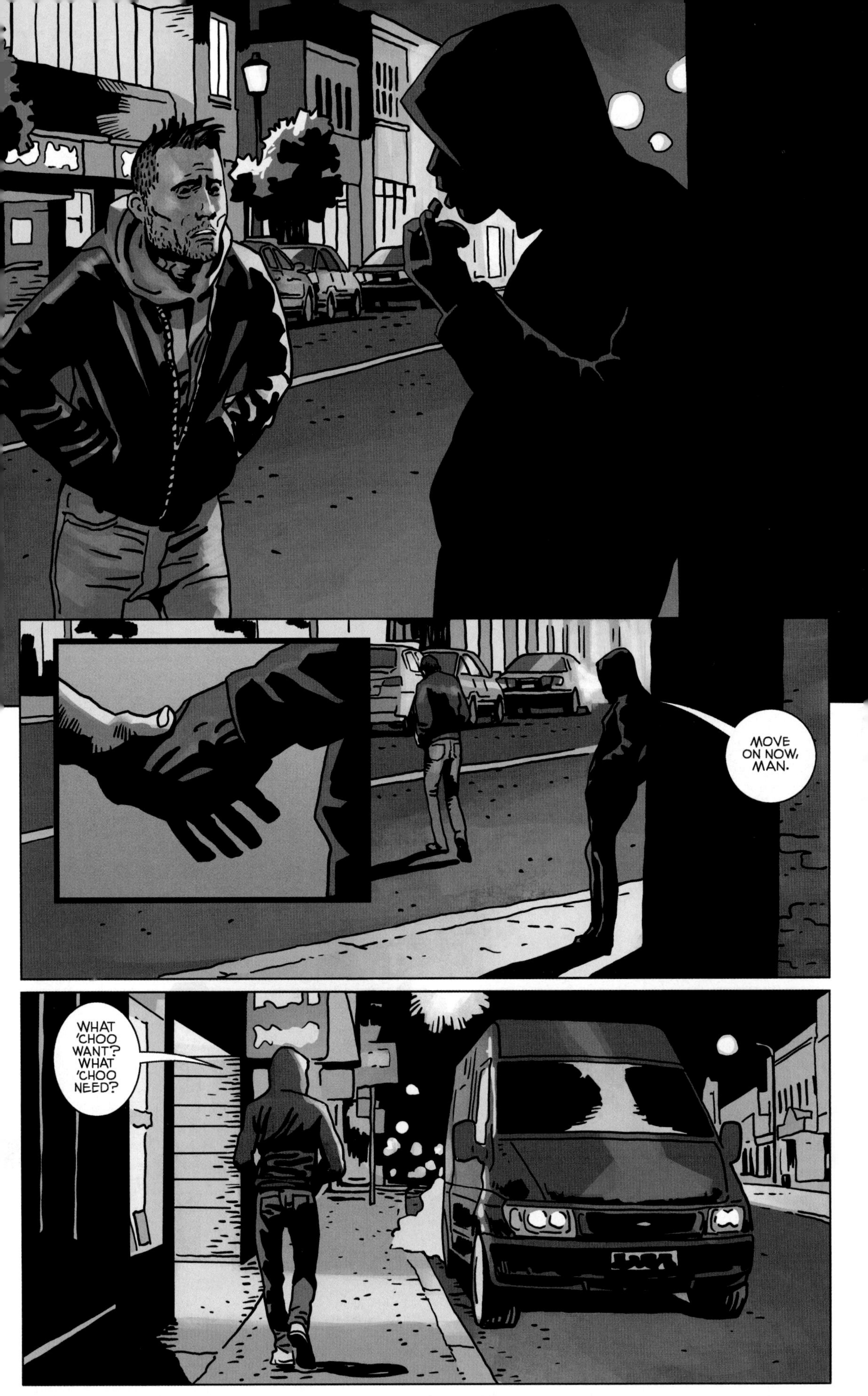
MOVE ON NOW, MAN.
WHAT 'CHOO WANT? WHAT 'CHOO NEED?

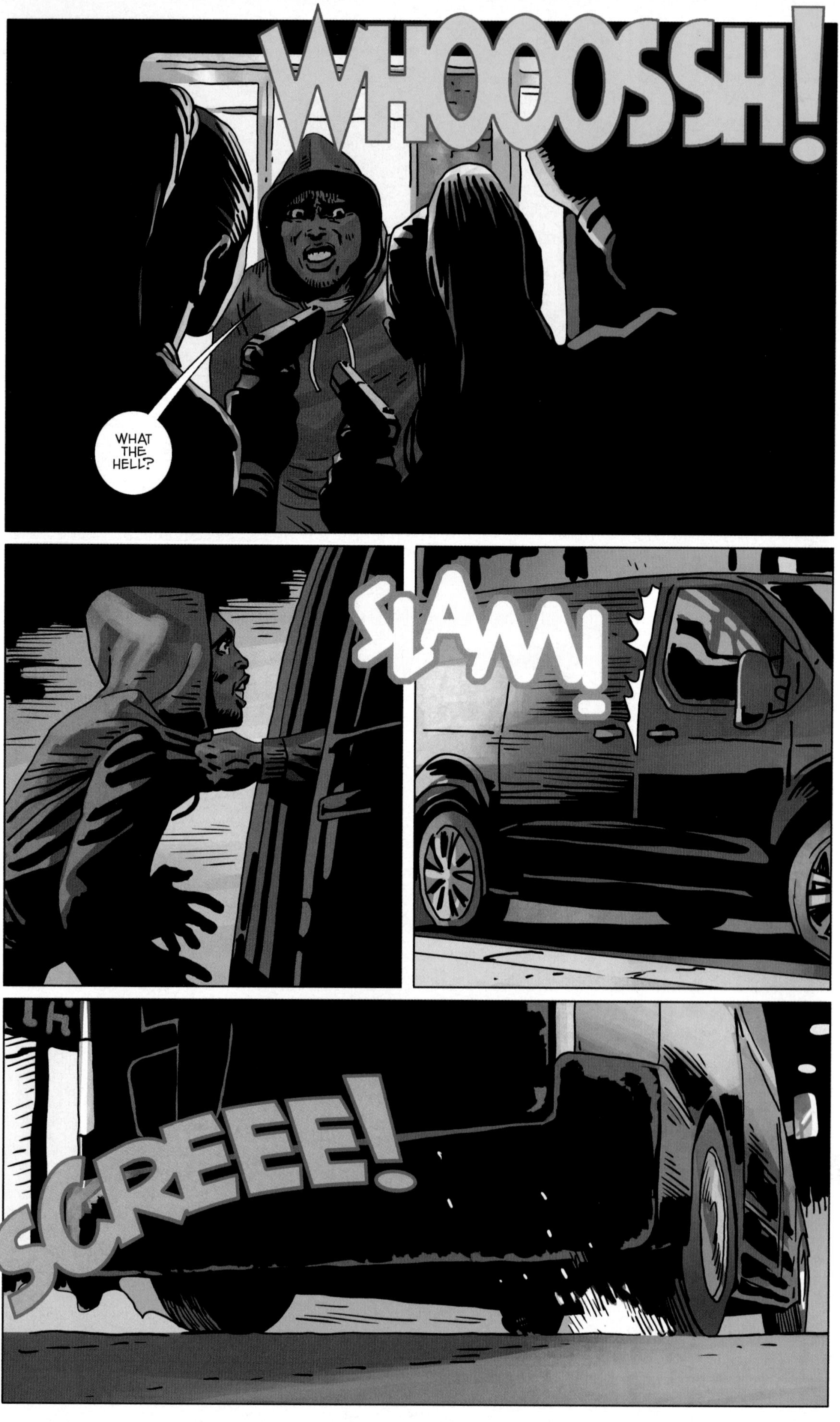
WHOOOSSH!
WHAT THE HELL?
SLAM!
SCREEE!

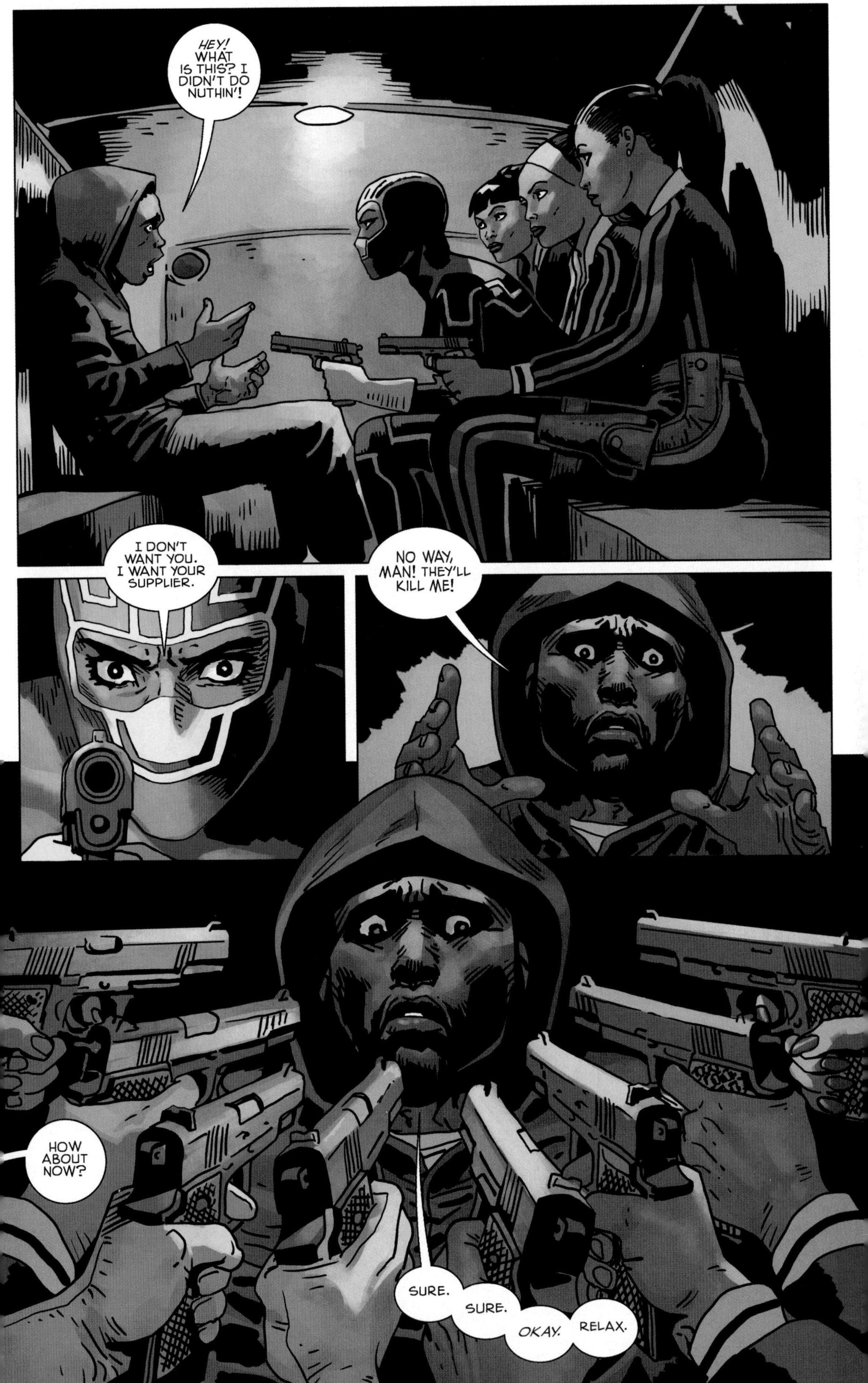
HEY! WHAT IS THIS? I DIDN'T DO NUTHIN'!
I DON'T WANT YOU. I WANT YOUR SUPPLIER.
NO WAY, MAN! THEY'LL KILL ME!
HOW ABOUT NOW?
SURE.
SURE.
OKAY.
RELAX.

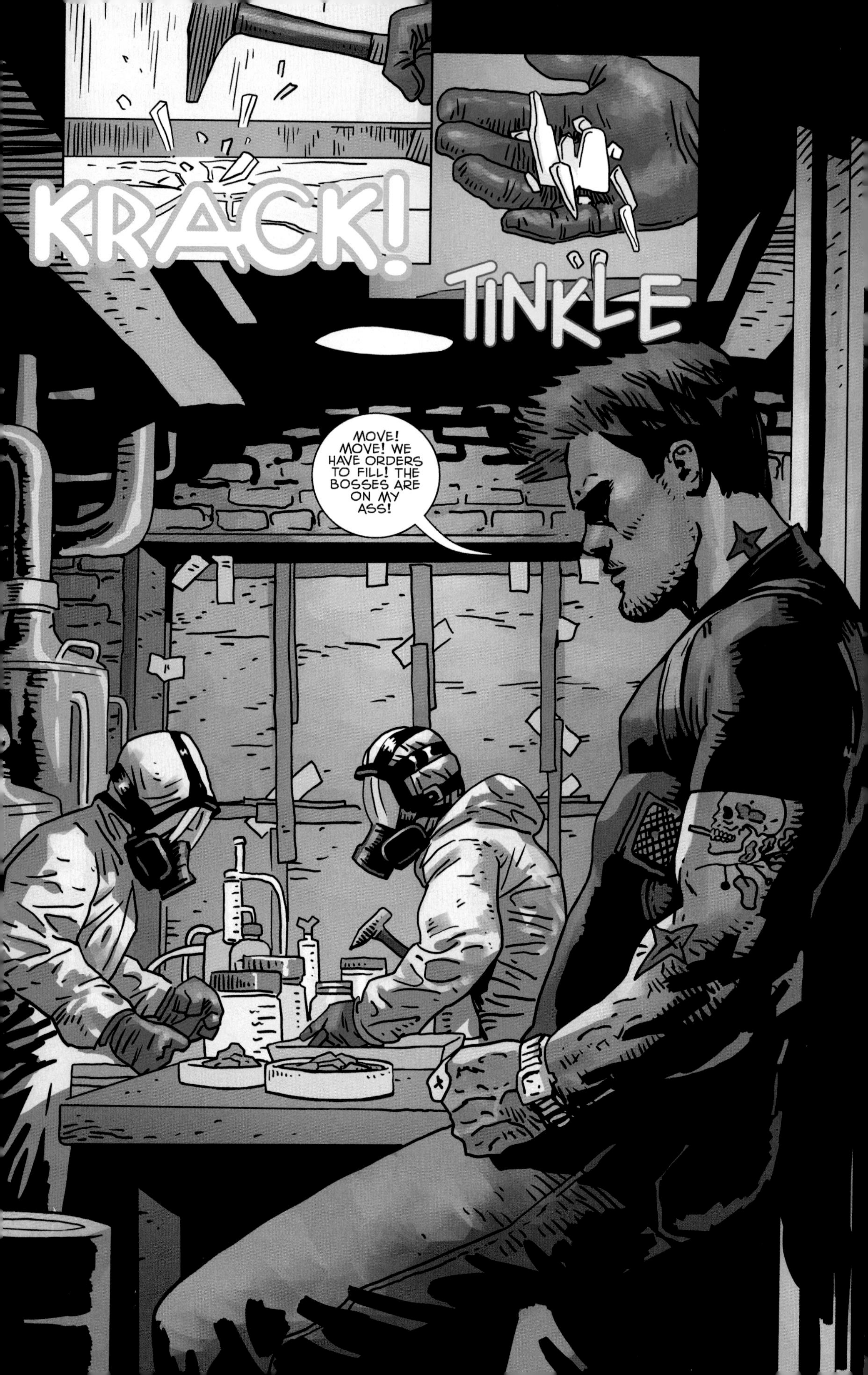
KRACK!
TINKLE
MOVE! MOVE! WE HAVE ORDERS TO FILL! THE BOSSES ARE ON MY ASS!

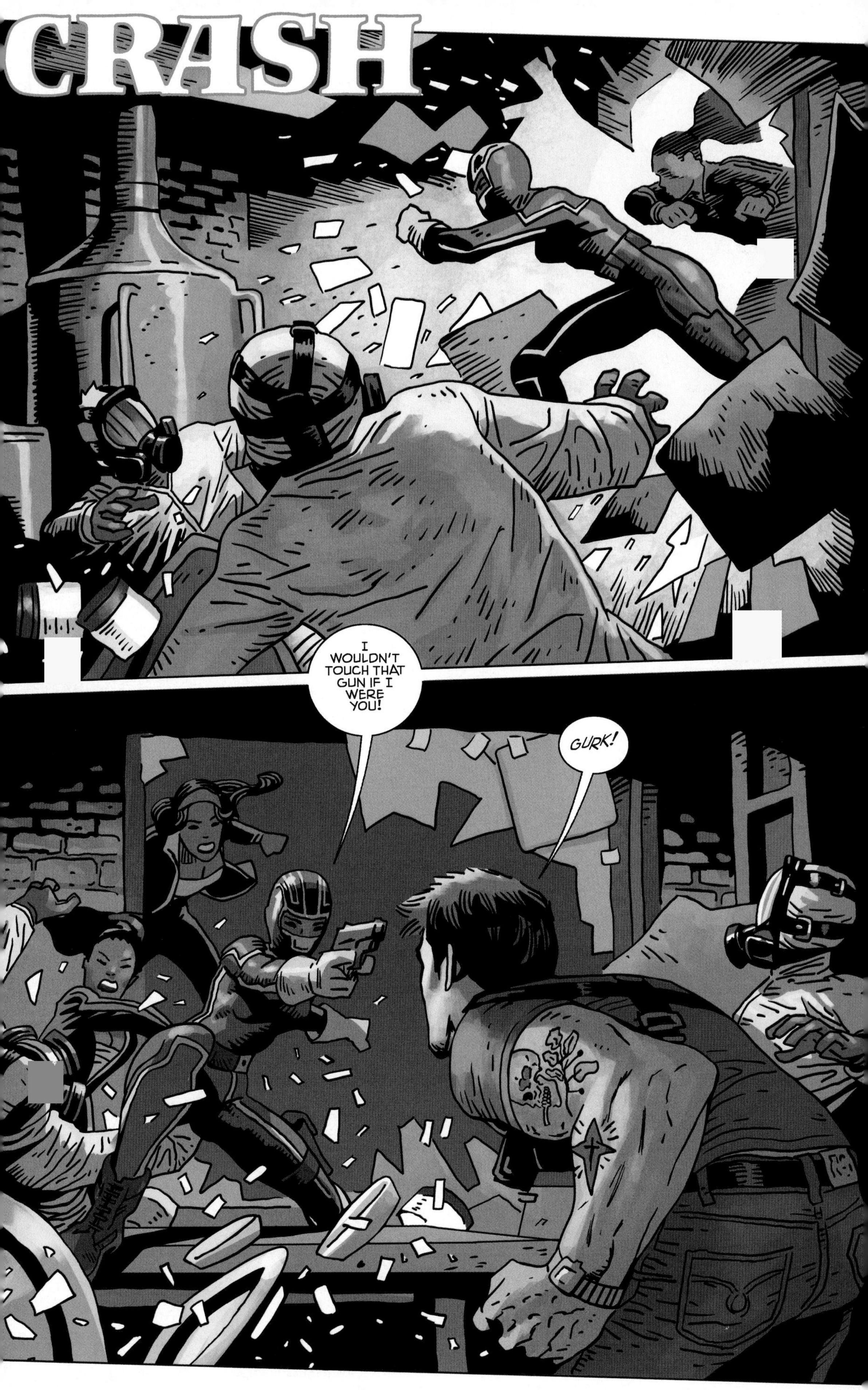
CRASH
I WOULDN'T TOUCH THAT GUN IF I WERE YOU!
GURK!

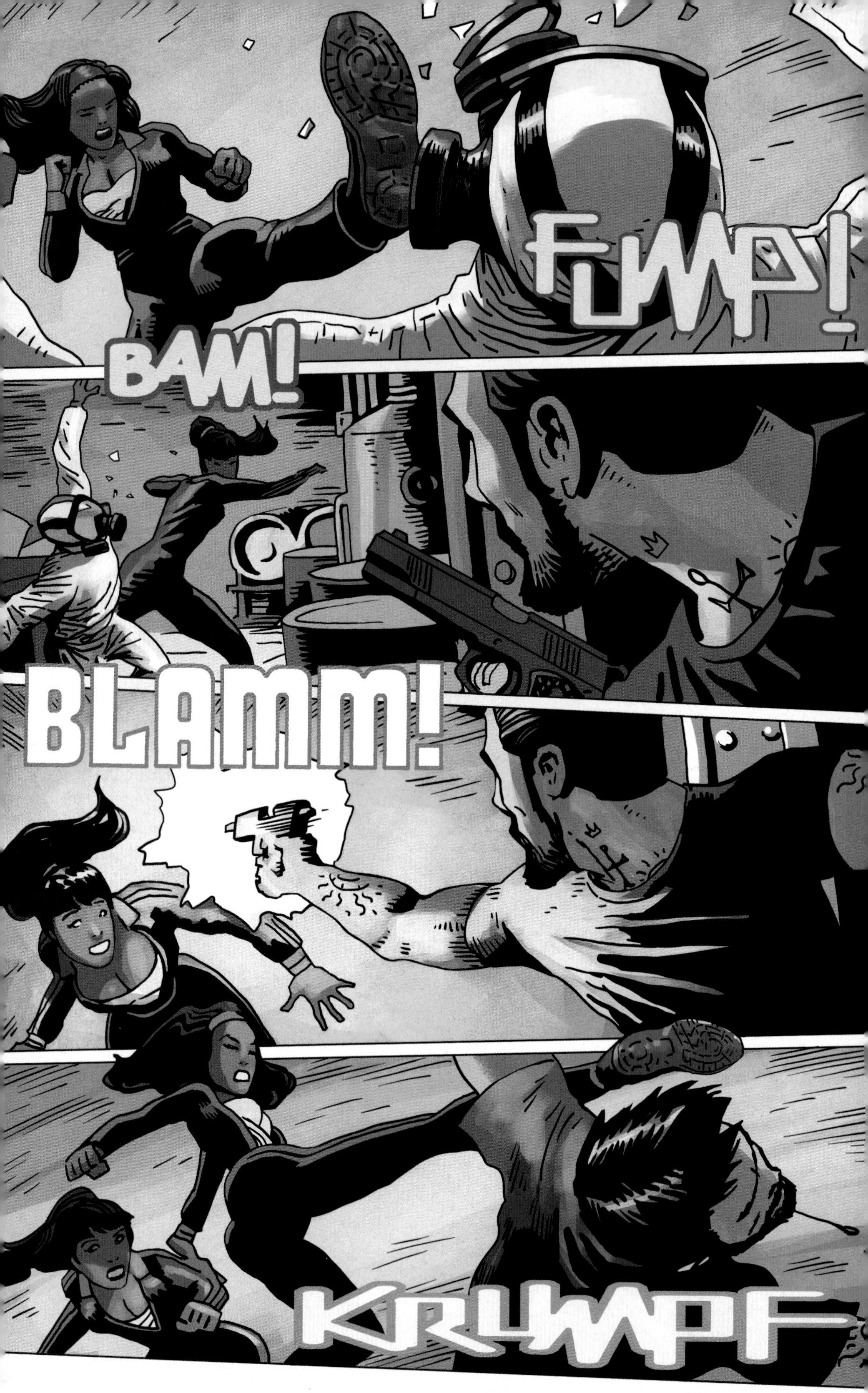
FUMP!
BAM!
BLAMM!
KRUMPF

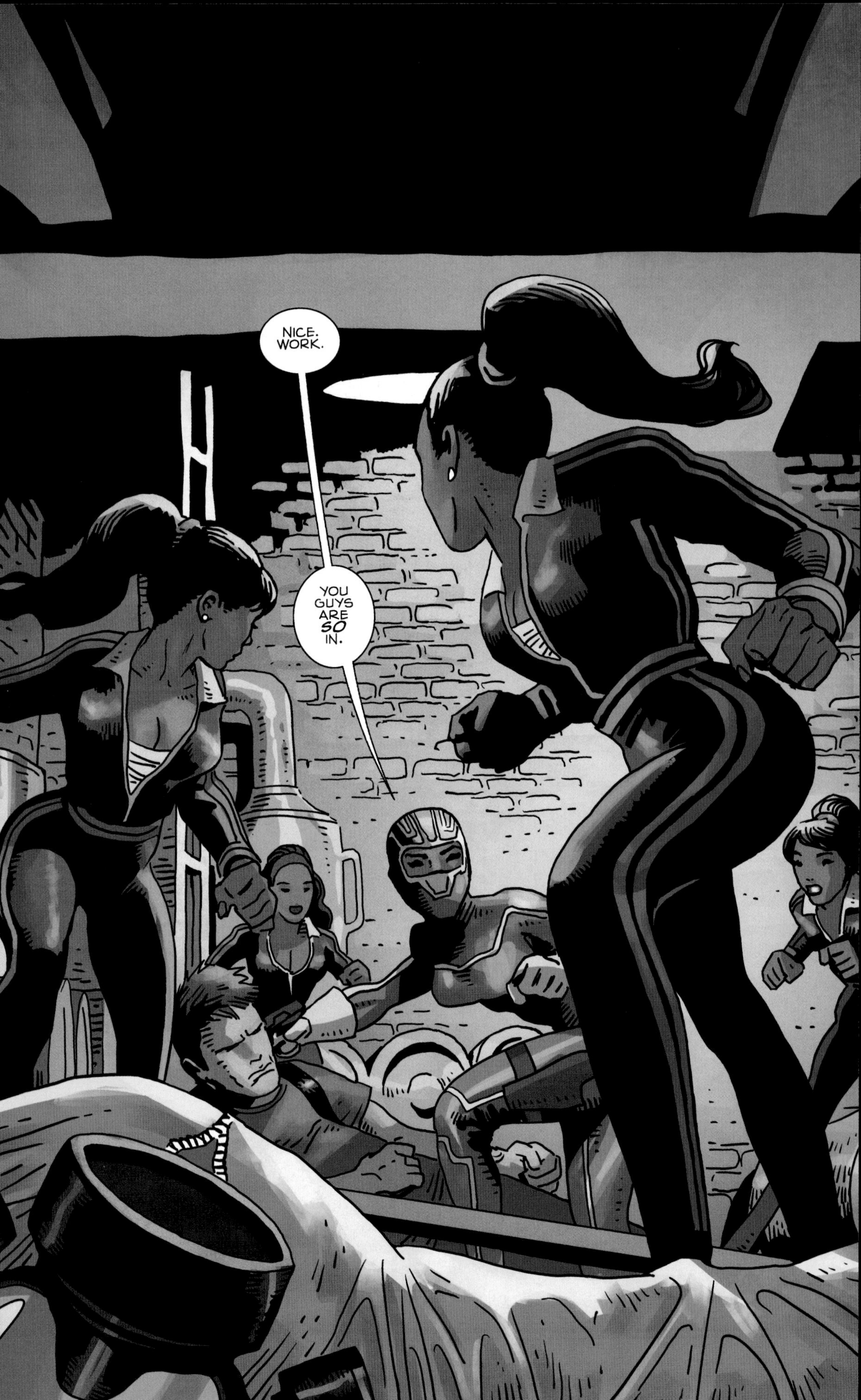
NICE. WORK.
YOU GUYS ARE SO IN.

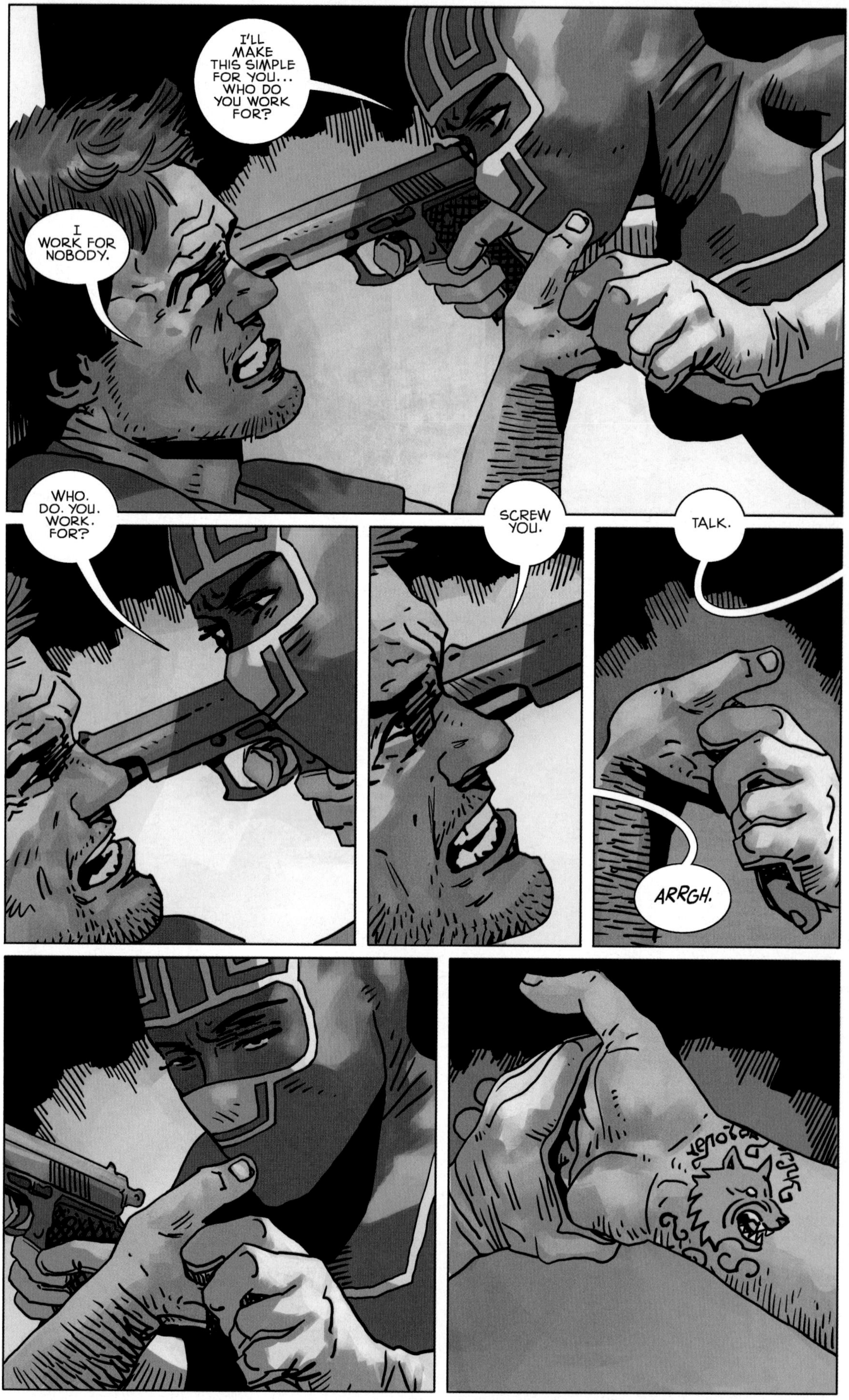
I'LL MAKE THIS SIMPLE FOR YOU... WHO DO YOU WORK FOR?
I WORK FOR NOBODY.
WHO. DO. YOU. WORK. FOR?
SCREW YOU.
TALK.
ARRGH.

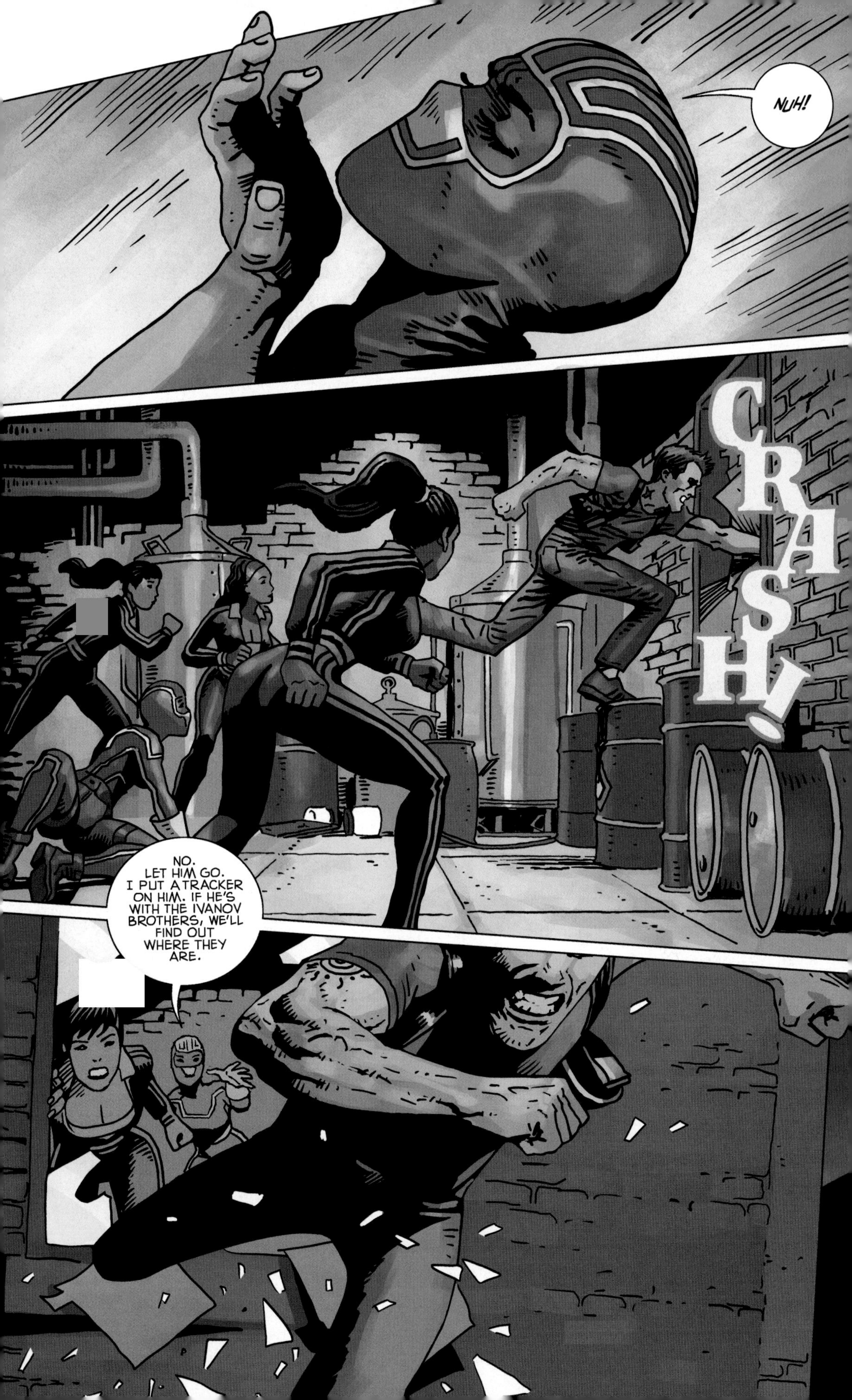
NUH!
CRASH!
NO. LET HIM GO. I PUT A TRACKER ON HIM. IF HE'S WITH THE IVANOV BROTHERS, WE'LL FIND OUT WHERE THEY ARE.

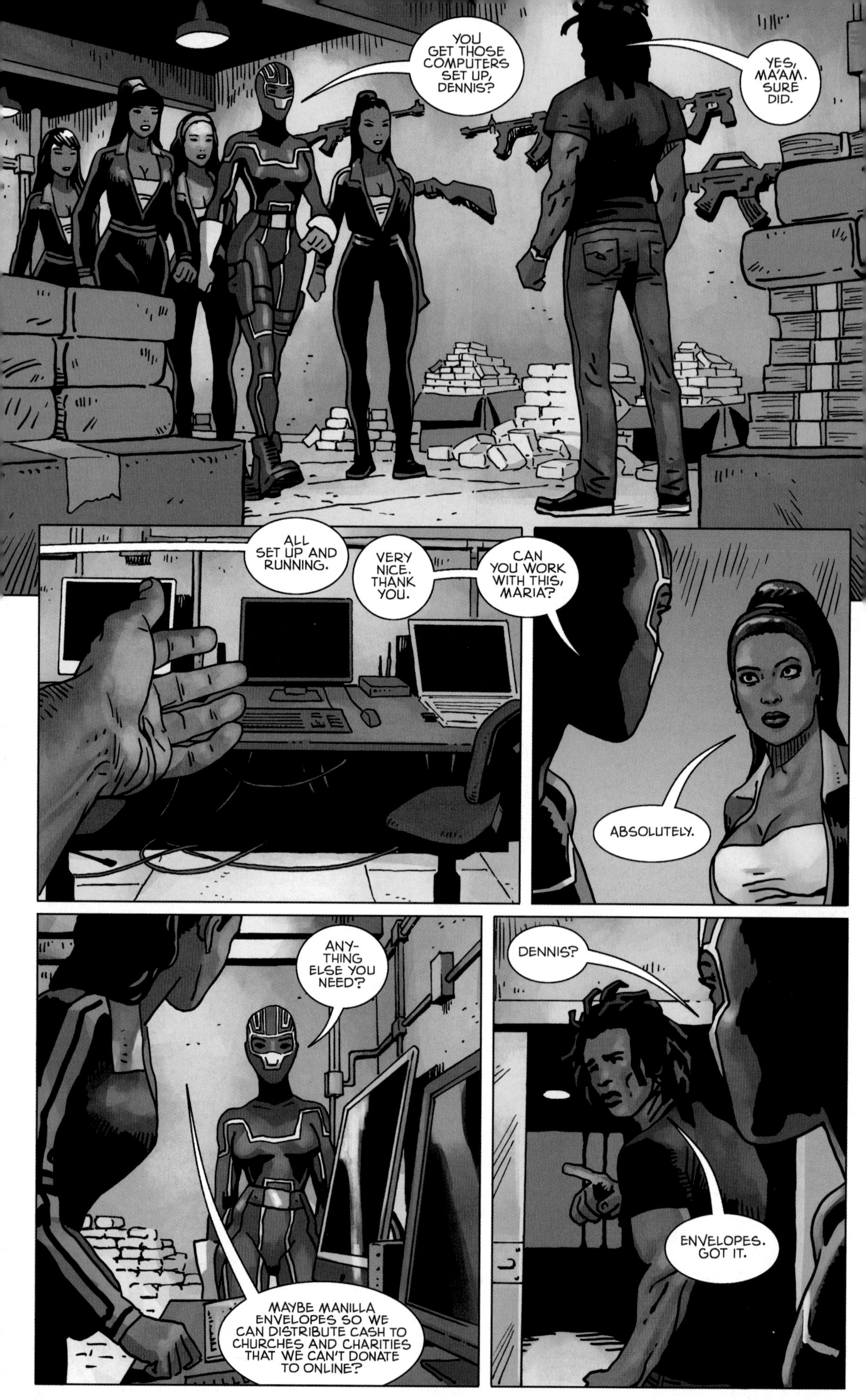
YOU GET THOSE COMPUTERS SET UP, DENNIS?
YES, MA'AM. SURE DID.
ALL SET UP AND RUNNING.
VERY NICE. THANK YOU.
CAN YOU WORK WITH THIS, MARIA?
ABSOLUTELY.
ANY-THING ELSE YOU NEED?
MAYBE MANILLA ENVELOPES SO WE CAN DISTRIBUTE CASH TO CHURCHES AND CHARITIES THAT WE CAN'T DONATE TO ONLINE?
DENNIS?
ENVELOPES. GOT IT.

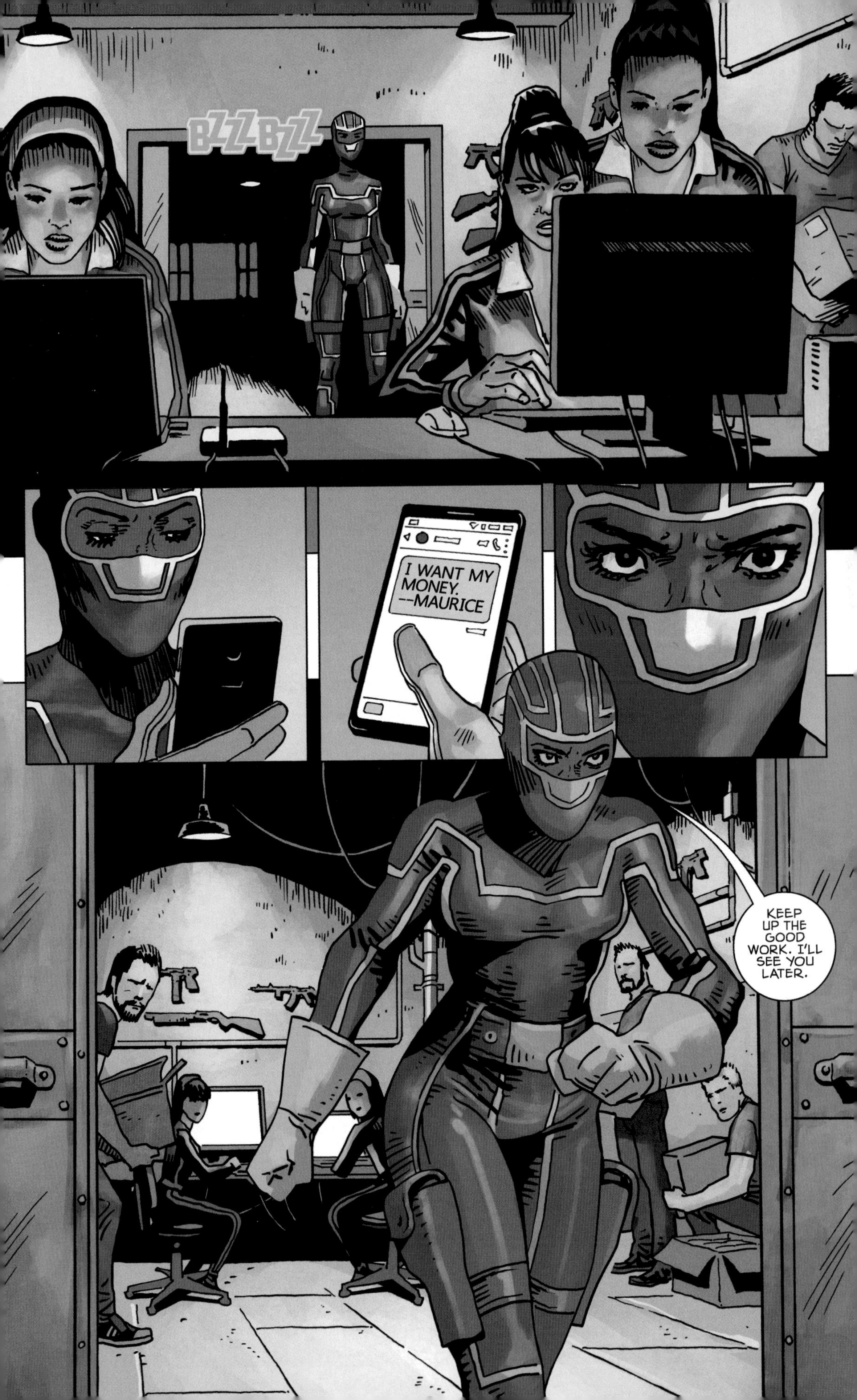
BZZZ BZZZ
I WANT MY MONEY. --MAURICE
KEEP UP THE GOOD WORK. I'LL SEE YOU LATER.

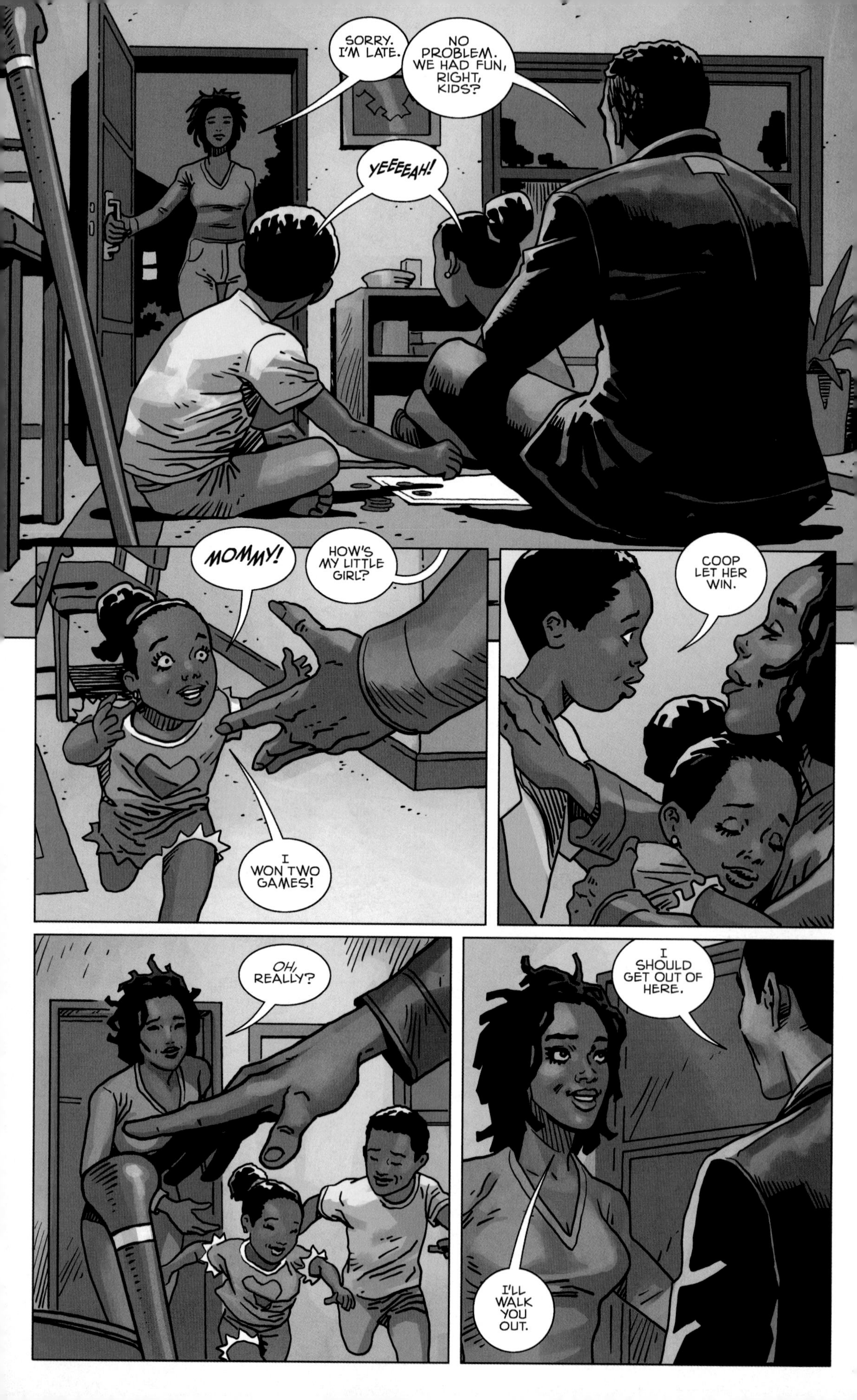
SORRY. I'M LATE.
NO PROBLEM. WE HAD FUN, RIGHT, KIDS?
YEEEEAH!
MOMMY!
HOW'S MY LITTLE GIRL?
I WON TWO GAMES!
COOP LET HER WIN.
OH, REALLY?
I SHOULD GET OUT OF HERE.
I'LL WALK YOU OUT.

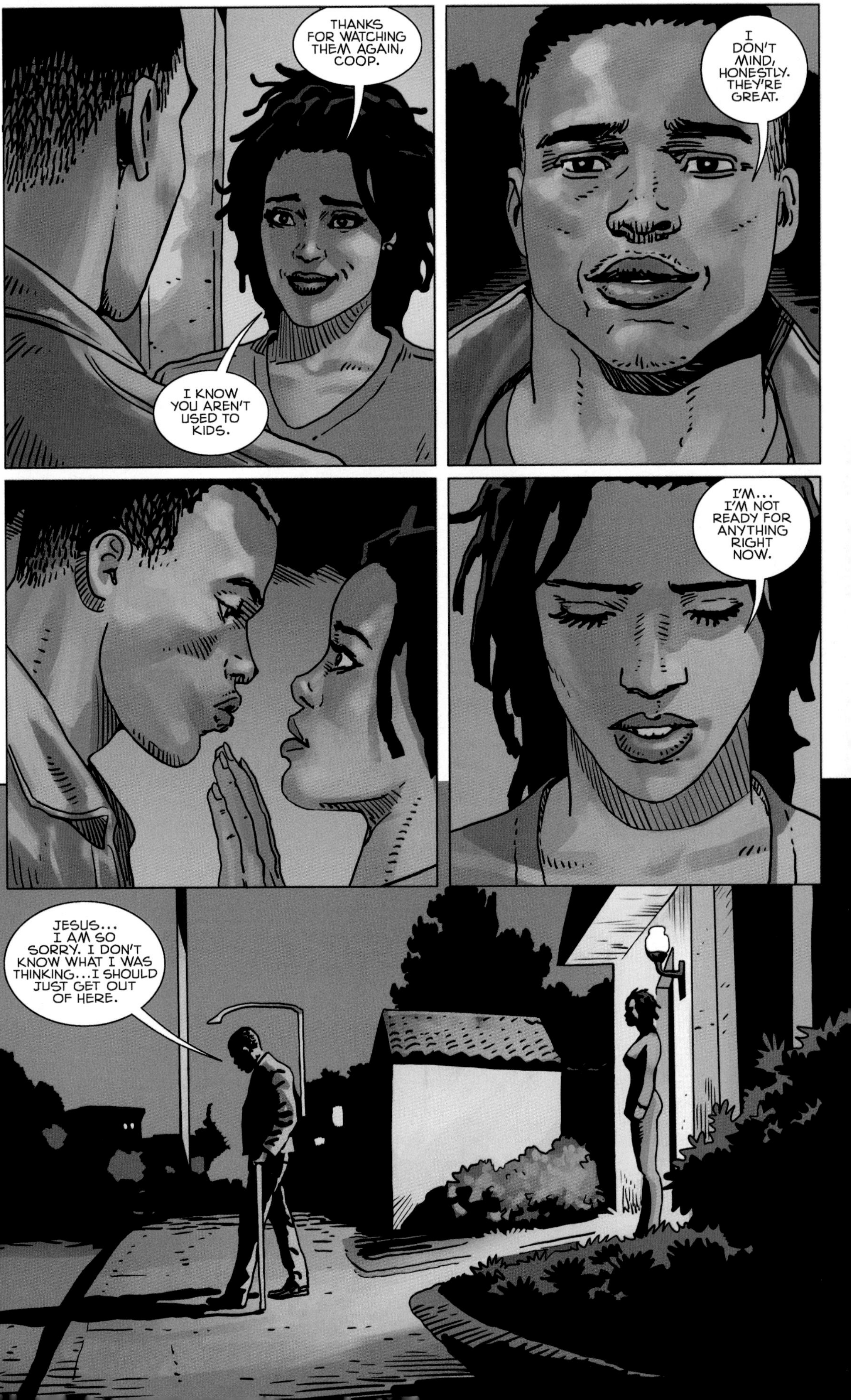

THANKS FOR WATCHING THEM AGAIN, COOP.
I KNOW YOU AREN'T USED TO KIDS.
I DON'T MIND, HONESTLY. THEY'RE GREAT.
I'M... I'M NOT READY FOR ANYTHING RIGHT NOW.
JESUS... I AM SO SORRY. I DON'T KNOW WHAT I WAS THINKING...I SHOULD JUST GET OUT OF HERE.

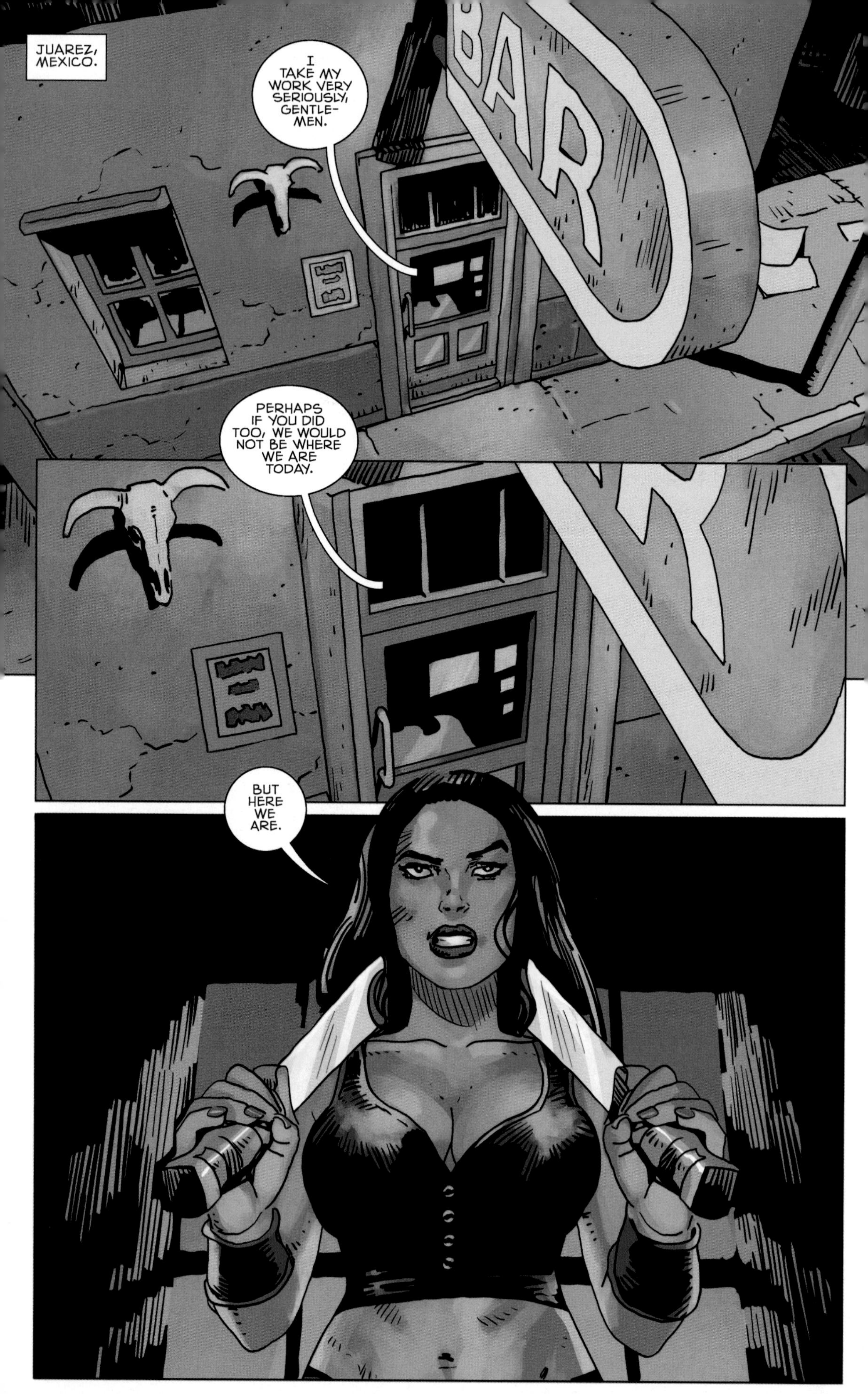
JUAREZ, MEXICO.
I TAKE MY WORK VERY SERIOUSLY, GENTLE-MEN.
BAR
PERHAPS IF YOU DID TOO, WE WOULD NOT BE WHERE WE ARE TODAY.
BUT HERE WE ARE.

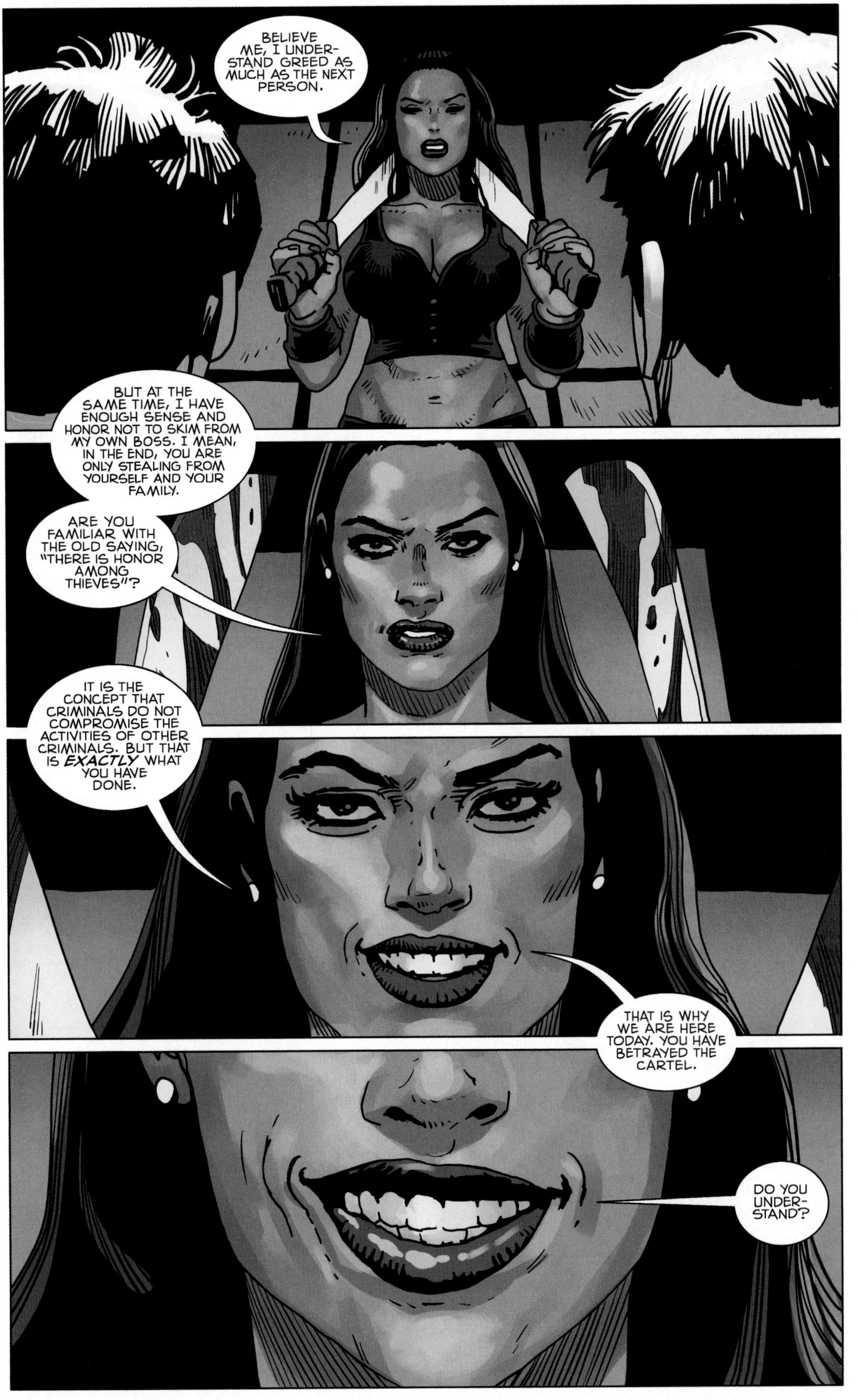
BELIEVE ME, I UNDERSTAND GREED AS MUCH AS THE NEXT PERSON.
BUT AT THE SAME TIME, I HAVE ENOUGH SENSE AND HONOR NOT TO SKIM FROM MY OWN BOSS. I MEAN, IN THE END, YOU ARE ONLY STEALING FROM YOURSELF AND YOUR FAMILY.
ARE YOU FAMILIAR WITH THE OLD SAYING, "THERE IS HONOR AMONG THIEVES"?
IT IS THE CONCEPT THAT CRIMINALS DO NOT COMPROMISE THE ACTIVITIES OF OTHER CRIMINALS. BUT THAT IS *EXACTLY* WHAT YOU HAVE DONE.
THAT IS WHY WE ARE HERE TODAY. YOU HAVE BETRAYED THE CARTEL.
DO YOU UNDERSTAND?

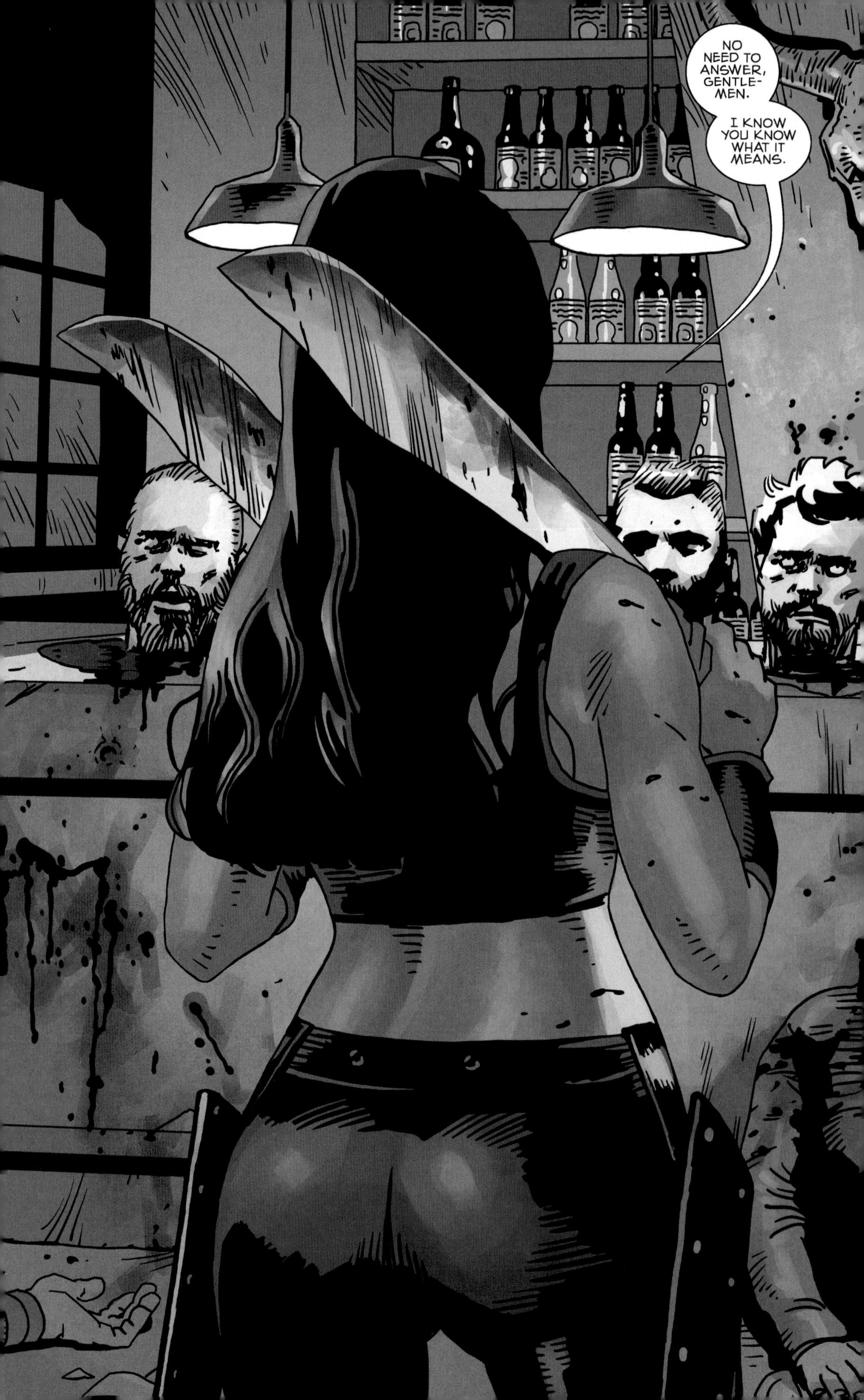
NO NEED TO ANSWER, GENTLE-MEN.
I KNOW YOU KNOW WHAT IT MEANS.

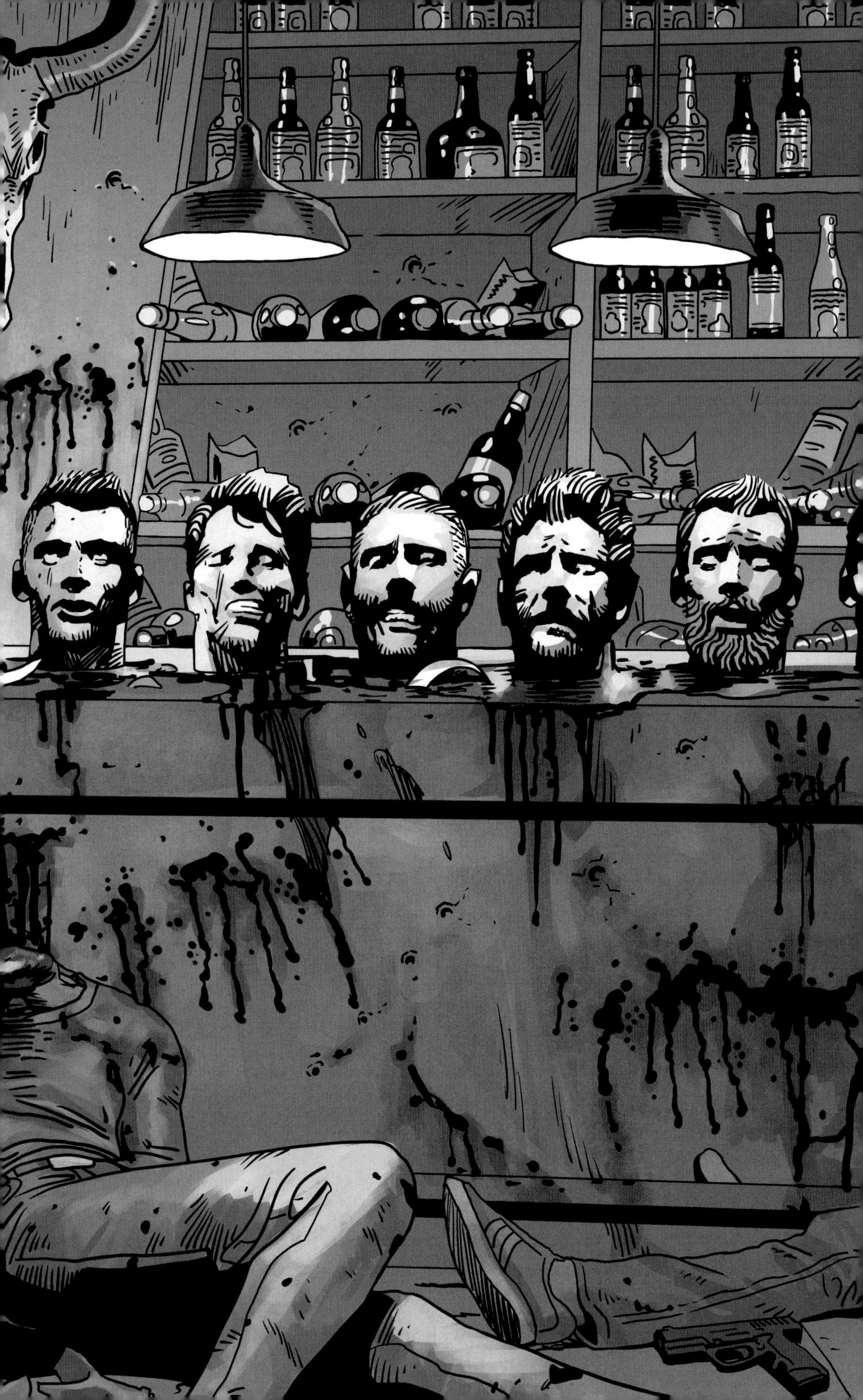

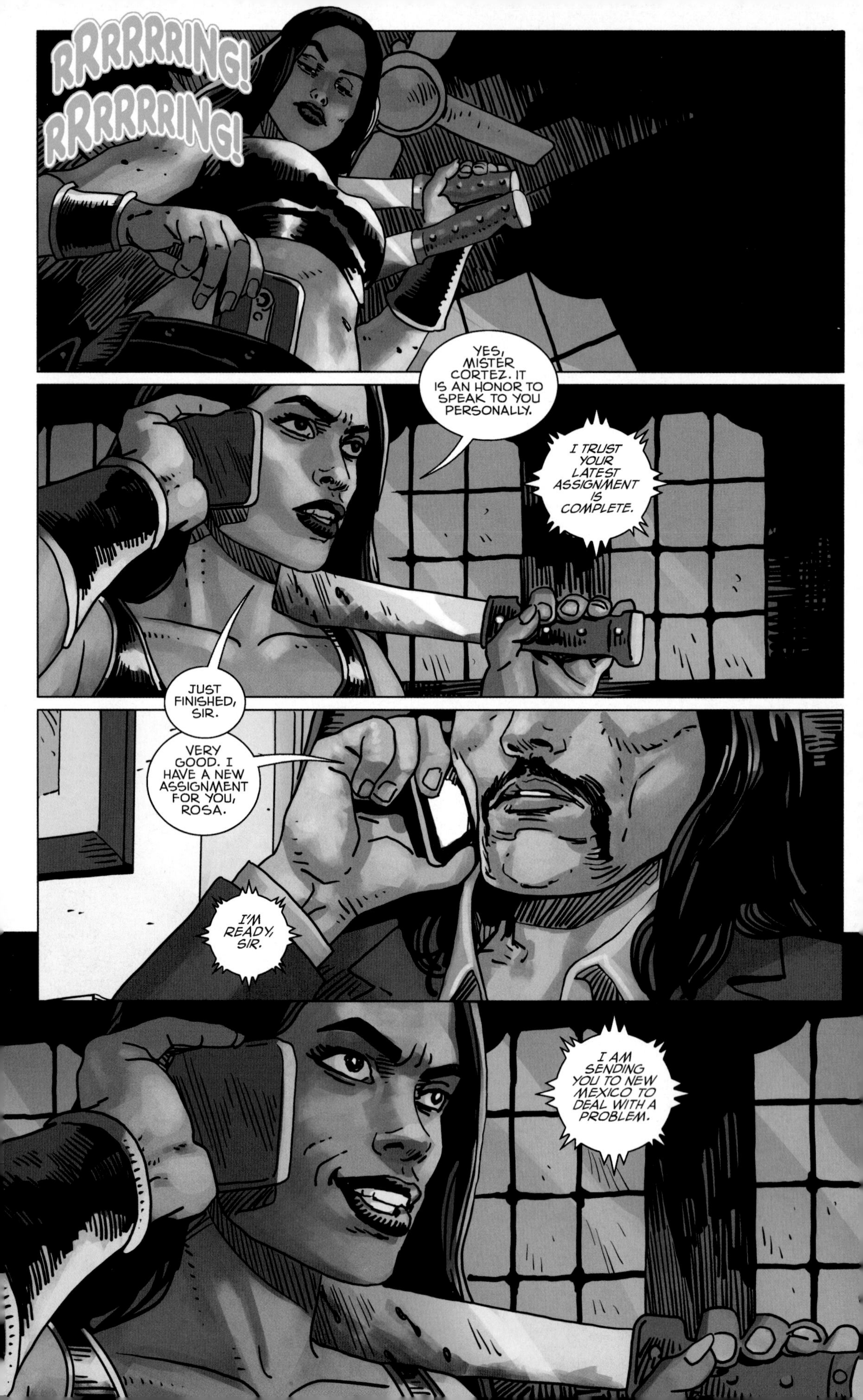
RRRRRRING!
RRRRRRING!
YES, MISTER CORTEZ. IT IS AN HONOR TO SPEAK TO YOU PERSONALLY.
I TRUST YOUR LATEST ASSIGNMENT IS COMPLETE.
JUST FINISHED, SIR.
VERY GOOD. I HAVE A NEW ASSIGNMENT FOR YOU, ROSA.
I'M READY, SIR.
I AM SENDING YOU TO NEW MEXICO TO DEAL WITH A PROBLEM.

THREE

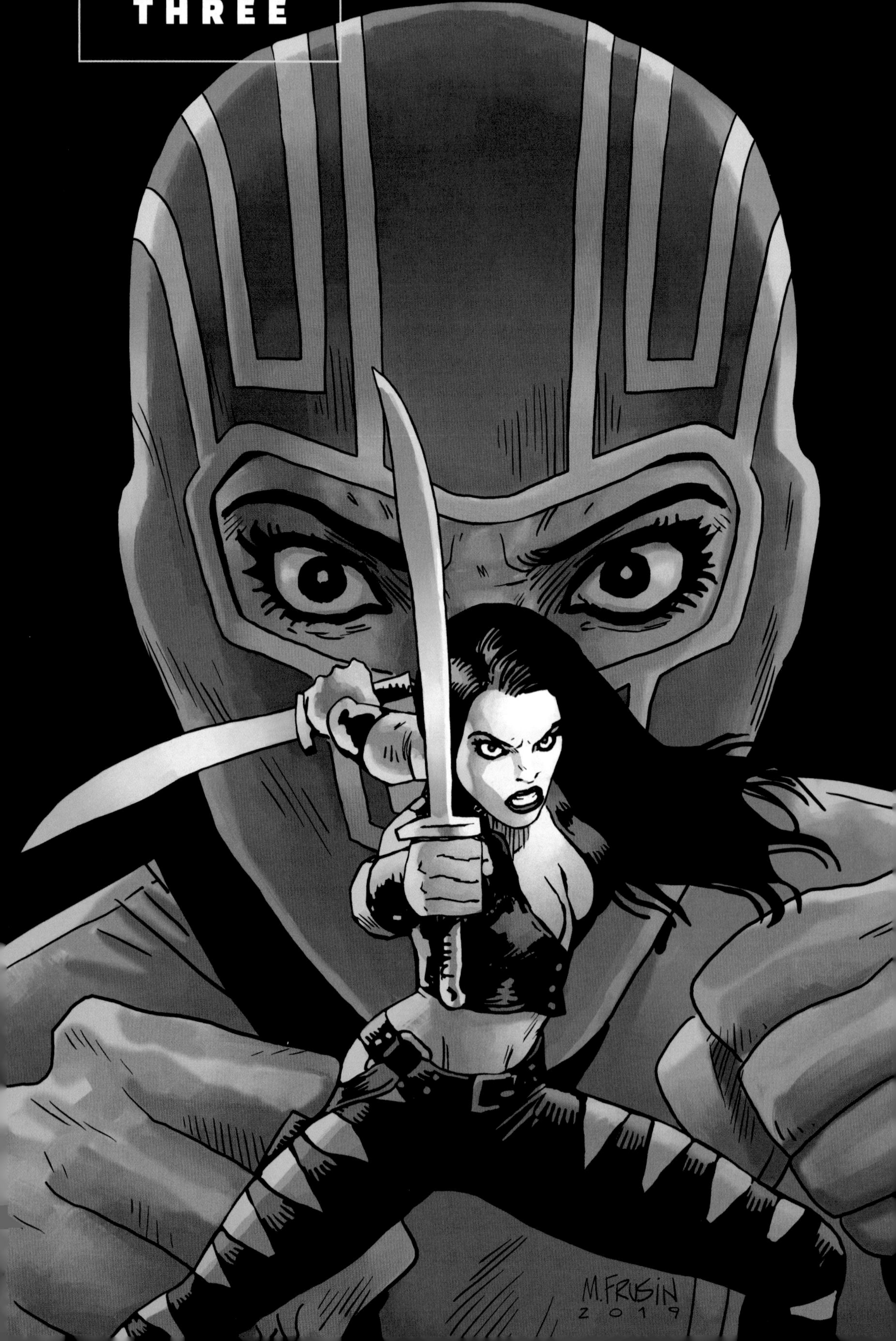
M. FRUSIN
2019

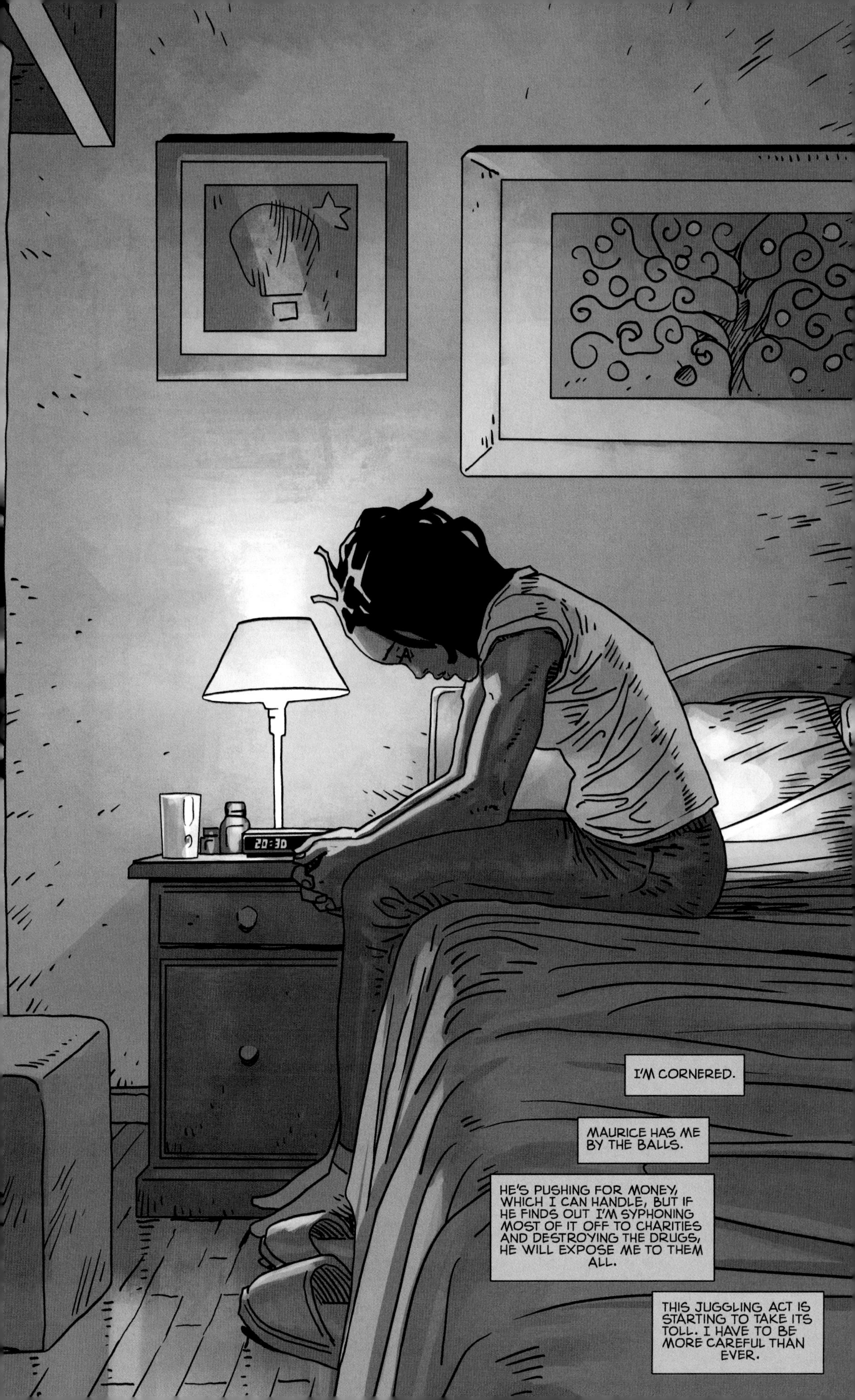
20:30
I'M CORNERED.
MAURICE HAS ME BY THE BALLS.
HE'S PUSHING FOR MONEY, WHICH I CAN HANDLE, BUT IF HE FINDS OUT I'M SYPHONING MOST OF IT OFF TO CHARITIES AND DESTROYING THE DRUGS, HE WILL EXPOSE ME TO THEM ALL.
THIS JUGGLING ACT IS STARTING TO TAKE ITS TOLL. I HAVE TO BE MORE CAREFUL THAN EVER.

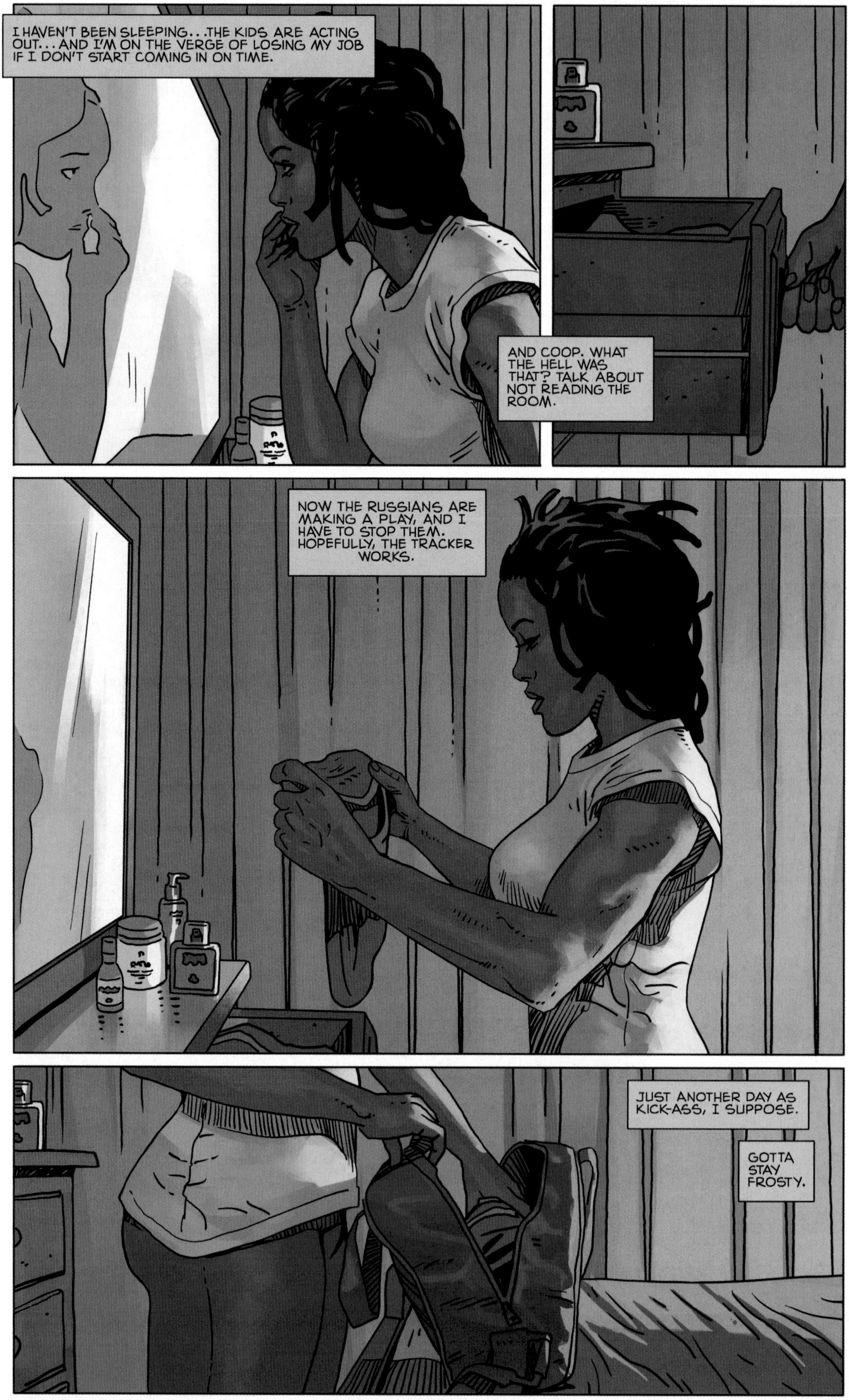
I HAVEN'T BEEN SLEEPING. . .THE KIDS ARE ACTING OUT. . . AND I'M ON THE VERGE OF LOSING MY JOB IF I DON'T START COMING IN ON TIME.
AND COOP. WHAT THE HELL WAS THAT? TALK ABOUT NOT READING THE ROOM.
NOW THE RUSSIANS ARE MAKING A PLAY, AND I HAVE TO STOP THEM. HOPEFULLY, THE TRACKER WORKS.
JUST ANOTHER DAY AS KICK-ASS, I SUPPOSE.
GOTTA STAY FROSTY.

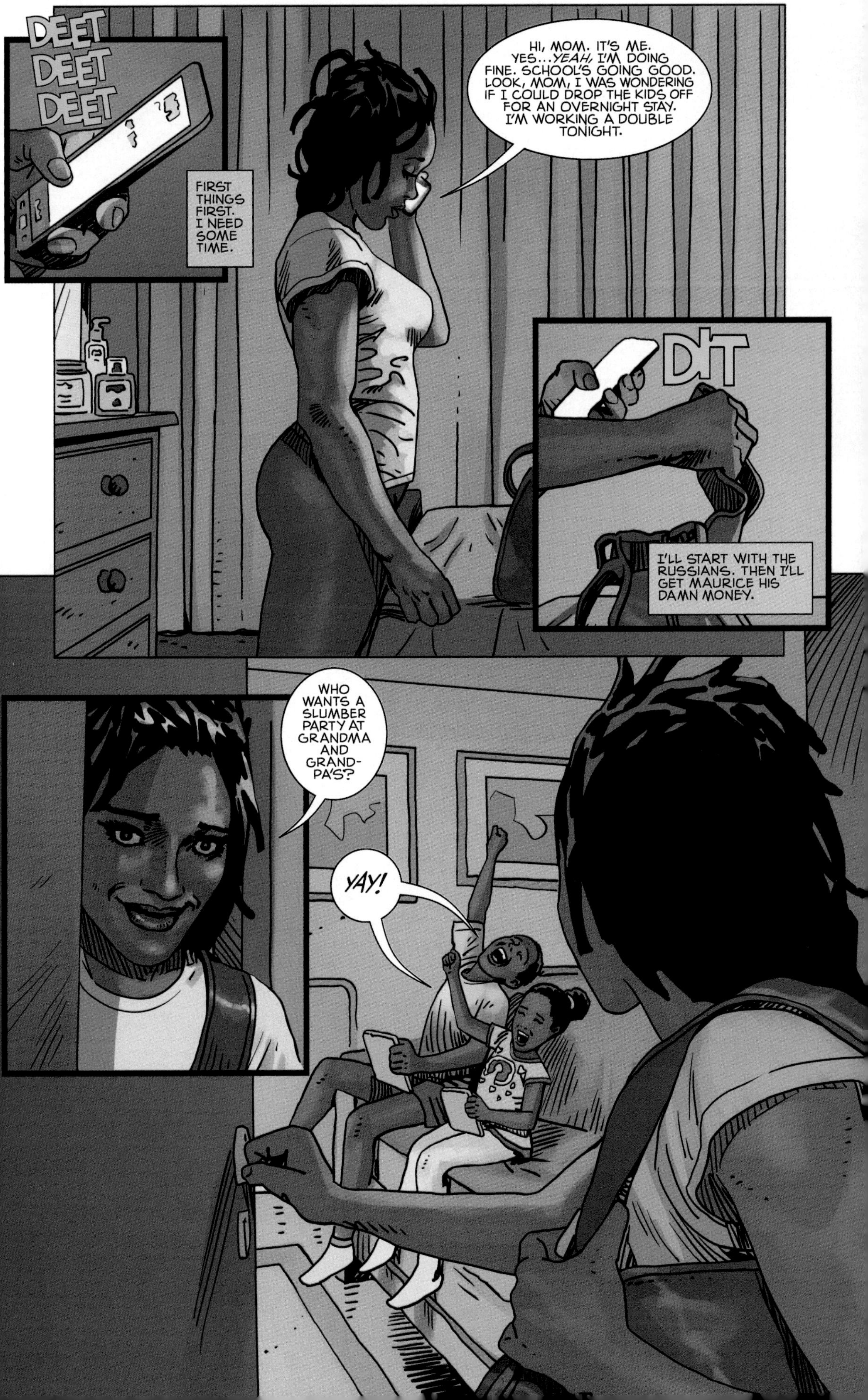
DEET DEET DEET
FIRST THINGS FIRST. I NEED SOME TIME.
HI, MOM. IT'S ME. YES... YEAH, I'M DOING FINE. SCHOOL'S GOING GOOD. LOOK, MOM, I WAS WONDERING IF I COULD DROP THE KIDS OFF FOR AN OVERNIGHT STAY. I'M WORKING A DOUBLE TONIGHT.
DIT
I'LL START WITH THE RUSSIANS. THEN I'LL GET MAURICE HIS DAMN MONEY.
WHO WANTS A SLUMBER PARTY AT GRANDMA AND GRAND-PA'S?
YAY!

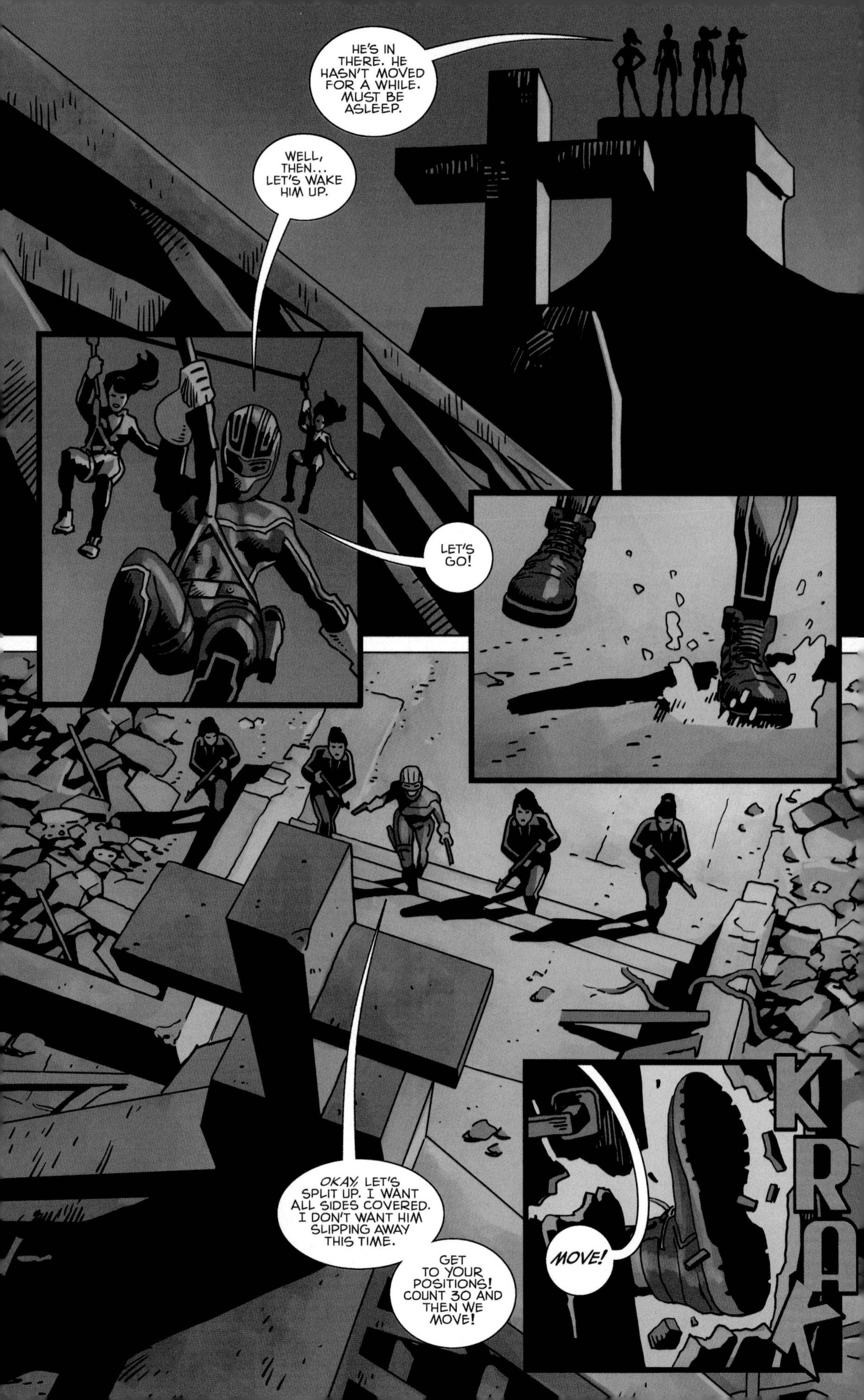
HE'S IN THERE. HE HASN'T MOVED FOR A WHILE. MUST BE ASLEEP.
WELL, THEN... LET'S WAKE HIM UP.
LET'S GO!
OKAY, LET'S SPLIT UP. I WANT ALL SIDES COVERED. I DON'T WANT HIM SLIPPING AWAY THIS TIME.
GET TO YOUR POSITIONS! COUNT 30 AND THEN WE MOVE!
MOVE!
KRA

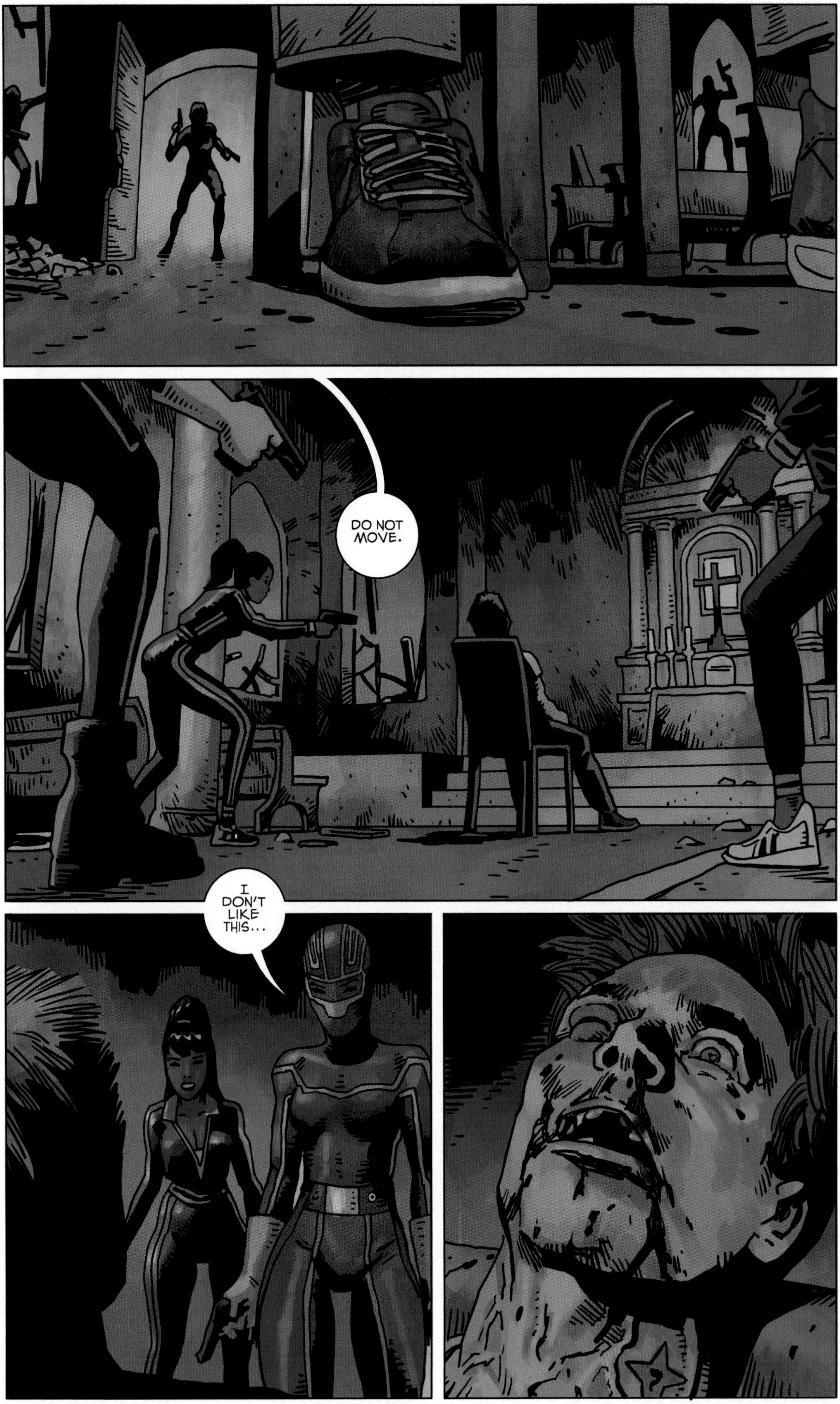
DO NOT MOVE.
I DON'T LIKE THIS...

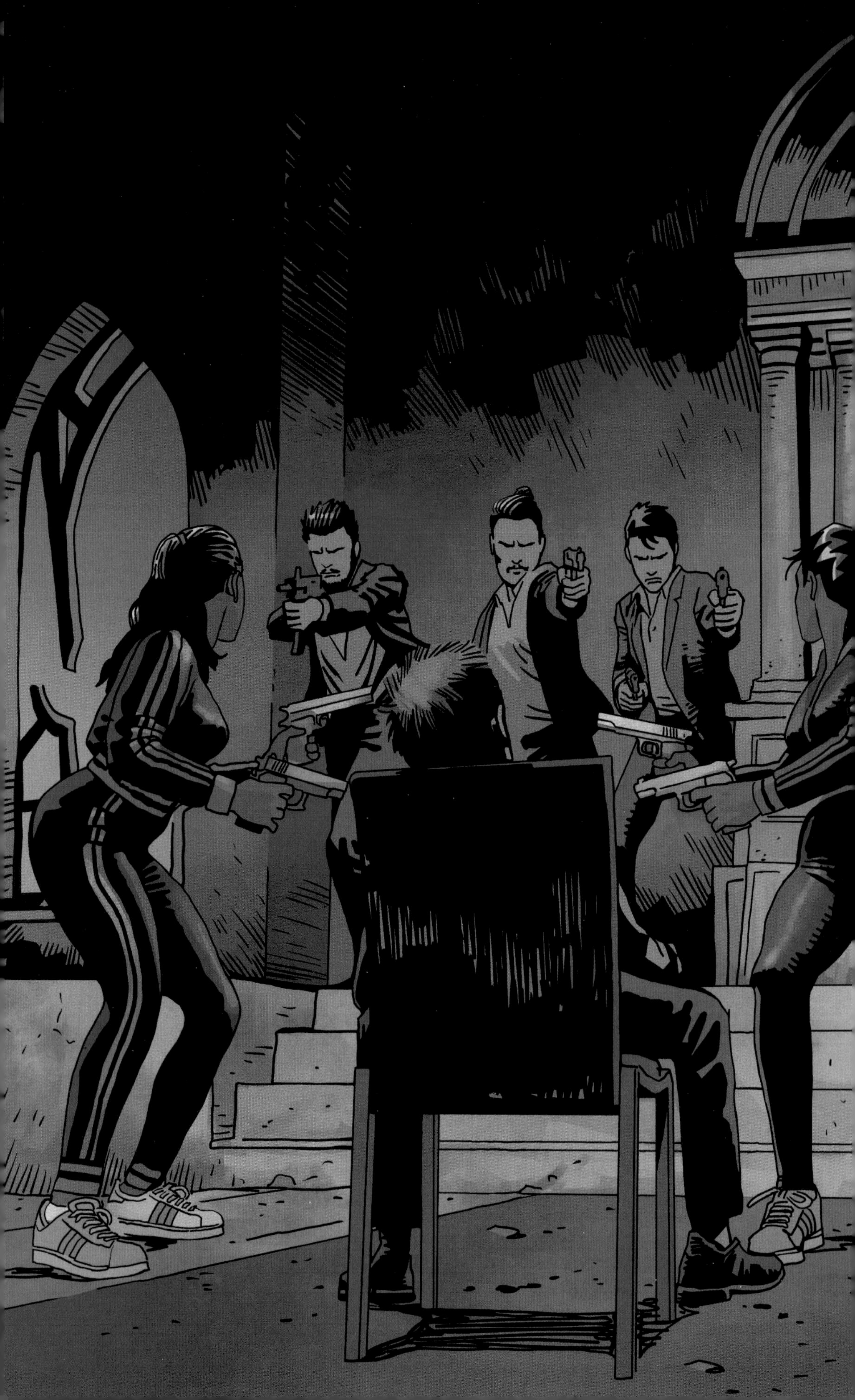

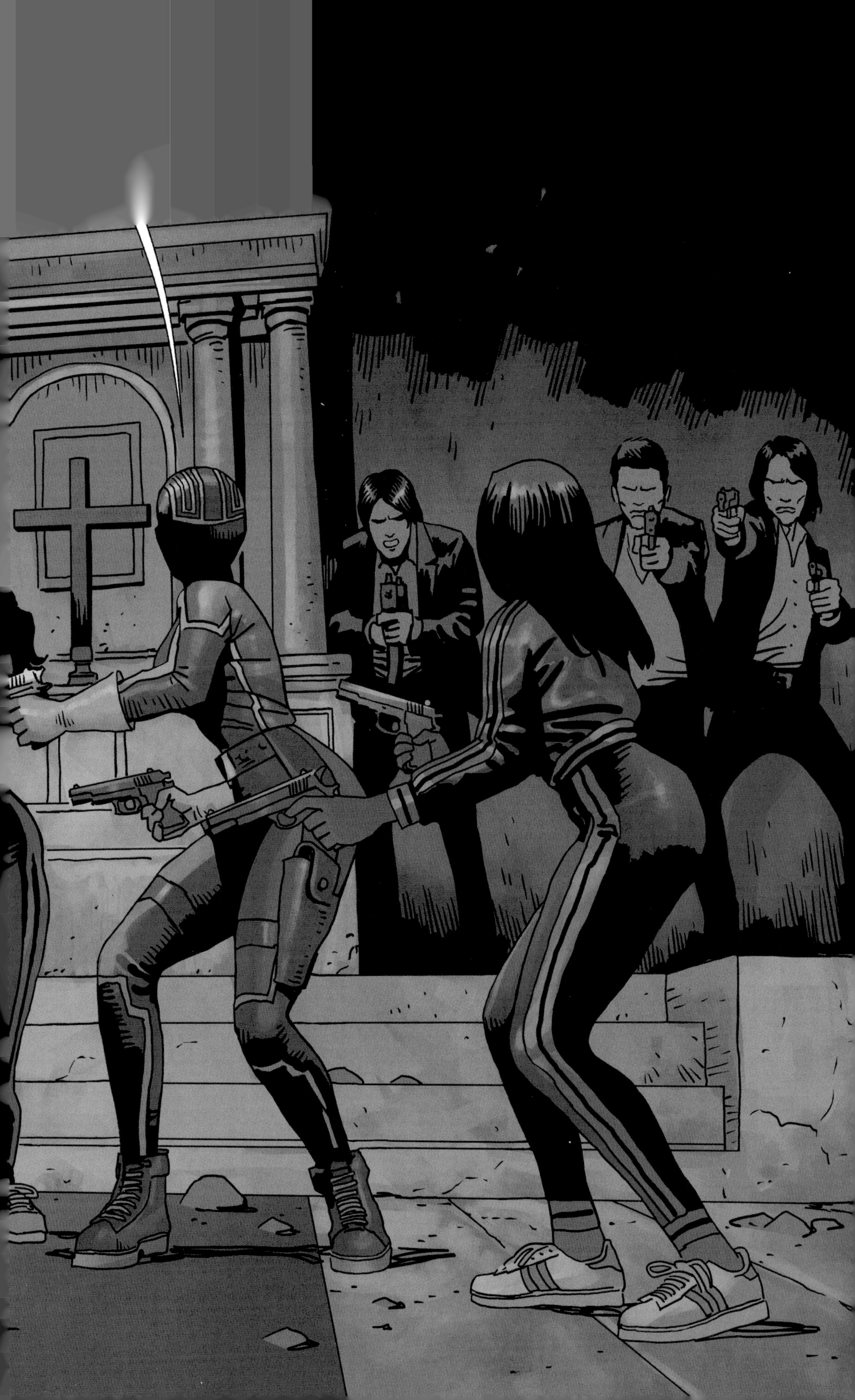

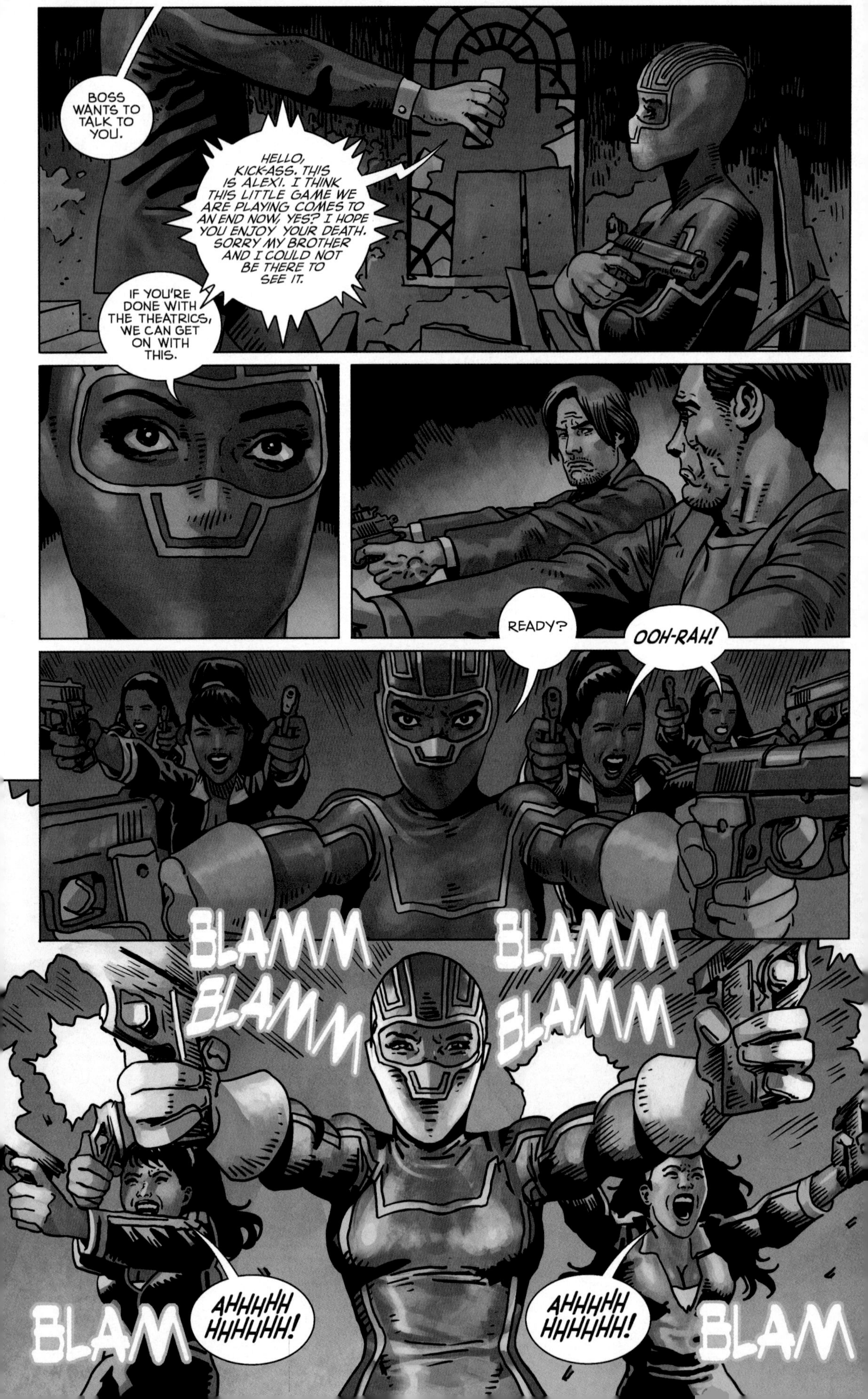
BOSS WANTS TO TALK TO YOU.
HELLO, KICK-ASS. THIS IS ALEXI. I THINK THIS LITTLE GAME WE ARE PLAYING COMES TO AN END NOW, YES? I HOPE YOU ENJOY YOUR DEATH. SORRY MY BROTHER AND I COULD NOT BE THERE TO SEE IT.
IF YOU'RE DONE WITH THE THEATRICS, WE CAN GET ON WITH THIS.
READY?
OOH-RAH!
BLAMM
BLAMM
BLAMM
BLAMM
BLAM
AHHHHH HHHHHH!
AHHHHH HHHHHH!
BLAM

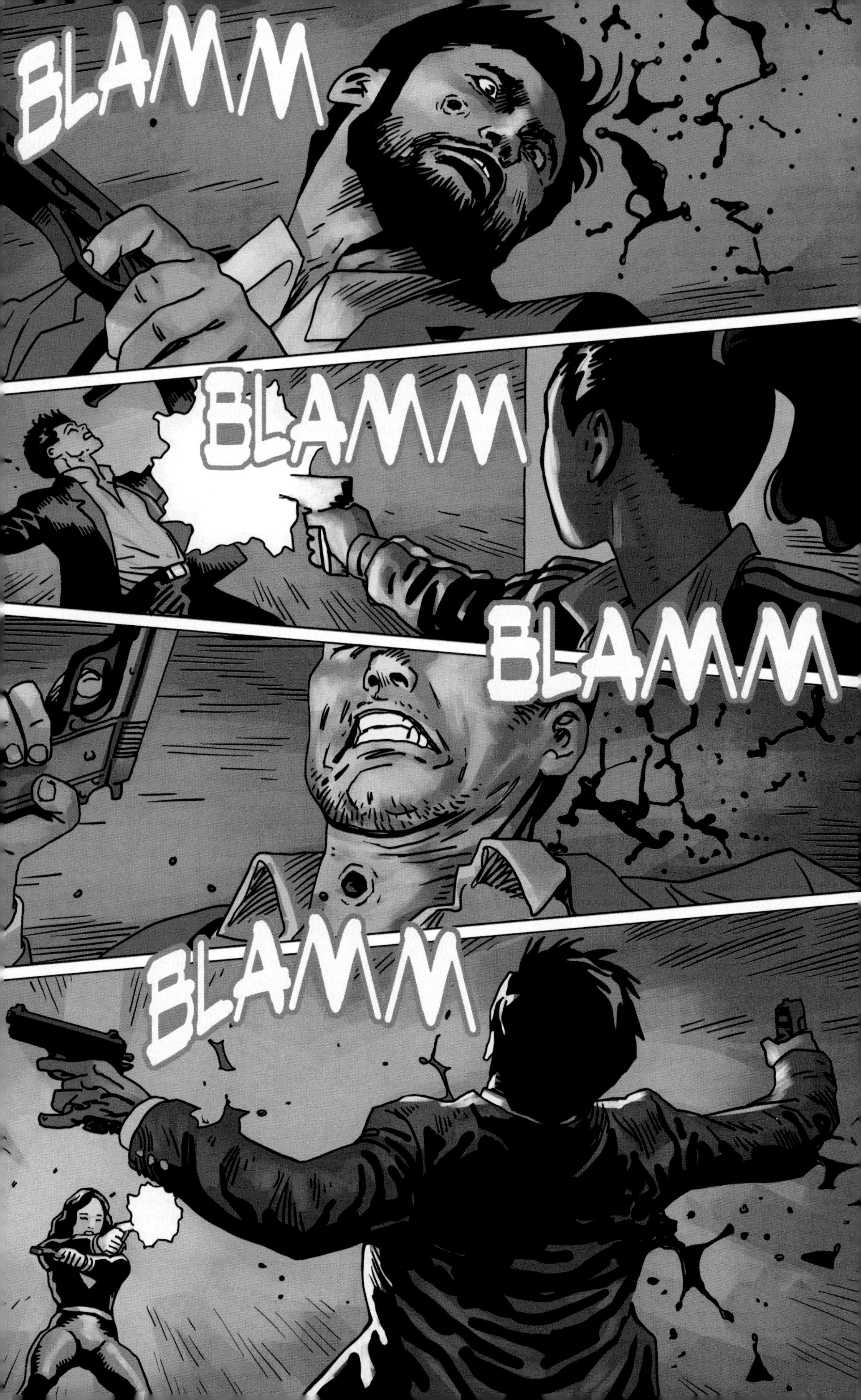
BLAMM
BLAMM
BLAMM
BLAMM

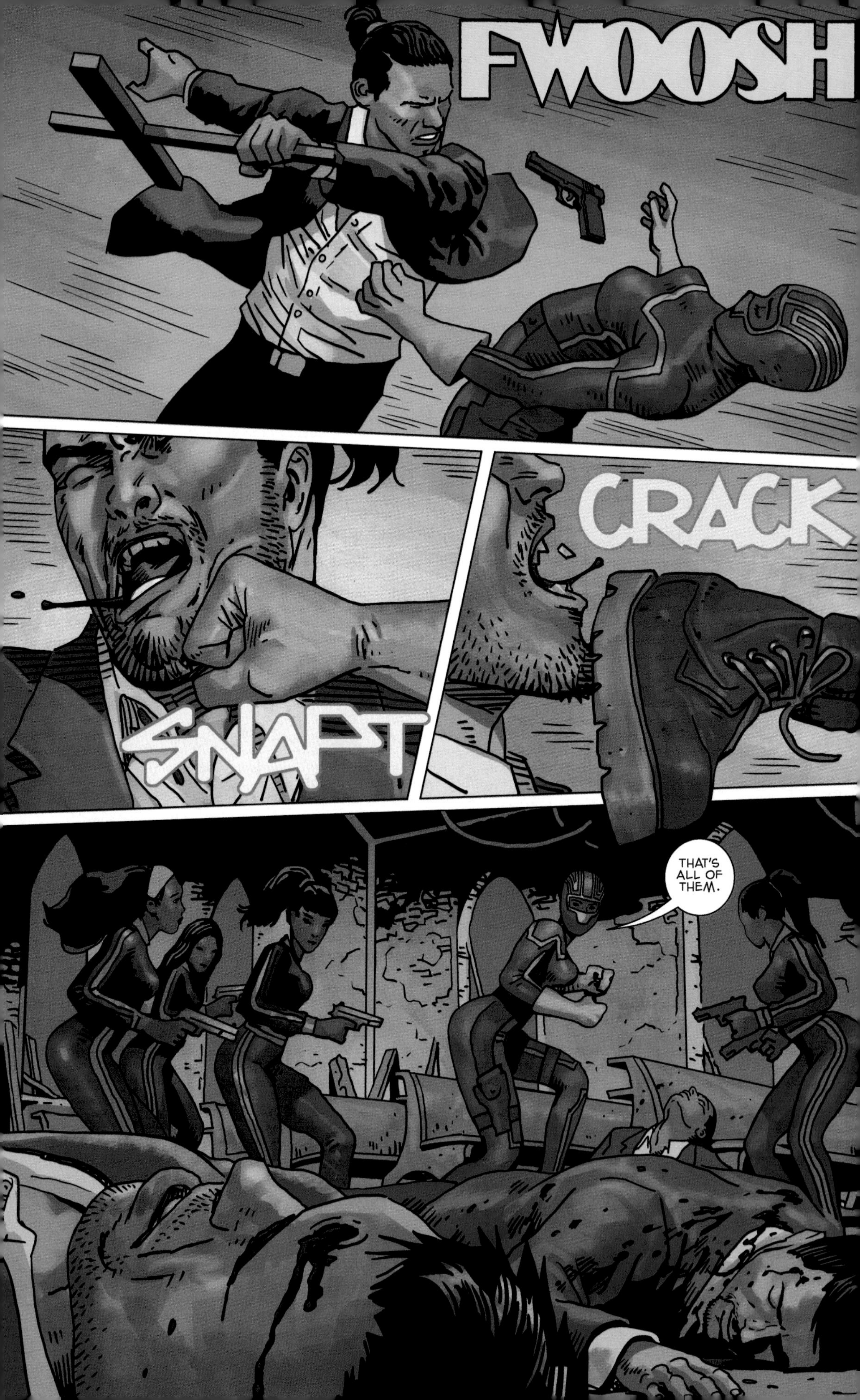
FWOOSH
SNAPT
CRACK
THAT'S ALL OF THEM.

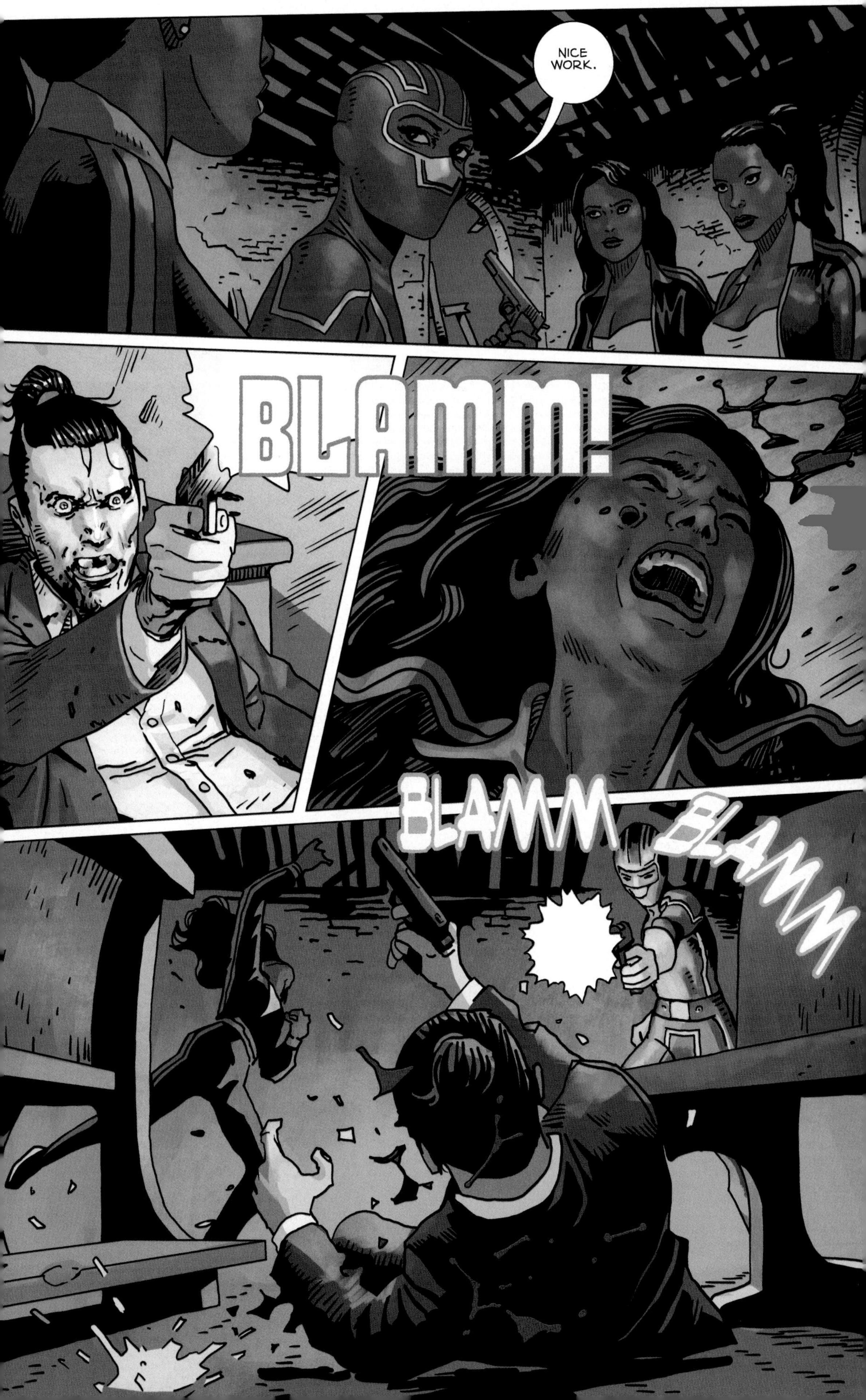
NICE WORK.
BLAMM!
BLAMM
BLAMM

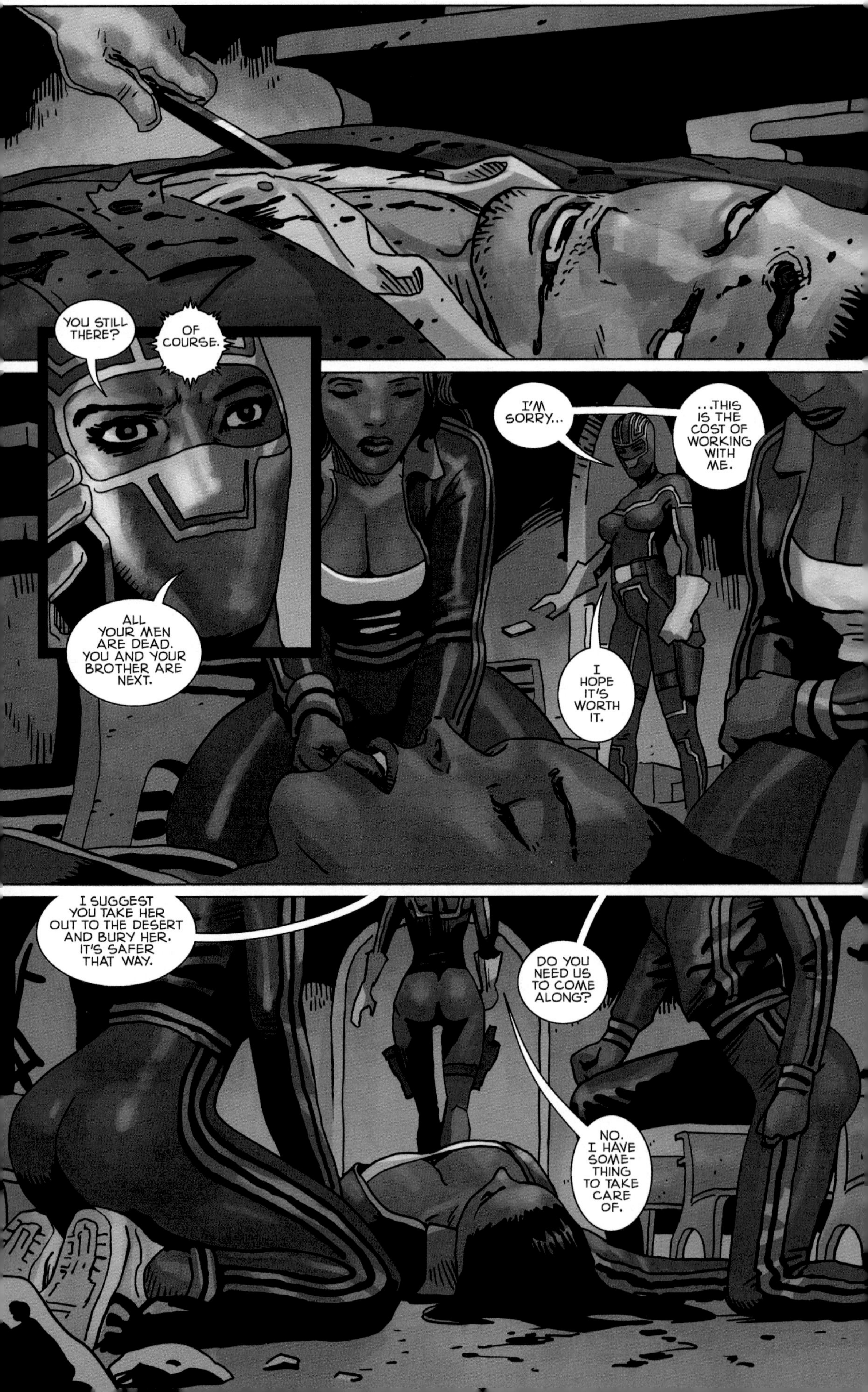
YOU STILL THERE?
OF COURSE.
ALL YOUR MEN ARE DEAD. YOU AND YOUR BROTHER ARE NEXT.
I'M SORRY...
...THIS IS THE COST OF WORKING WITH ME.
I HOPE IT'S WORTH IT.
I SUGGEST YOU TAKE HER OUT TO THE DESERT AND BURY HER. IT'S SAFER THAT WAY.
DO YOU NEED US TO COME ALONG?
NO. I HAVE SOME-THING TO TAKE CARE OF.

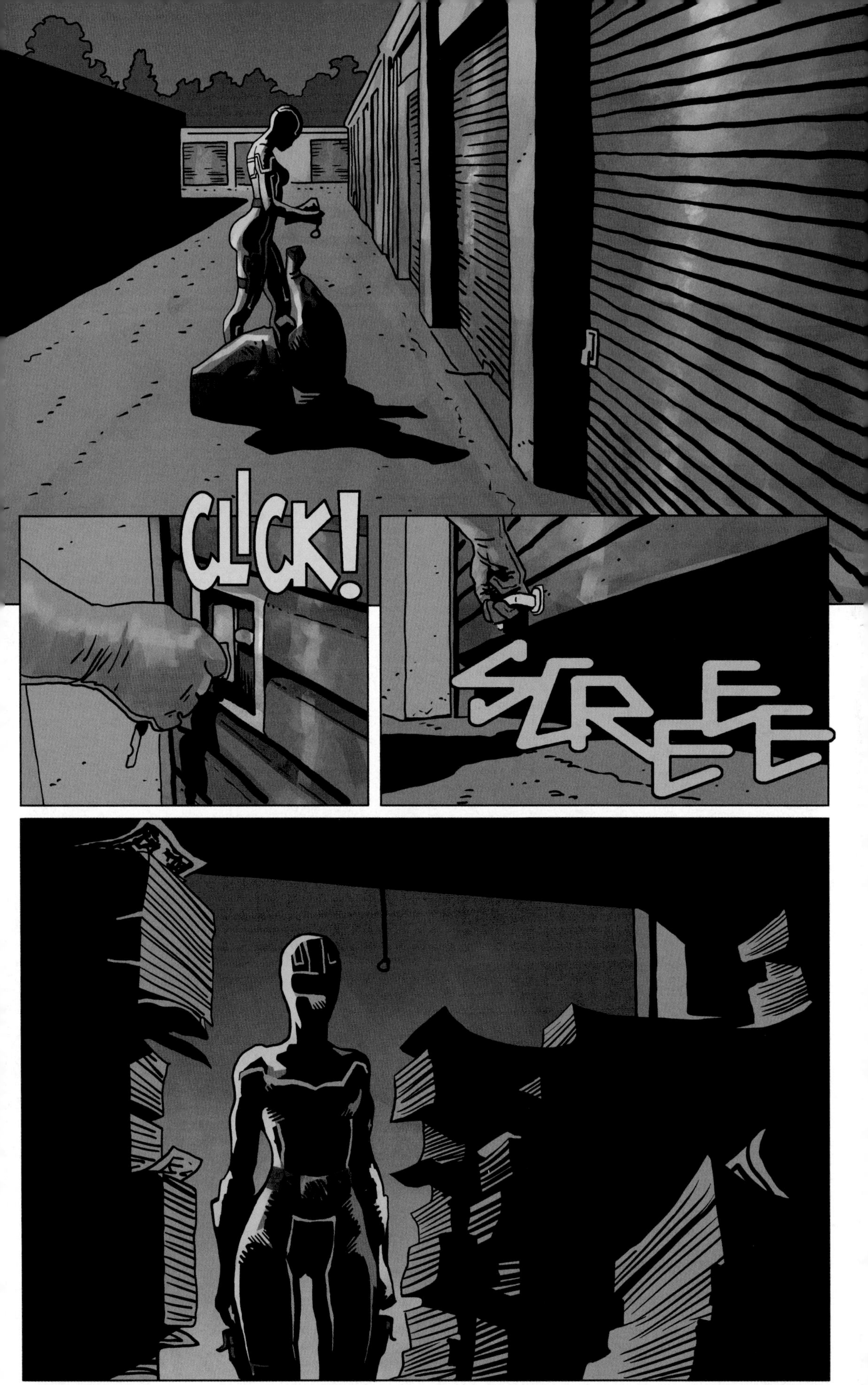
CLICK!
SCREEE

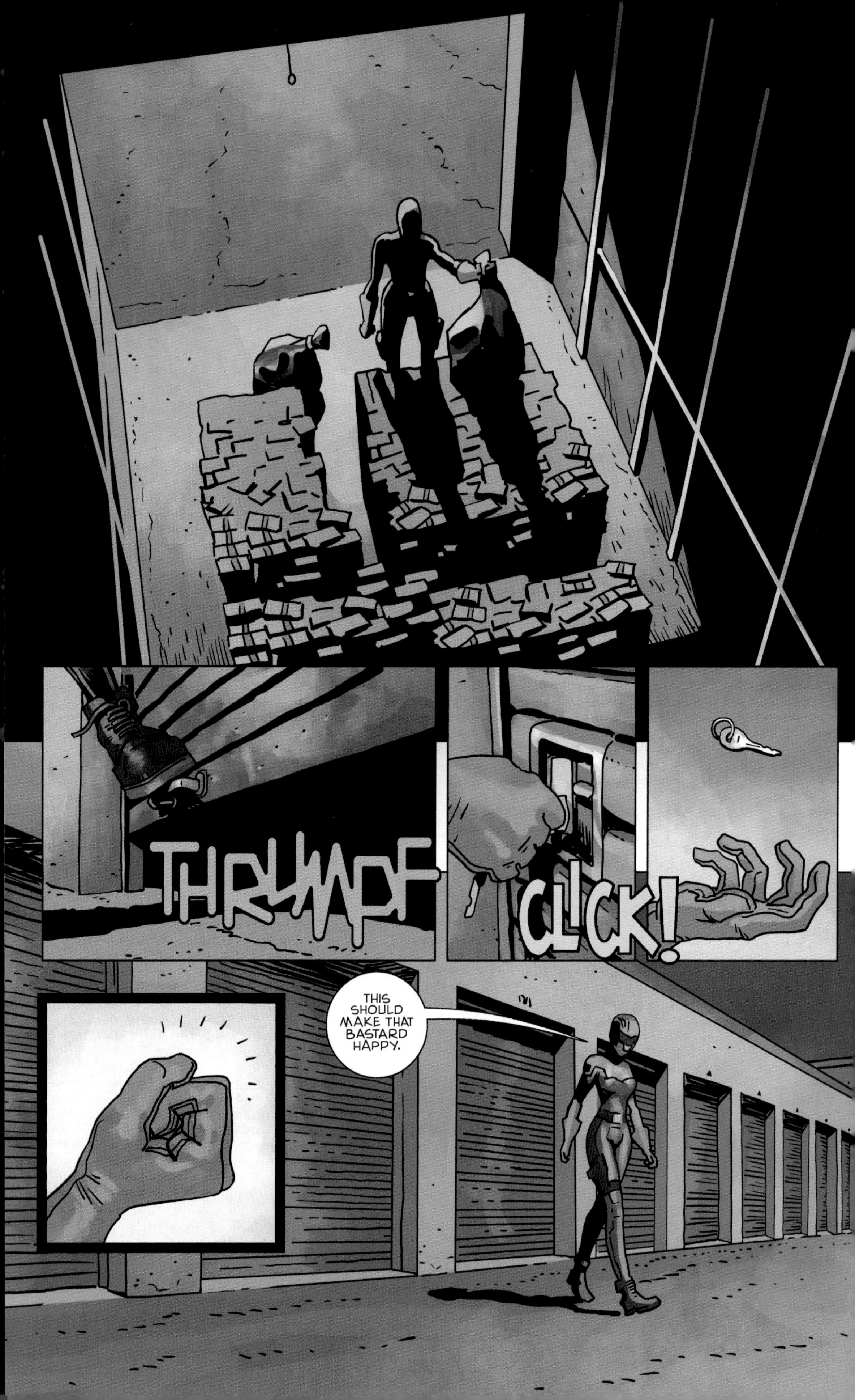
THRUMPF
CLICK!
THIS SHOULD MAKE THAT BASTARD HAPPY.

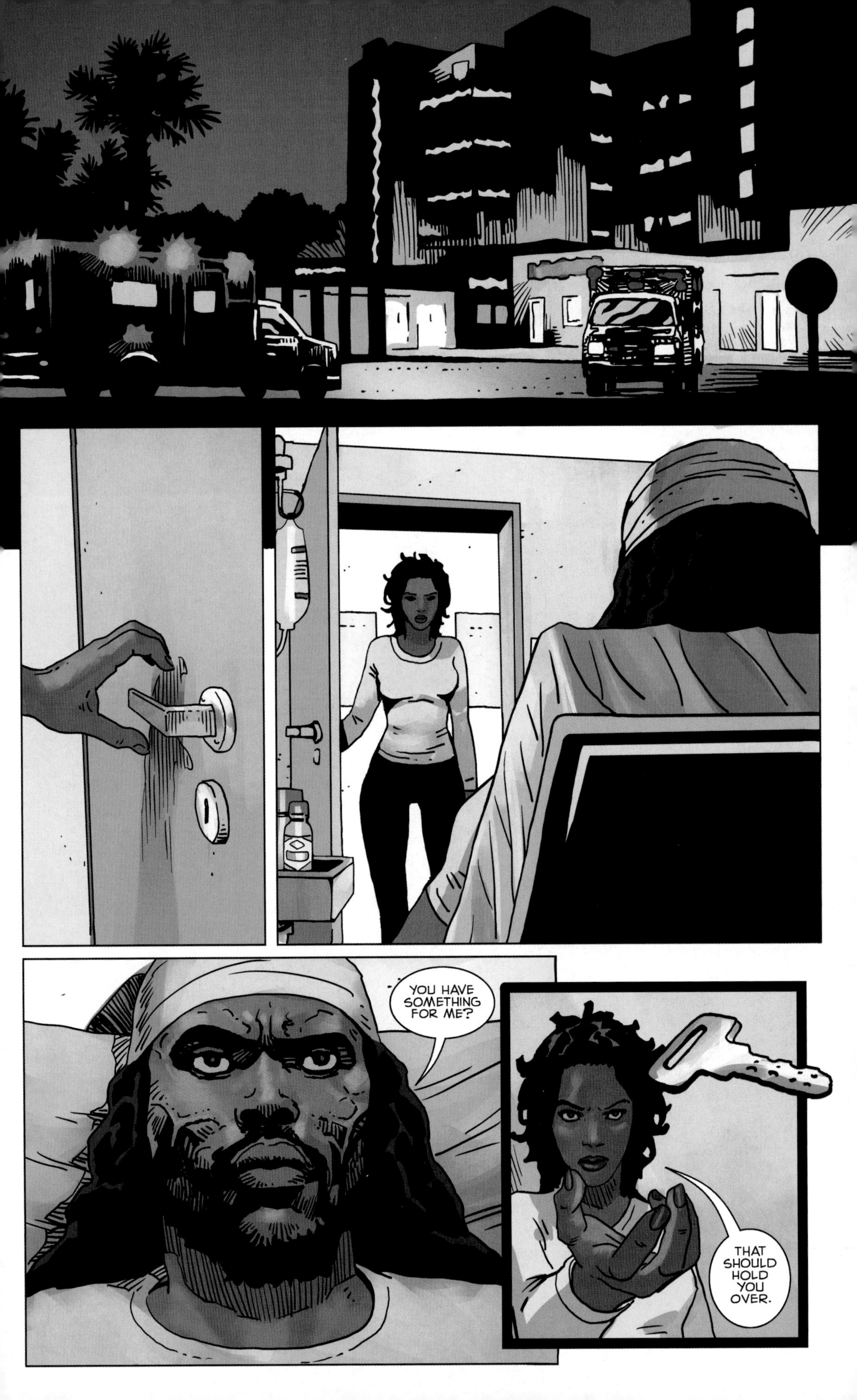
YOU HAVE SOMETHING FOR ME?
THAT SHOULD HOLD YOU OVER.

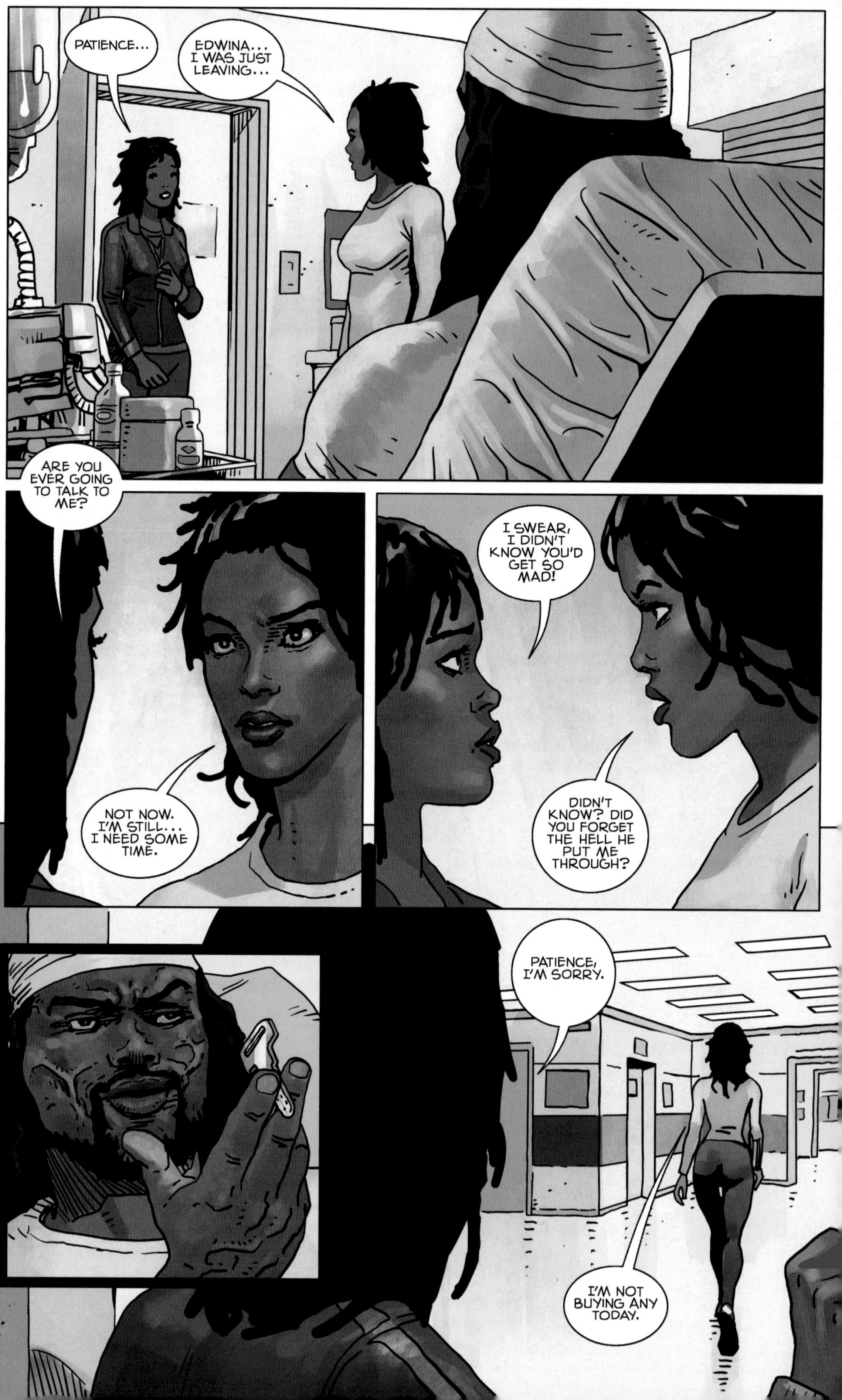
PATIENCE...
EDWINA... I WAS JUST LEAVING...
ARE YOU EVER GOING TO TALK TO ME?
NOT NOW. I'M STILL... I NEED SOME TIME.
I SWEAR, I DIDN'T KNOW YOU'D GET SO MAD!
DIDN'T KNOW? DID YOU FORGET THE HELL HE PUT ME THROUGH?
PATIENCE, I'M SORRY.
I'M NOT BUYING ANY TODAY.

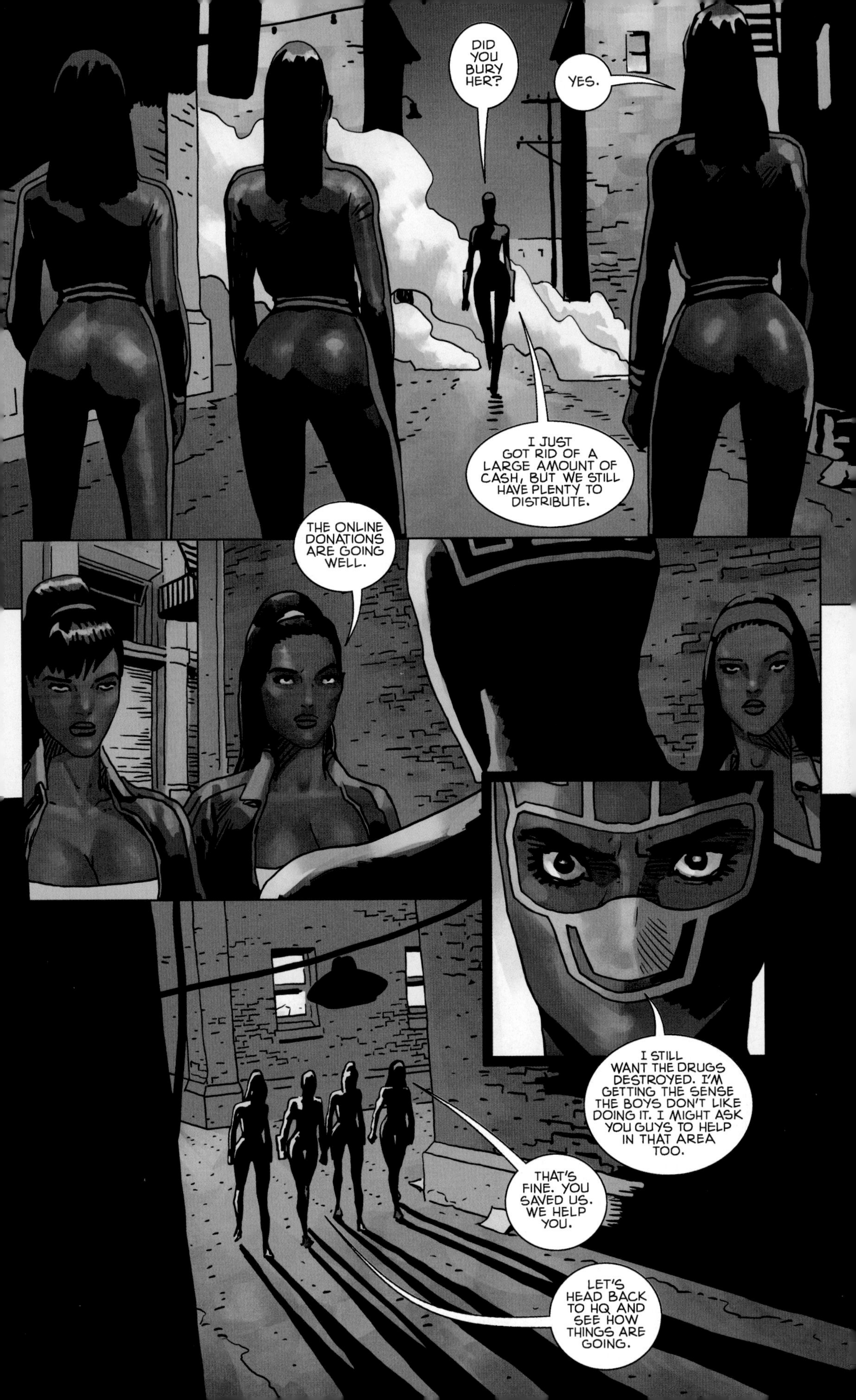
DID YOU BURY HER?
YES.
I JUST GOT RID OF A LARGE AMOUNT OF CASH, BUT WE STILL HAVE PLENTY TO DISTRIBUTE.
THE ONLINE DONATIONS ARE GOING WELL.
I STILL WANT THE DRUGS DESTROYED. I'M GETTING THE SENSE THE BOYS DON'T LIKE DOING IT. I MIGHT ASK YOU GUYS TO HELP IN THAT AREA TOO.
THAT'S FINE. YOU SAVED US. WE HELP YOU.
LET'S HEAD BACK TO HQ AND SEE HOW THINGS ARE GOING.

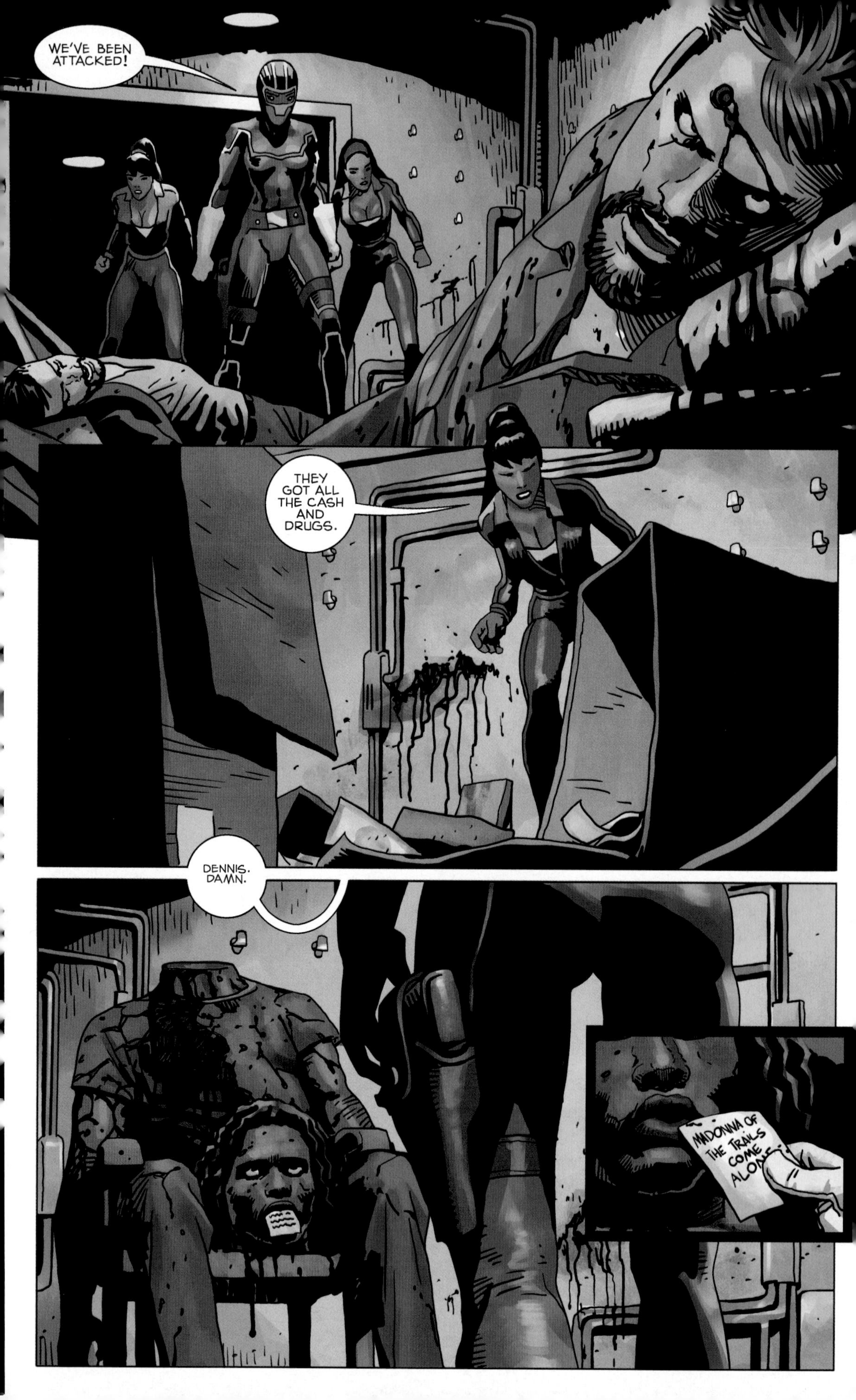
WE'VE BEEN ATTACKED!
THEY GOT ALL THE CASH AND DRUGS.
DENNIS. DAMN.
MADONNA OF THE TRAILS COME ALON

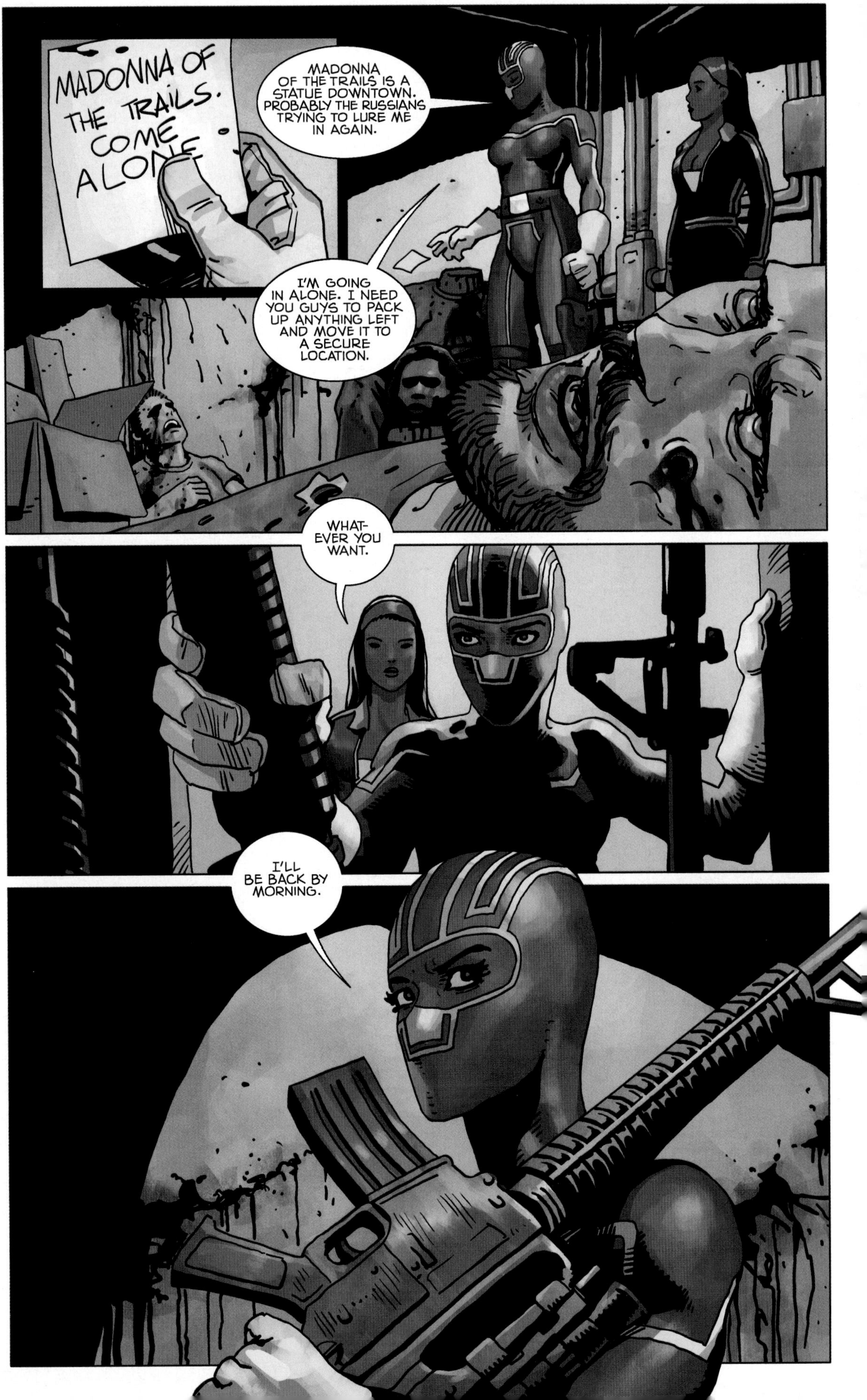
MADONNA OF THE TRAILS. COME ALONE
MADONNA OF THE TRAILS IS A STATUE DOWNTOWN. PROBABLY THE RUSSIANS TRYING TO LURE ME IN AGAIN.
I'M GOING IN ALONE. I NEED YOU GUYS TO PACK UP ANYTHING LEFT AND MOVE IT TO A SECURE LOCATION.
WHAT-EVER YOU WANT.
I'LL BE BACK BY MORNING.

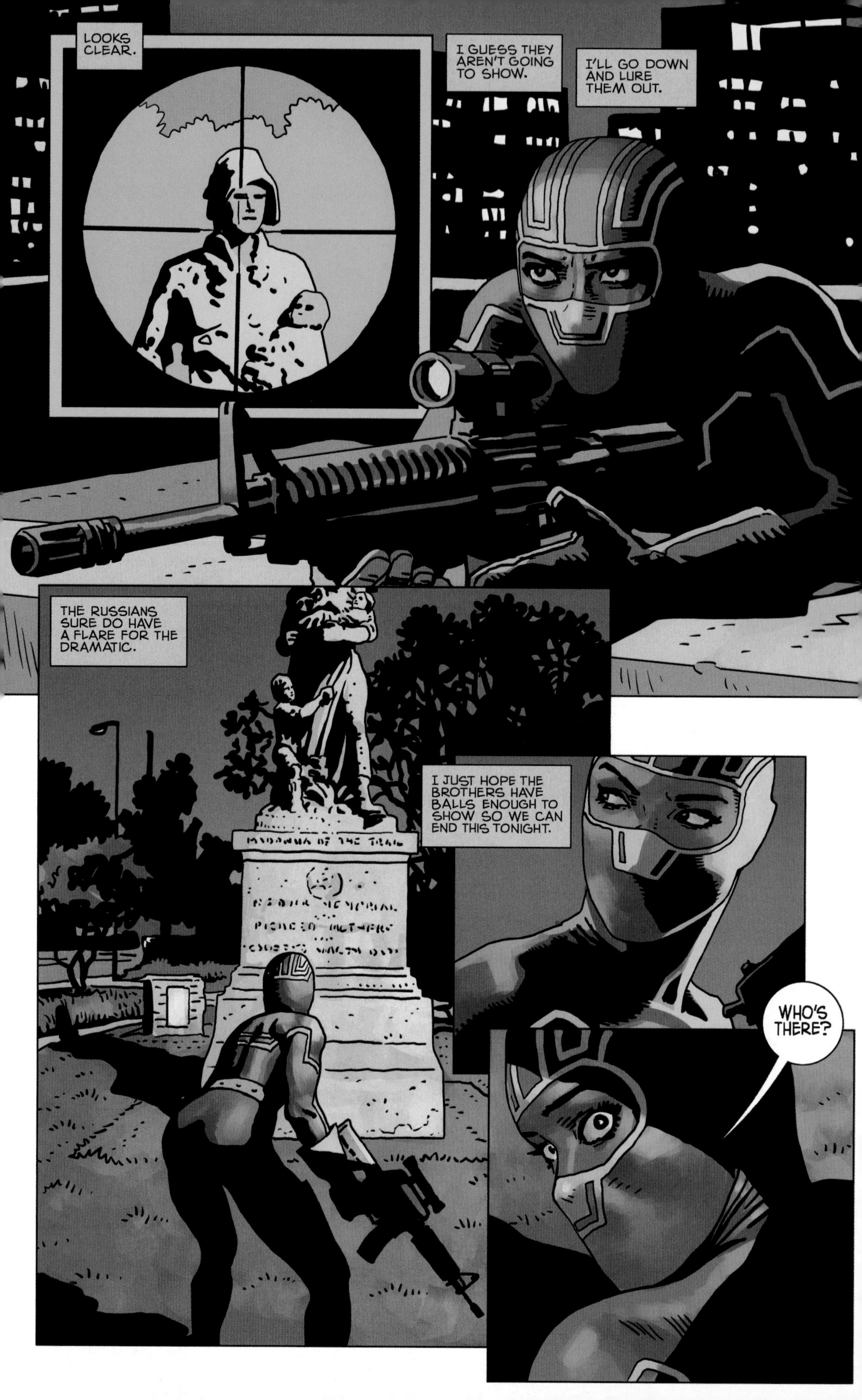
LOOKS CLEAR.
I GUESS THEY AREN'T GOING TO SHOW.
I'LL GO DOWN AND LURE THEM OUT.
THE RUSSIANS SURE DO HAVE A FLARE FOR THE DRAMATIC.
I JUST HOPE THE BROTHERS HAVE BALLS ENOUGH TO SHOW SO WE CAN END THIS TONIGHT.
WHO'S THERE?

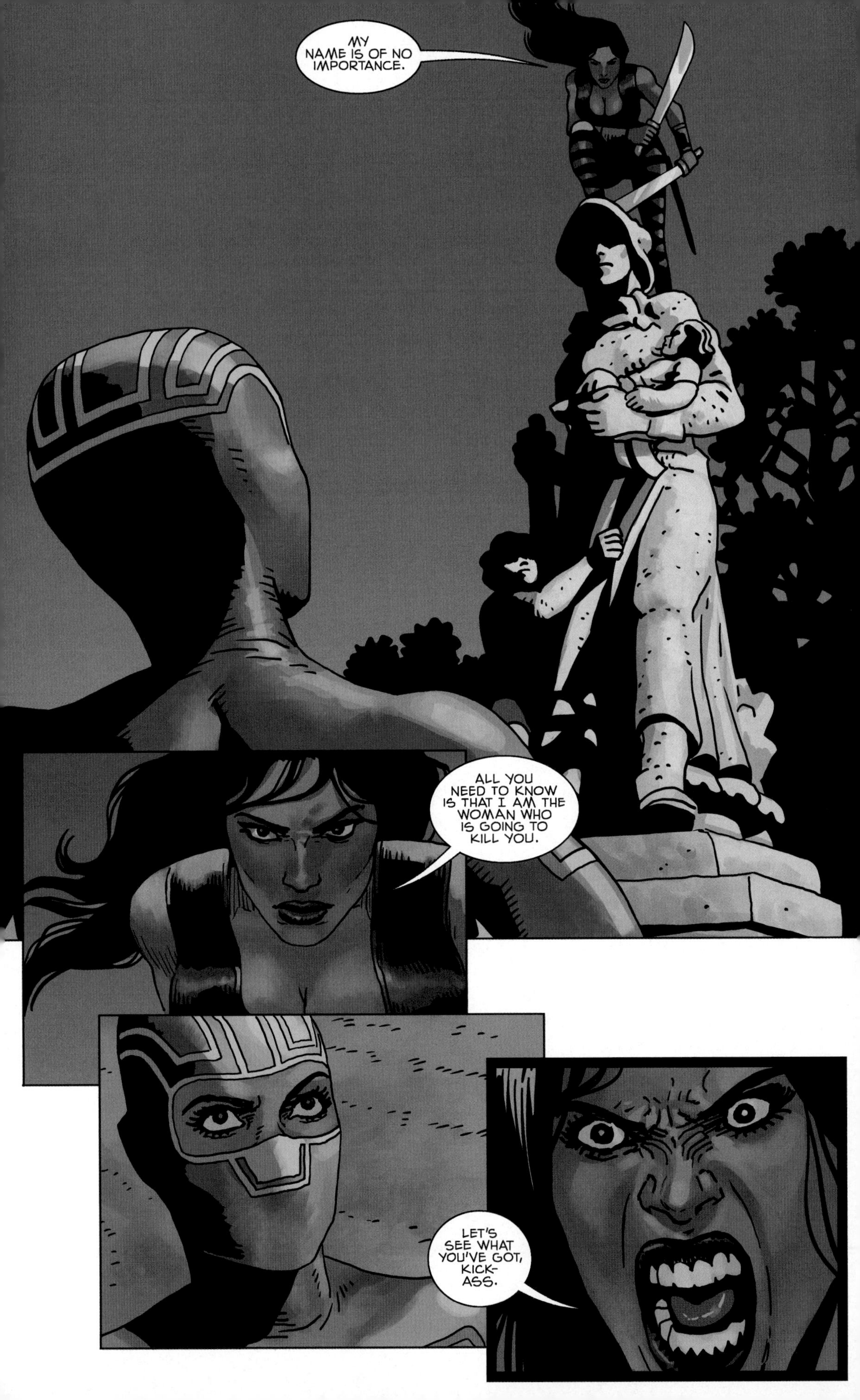
MY NAME IS OF NO IMPORTANCE.
ALL YOU NEED TO KNOW IS THAT I AM THE WOMAN WHO IS GOING TO KILL YOU.
LET'S SEE WHAT YOU'VE GOT, KICK-ASS.

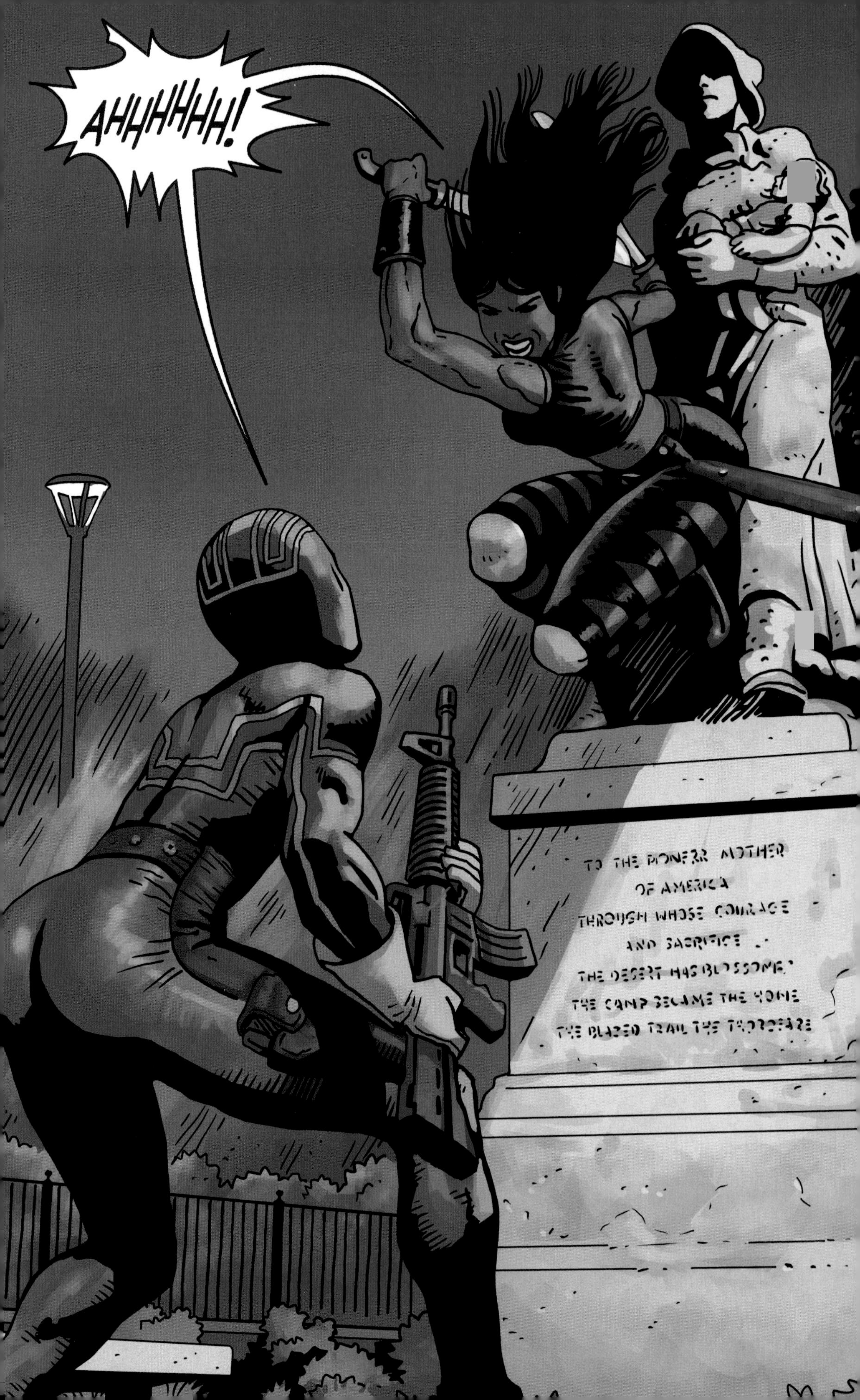
AHHHHHH!
TO THE PIONEER MOTHER
OF AMERICA
THROUGH WHOSE COURAGE
AND SACRIFICE
THE DESERT HAS BLOSSOMED
THE CAMP BECAME THE HOME
THE BLAZED TRAIL THE THOROFARE

FOUR

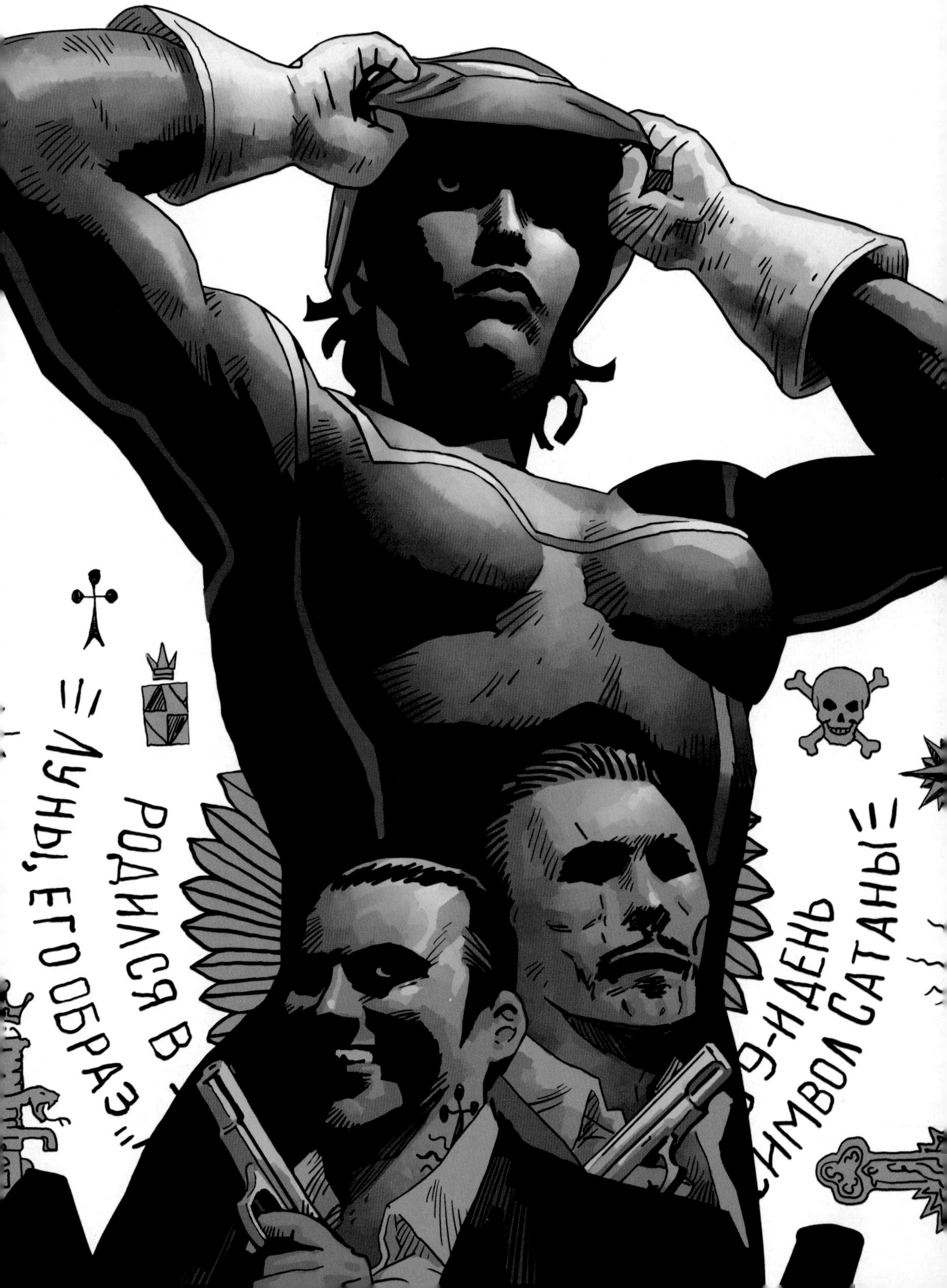

РОДИЛСЯ В
ЛУНЫ, ЕГО ОБРАЗ
9-Й ДЕНЬ
СИМВОЛ САТАНЫ

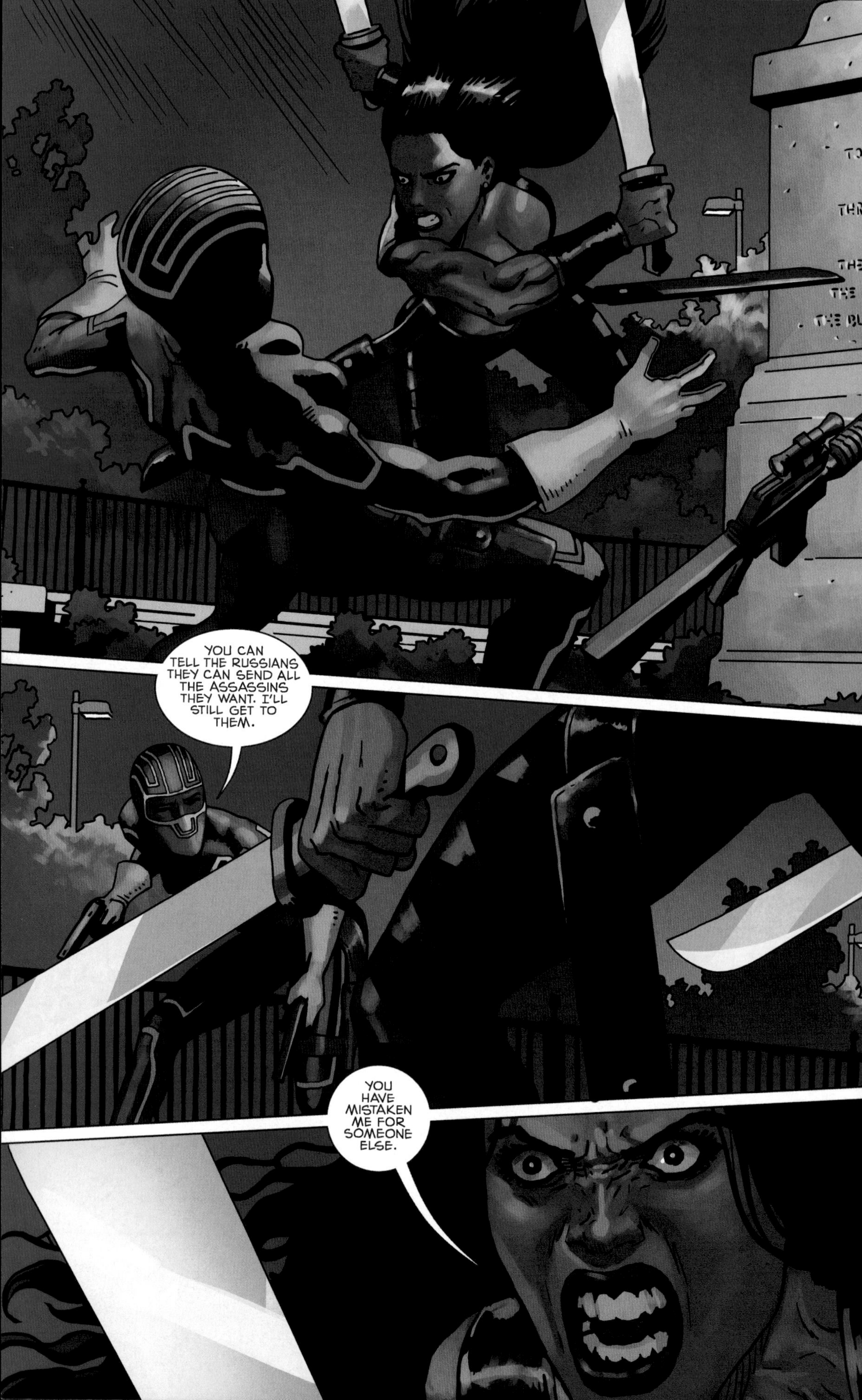
YOU CAN TELL THE RUSSIANS THEY CAN SEND ALL THE ASSASSINS THEY WANT. I'LL STILL GET TO THEM.
YOU HAVE MISTAKEN ME FOR SOMEONE ELSE.

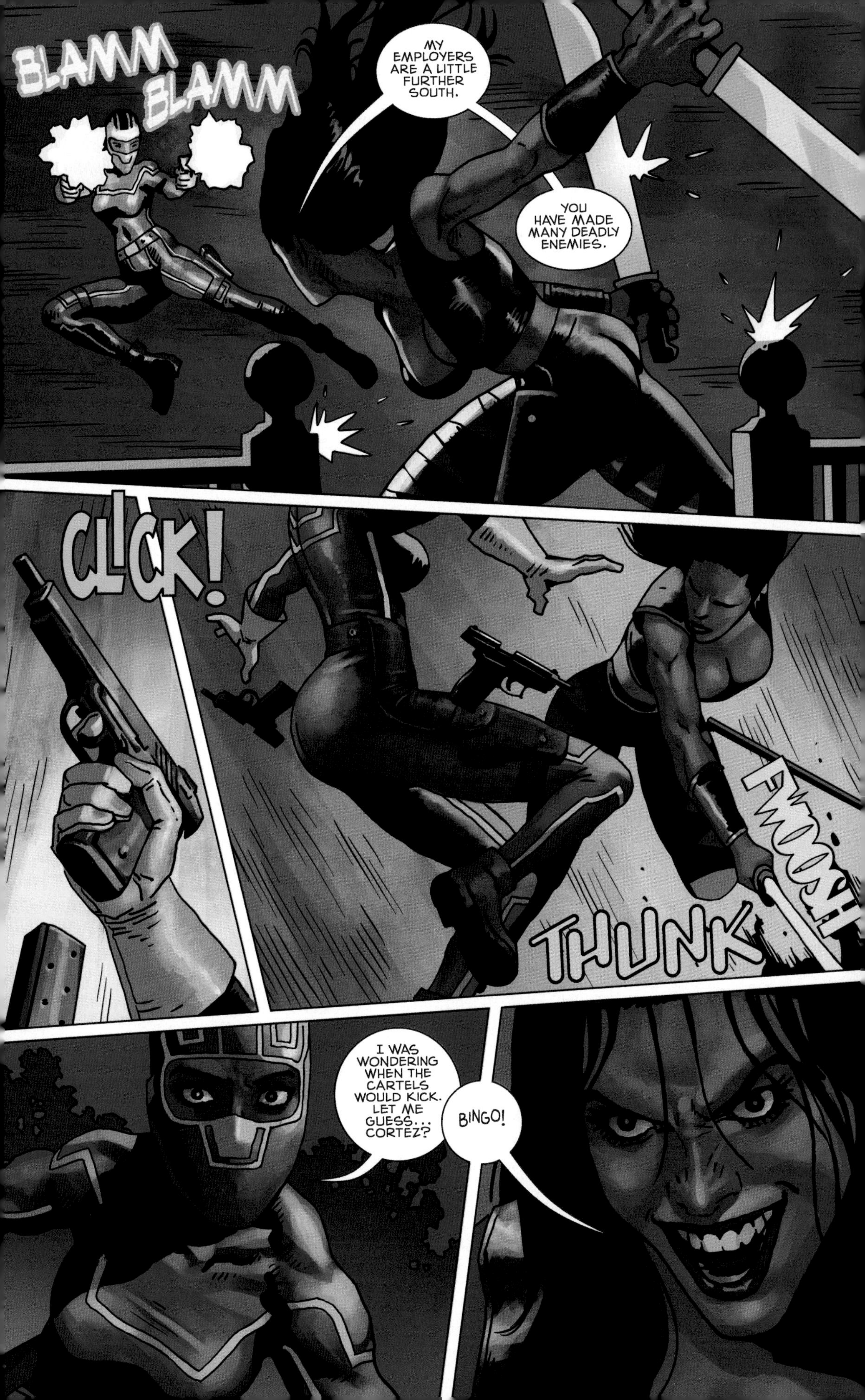
BLAMM BLAMM
MY EMPLOYERS ARE A LITTLE FURTHER SOUTH.
YOU HAVE MADE MANY DEADLY ENEMIES.
CLICK!
FWOOSH!
THUNK
I WAS WONDERING WHEN THE CARTELS WOULD KICK. LET ME GUESS... CORTEZ?
BINGO!

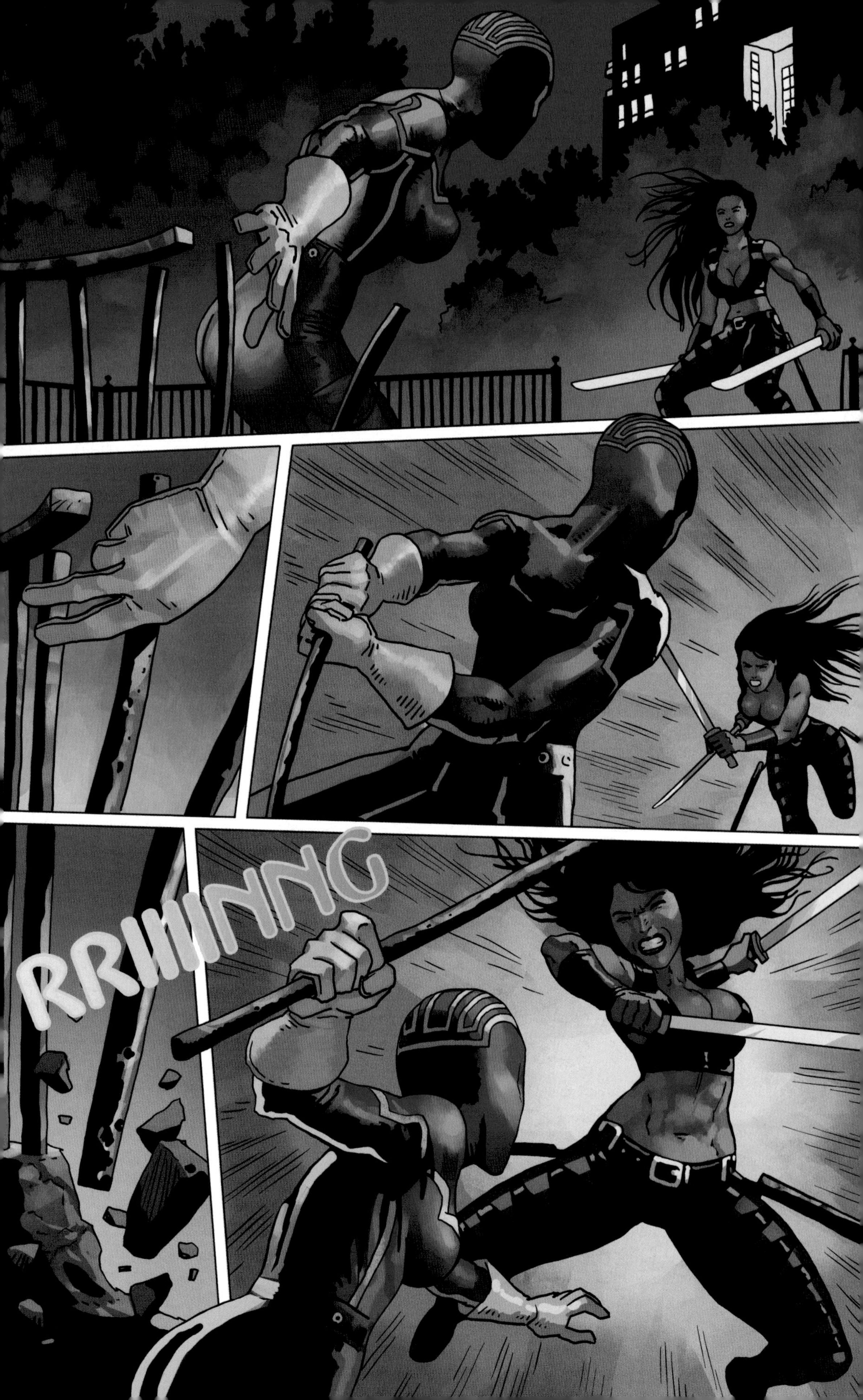
RRIIIINNG

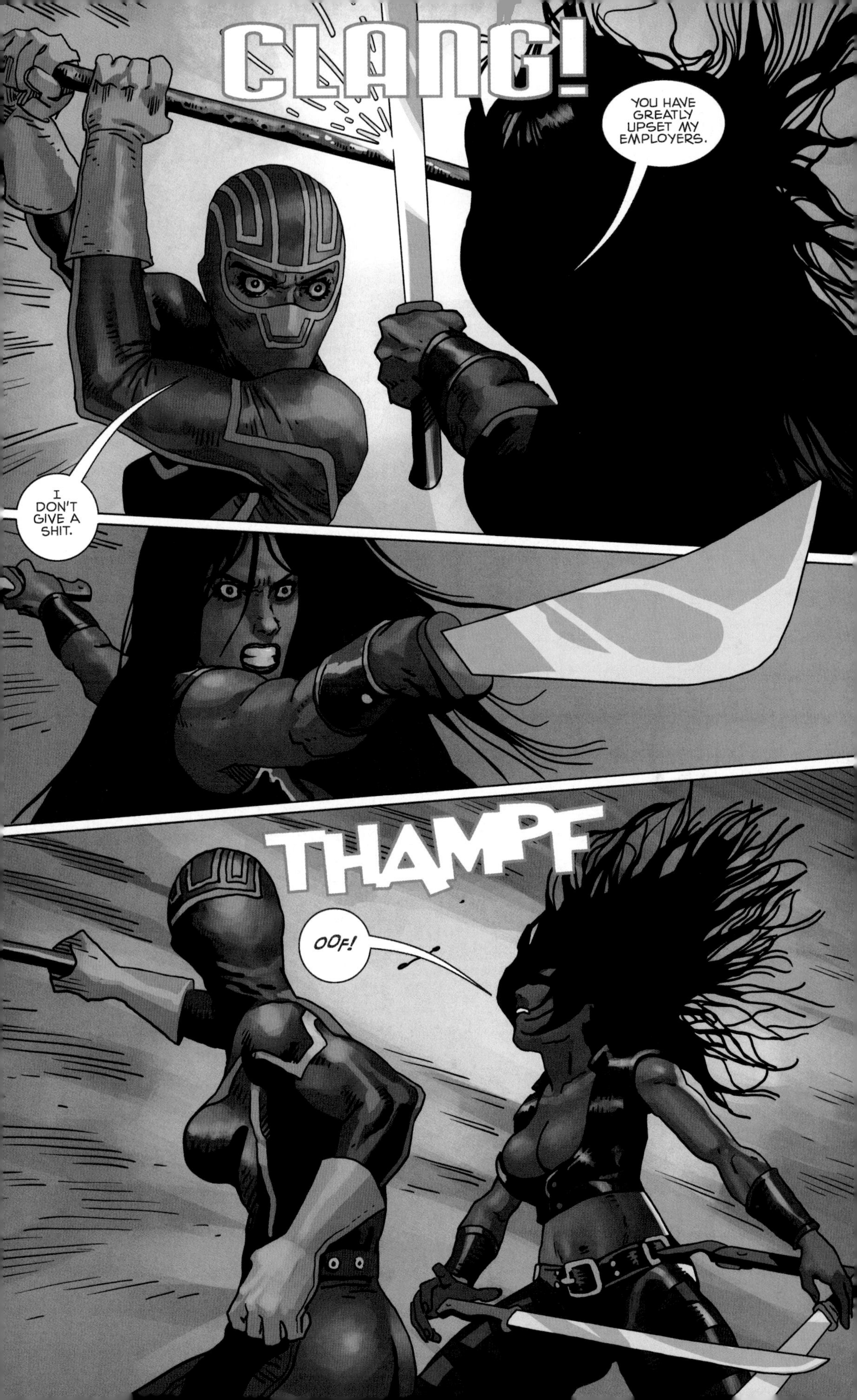
CLANG!
YOU HAVE GREATLY UPSET MY EMPLOYERS.
I DON'T GIVE A SHIT.
THAMPF
OOF!

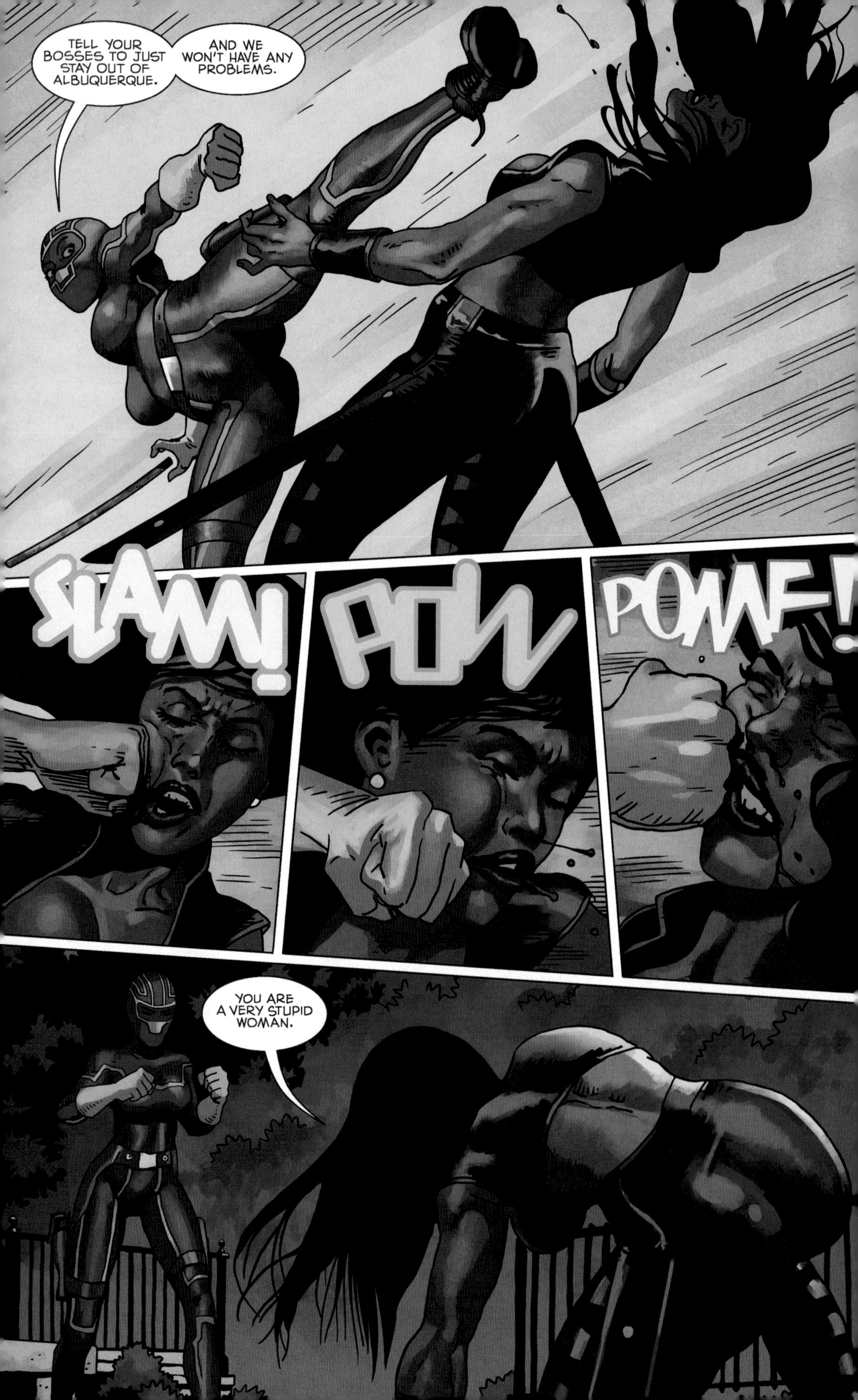
TELL YOUR BOSSES TO JUST STAY OUT OF ALBUQUERQUE.
AND WE WON'T HAVE ANY PROBLEMS.
SLAM!
POW
POWF!
YOU ARE A VERY STUPID WOMAN.

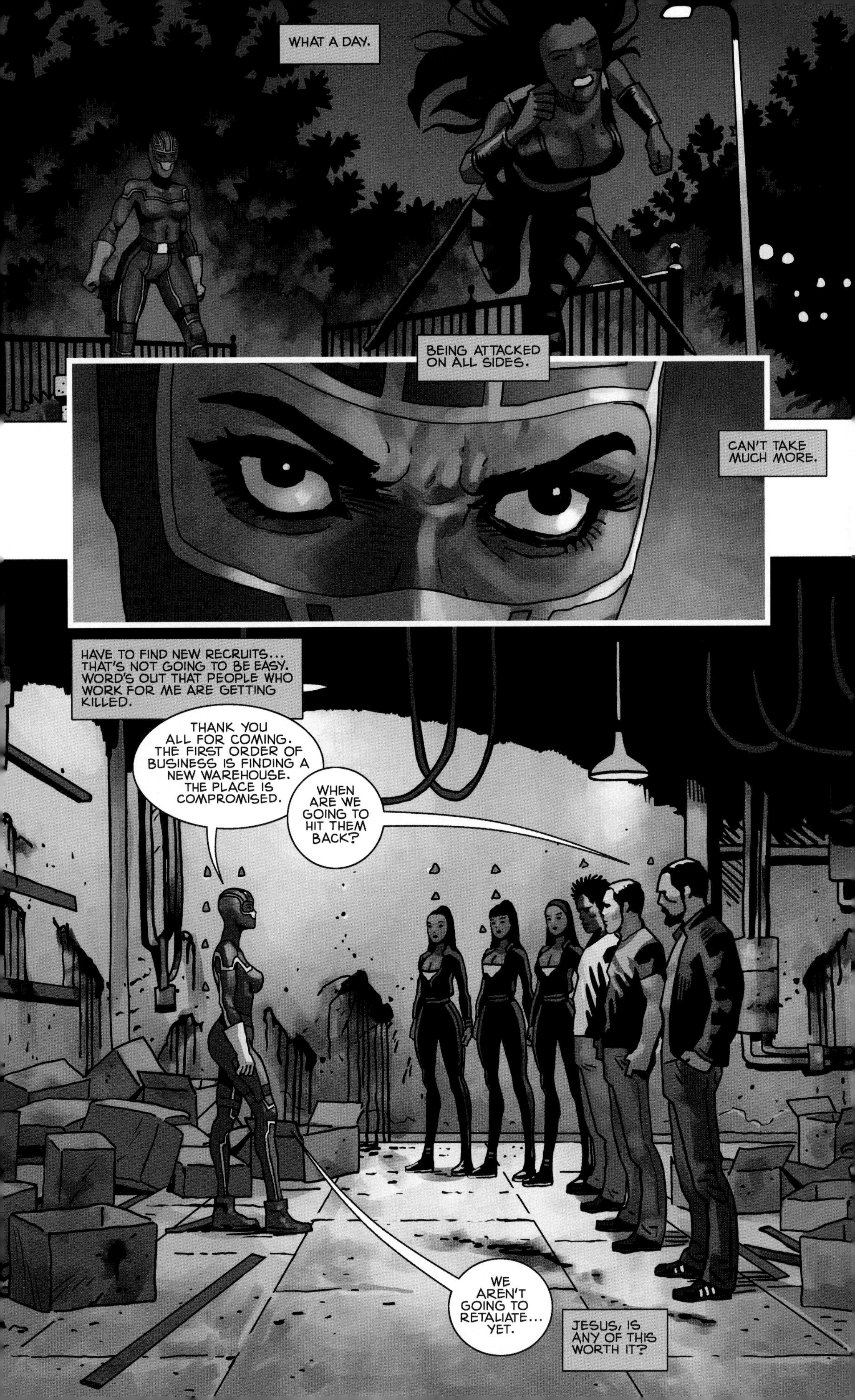
WHAT A DAY.
BEING ATTACKED ON ALL SIDES.
CAN'T TAKE MUCH MORE.
HAVE TO FIND NEW RECRUITS... THAT'S NOT GOING TO BE EASY. WORD'S OUT THAT PEOPLE WHO WORK FOR ME ARE GETTING KILLED.
THANK YOU ALL FOR COMING. THE FIRST ORDER OF BUSINESS IS FINDING A NEW WAREHOUSE. THE PLACE IS COMPROMISED.
WHEN ARE WE GOING TO HIT THEM BACK?
WE AREN'T GOING TO RETALIATE... YET.
JESUS, IS ANY OF THIS WORTH IT?

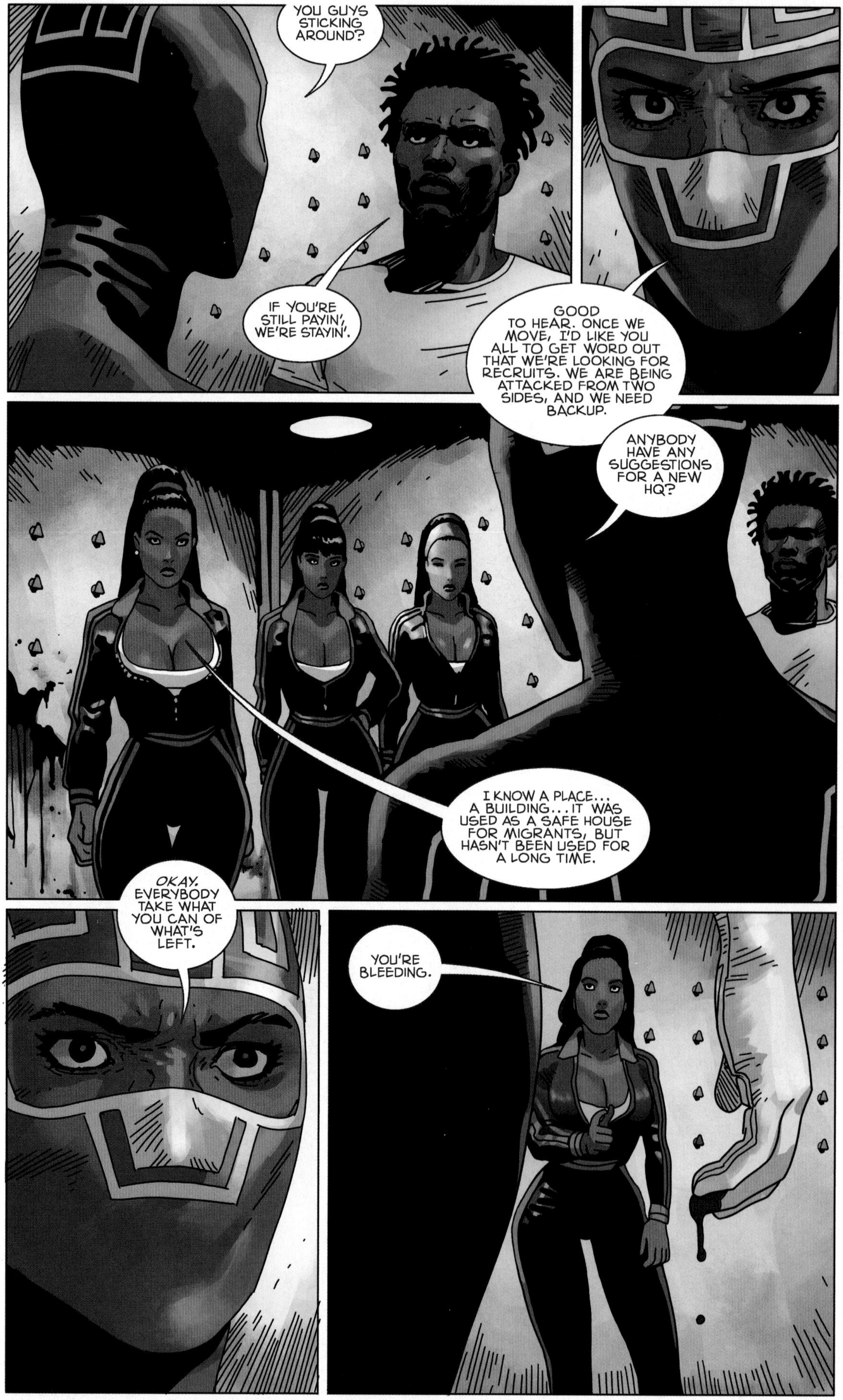
YOU GUYS STICKING AROUND?
IF YOU'RE STILL PAYIN', WE'RE STAYIN'.
GOOD TO HEAR. ONCE WE MOVE, I'D LIKE YOU ALL TO GET WORD OUT THAT WE'RE LOOKING FOR RECRUITS. WE ARE BEING ATTACKED FROM TWO SIDES, AND WE NEED BACKUP.
ANYBODY HAVE ANY SUGGESTIONS FOR A NEW HQ?
I KNOW A PLACE... A BUILDING...IT WAS USED AS A SAFE HOUSE FOR MIGRANTS, BUT HASN'T BEEN USED FOR A LONG TIME.
OKAY. EVERYBODY TAKE WHAT YOU CAN OF WHAT'S LEFT.
YOU'RE BLEEDING.

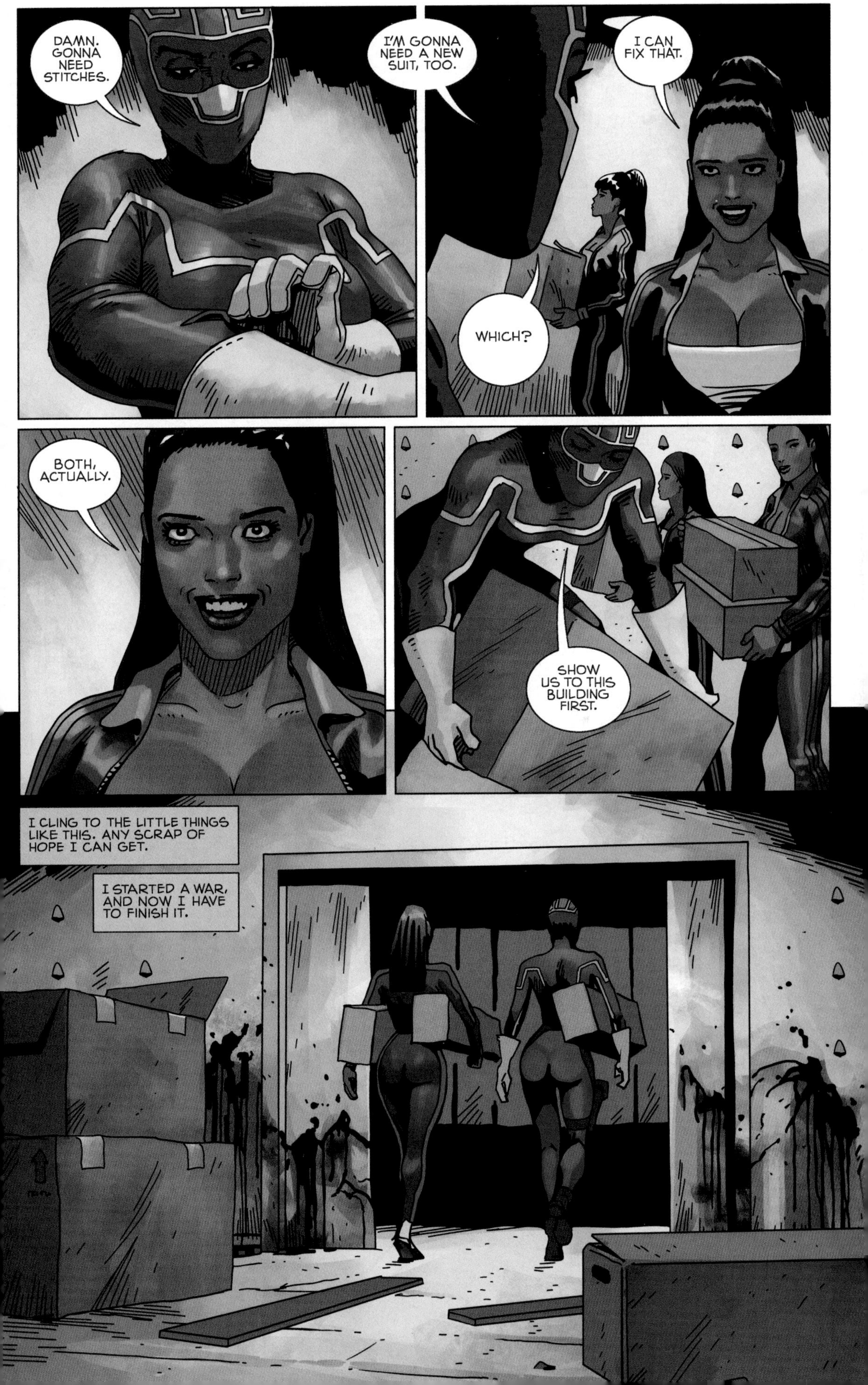
DAMN. GONNA NEED STITCHES.
I'M GONNA NEED A NEW SUIT, TOO.
I CAN FIX THAT.
WHICH?
BOTH, ACTUALLY.
SHOW US TO THIS BUILDING FIRST.
I CLING TO THE LITTLE THINGS LIKE THIS. ANY SCRAP OF HOPE I CAN GET.
I STARTED A WAR, AND NOW I HAVE TO FINISH IT.

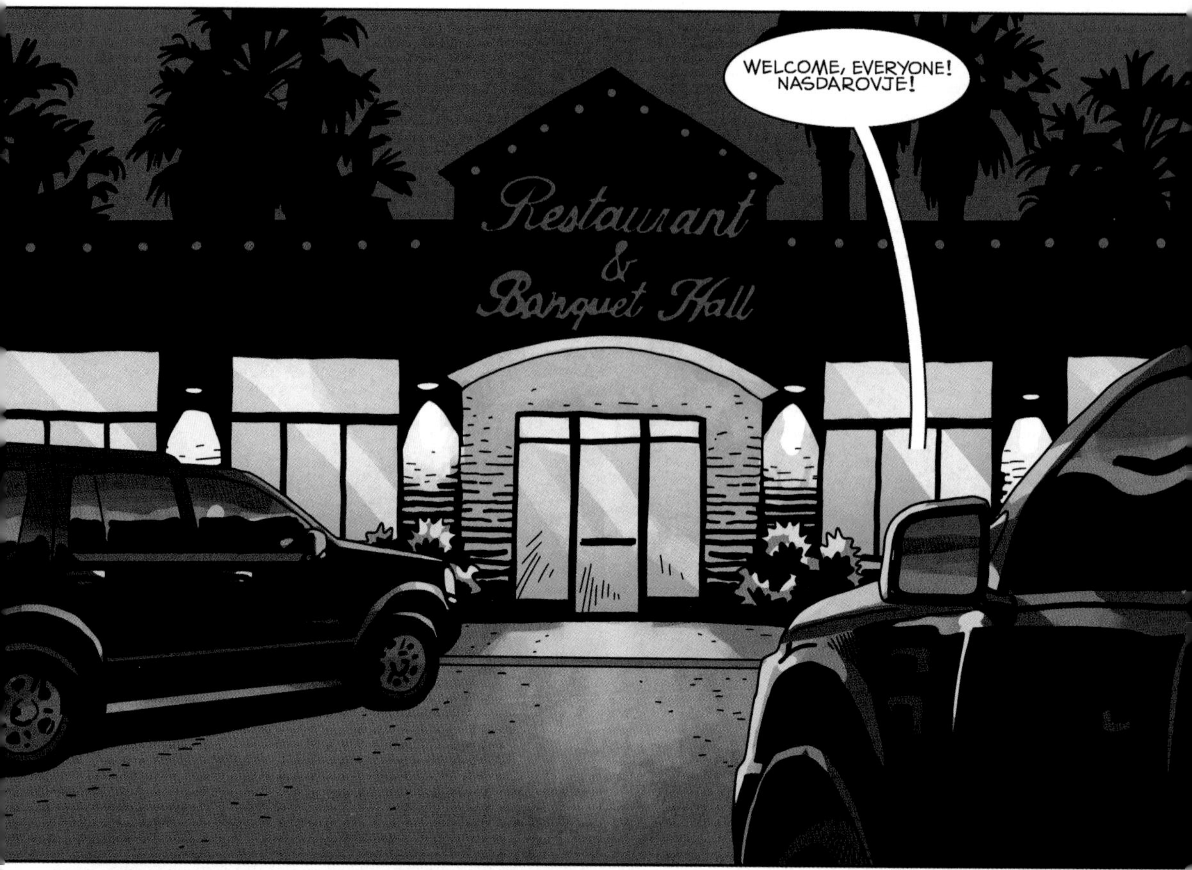
Restaurant & Banquet Hall
WELCOME, EVERYONE! NASDAROVJE!

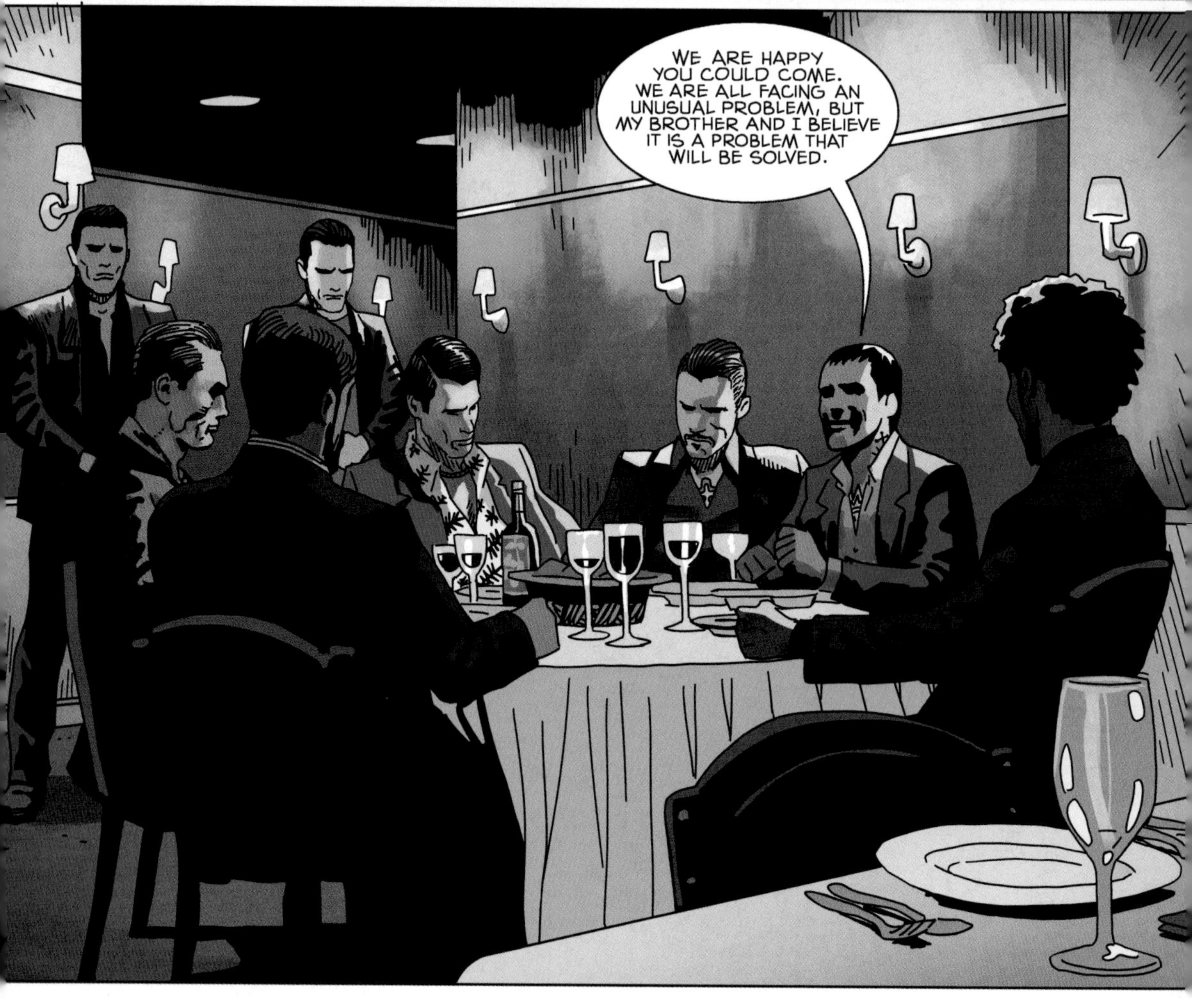
WE ARE HAPPY YOU COULD COME. WE ARE ALL FACING AN UNUSUAL PROBLEM, BUT MY BROTHER AND I BELIEVE IT IS A PROBLEM THAT WILL BE SOLVED.

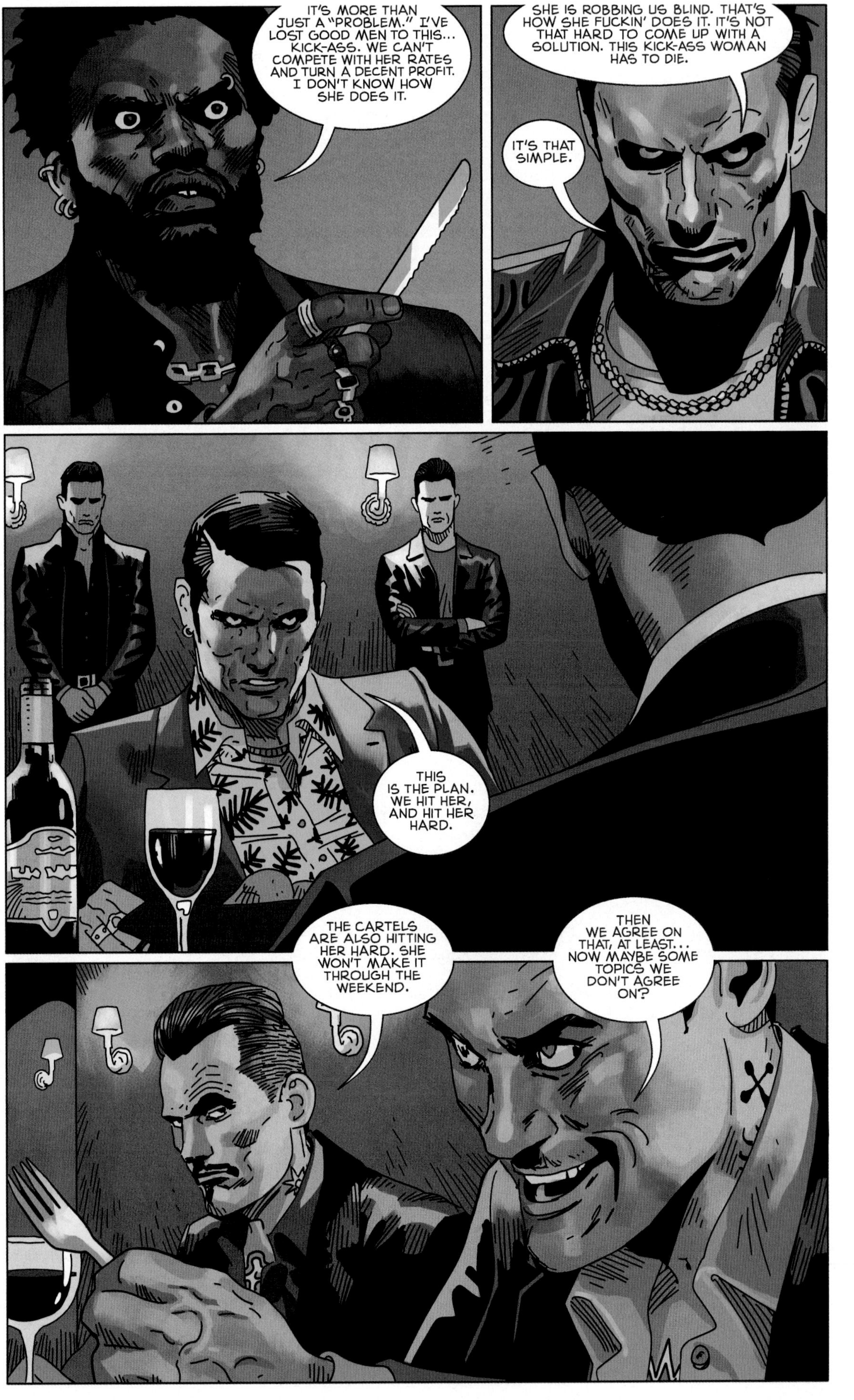
IT'S MORE THAN JUST A "PROBLEM." I'VE LOST GOOD MEN TO THIS... KICK-ASS. WE CAN'T COMPETE WITH HER RATES AND TURN A DECENT PROFIT. I DON'T KNOW HOW SHE DOES IT.
SHE IS ROBBING US BLIND. THAT'S HOW SHE FUCKIN' DOES IT. IT'S NOT THAT HARD TO COME UP WITH A SOLUTION. THIS KICK-ASS WOMAN HAS TO DIE.
IT'S THAT SIMPLE.
THIS IS THE PLAN. WE HIT HER, AND HIT HER HARD.
THE CARTELS ARE ALSO HITTING HER HARD. SHE WON'T MAKE IT THROUGH THE WEEKEND.
THEN WE AGREE ON THAT, AT LEAST... NOW MAYBE SOME TOPICS WE DON'T AGREE ON?

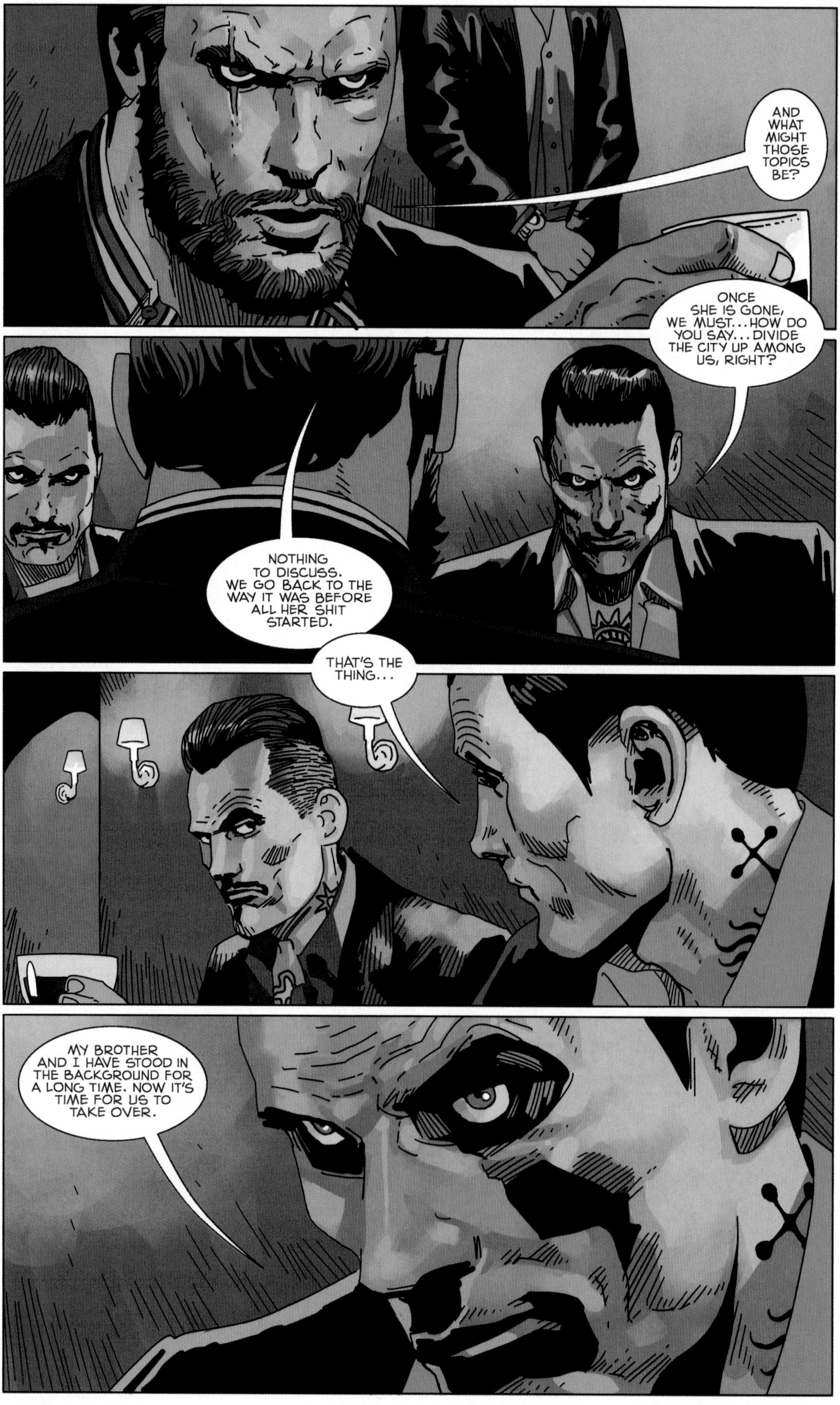
AND WHAT MIGHT THOSE TOPICS BE?
ONCE SHE IS GONE, WE MUST... HOW DO YOU SAY... DIVIDE THE CITY UP AMONG US, RIGHT?
NOTHING TO DISCUSS. WE GO BACK TO THE WAY IT WAS BEFORE ALL HER SHIT STARTED.
THAT'S THE THING...
MY BROTHER AND I HAVE STOOD IN THE BACKGROUND FOR A LONG TIME. NOW IT'S TIME FOR US TO TAKE OVER.

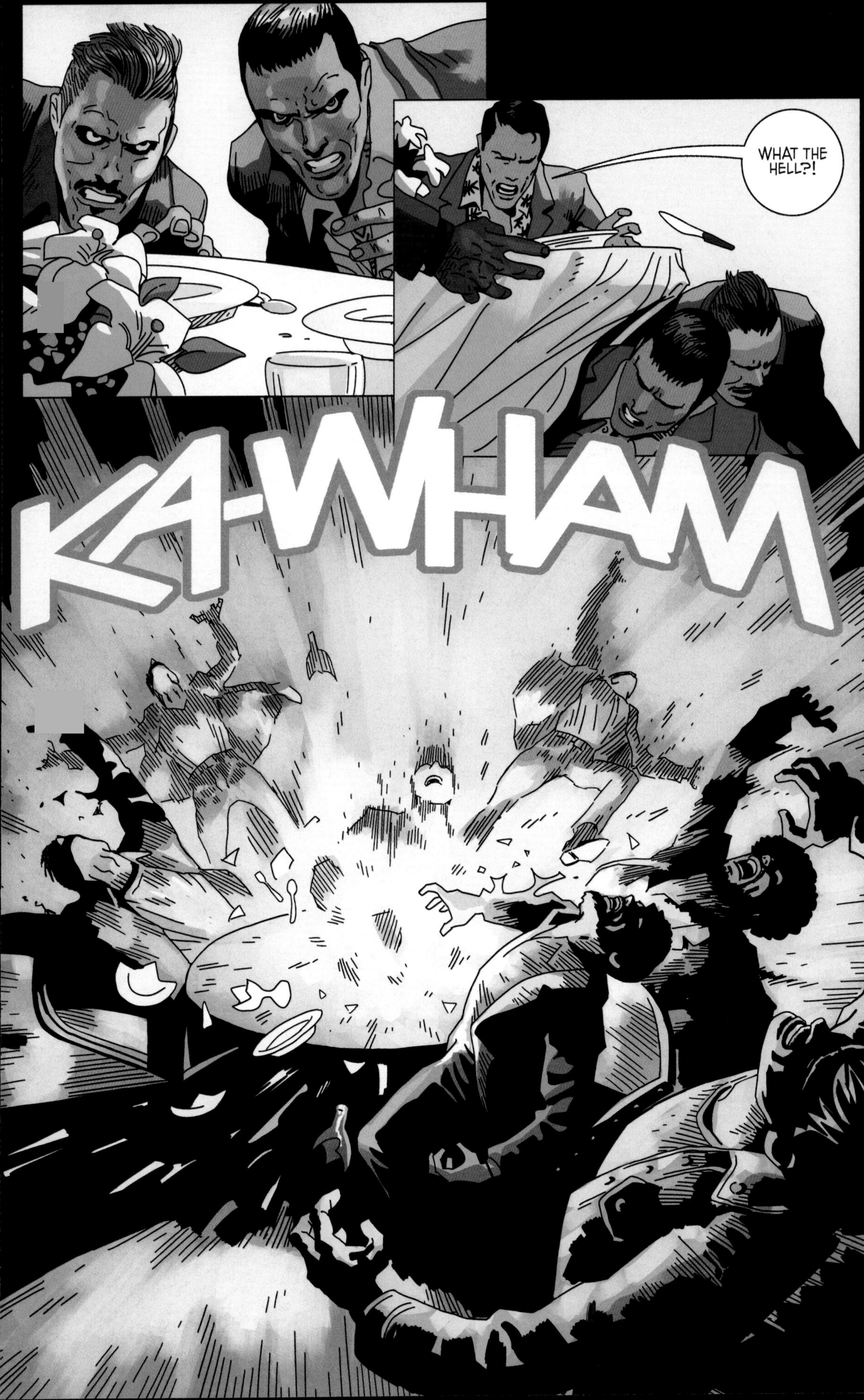
WHAT THE HELL?!
KA-WHAM

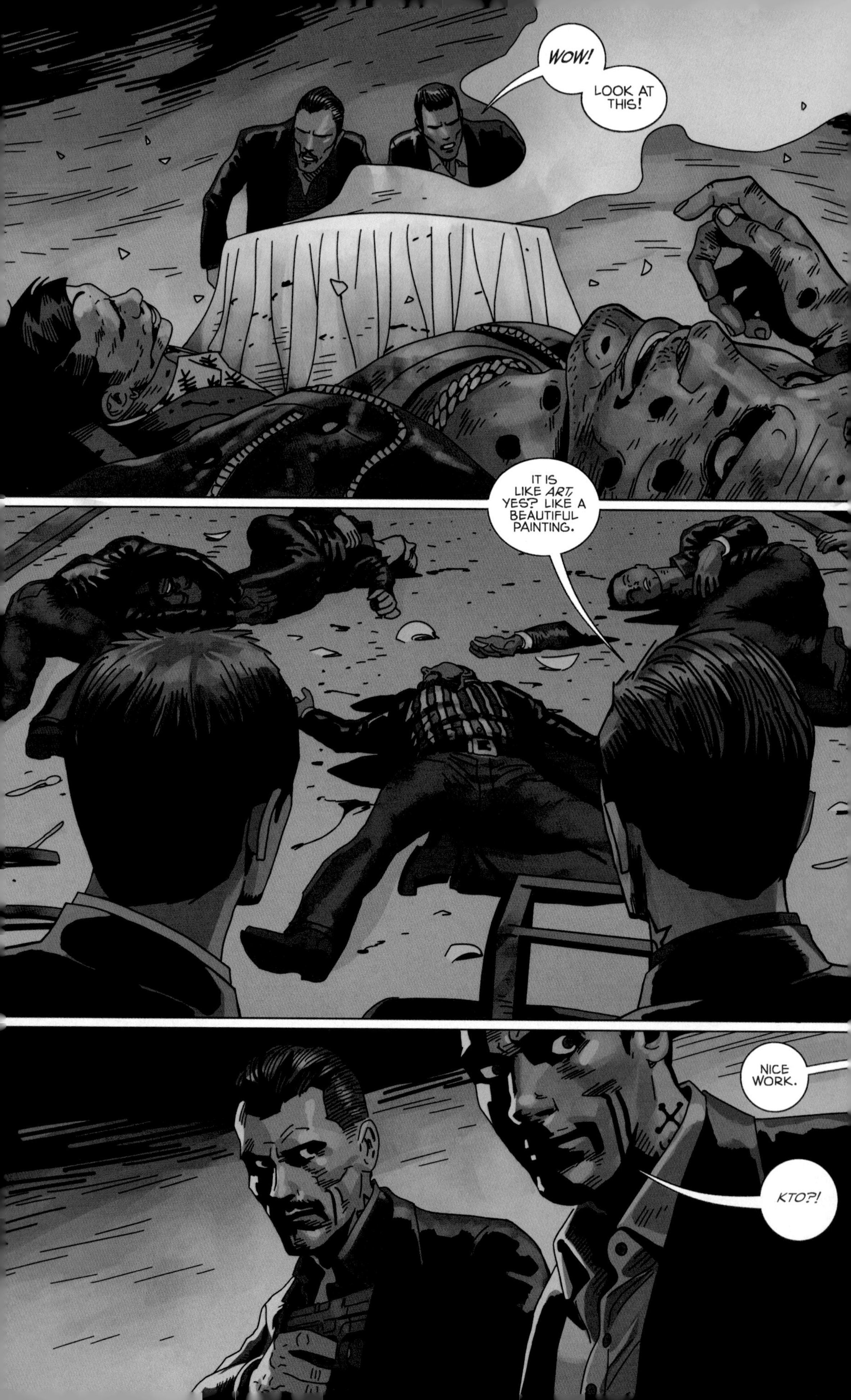
WOW!
LOOK AT THIS!
IT IS LIKE ART, YES? LIKE A BEAUTIFUL PAINTING.
NICE WORK.
KTO?!

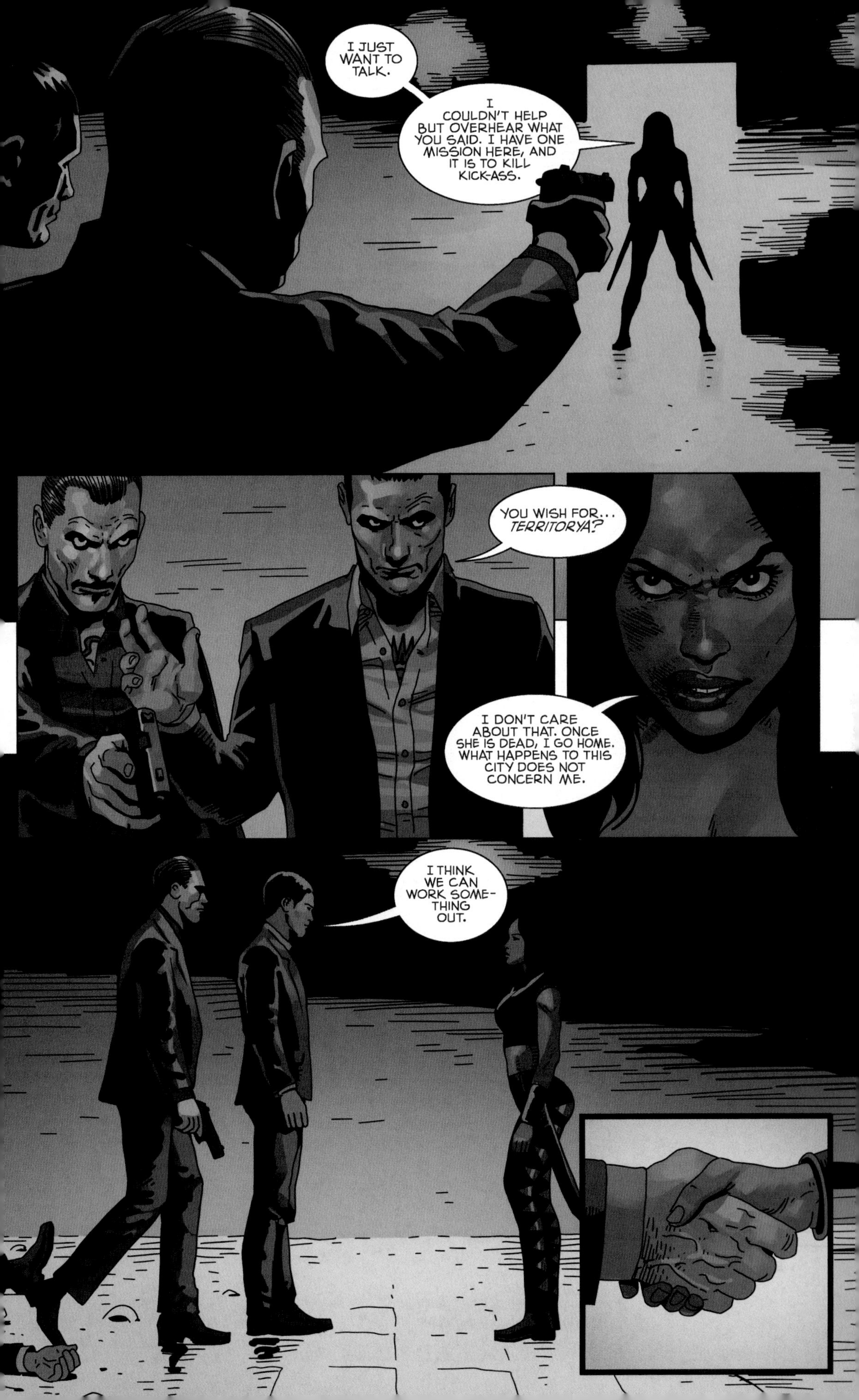
I JUST WANT TO TALK.
I COULDN'T HELP BUT OVERHEAR WHAT YOU SAID. I HAVE ONE MISSION HERE, AND IT IS TO KILL KICK-ASS.
YOU WISH FOR... *TERRITORYA?*
I DON'T CARE ABOUT THAT. ONCE SHE IS DEAD, I GO HOME. WHAT HAPPENS TO THIS CITY DOES NOT CONCERN ME.
I THINK WE CAN WORK SOME-THING OUT.

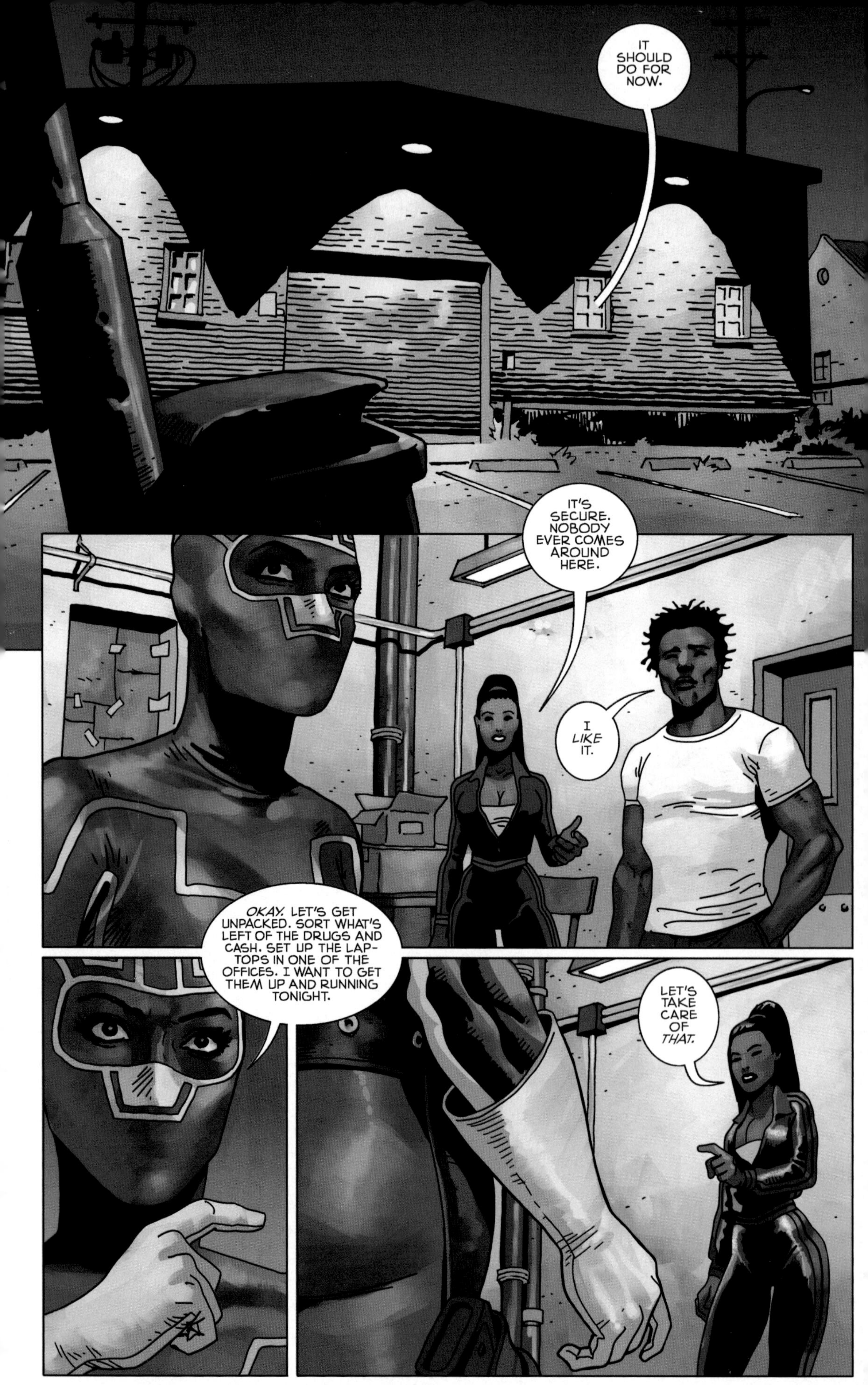
IT SHOULD DO FOR NOW.
IT'S SECURE. NOBODY EVER COMES AROUND HERE.
I LIKE IT.
OKAY. LET'S GET UNPACKED. SORT WHAT'S LEFT OF THE DRUGS AND CASH. SET UP THE LAPTOPS IN ONE OF THE OFFICES. I WANT TO GET THEM UP AND RUNNING TONIGHT.
LET'S TAKE CARE OF THAT.

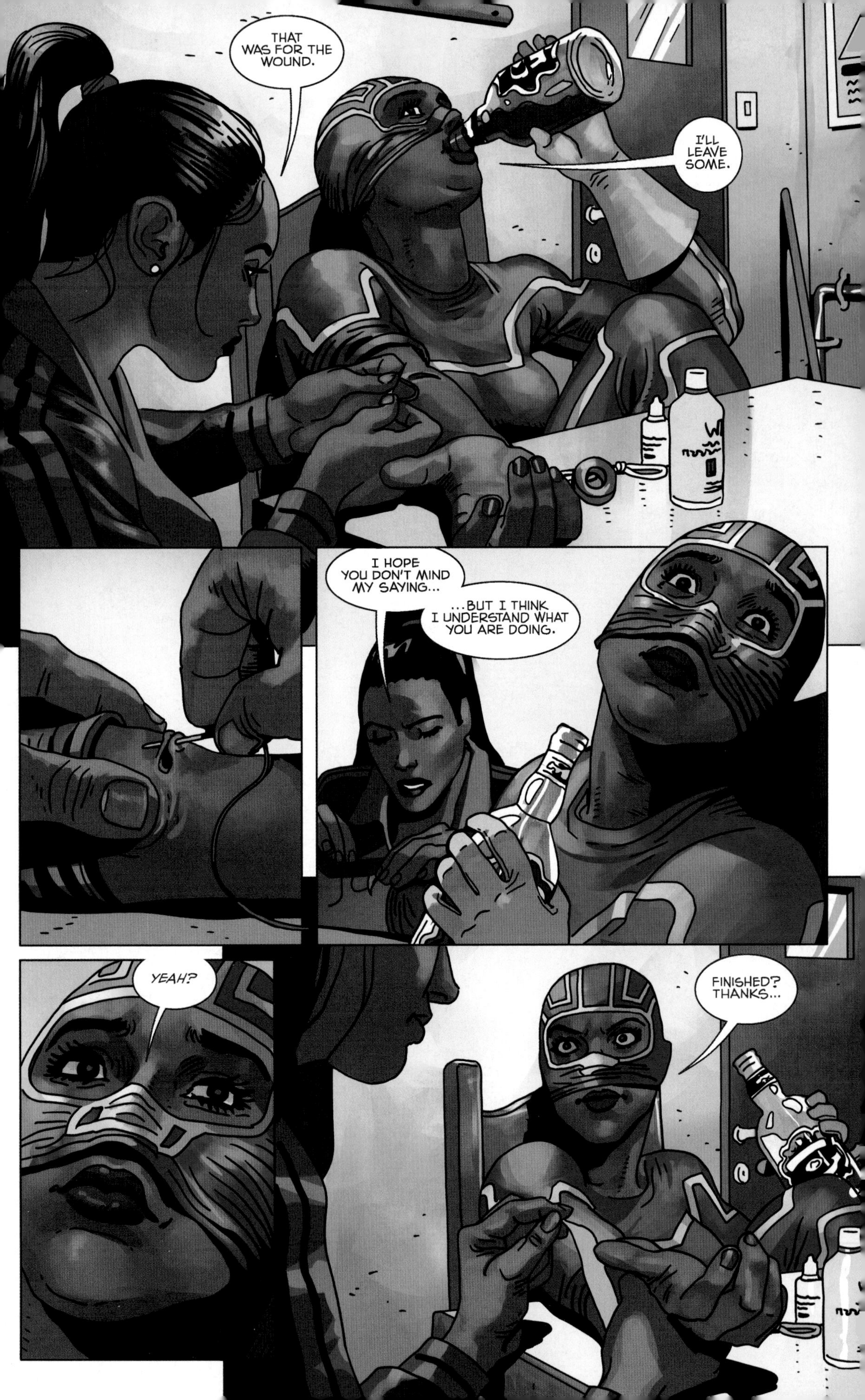
THAT WAS FOR THE WOUND.
I'LL LEAVE SOME.
I HOPE YOU DON'T MIND MY SAYING...
...BUT I THINK I UNDERSTAND WHAT YOU ARE DOING.
YEAH?
FINISHED? THANKS...

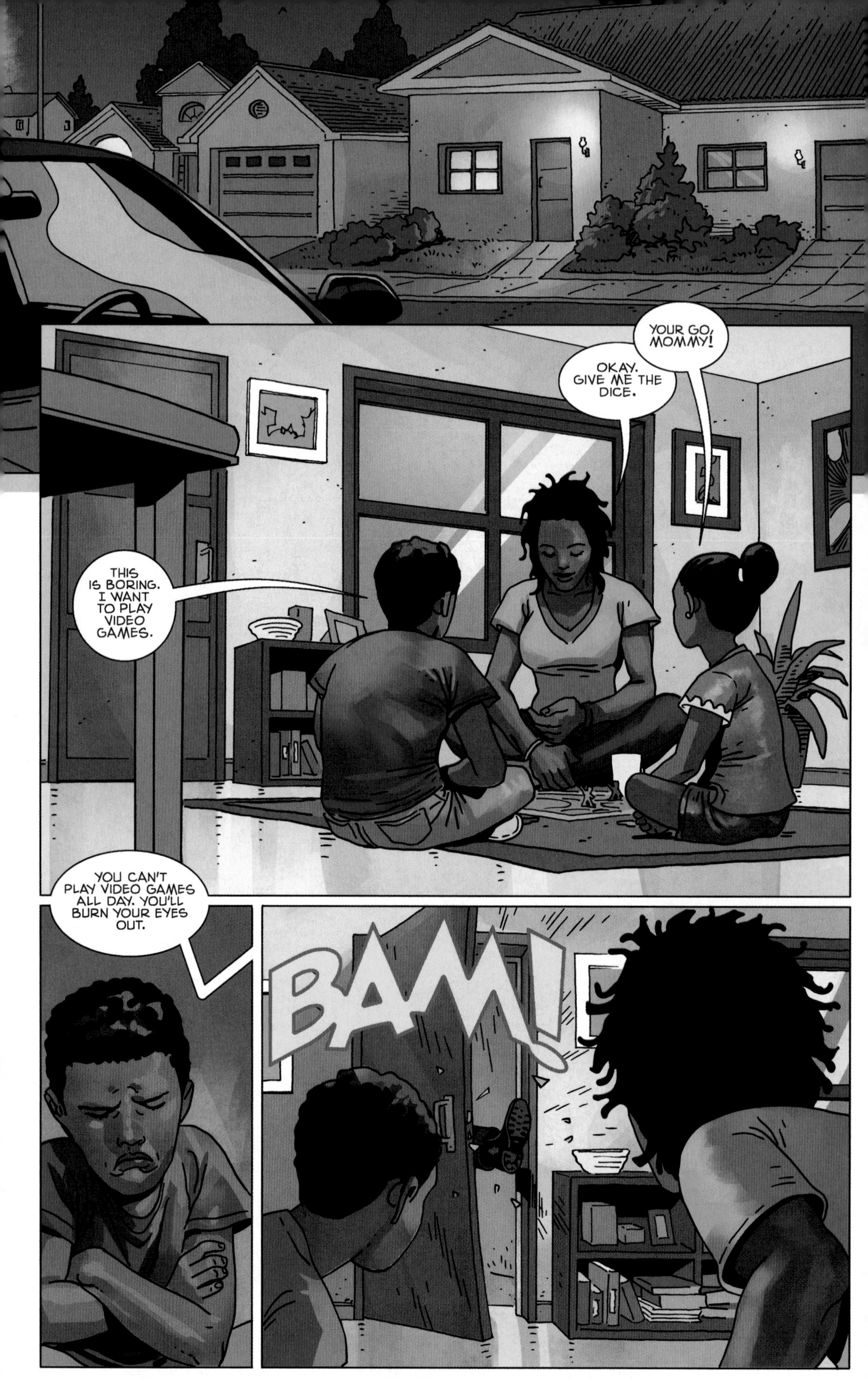
YOUR GO, MOMMY!
OKAY. GIVE ME THE DICE.
THIS IS BORING. I WANT TO PLAY VIDEO GAMES.
YOU CAN'T PLAY VIDEO GAMES ALL DAY. YOU'LL BURN YOUR EYES OUT.
BAM!

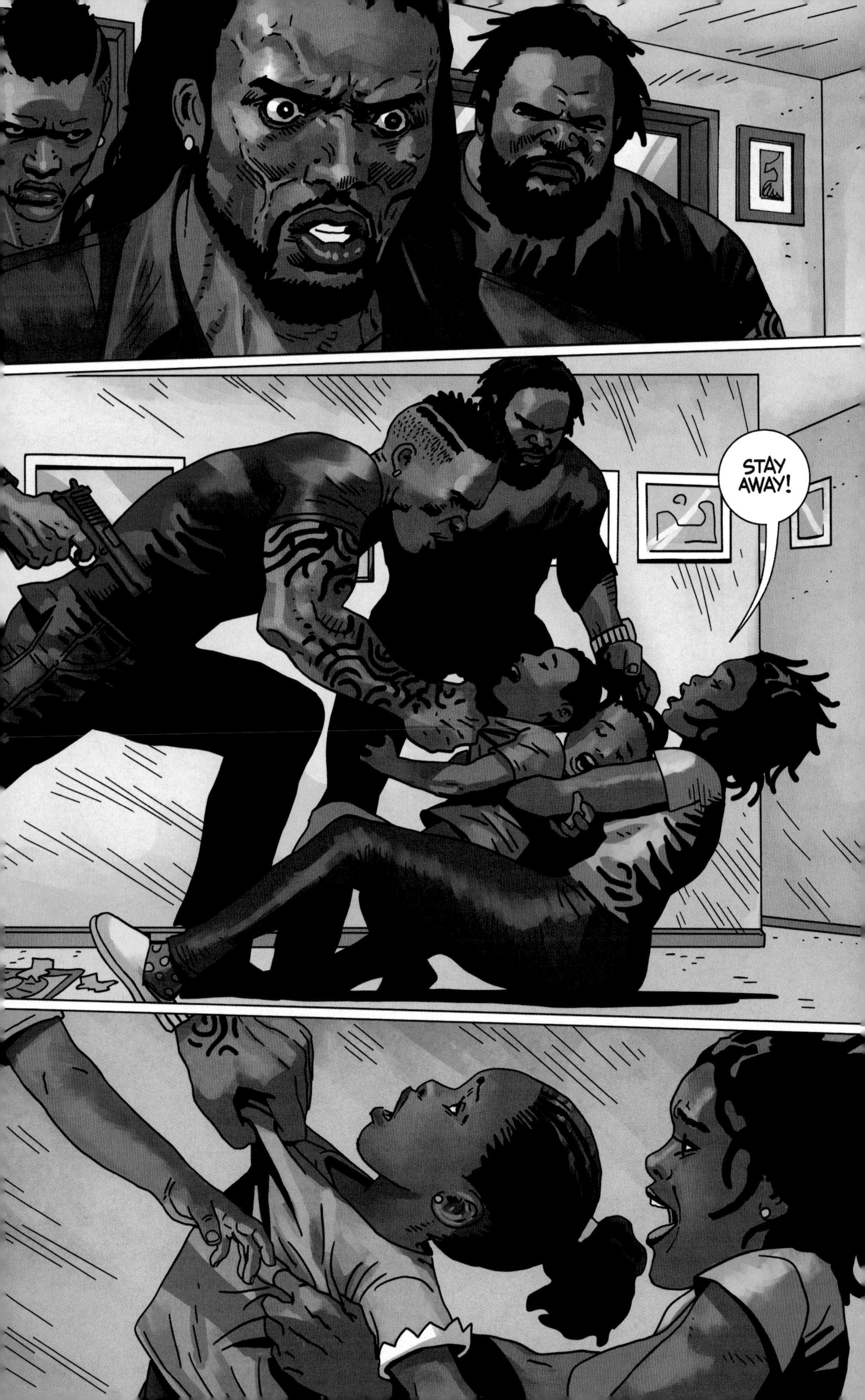
STAY AWAY!

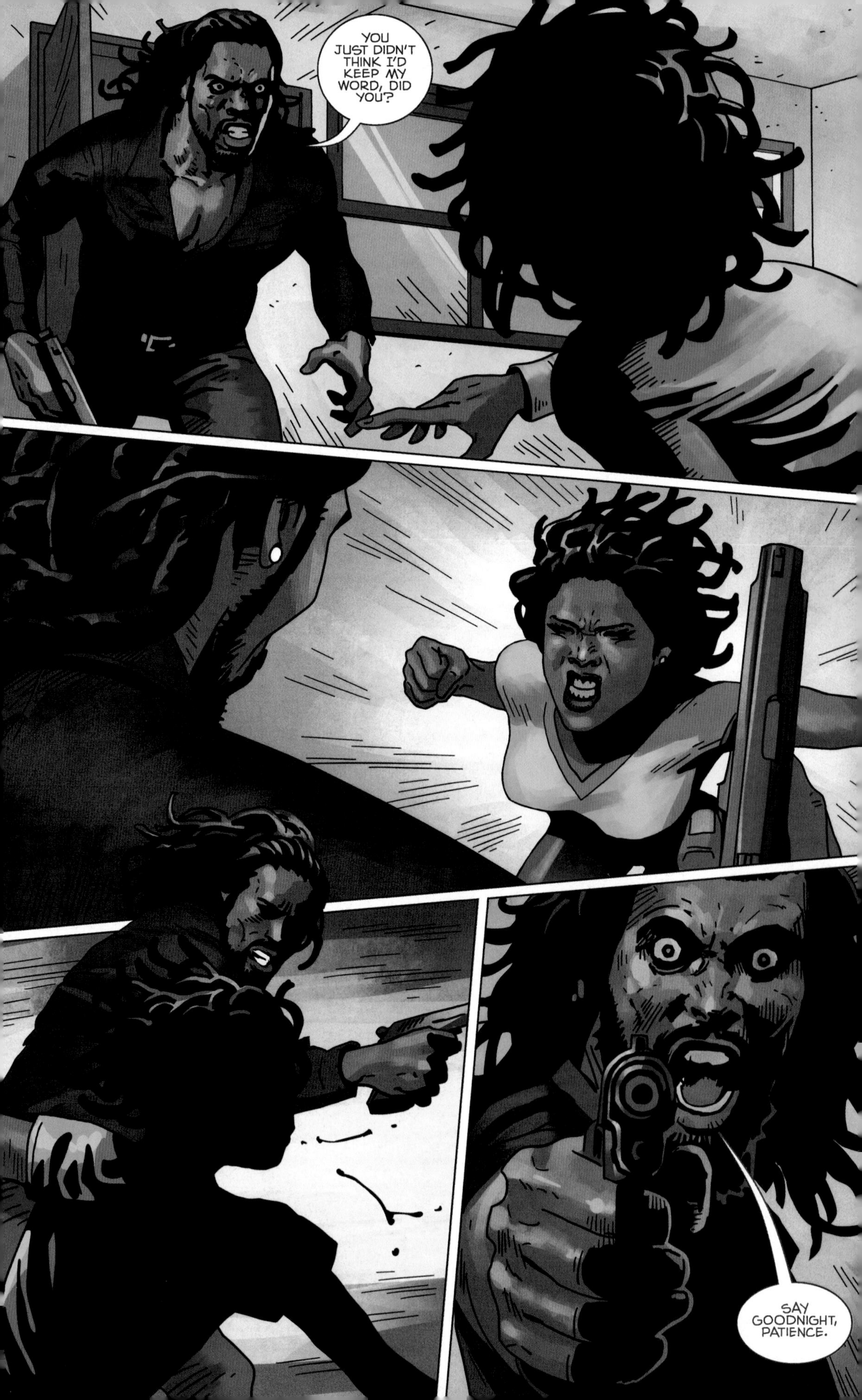
YOU JUST DIDN'T THINK I'D KEEP MY WORD, DID YOU?
SAY GOODNIGHT, PATIENCE.

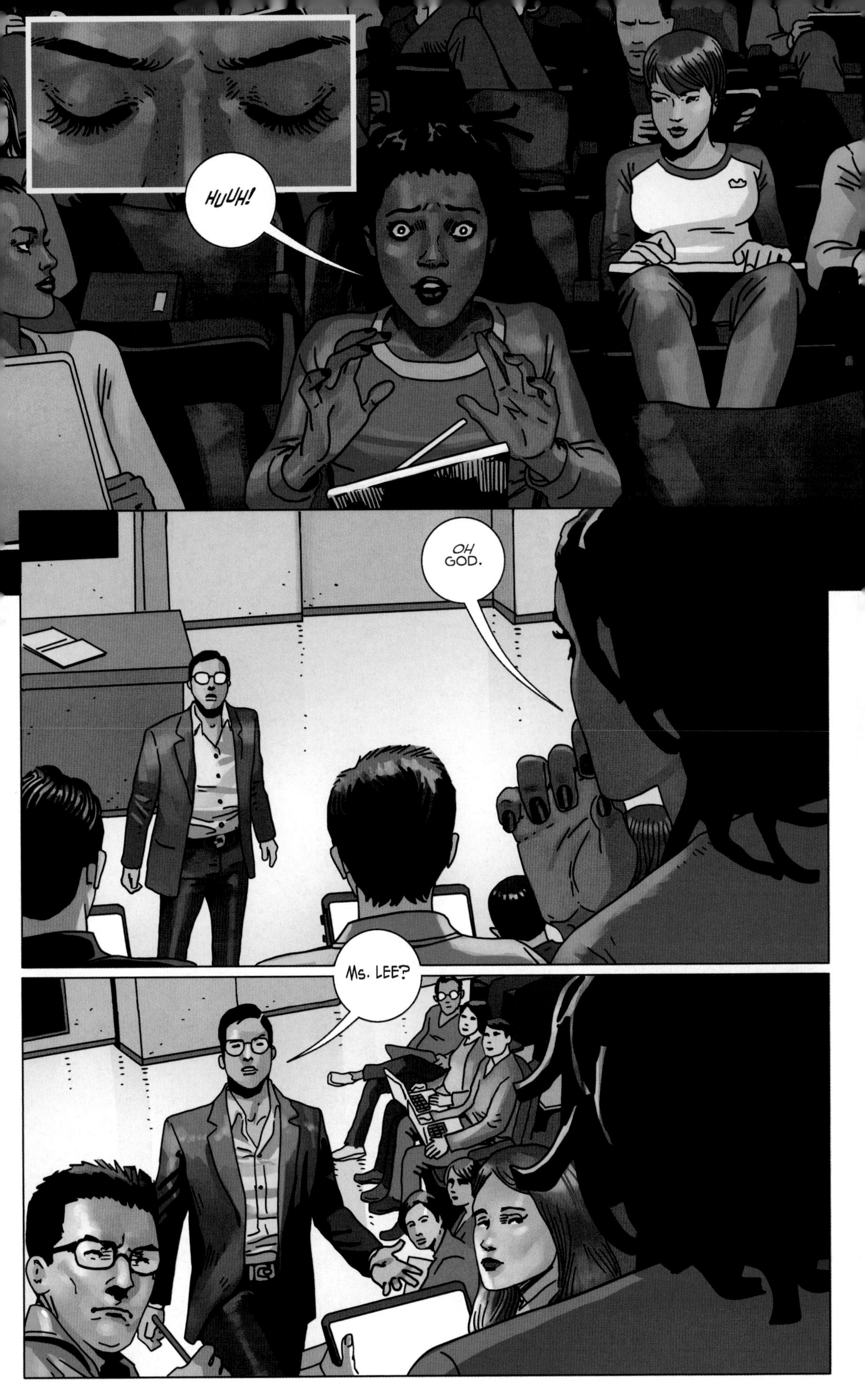
HUUH!
OH GOD.
Ms. LEE?

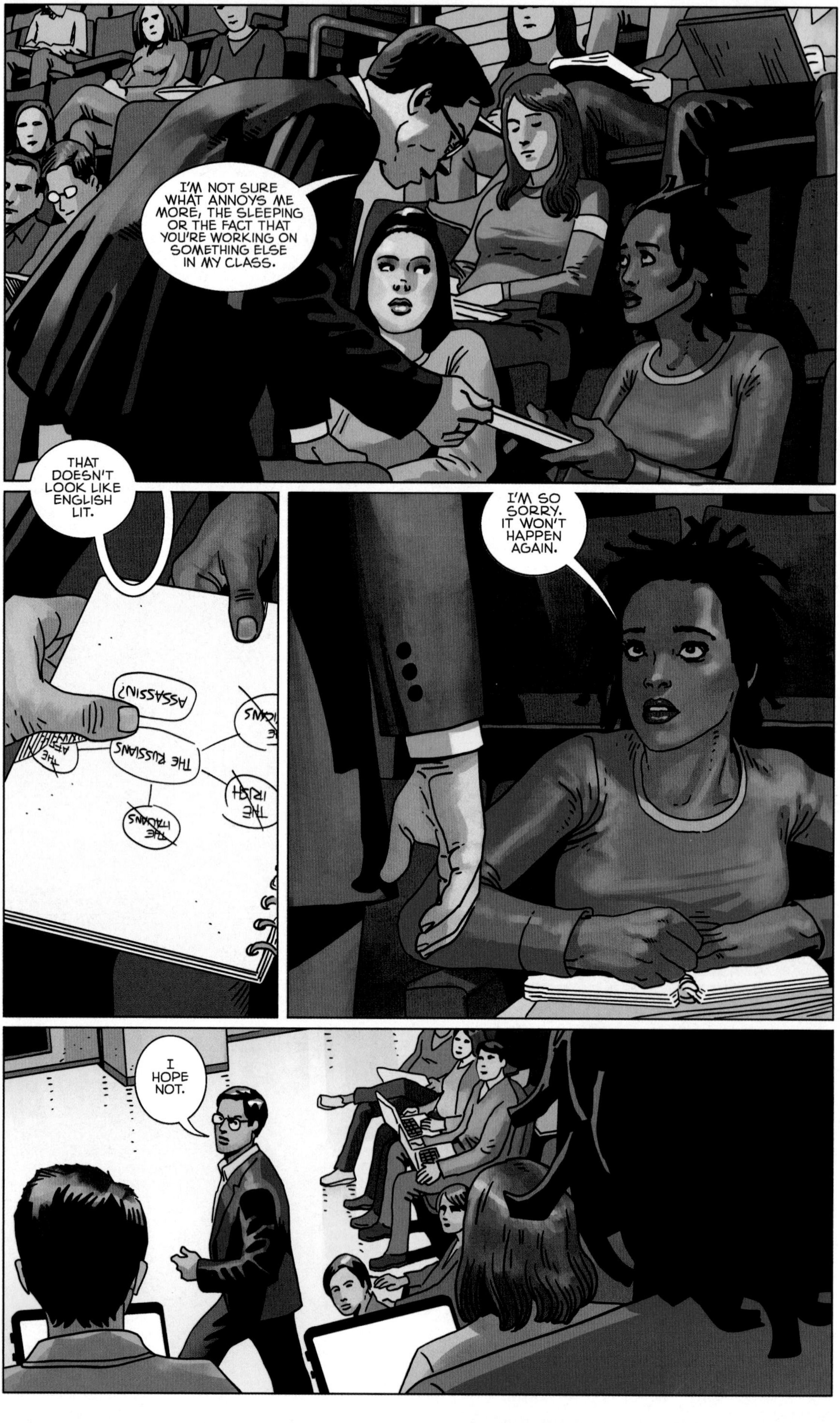
I'M NOT SURE WHAT ANNOYS ME MORE, THE SLEEPING OR THE FACT THAT YOU'RE WORKING ON SOMETHING ELSE IN MY CLASS.
THAT DOESN'T LOOK LIKE ENGLISH LIT.
ASSASSIN?
THE RUSSIANS
I'M SO SORRY. IT WON'T HAPPEN AGAIN.
I HOPE NOT.

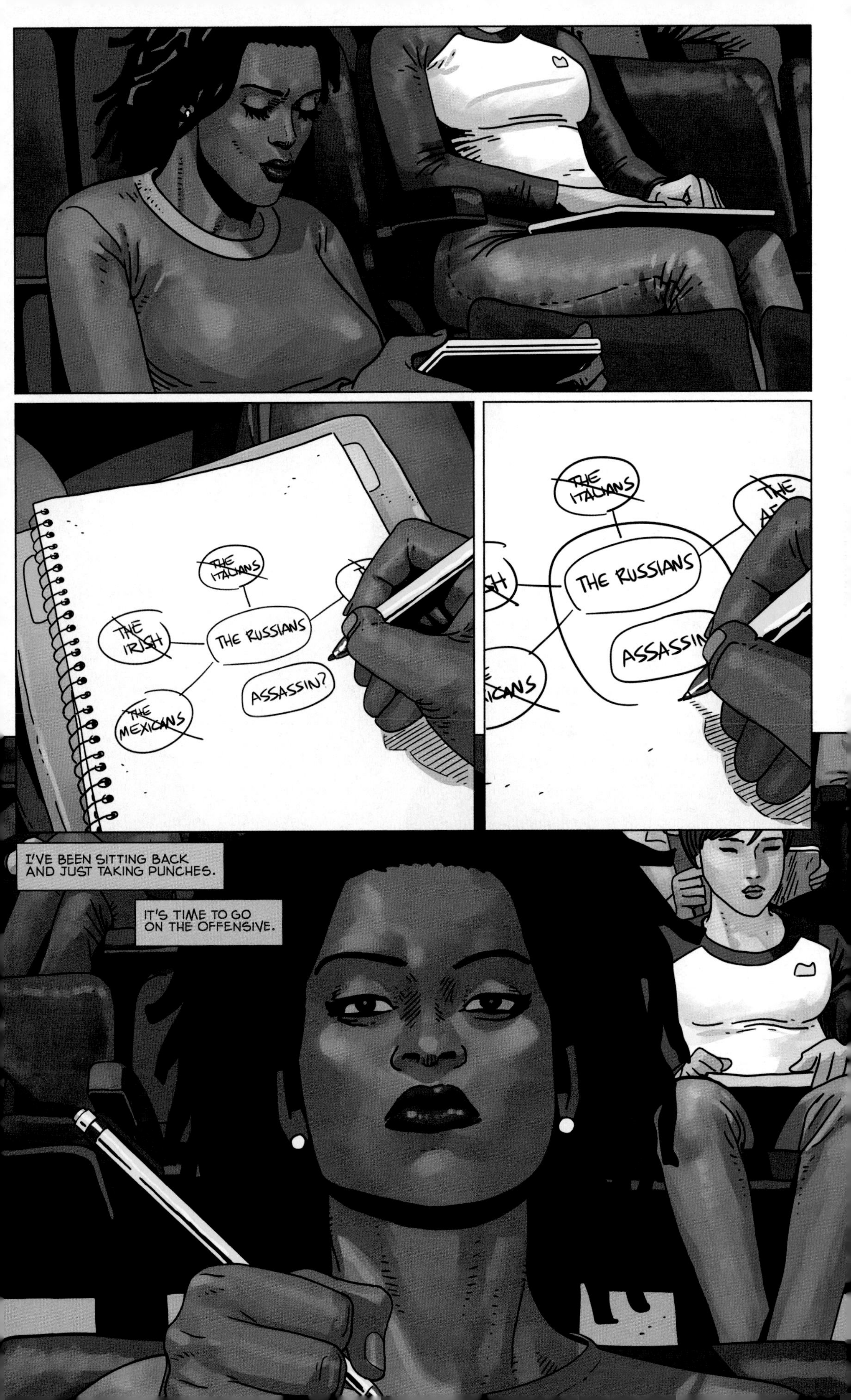
THE ITALIANS
THE IRISH
THE RUSSIANS
ASSASSIN?
THE MEXICANS
THE ITALIANS
THE RUSSIANS
I'VE BEEN SITTING BACK AND JUST TAKING PUNCHES.
IT'S TIME TO GO ON THE OFFENSIVE.

FIVE

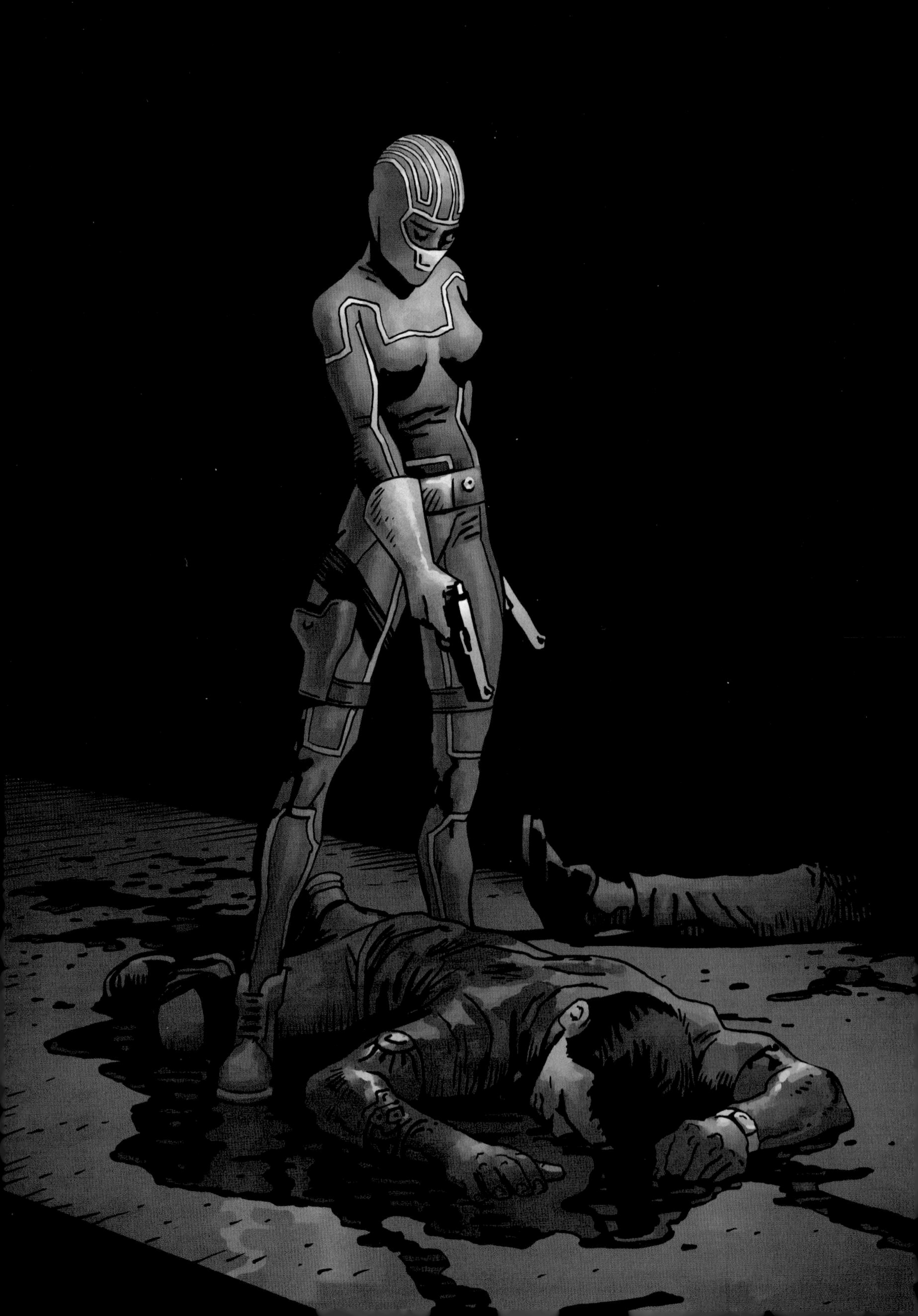

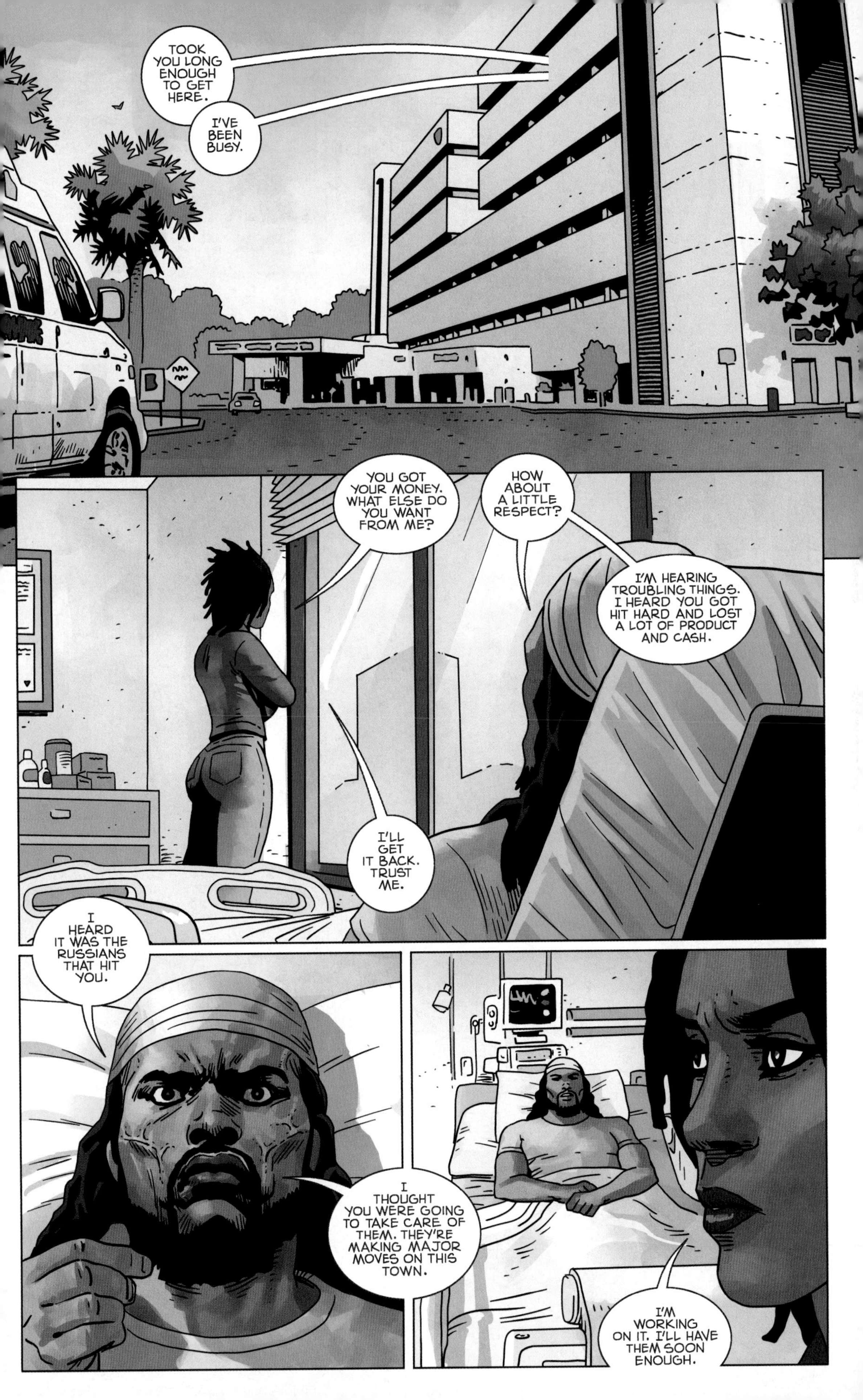
TOOK YOU LONG ENOUGH TO GET HERE.
I'VE BEEN BUSY.
YOU GOT YOUR MONEY. WHAT ELSE DO YOU WANT FROM ME?
HOW ABOUT A LITTLE RESPECT?
I'M HEARING TROUBLING THINGS. I HEARD YOU GOT HIT HARD AND LOST A LOT OF PRODUCT AND CASH.
I'LL GET IT BACK. TRUST ME.
I HEARD IT WAS THE RUSSIANS THAT HIT YOU.
I THOUGHT YOU WERE GOING TO TAKE CARE OF THEM. THEY'RE MAKING MAJOR MOVES ON THIS TOWN.
I'M WORKING ON IT. I'LL HAVE THEM SOON ENOUGH.

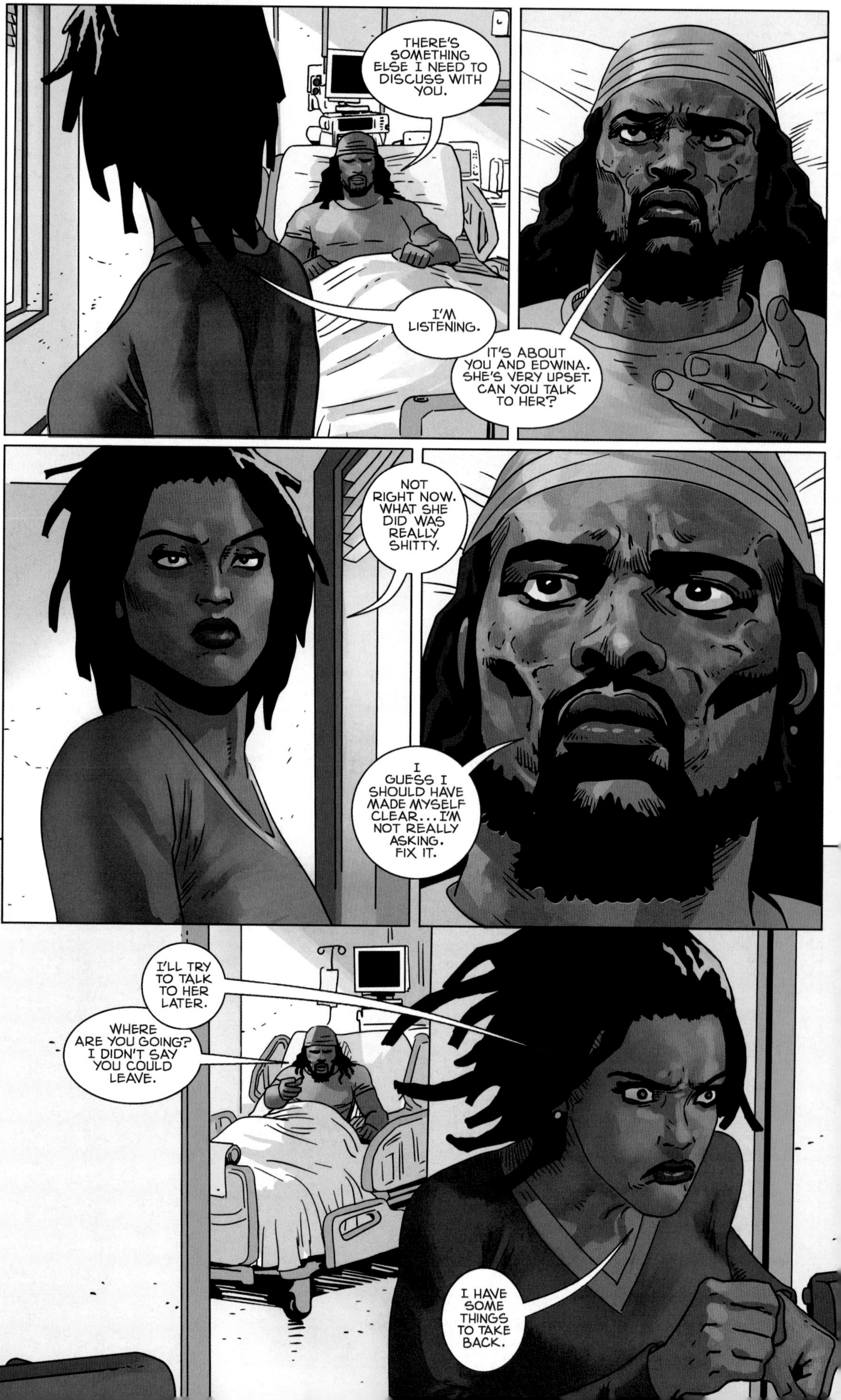
THERE'S SOMETHING ELSE I NEED TO DISCUSS WITH YOU.
I'M LISTENING.
IT'S ABOUT YOU AND EDWINA. SHE'S VERY UPSET. CAN YOU TALK TO HER?
NOT RIGHT NOW. WHAT SHE DID WAS REALLY SHITTY.
I GUESS I SHOULD HAVE MADE MYSELF CLEAR... I'M NOT REALLY ASKING. FIX IT.
I'LL TRY TO TALK TO HER LATER.
WHERE ARE YOU GOING? I DIDN'T SAY YOU COULD LEAVE.
I HAVE SOME THINGS TO TAKE BACK.

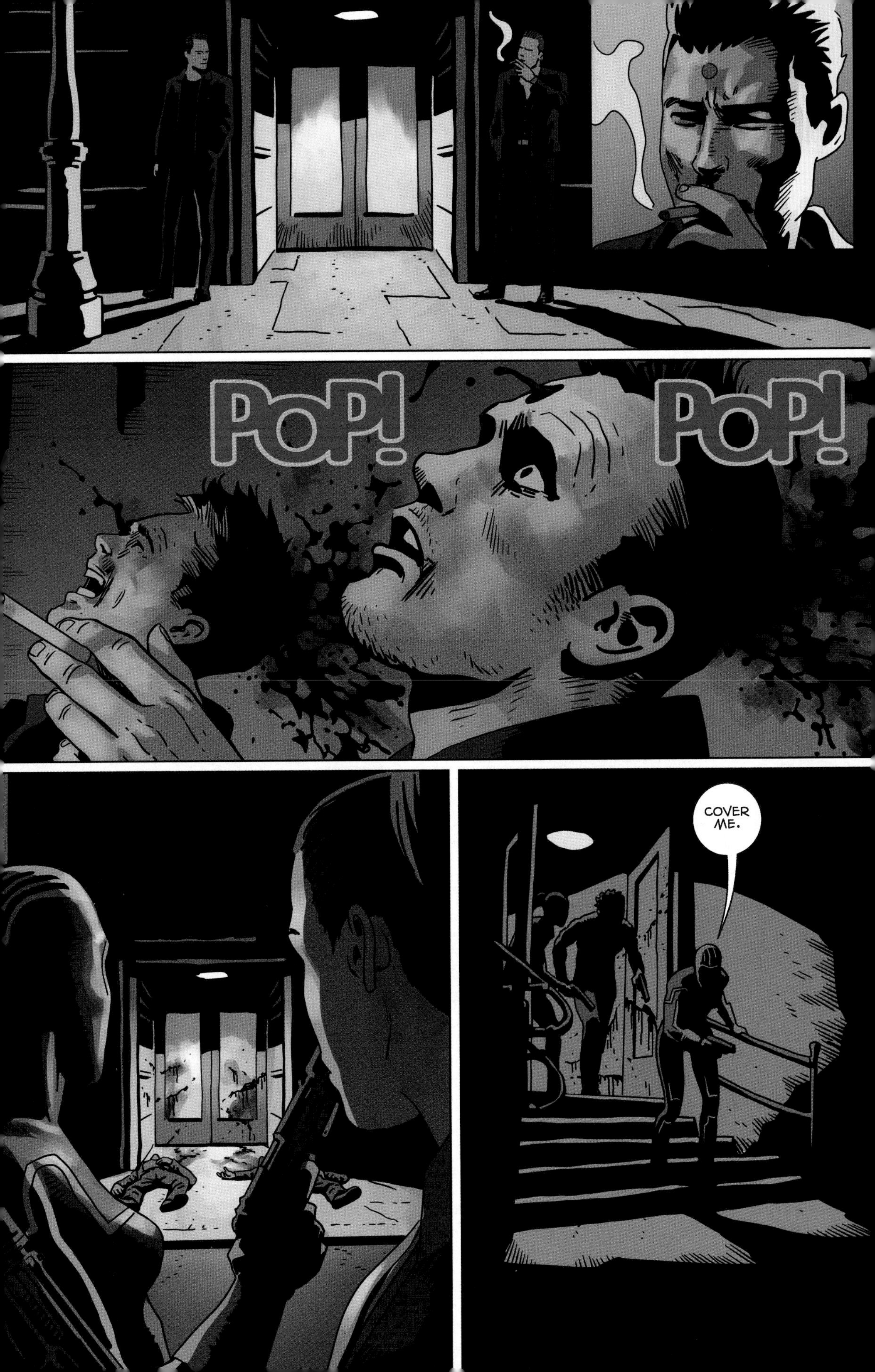
POP!
POP!
COVER ME.

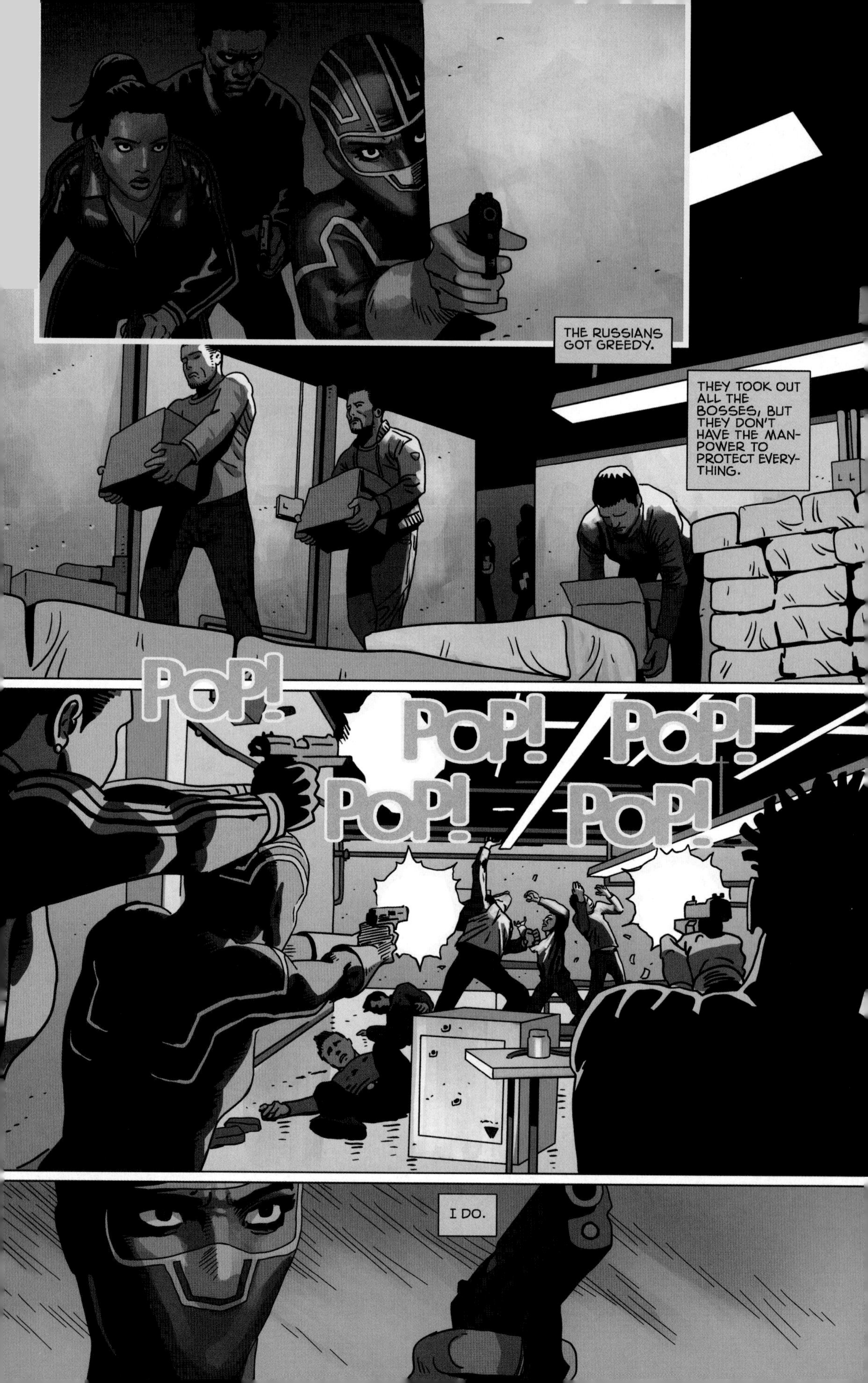
THE RUSSIANS GOT GREEDY.
THEY TOOK OUT ALL THE BOSSES, BUT THEY DON'T HAVE THE MAN-POWER TO PROTECT EVERY-THING.
POP!
POP!
POP!
POP!
POP!
I DO.

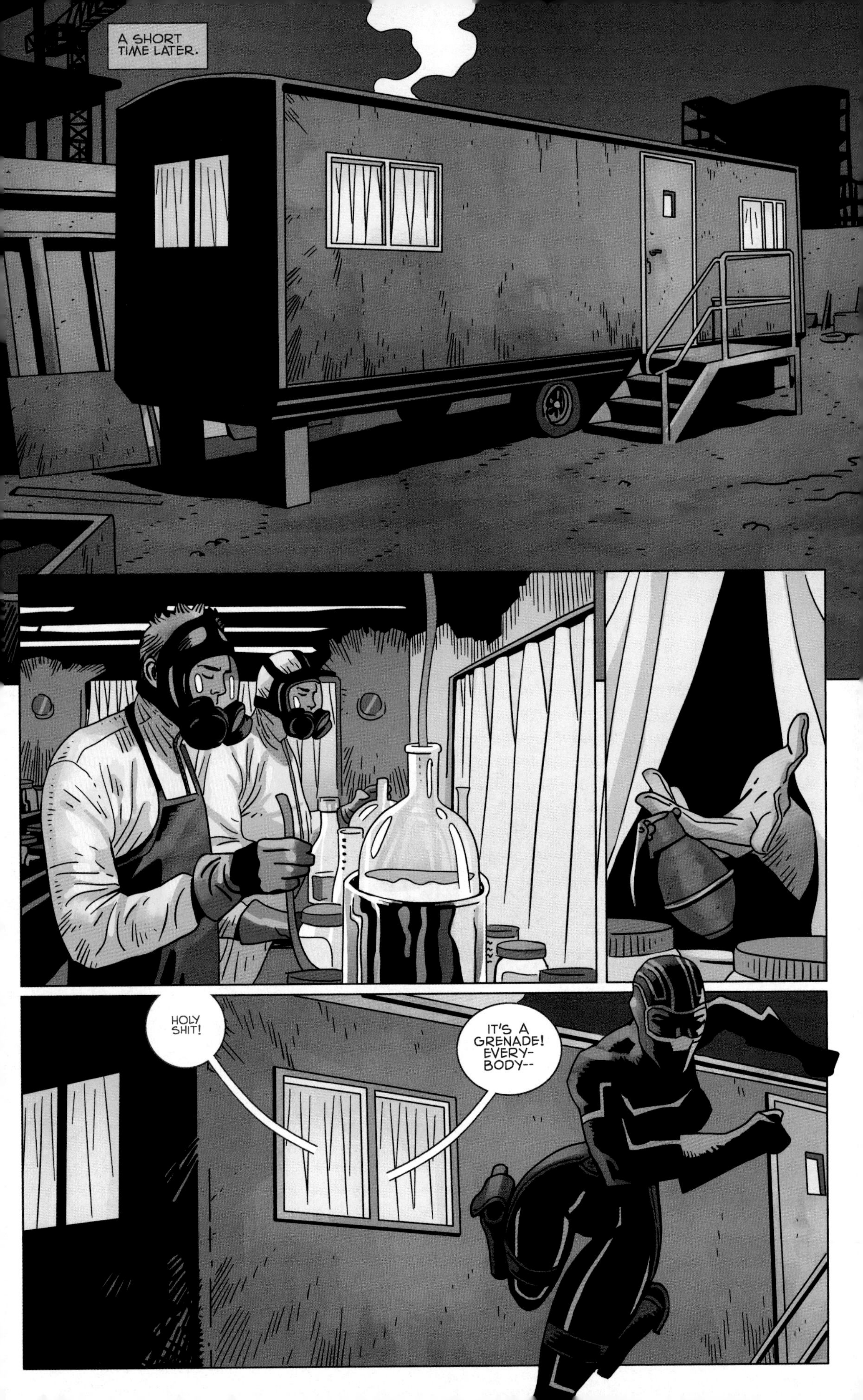
A SHORT TIME LATER.
HOLY SHIT!
IT'S A GRENADE! EVERY-BODY--

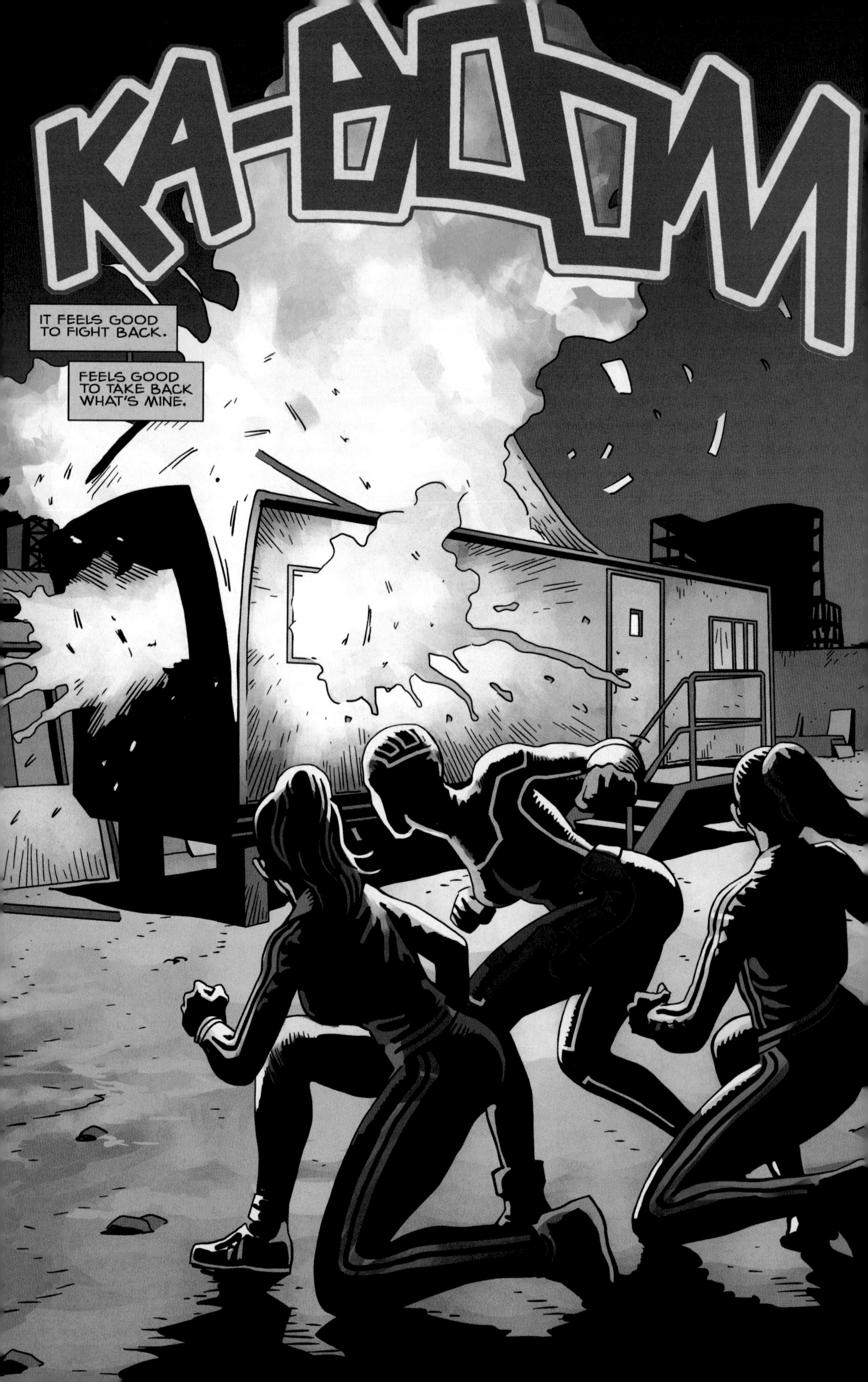
KA-BOOM
IT FEELS GOOD TO FIGHT BACK.
FEELS GOOD TO TAKE BACK WHAT'S MINE.

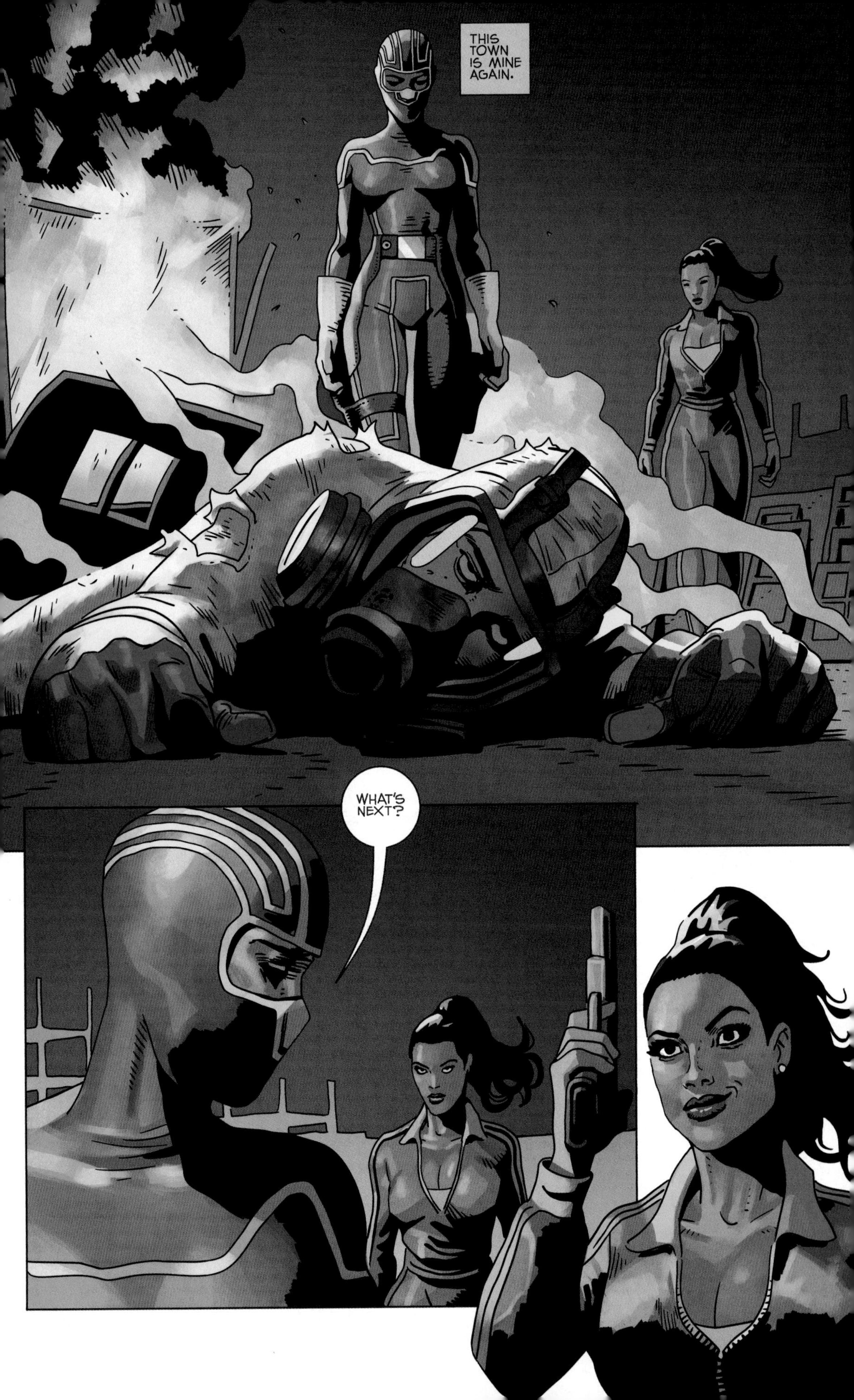
THIS TOWN IS MINE AGAIN.
WHAT'S NEXT?

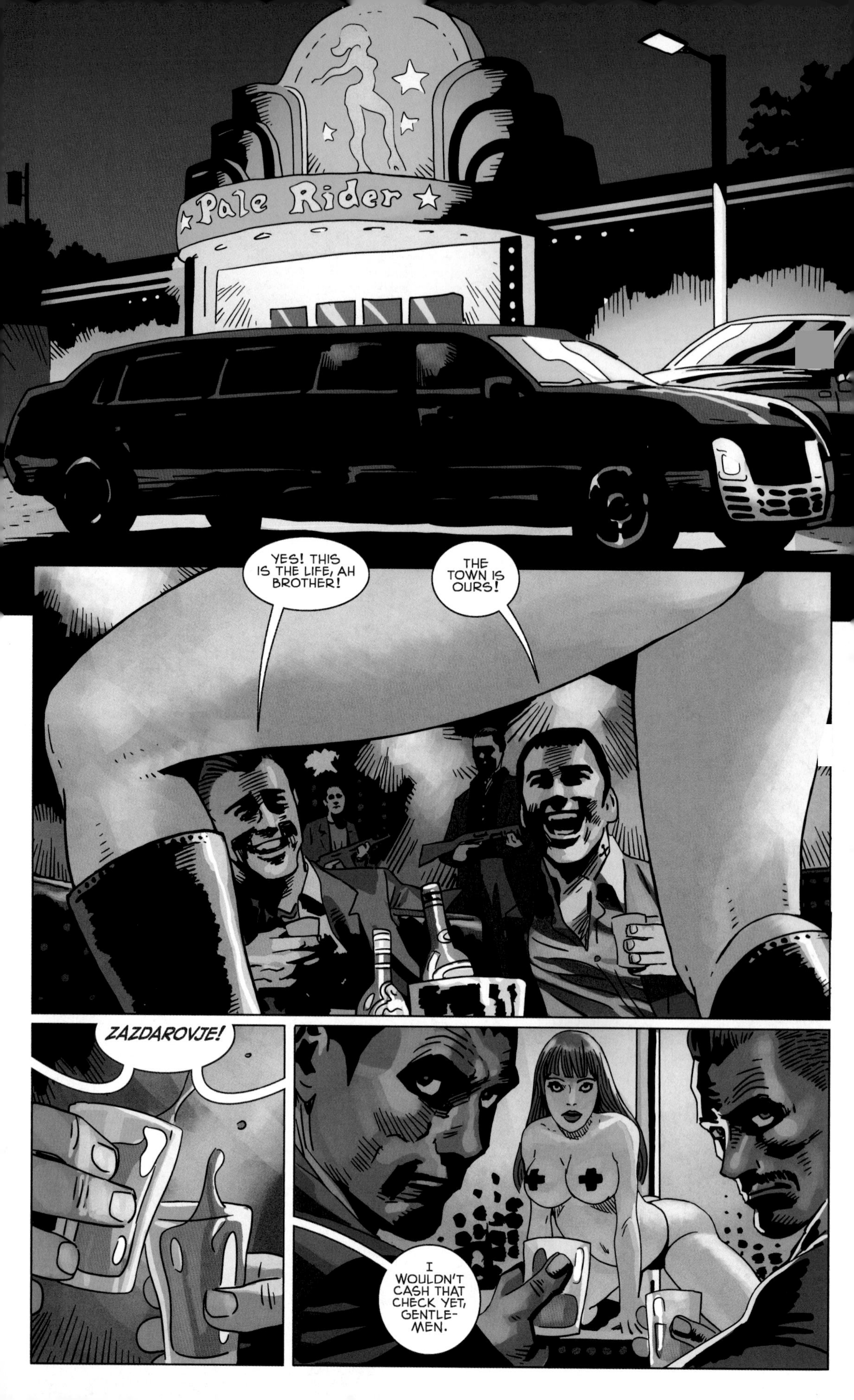
Pale Rider
YES! THIS IS THE LIFE, AH BROTHER!
THE TOWN IS OURS!
ZAZDAROVJE!
I WOULDN'T CASH THAT CHECK YET, GENTLE-MEN.

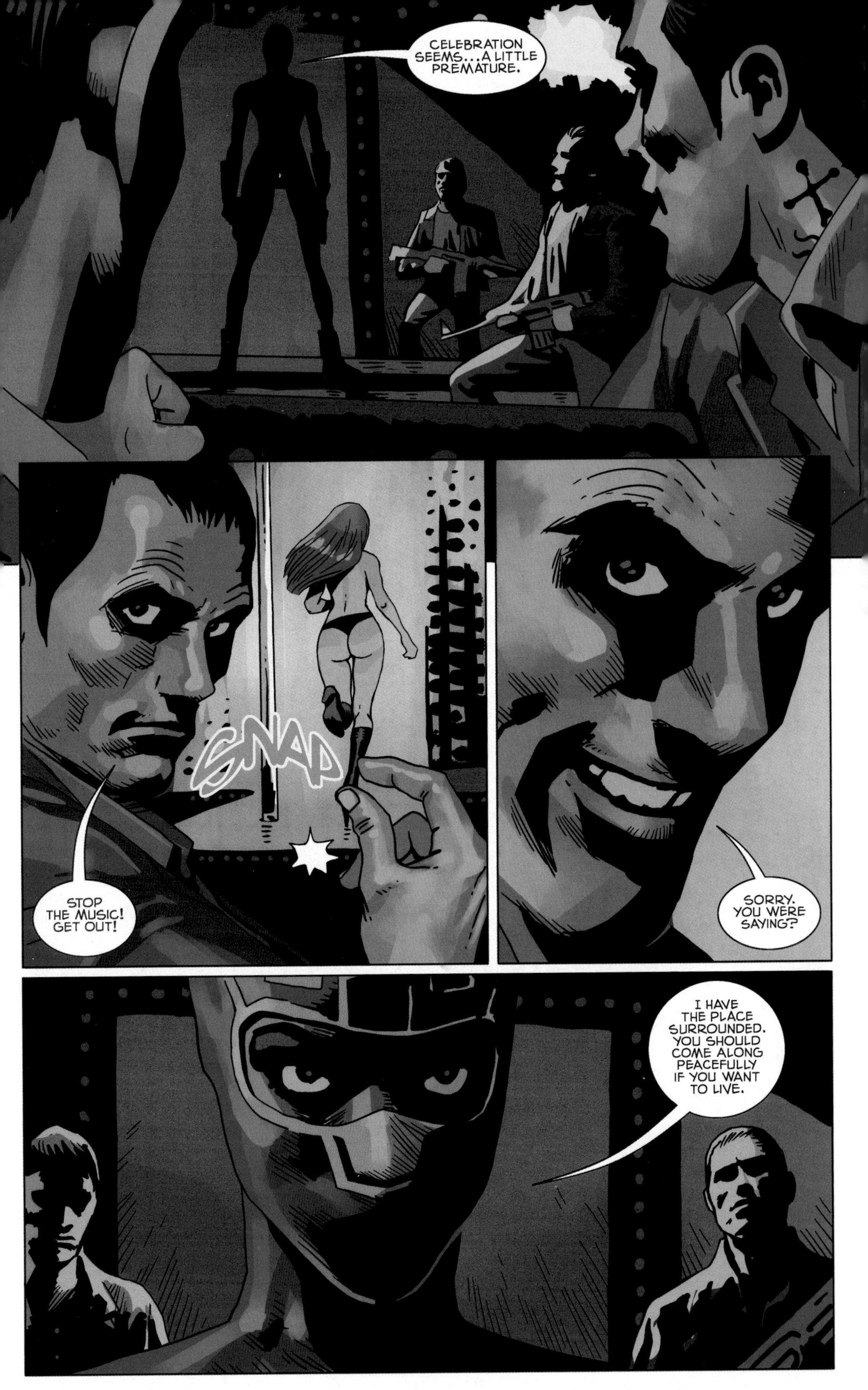
CELEBRATION SEEMS...A LITTLE PREMATURE.
SNAP
STOP THE MUSIC! GET OUT!
SORRY. YOU WERE SAYING?
I HAVE THE PLACE SURROUNDED. YOU SHOULD COME ALONG PEACEFULLY IF YOU WANT TO LIVE.

HA HA
HA!

HAHAHA!

HAHA!

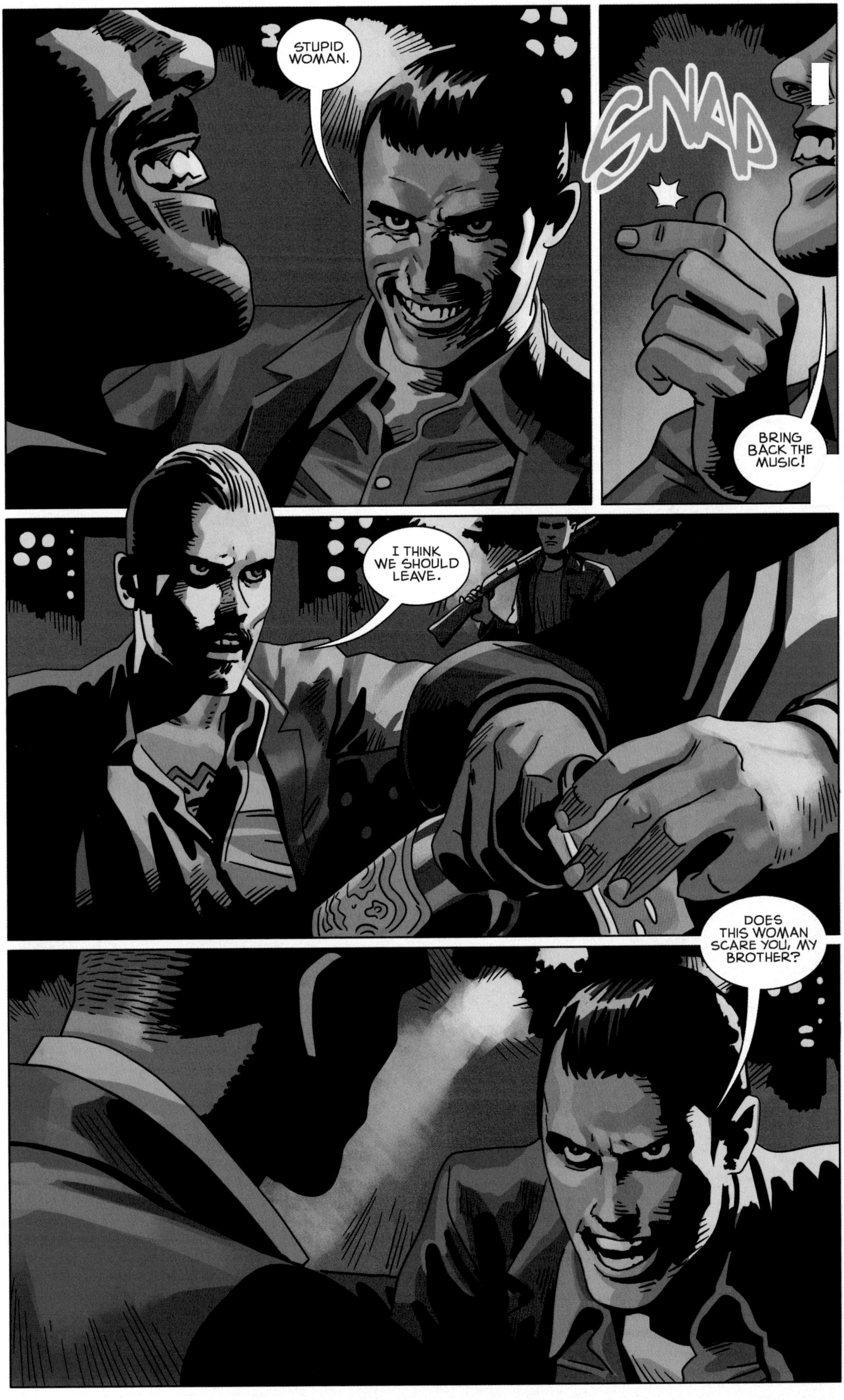
STUPID WOMAN.
SNAP
BRING BACK THE MUSIC!
I THINK WE SHOULD LEAVE.
DOES THIS WOMAN SCARE YOU, MY BROTHER?

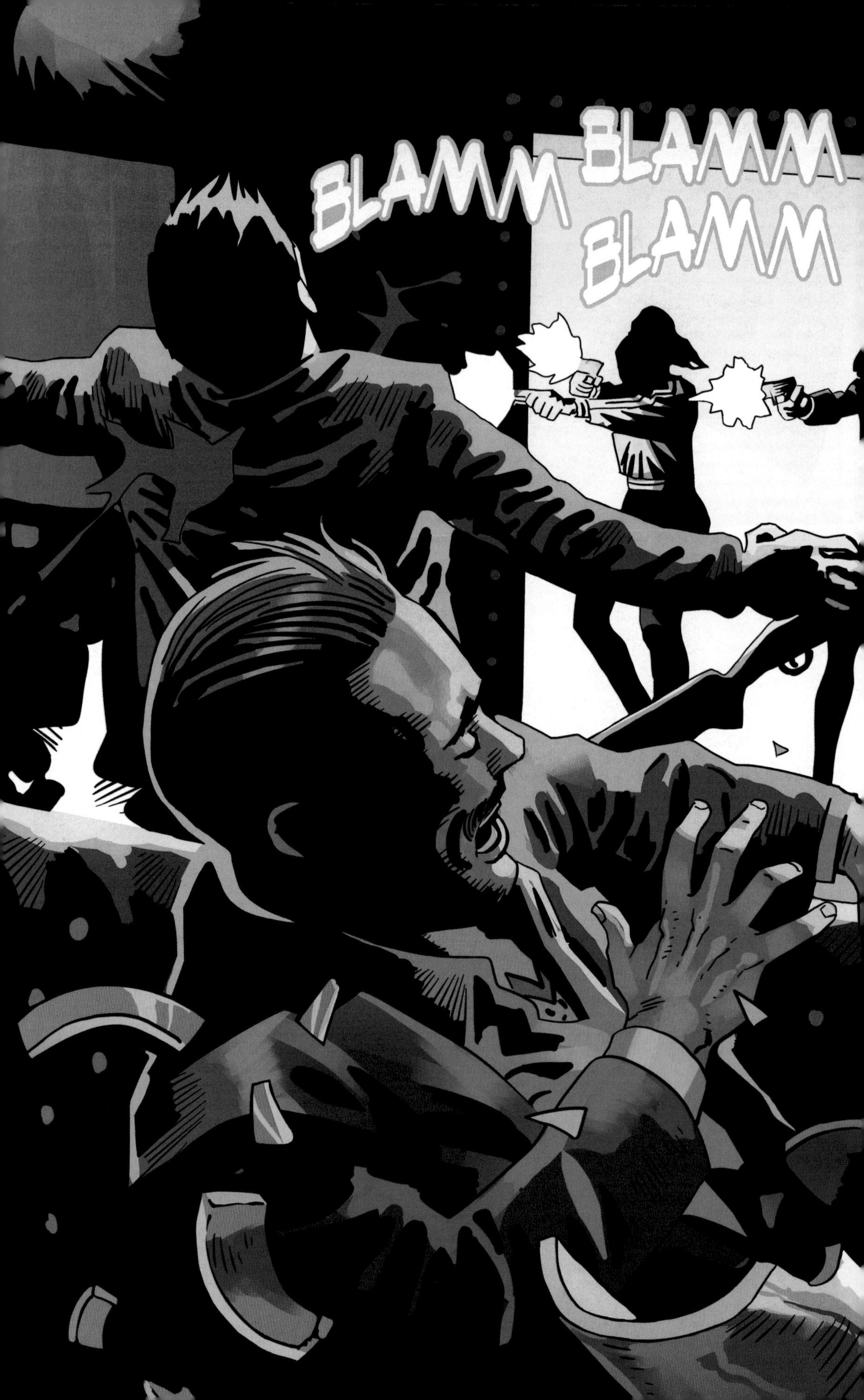
BLAMM
BLAMM
BLAMM

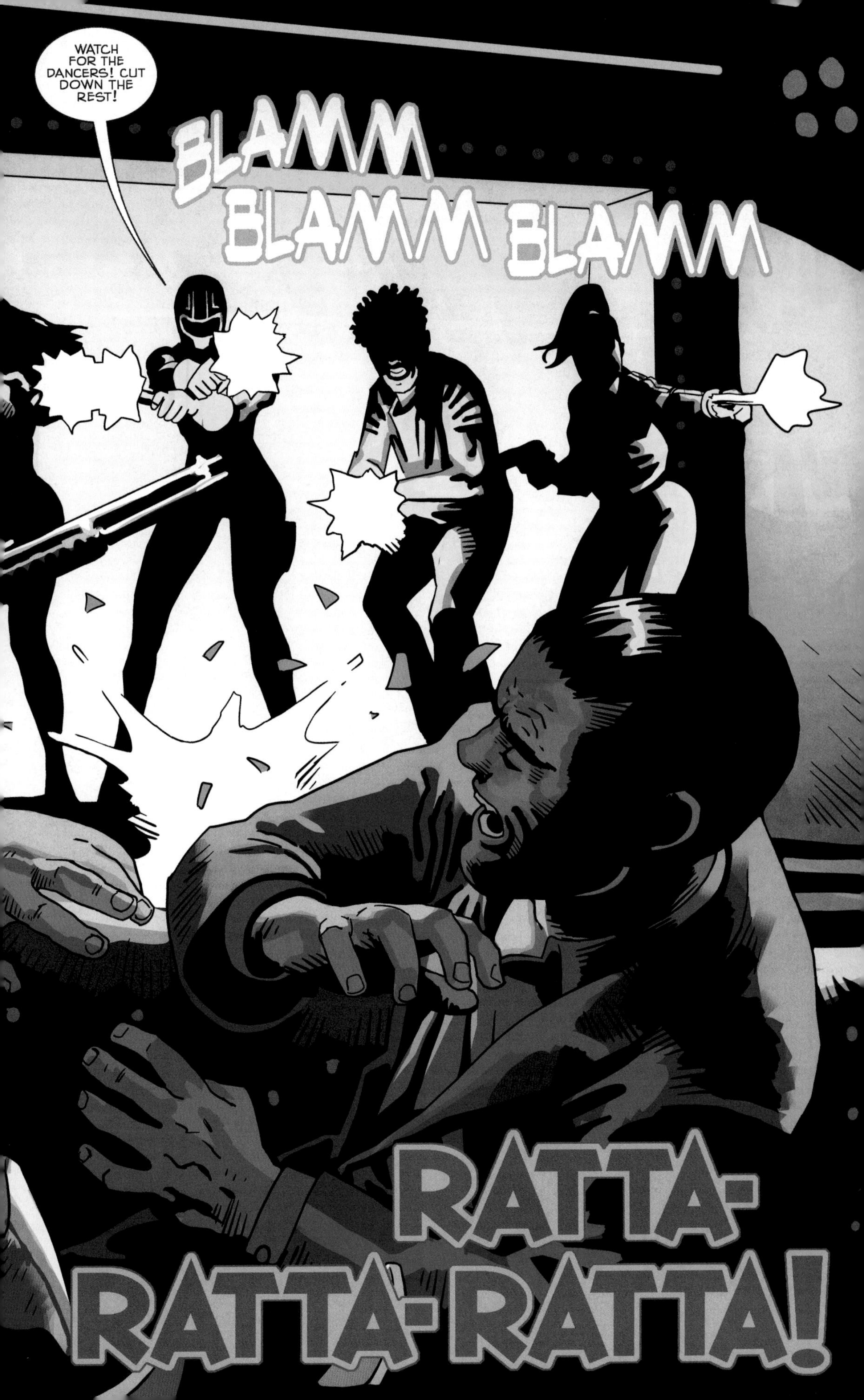
WATCH FOR THE DANCERS! CUT DOWN THE REST!
BLAMM BLAMM BLAMM
RATTA-RATTA-RATTA!

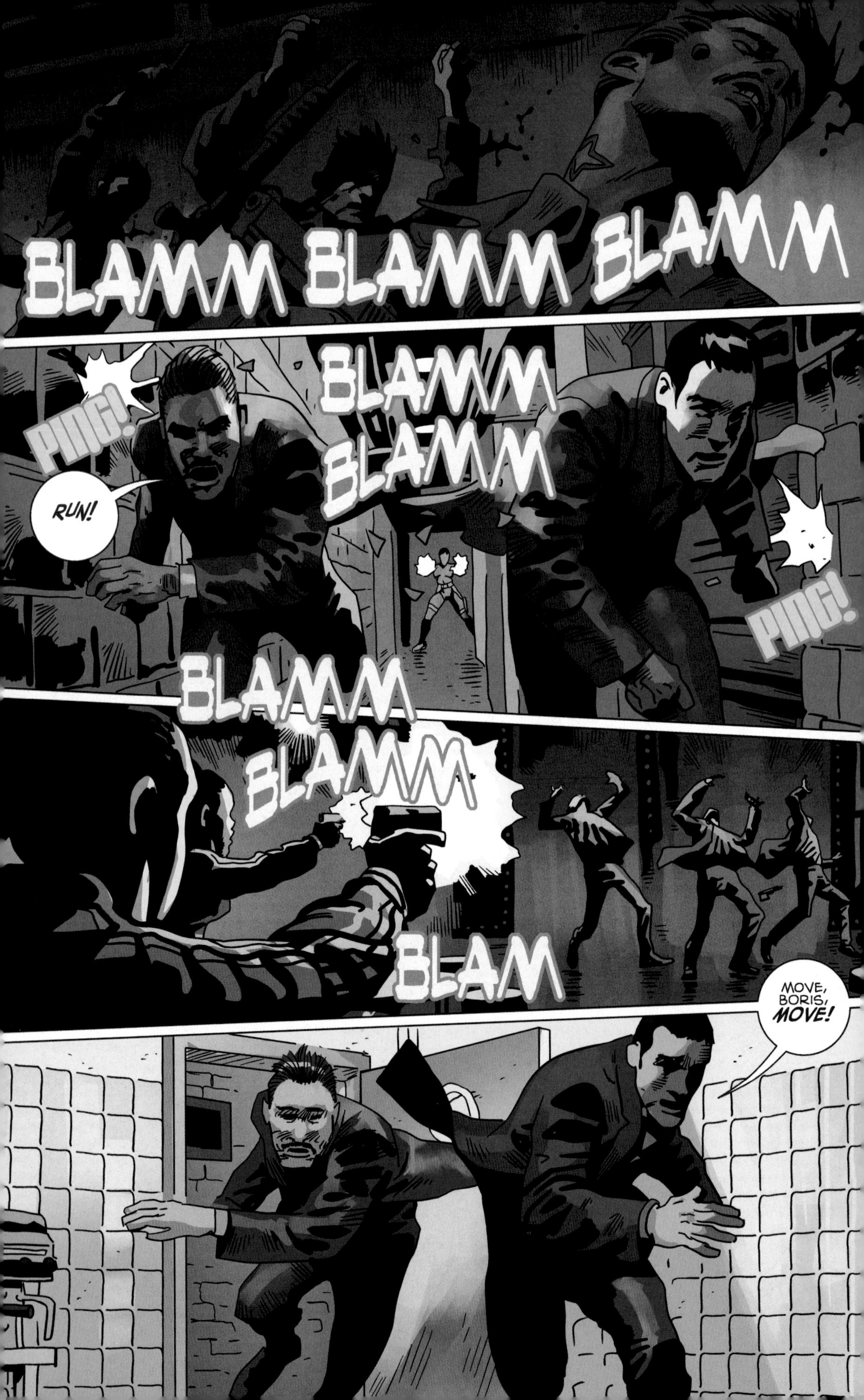
BLAMM BLAMM BLAMM
PING!
BLAMM
BLAMM
RUN!
PING!
BLAMM
BLAMM
BLAM
MOVE, BORIS, MOVE!

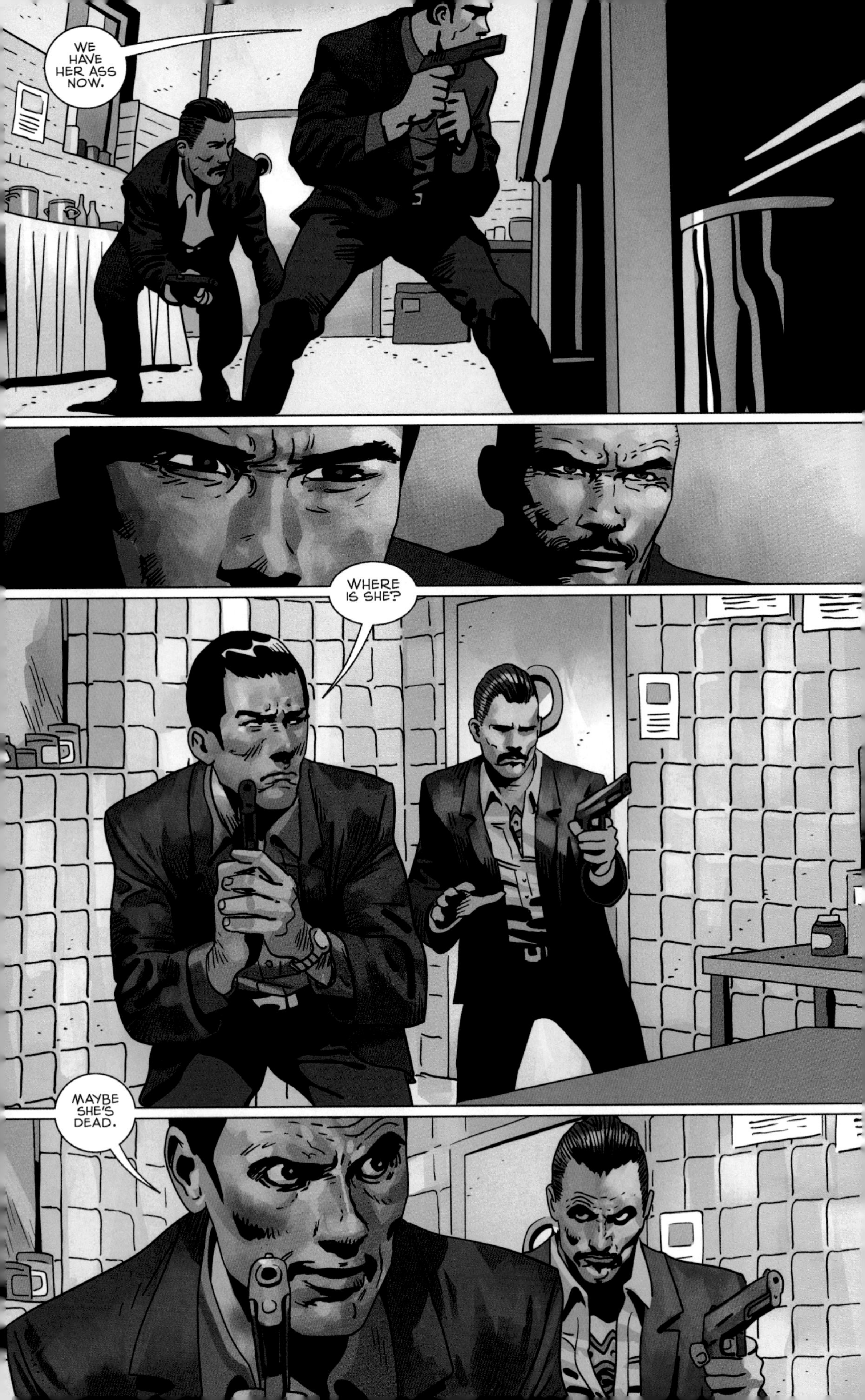
WE HAVE HER ASS NOW.
WHERE IS SHE?
MAYBE SHE'S DEAD.

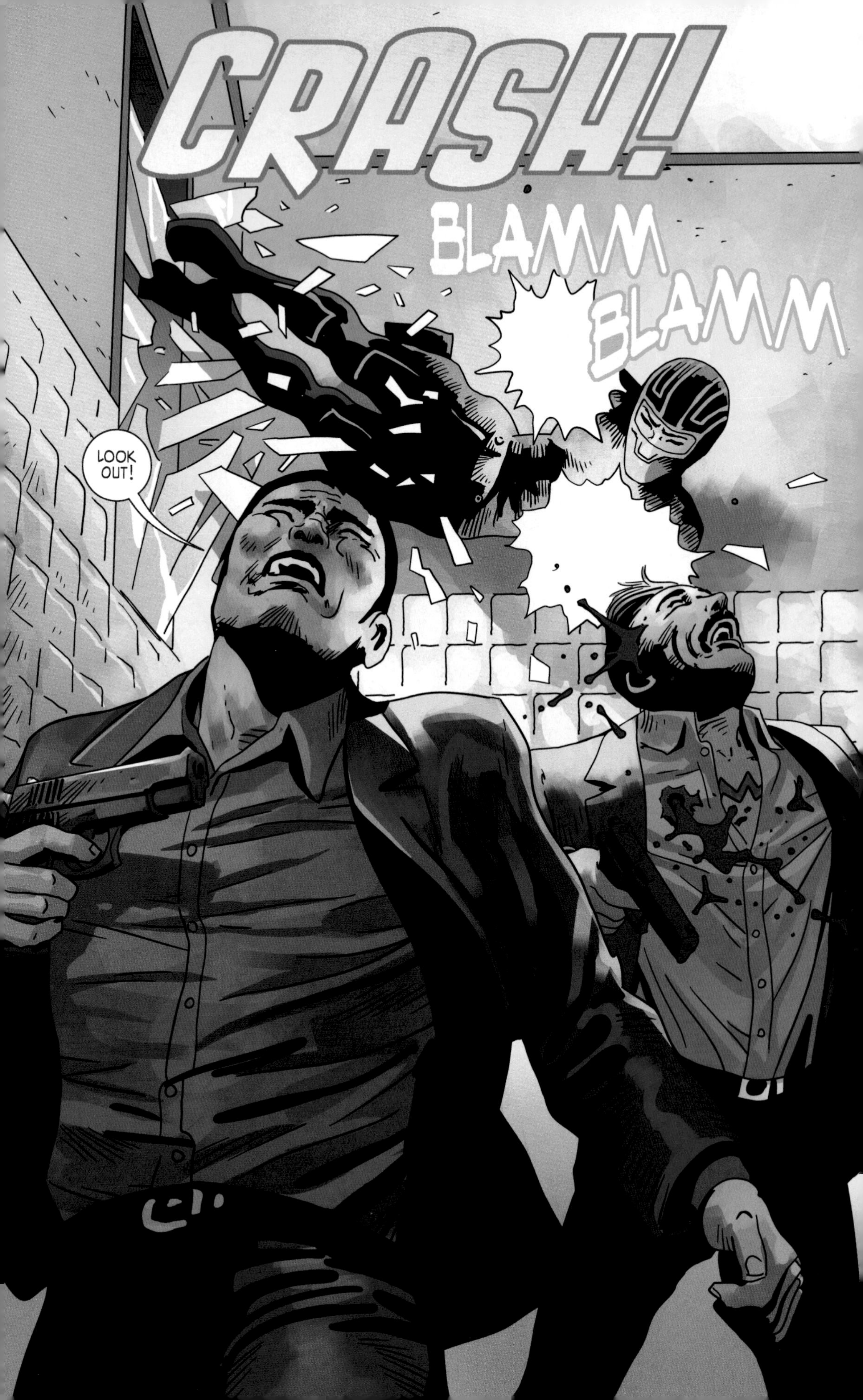
CRASH!
LOOK OUT!
BLAMM
BLAMM

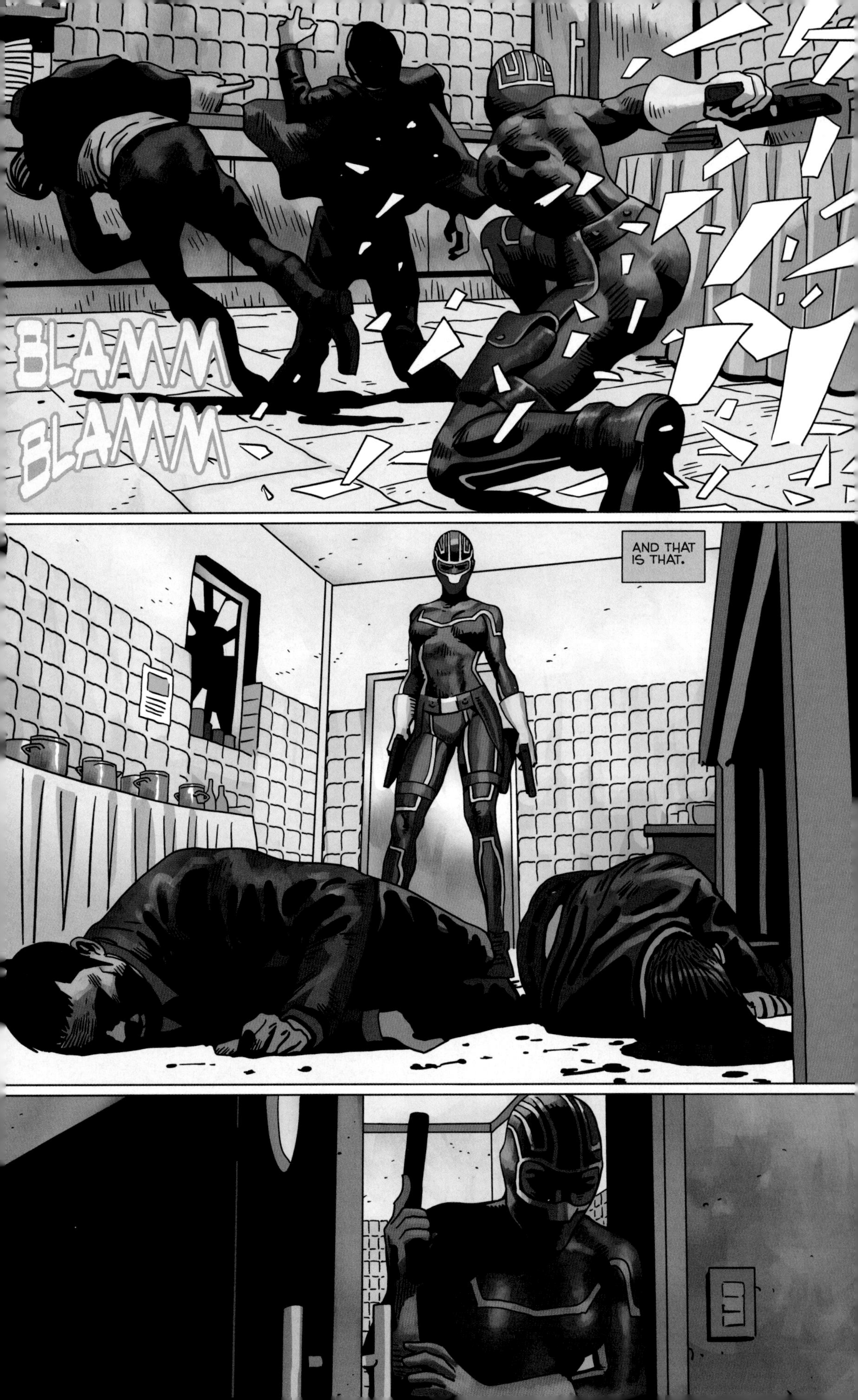
BLAMM
BLAMM
AND THAT IS THAT.

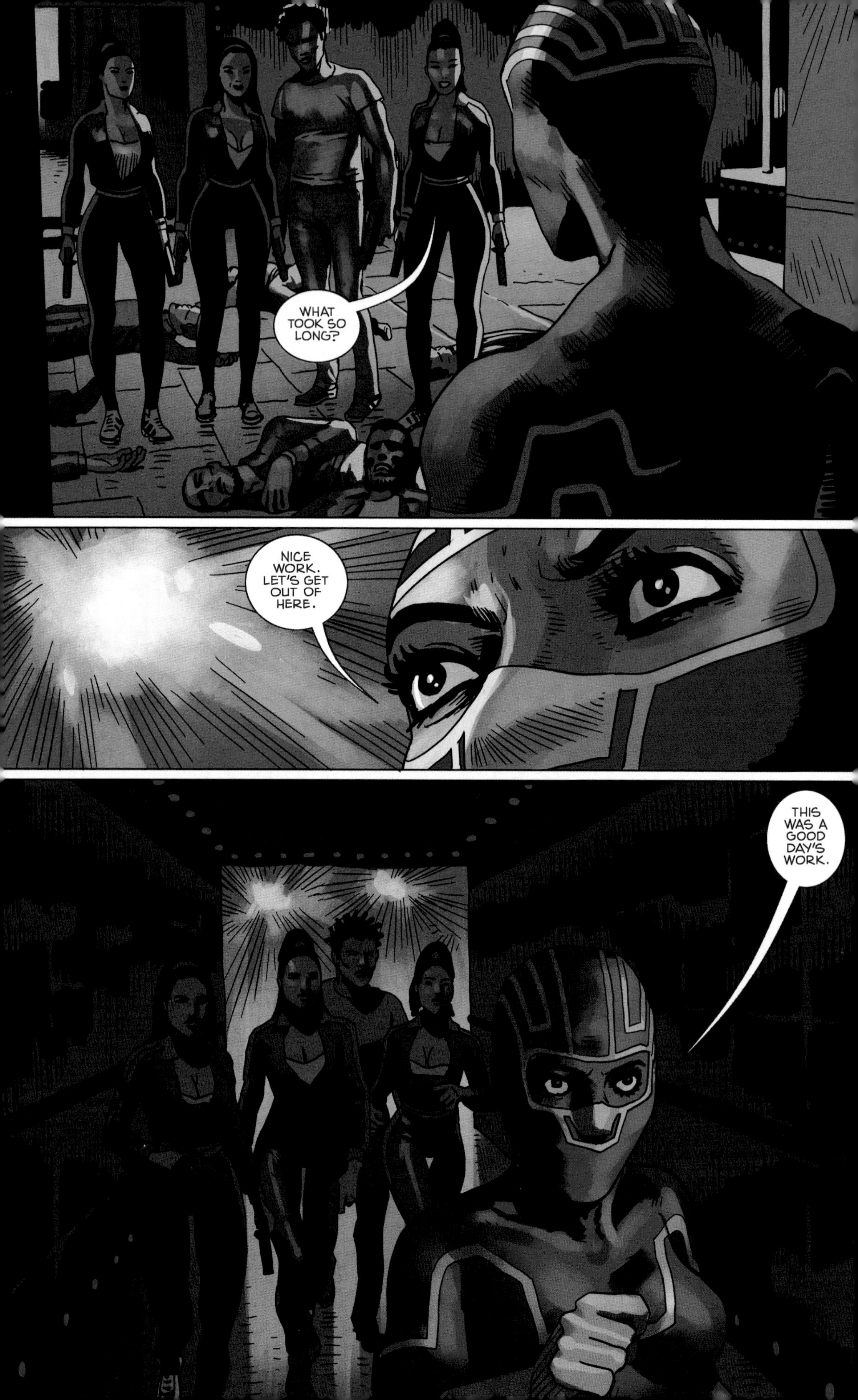
WHAT TOOK SO LONG?
NICE WORK. LET'S GET OUT OF HERE.
THIS WAS A GOOD DAY'S WORK.

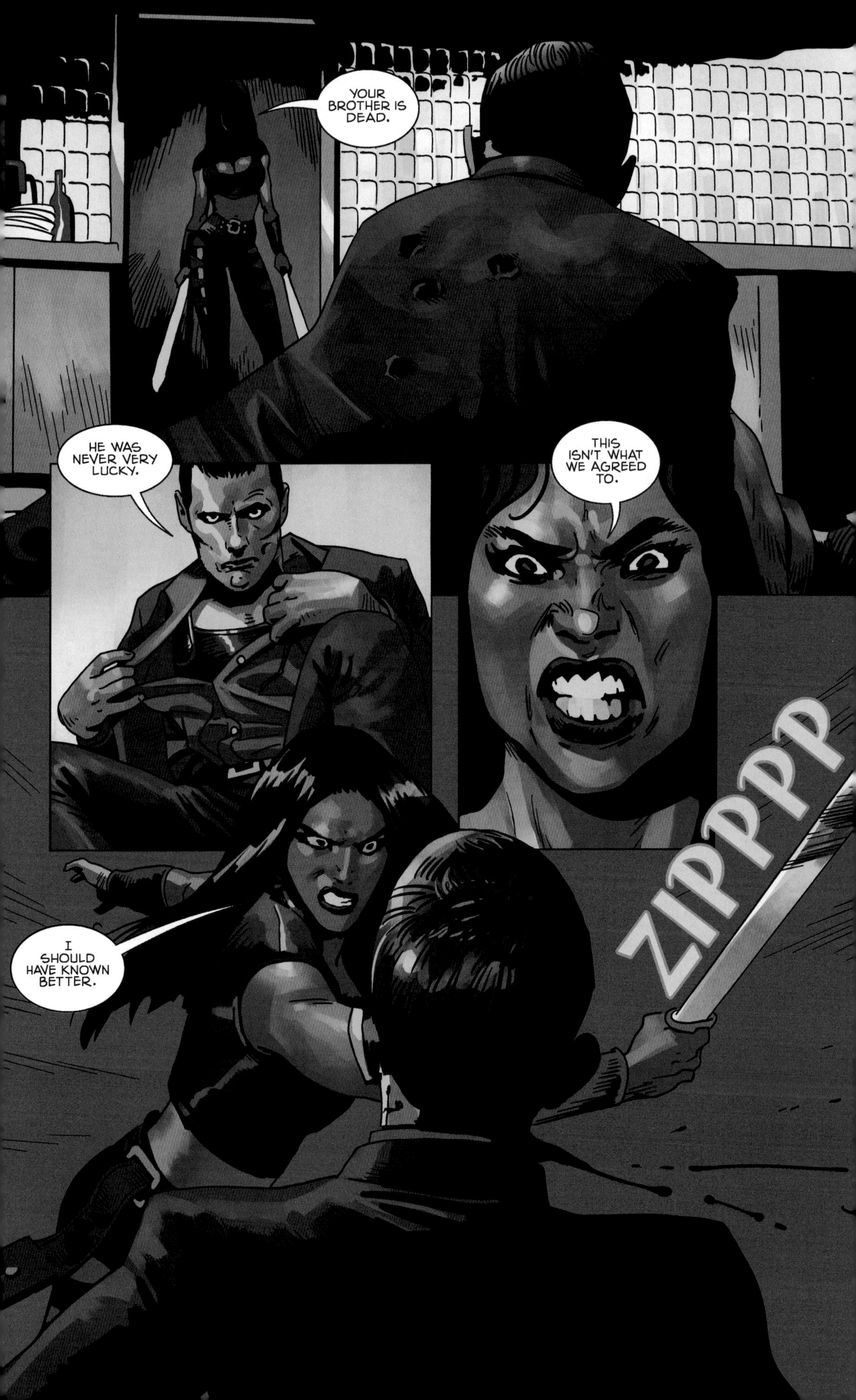
YOUR BROTHER IS DEAD.
HE WAS NEVER VERY LUCKY.
THIS ISN'T WHAT WE AGREED TO.
I SHOULD HAVE KNOWN BETTER.
ZIPPPP

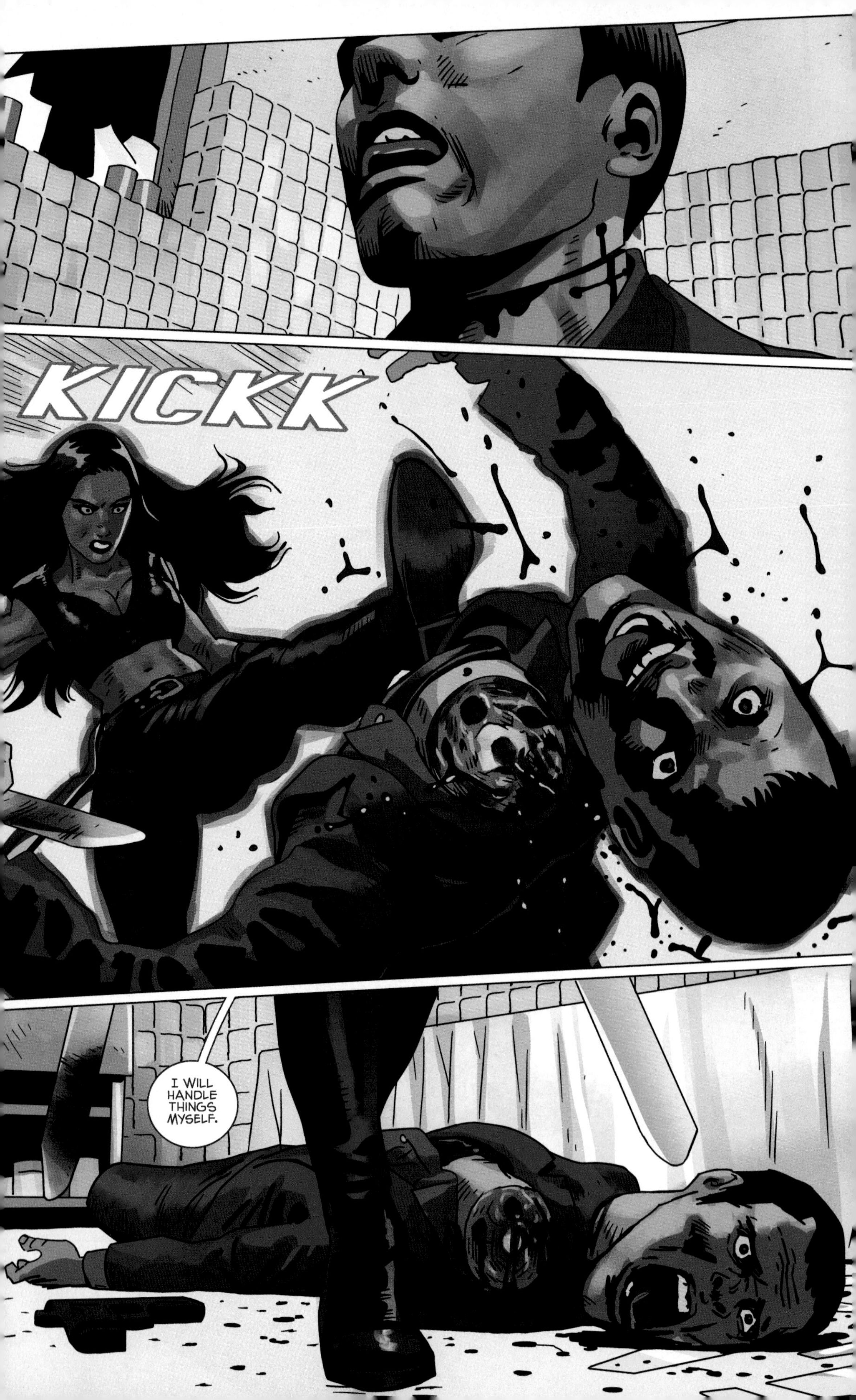
KICKK
I WILL HANDLE THINGS MYSELF.

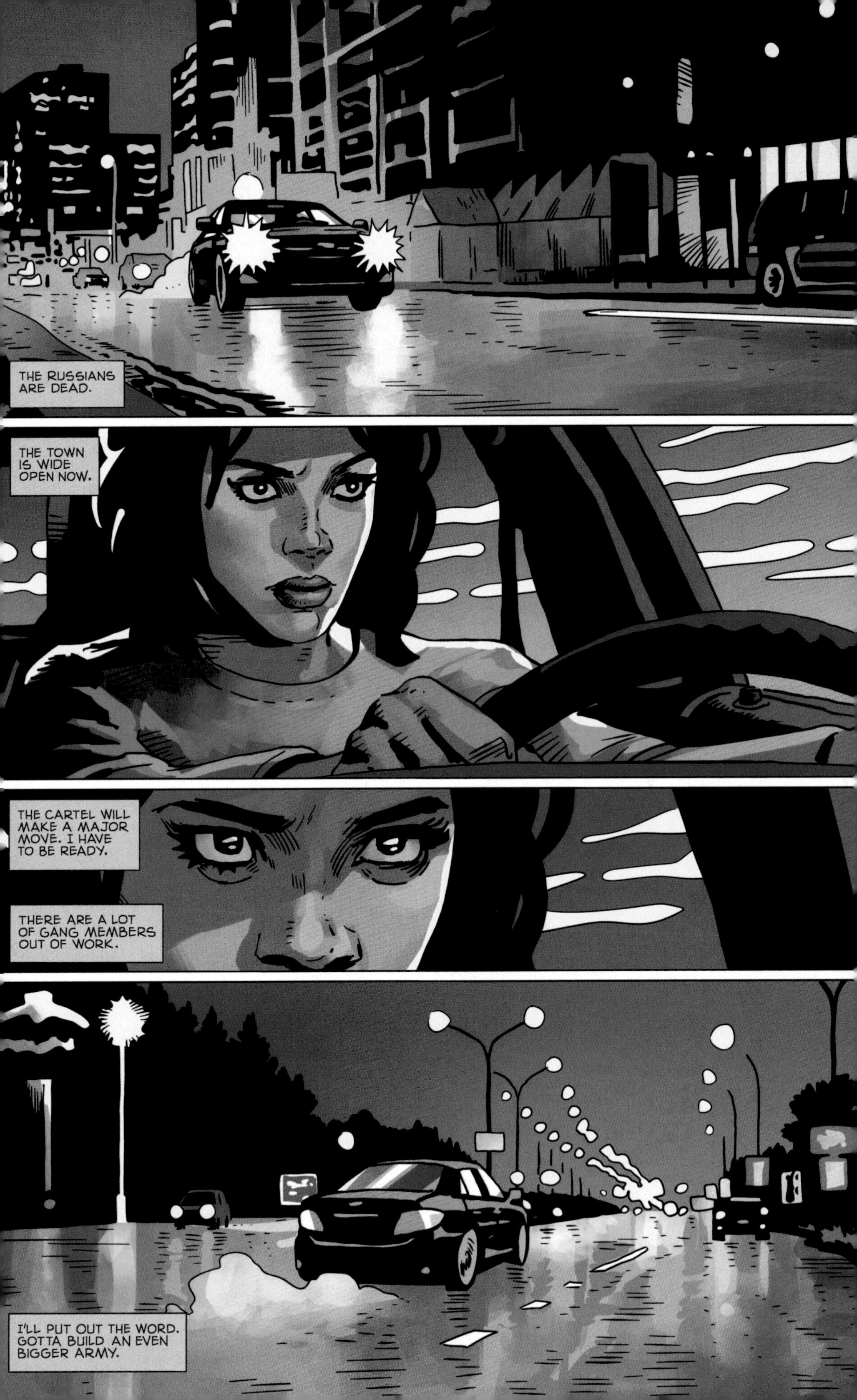
THE RUSSIANS ARE DEAD.
THE TOWN IS WIDE OPEN NOW.
THE CARTEL WILL MAKE A MAJOR MOVE. I HAVE TO BE READY.
THERE ARE A LOT OF GANG MEMBERS OUT OF WORK.
I'LL PUT OUT THE WORD. GOTTA BUILD AN EVEN BIGGER ARMY.

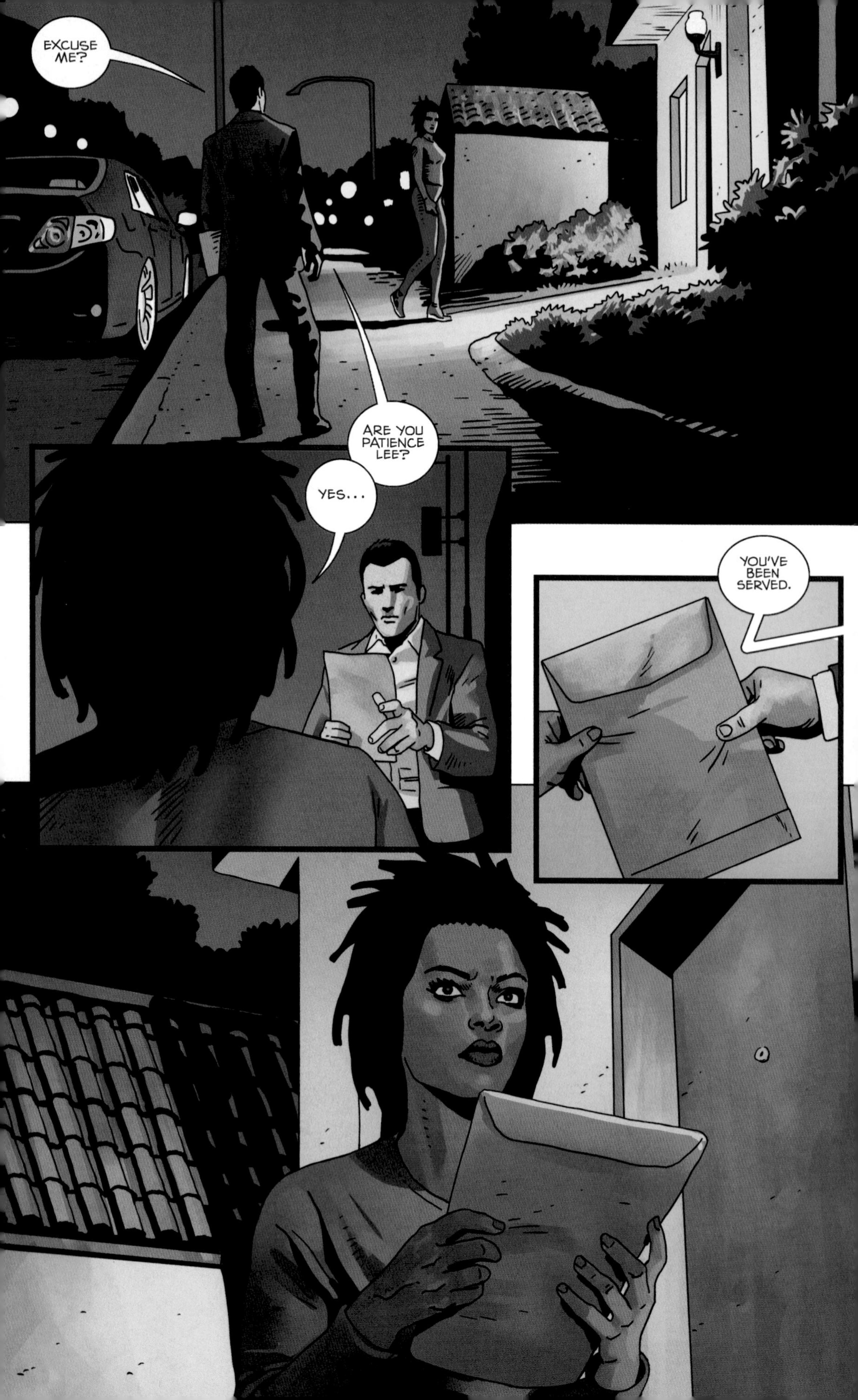
EXCUSE ME?
ARE YOU PATIENCE LEE?
YES...
YOU'VE BEEN SERVED.

SIX

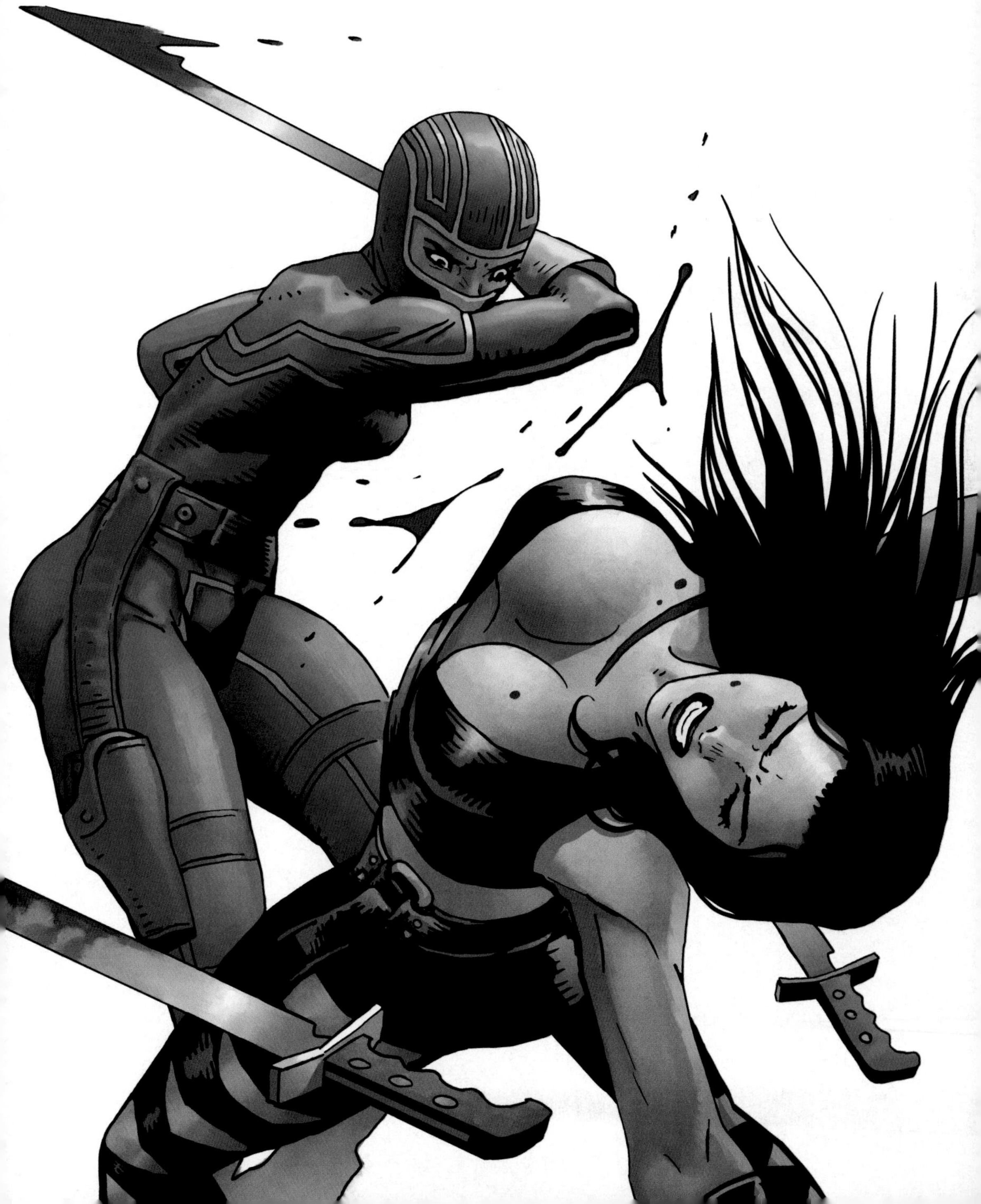

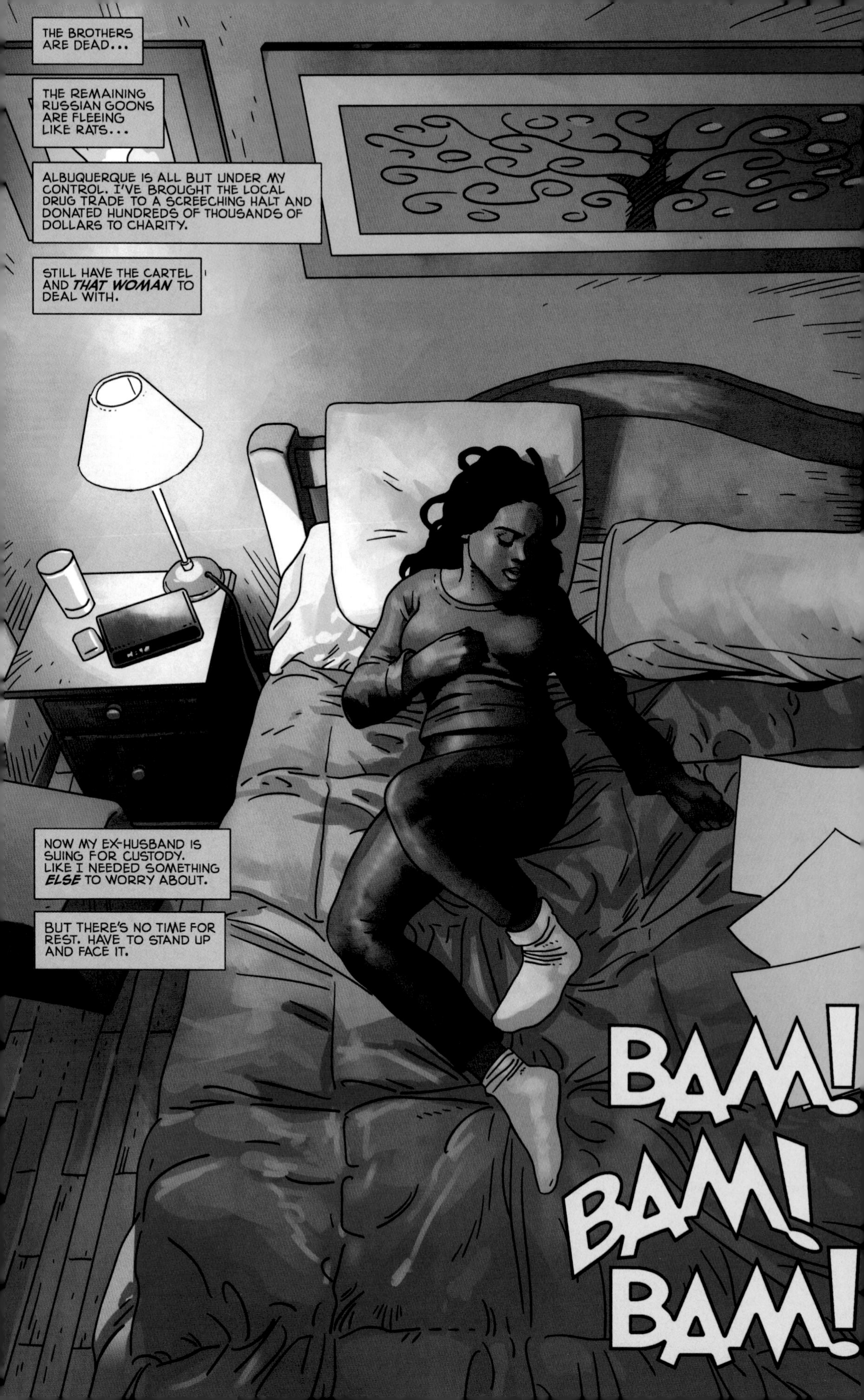
THE BROTHERS ARE DEAD...
THE REMAINING RUSSIAN GOONS ARE FLEEING LIKE RATS...
ALBUQUERQUE IS ALL BUT UNDER MY CONTROL. I'VE BROUGHT THE LOCAL DRUG TRADE TO A SCREECHING HALT AND DONATED HUNDREDS OF THOUSANDS OF DOLLARS TO CHARITY.
STILL HAVE THE CARTEL AND *THAT WOMAN* TO DEAL WITH.
NOW MY EX-HUSBAND IS SUING FOR CUSTODY. LIKE I NEEDED SOMETHING *ELSE* TO WORRY ABOUT.
BUT THERE'S NO TIME FOR REST. HAVE TO STAND UP AND FACE IT.
BAM!
BAM!
BAM!

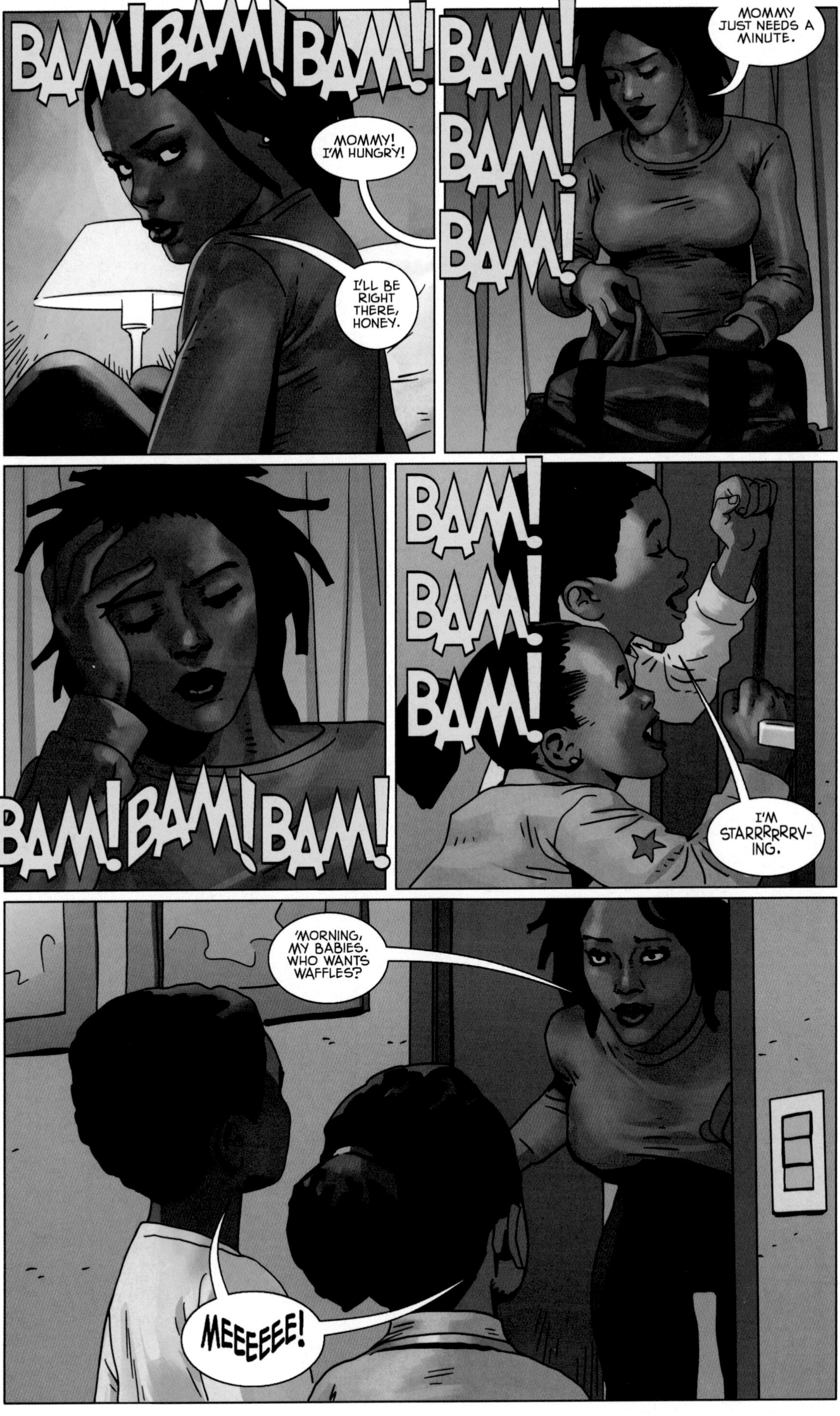
BAM! BAM! BAM! BAM!
MOMMY! I'M HUNGRY!
I'LL BE RIGHT THERE, HONEY.
MOMMY JUST NEEDS A MINUTE.
BAM! BAM! BAM!
BAM! BAM! BAM!
BAM! BAM! BAM!
I'M STARRRRRRV-ING.
'MORNING, MY BABIES. WHO WANTS WAFFLES?
MEEEEEE!

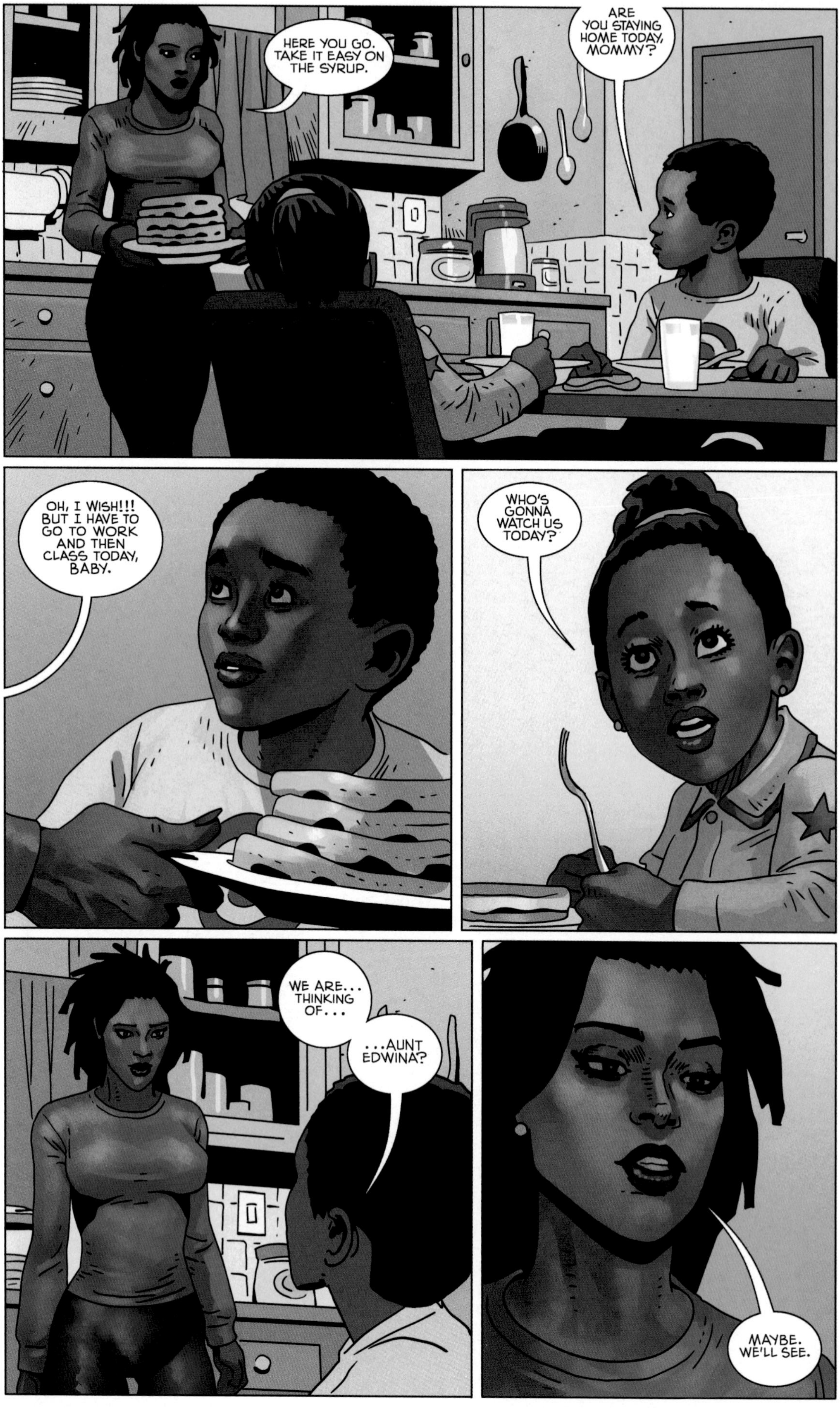
HERE YOU GO. TAKE IT EASY ON THE SYRUP.
ARE YOU STAYING HOME TODAY, MOMMY?
OH, I WISH!!! BUT I HAVE TO GO TO WORK AND THEN CLASS TODAY, BABY.
WHO'S GONNA WATCH US TODAY?
WE ARE... THINKING OF...
...AUNT EDWINA?
MAYBE. WE'LL SEE.

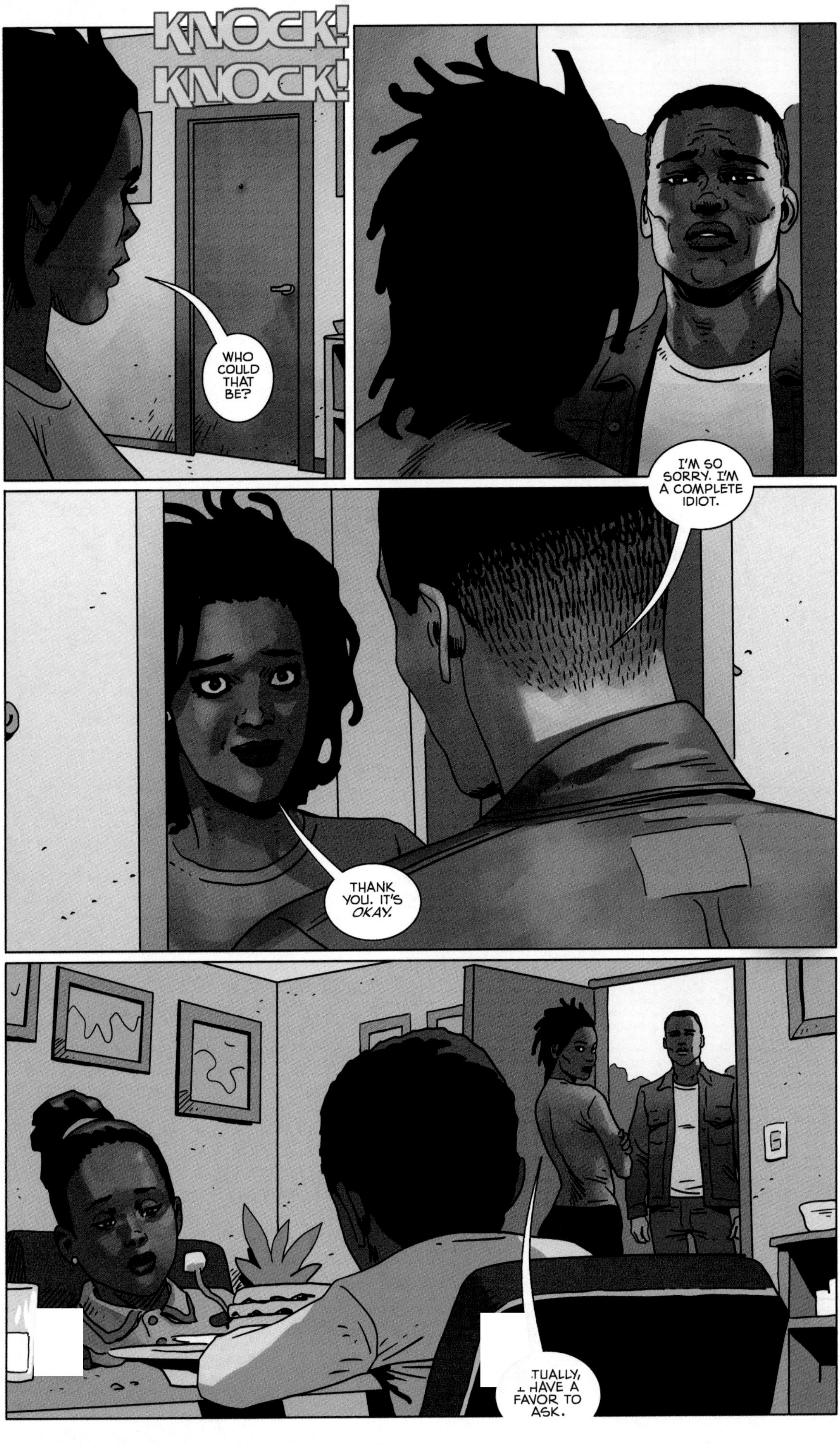
KNOCK! KNOCK!
WHO COULD THAT BE?
I'M SO SORRY. I'M A COMPLETE IDIOT.
THANK YOU. IT'S *OKAY.*
TUALLY, I HAVE A FAVOR TO ASK.

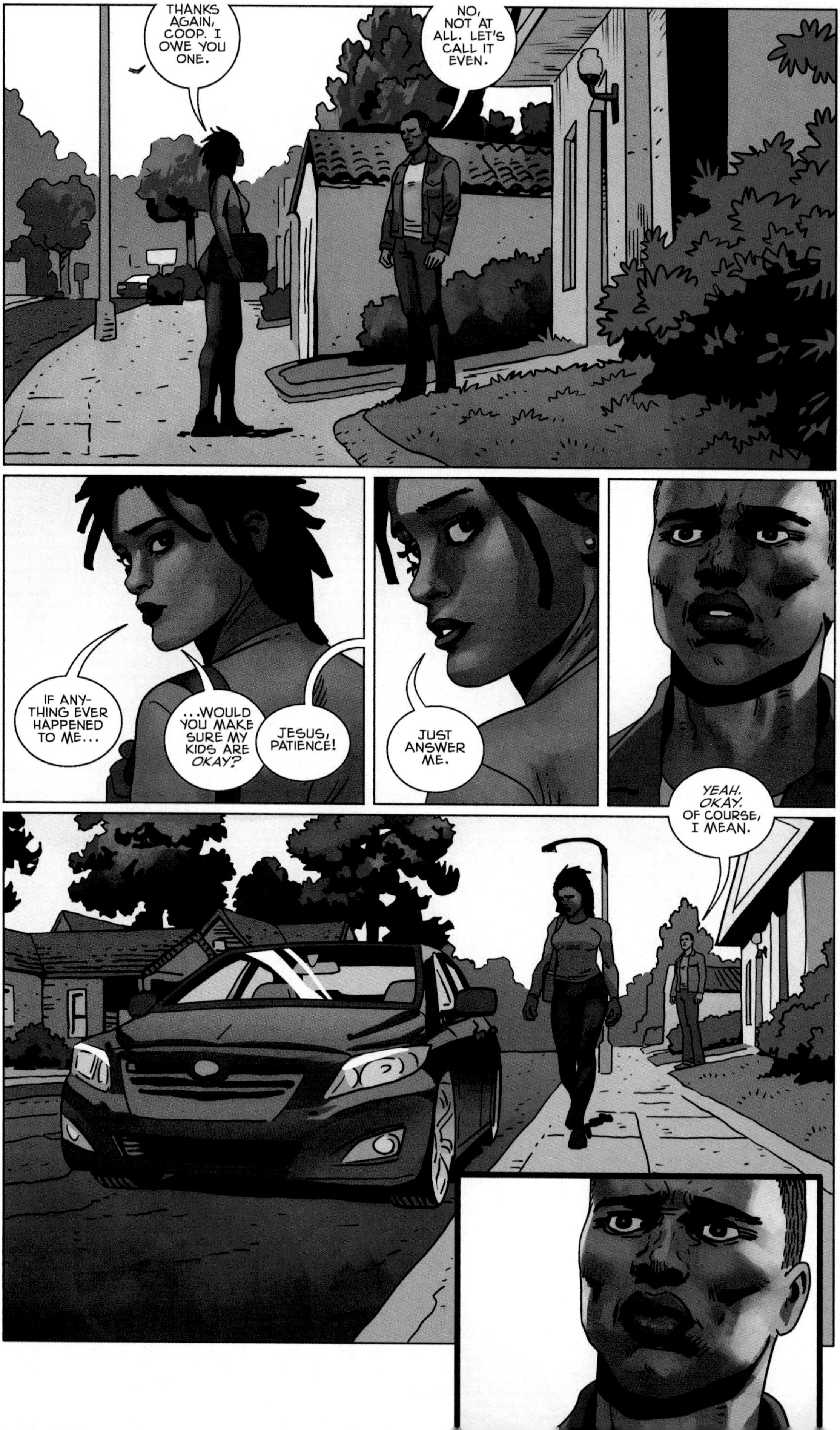
THANKS AGAIN, COOP. I OWE YOU ONE.
NO, NOT AT ALL. LET'S CALL IT EVEN.
IF ANYTHING EVER HAPPENED TO ME...
...WOULD YOU MAKE SURE MY KIDS ARE OKAY?
JESUS, PATIENCE!
JUST ANSWER ME.
YEAH. OKAY. OF COURSE, I MEAN.

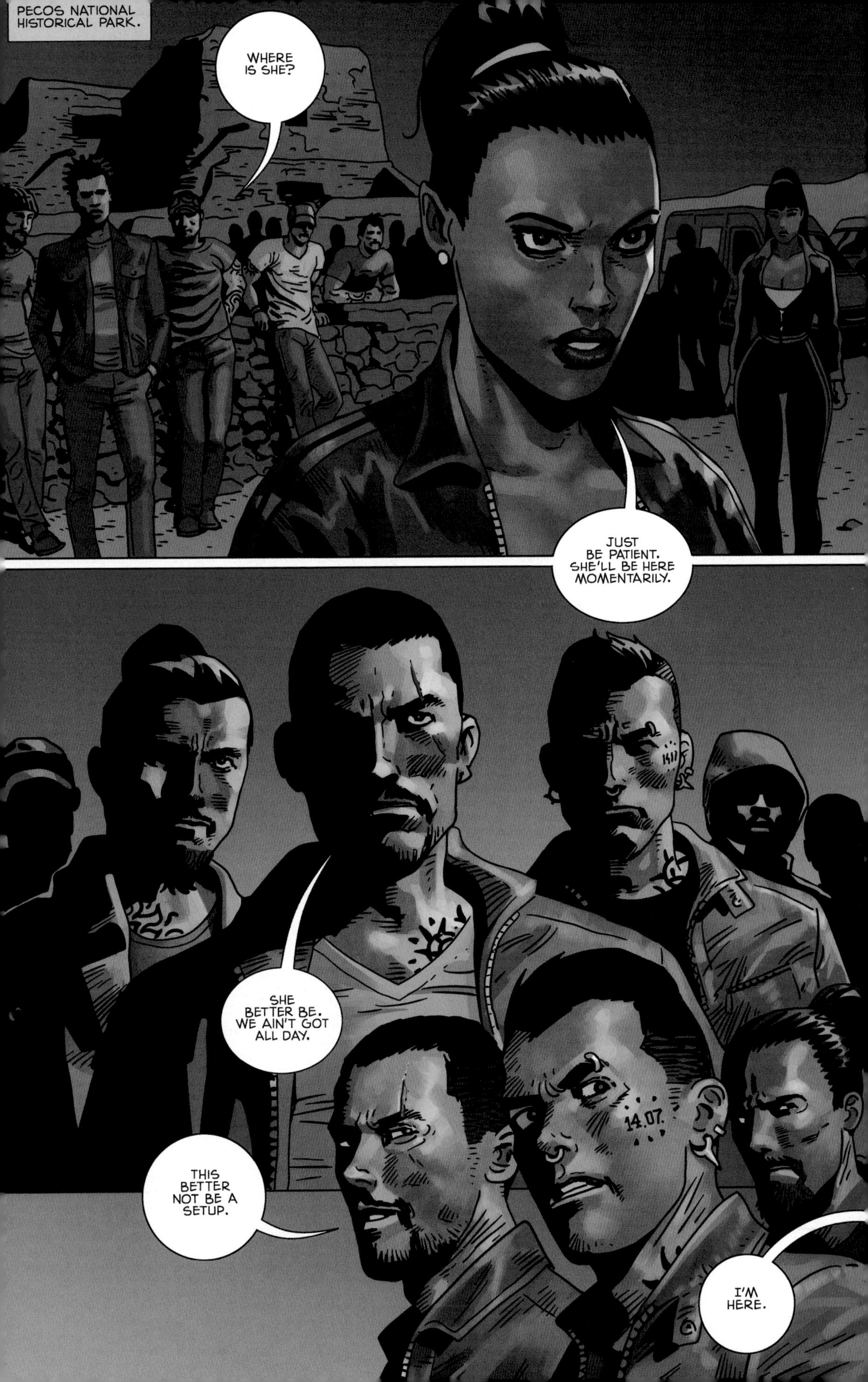
PECOS NATIONAL HISTORICAL PARK.
WHERE IS SHE?
JUST BE PATIENT. SHE'LL BE HERE MOMENTARILY.
SHE BETTER BE. WE AIN'T GOT ALL DAY.
THIS BETTER NOT BE A SETUP.
I'M HERE.

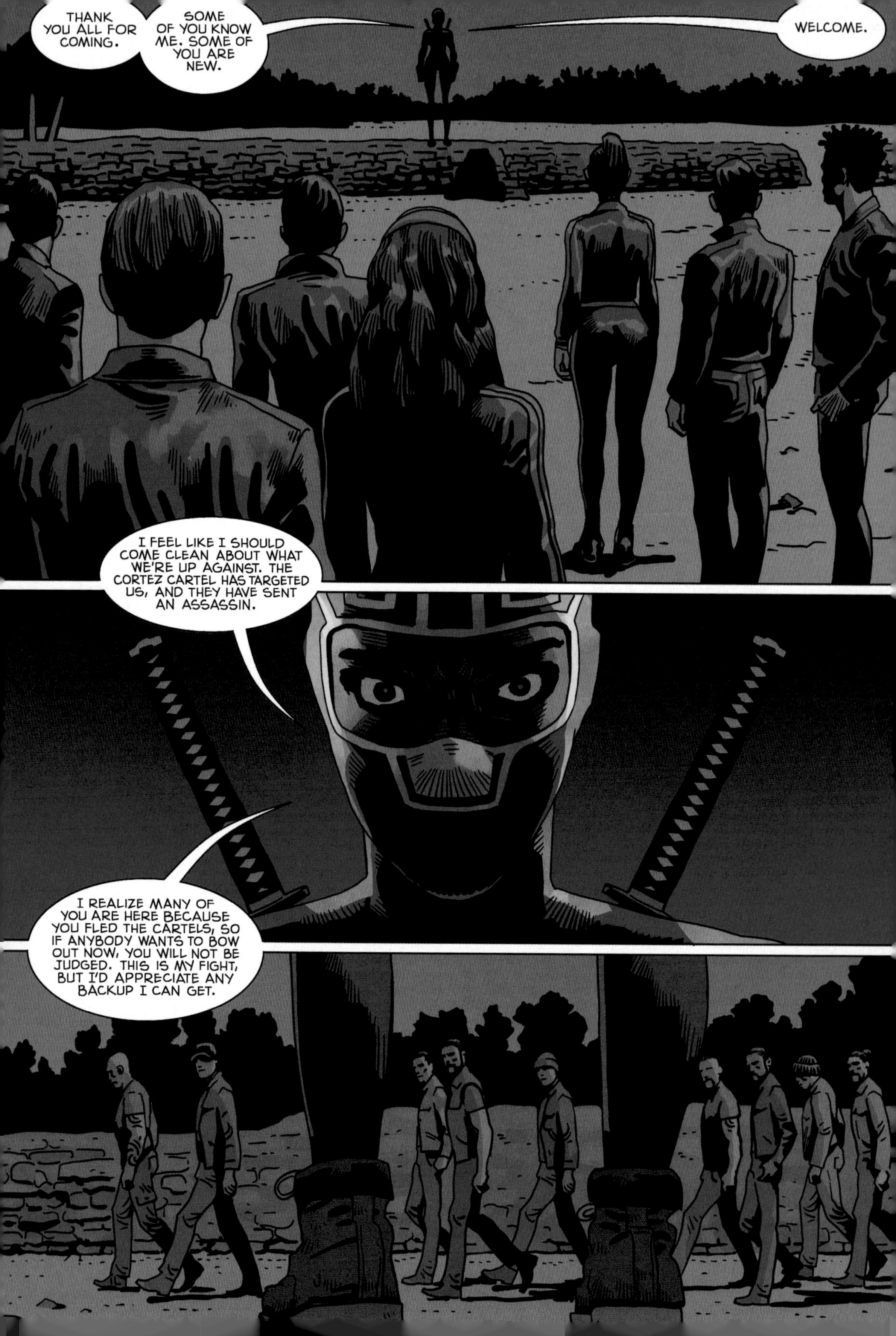
THANK YOU ALL FOR COMING.
SOME OF YOU KNOW ME. SOME OF YOU ARE NEW.
WELCOME.
I FEEL LIKE I SHOULD COME CLEAN ABOUT WHAT WE'RE UP AGAINST. THE CORTEZ CARTEL HAS TARGETED US, AND THEY HAVE SENT AN ASSASSIN.
I REALIZE MANY OF YOU ARE HERE BECAUSE YOU FLED THE CARTELS, SO IF ANYBODY WANTS TO BOW OUT NOW, YOU WILL NOT BE JUDGED. THIS IS MY FIGHT, BUT I'D APPRECIATE ANY BACKUP I CAN GET.

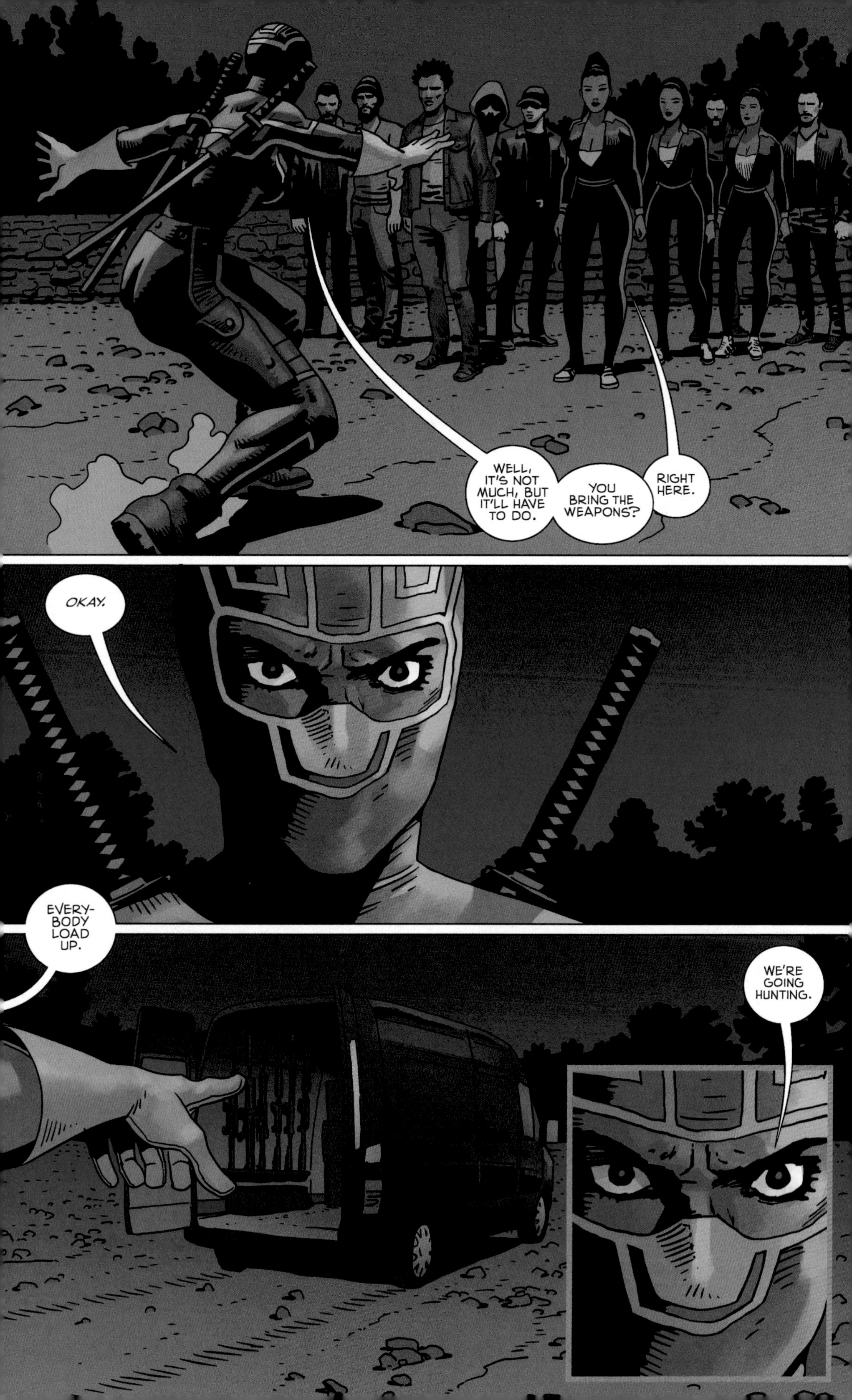
WELL, IT'S NOT MUCH, BUT IT'LL HAVE TO DO.
YOU BRING THE WEAPONS?
RIGHT HERE.
OKAY.
EVERY-BODY LOAD UP.
WE'RE GOING HUNTING.

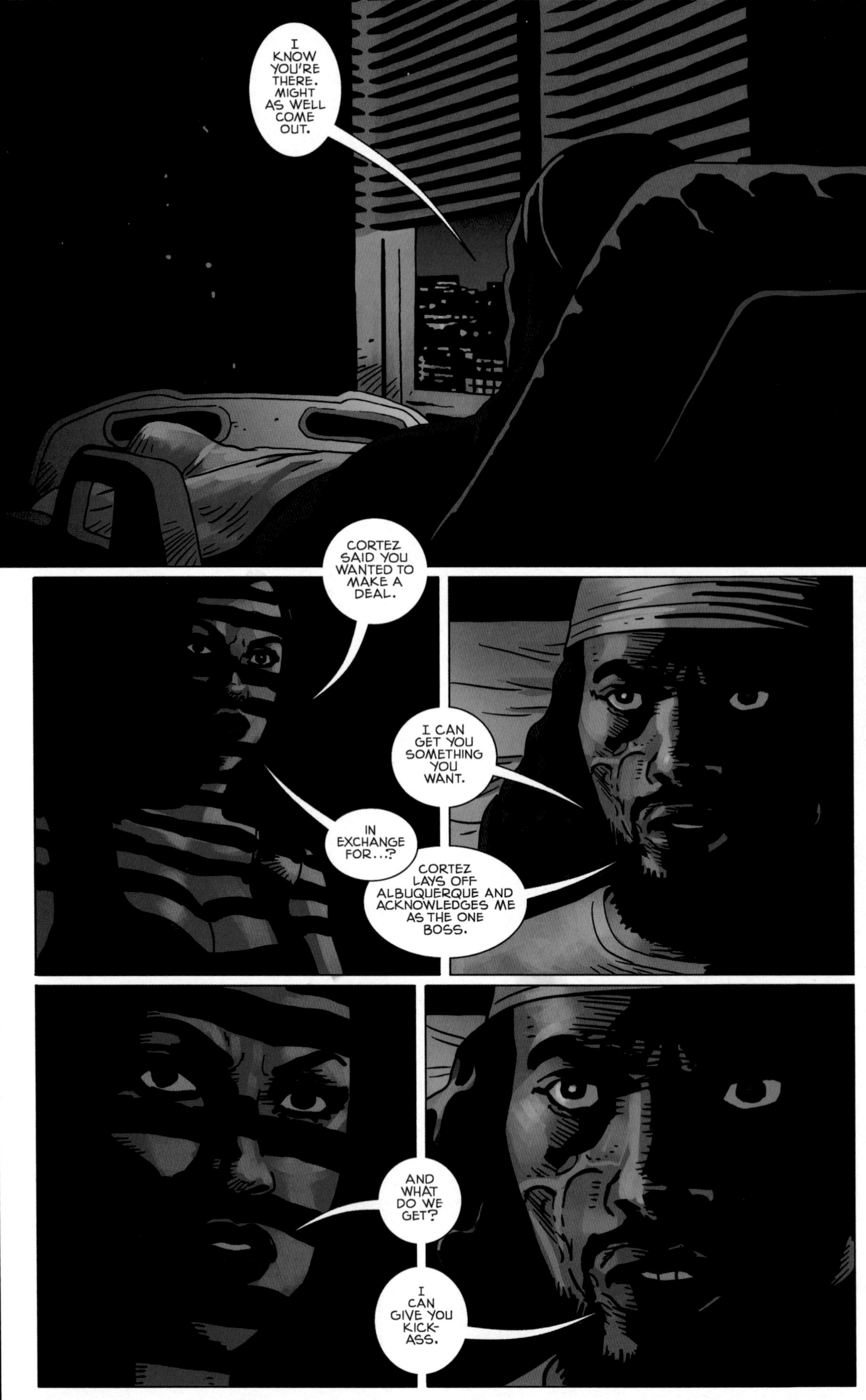
I KNOW YOU'RE THERE. MIGHT AS WELL COME OUT.
CORTEZ SAID YOU WANTED TO MAKE A DEAL.
I CAN GET YOU SOMETHING YOU WANT.
IN EXCHANGE FOR...?
CORTEZ LAYS OFF ALBUQUERQUE AND ACKNOWLEDGES ME AS THE ONE BOSS.
AND WHAT DO WE GET?
I CAN GIVE YOU KICK-ASS.

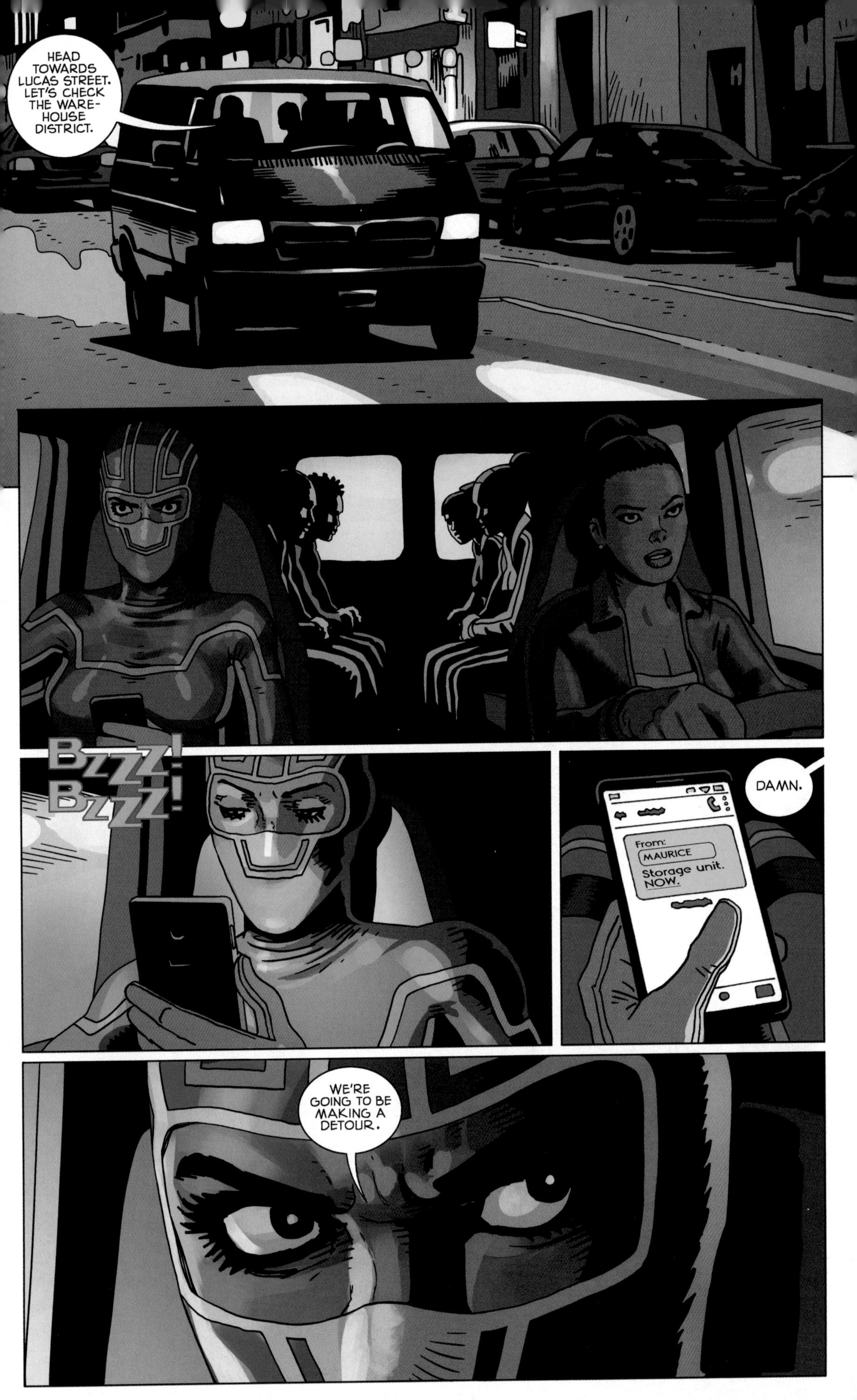
HEAD TOWARDS LUCAS STREET. LET'S CHECK THE WARE-HOUSE DISTRICT.
BZZZ! BZZZ!
From: MAURICE
Storage unit. NOW.
DAMN.
WE'RE GOING TO BE MAKING A DETOUR.

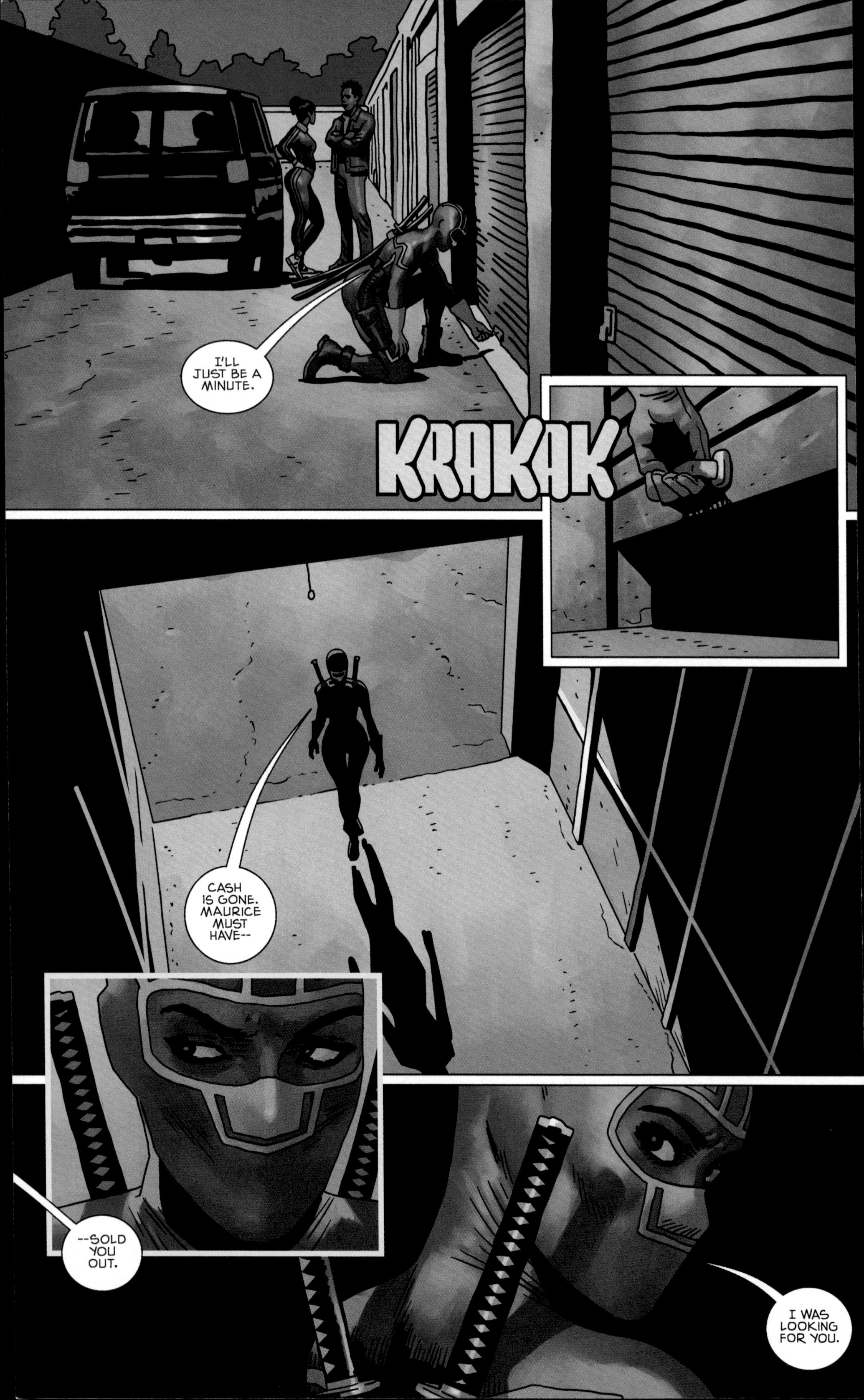
I'LL JUST BE A MINUTE.
KRAKAK
CASH IS GONE. MAURICE MUST HAVE--
--SOLD YOU OUT.
I WAS LOOKING FOR YOU.

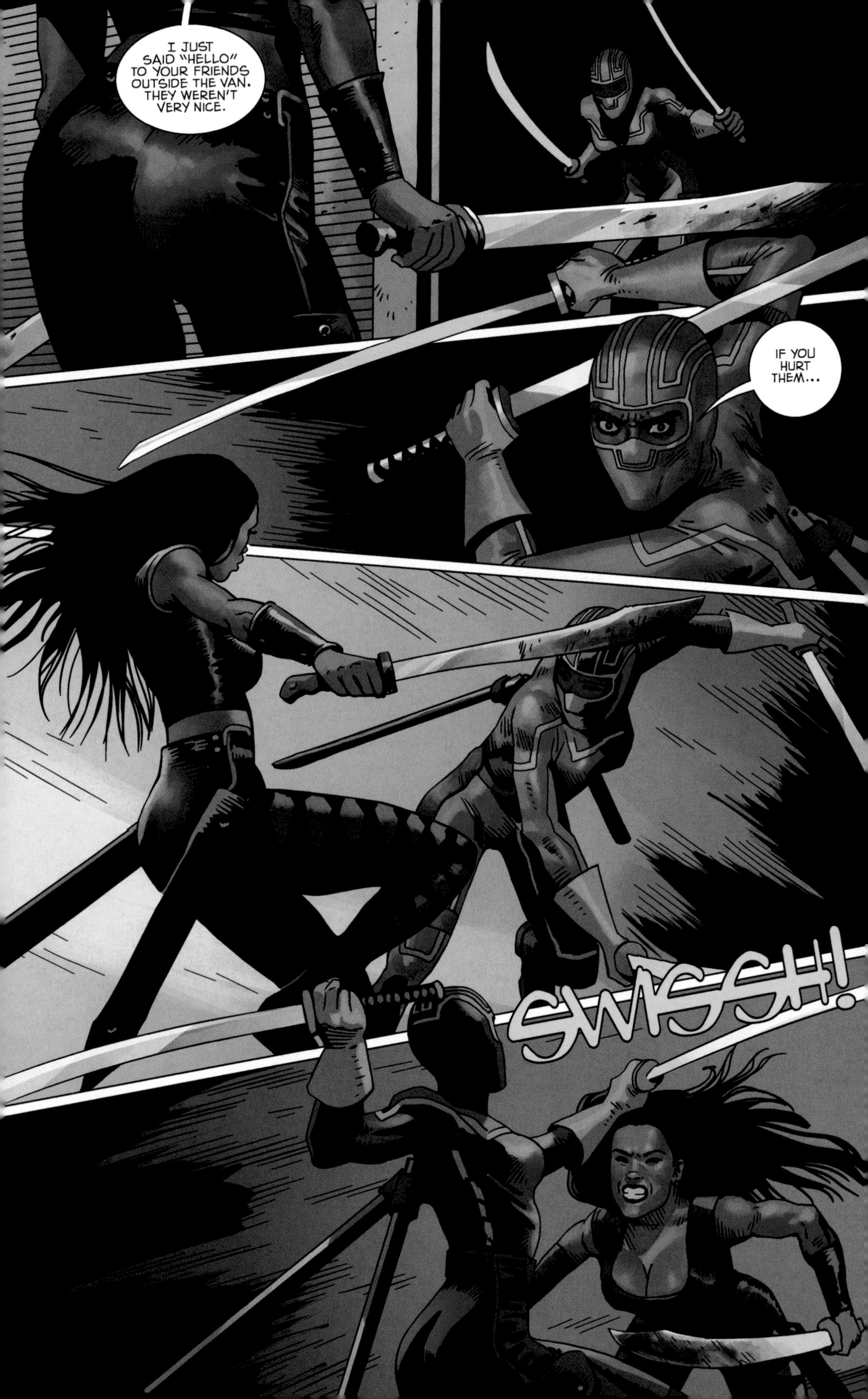

I JUST SAID "HELLO" TO YOUR FRIENDS OUTSIDE THE VAN. THEY WEREN'T VERY NICE.
IF YOU HURT THEM...
SWISSH!

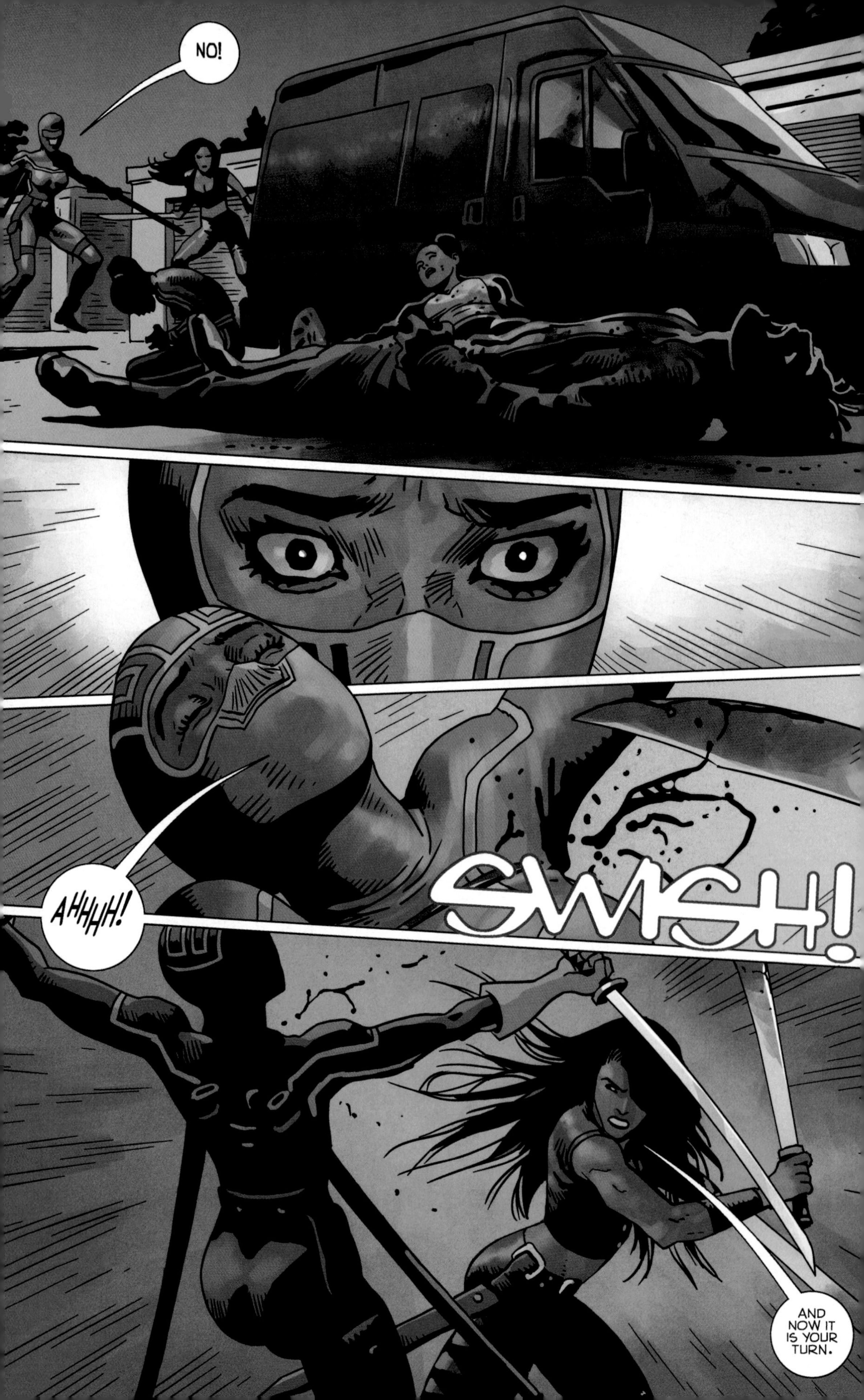
NO!
AHHHH!
SWISH!
AND NOW IT IS YOUR TURN.

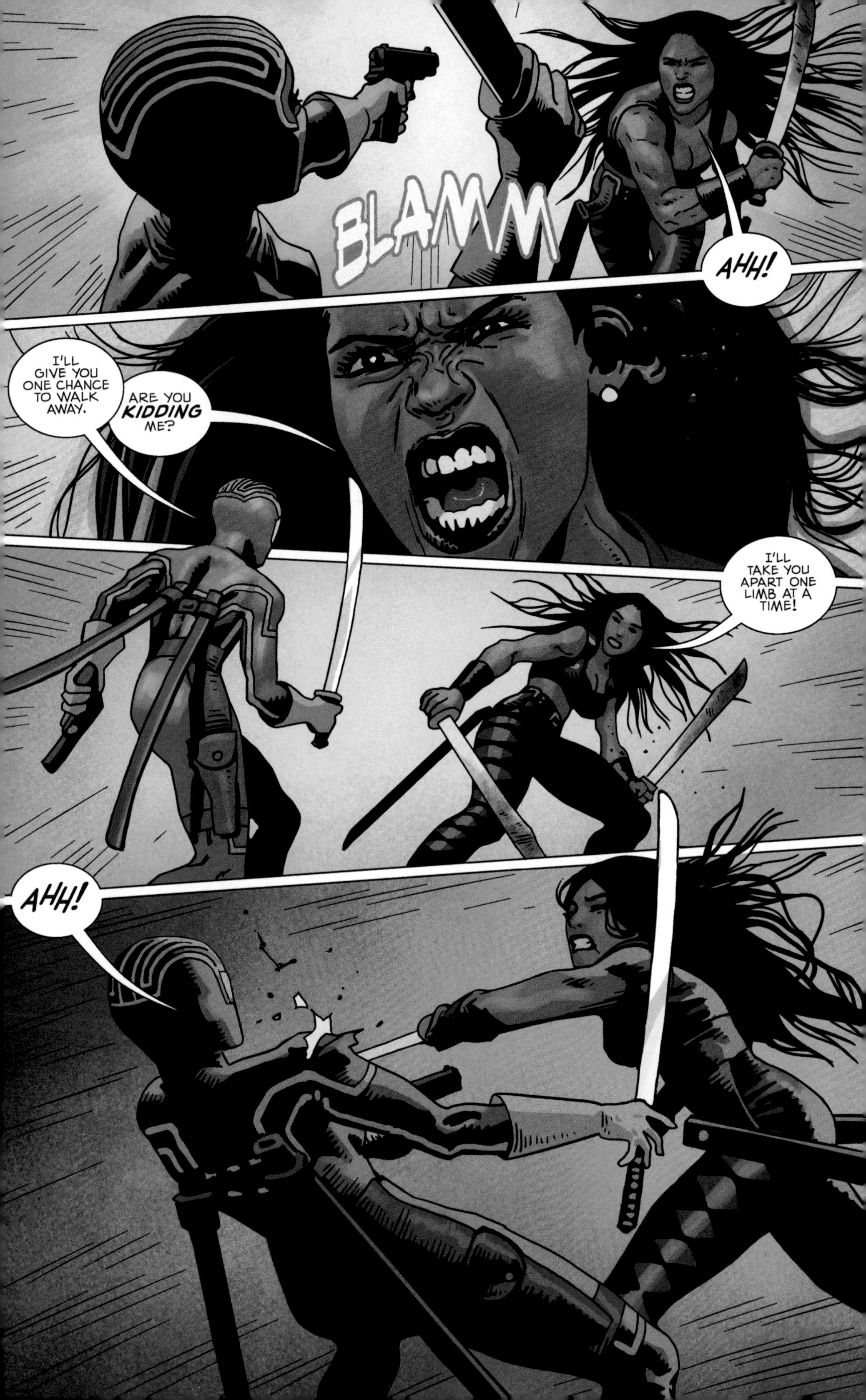
BLAMM
AHH!
I'LL GIVE YOU ONE CHANCE TO WALK AWAY.
ARE YOU KIDDING ME?
I'LL TAKE YOU APART ONE LIMB AT A TIME!
AHH!

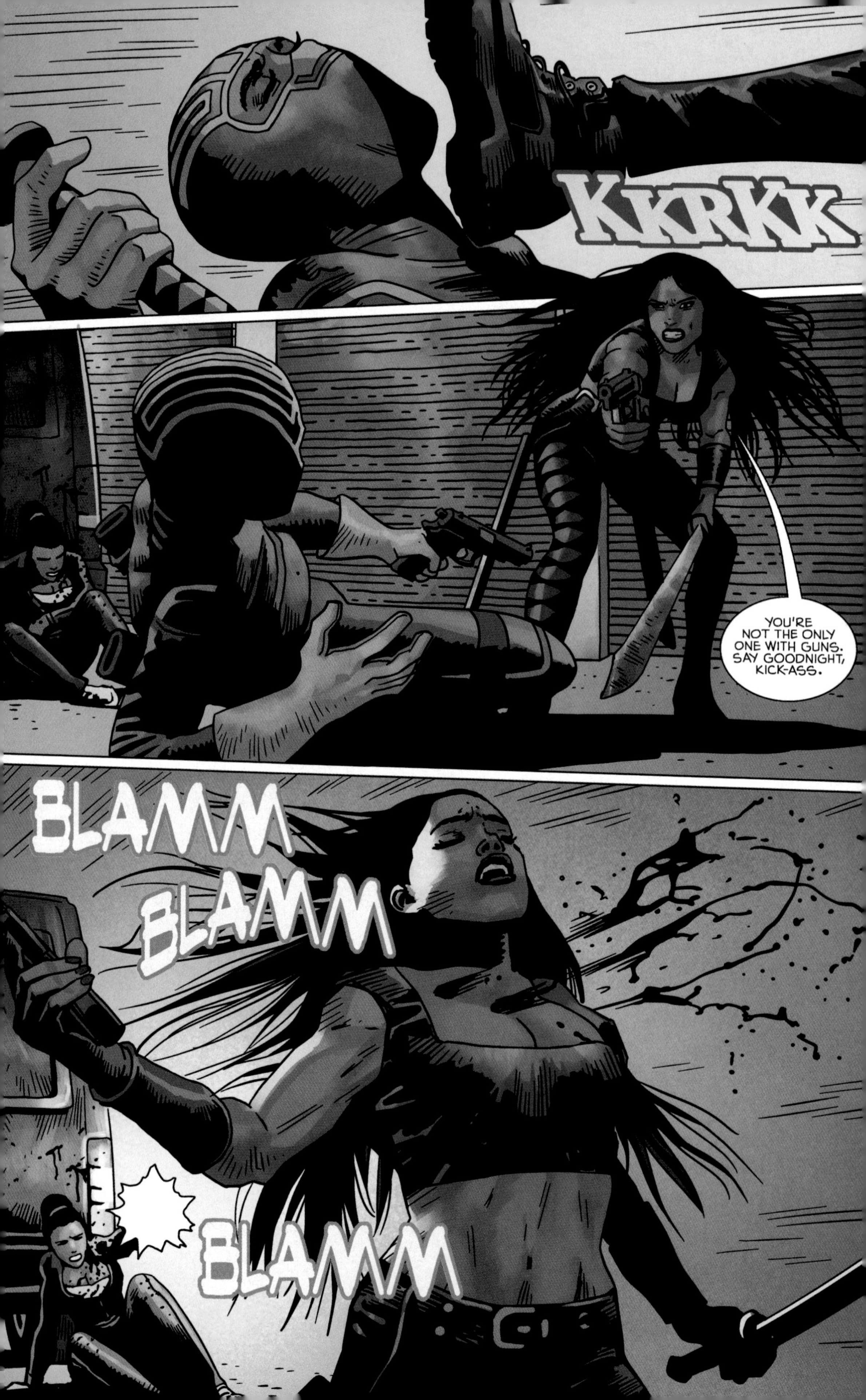
KKRKK
YOU'RE NOT THE ONLY ONE WITH GUNS. SAY GOODNIGHT, KICK-ASS.
BLAMM
BLAMM
BLAMM

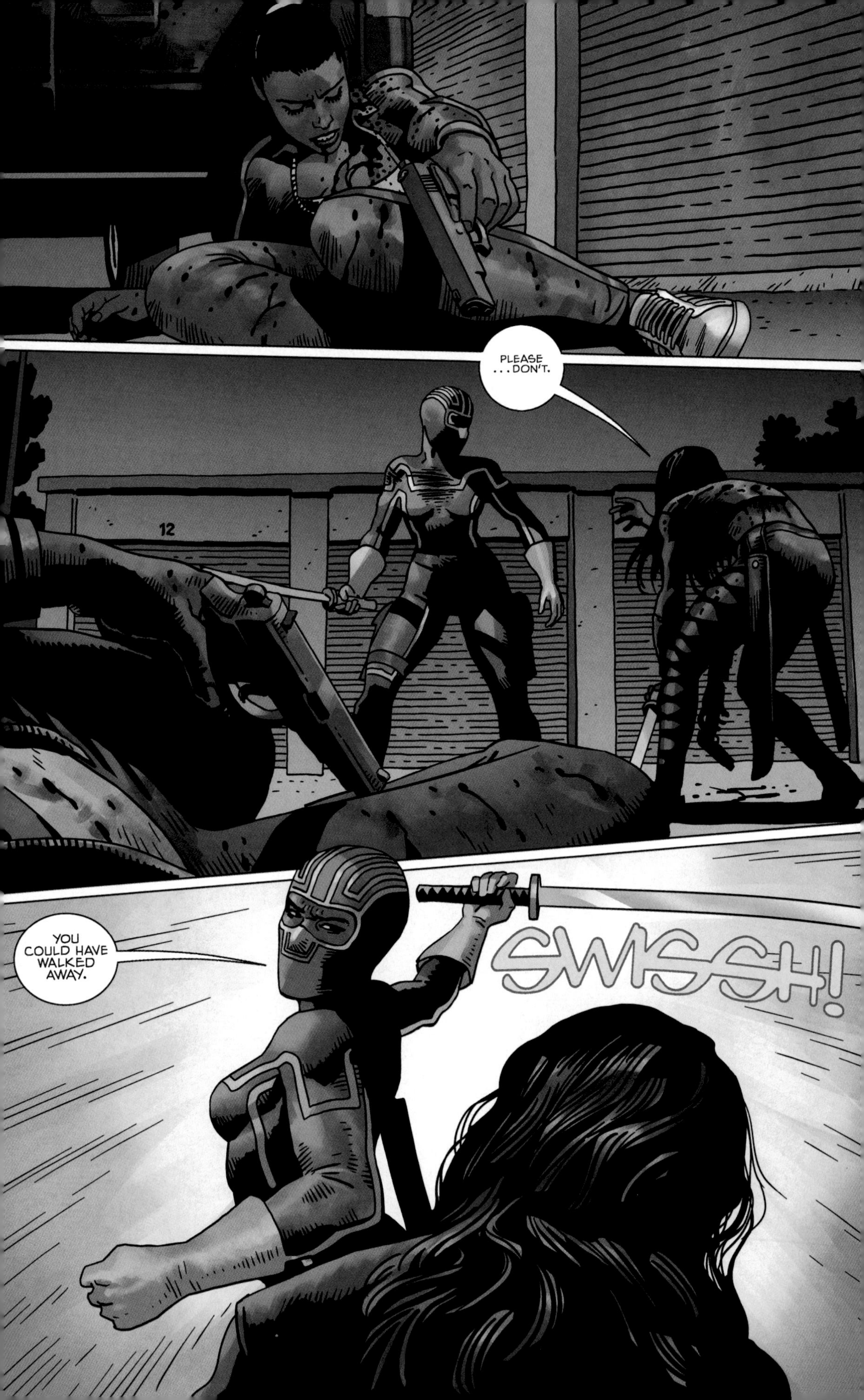

PLEASE ...DON'T.
12
YOU COULD HAVE WALKED AWAY.
SWISSH!

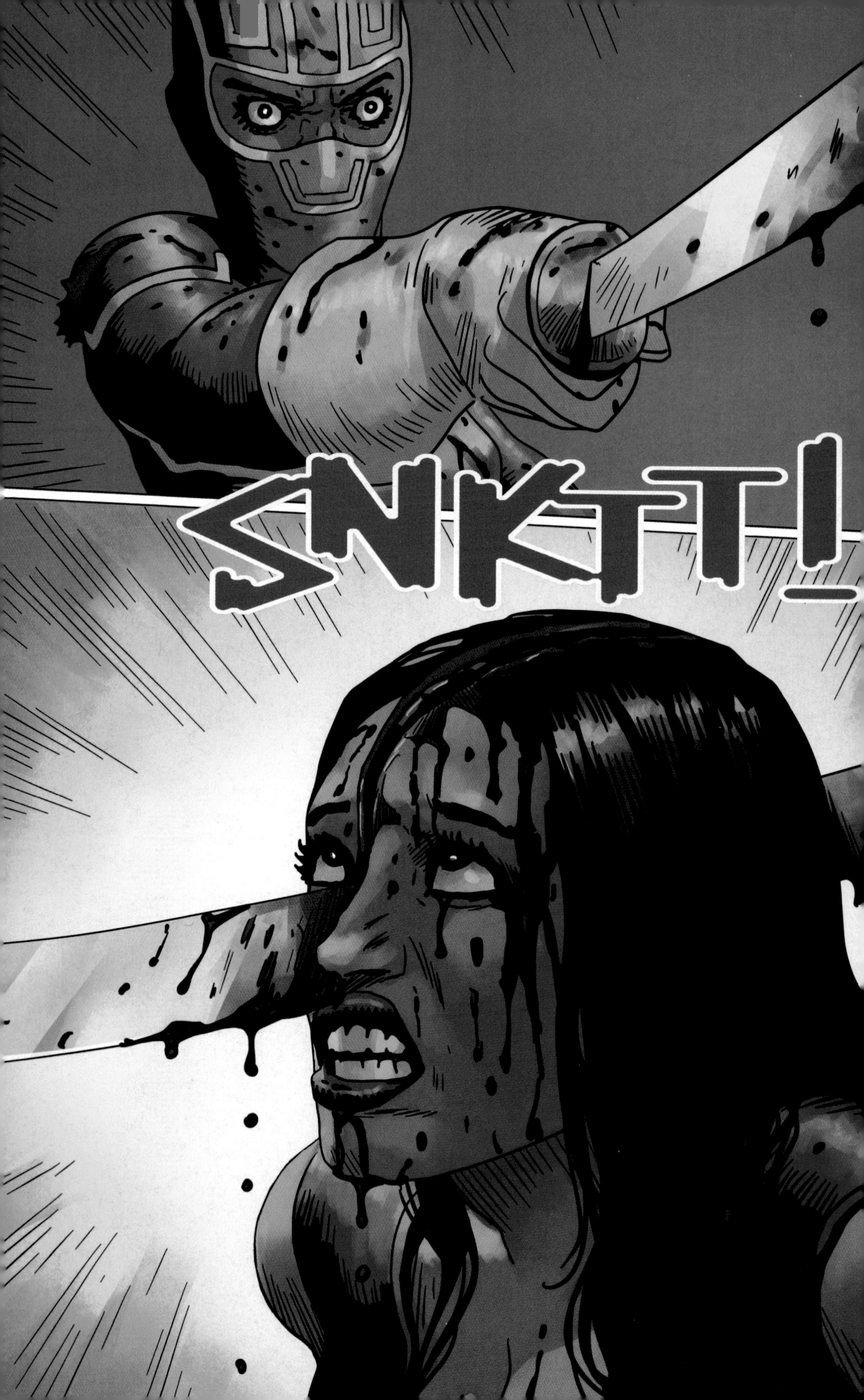
SNKT!

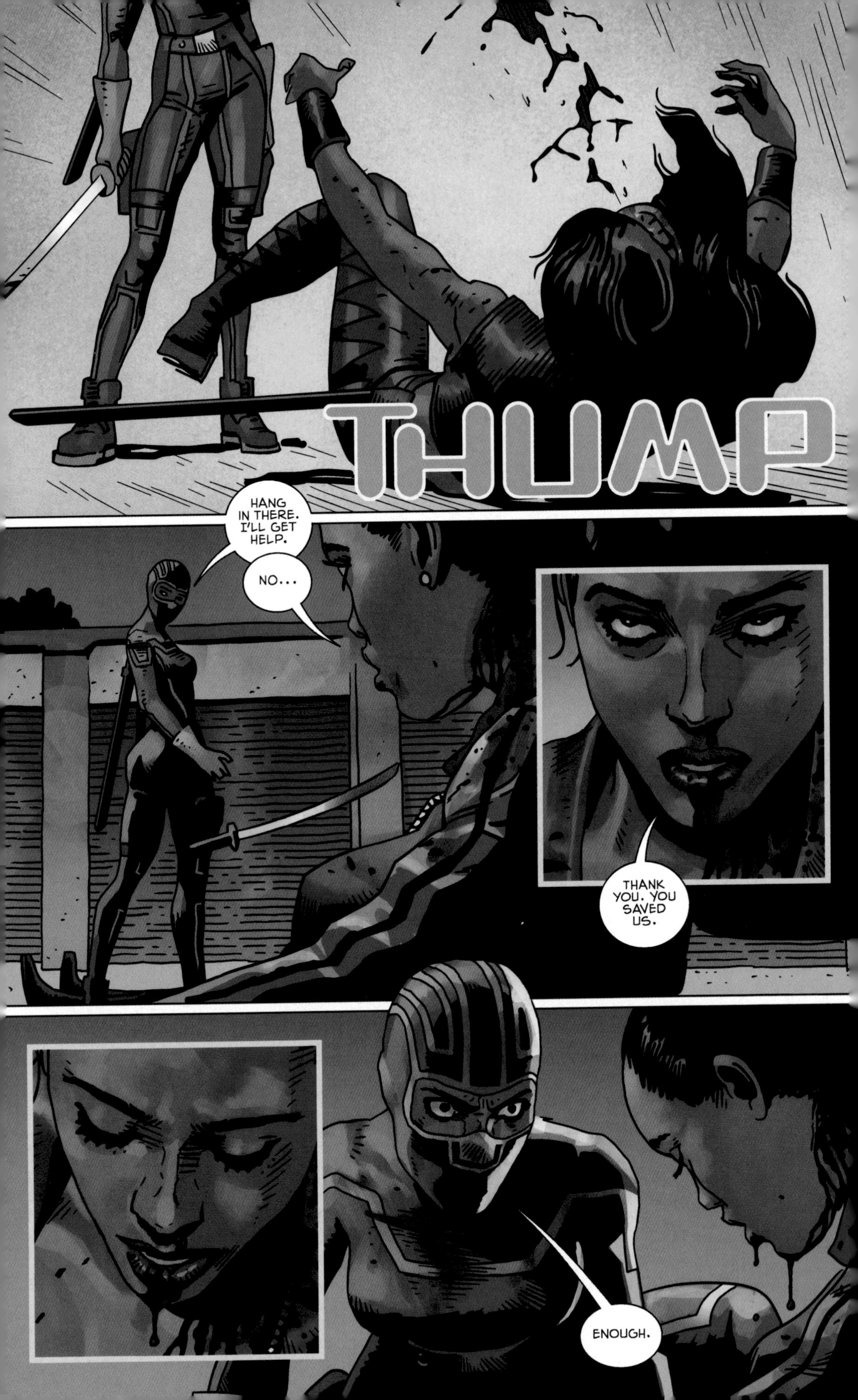
THUMP
HANG IN THERE. I'LL GET HELP.
NO...
THANK YOU. YOU SAVED US.
ENOUGH.

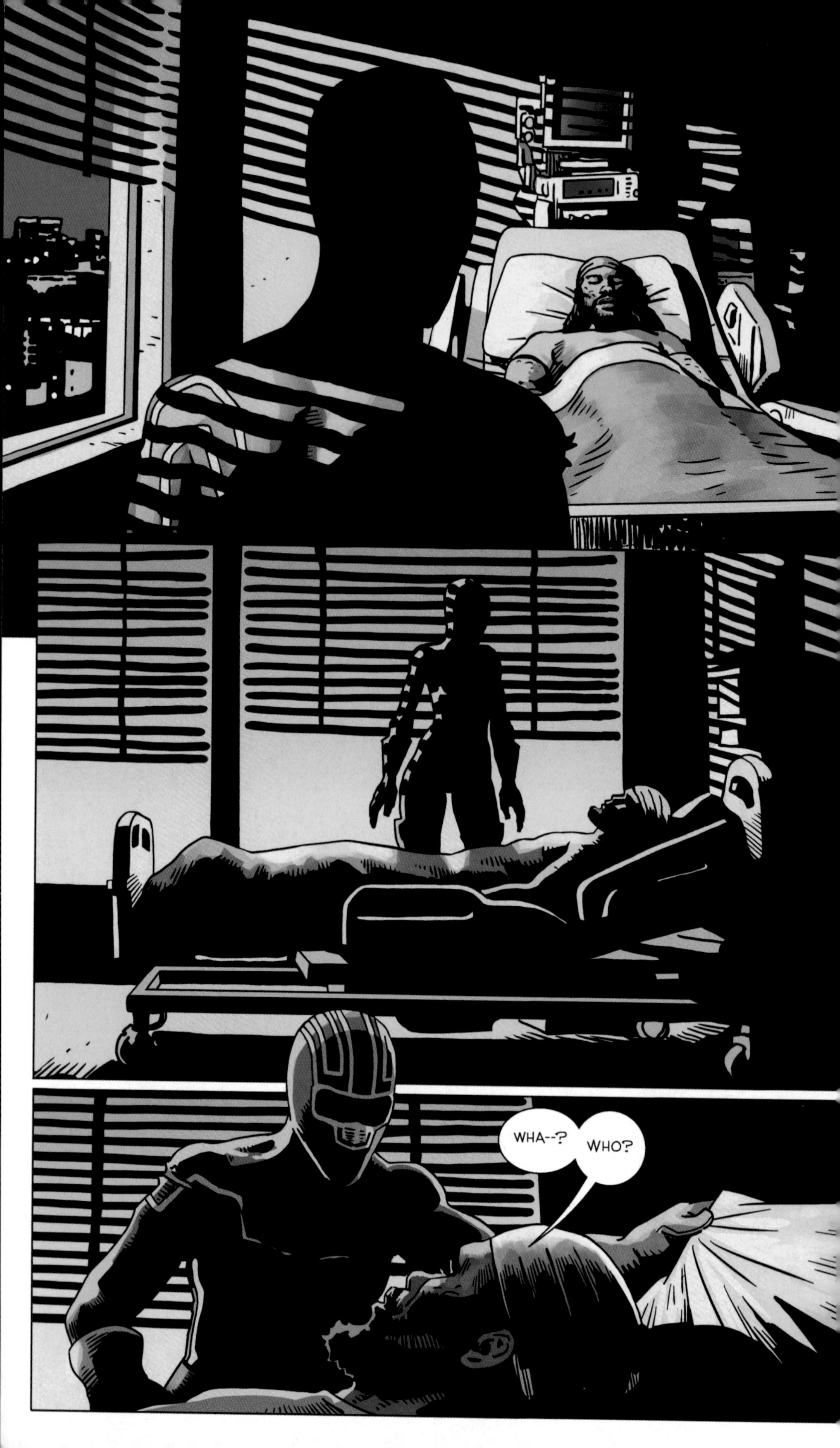
WHA--?
WHO?

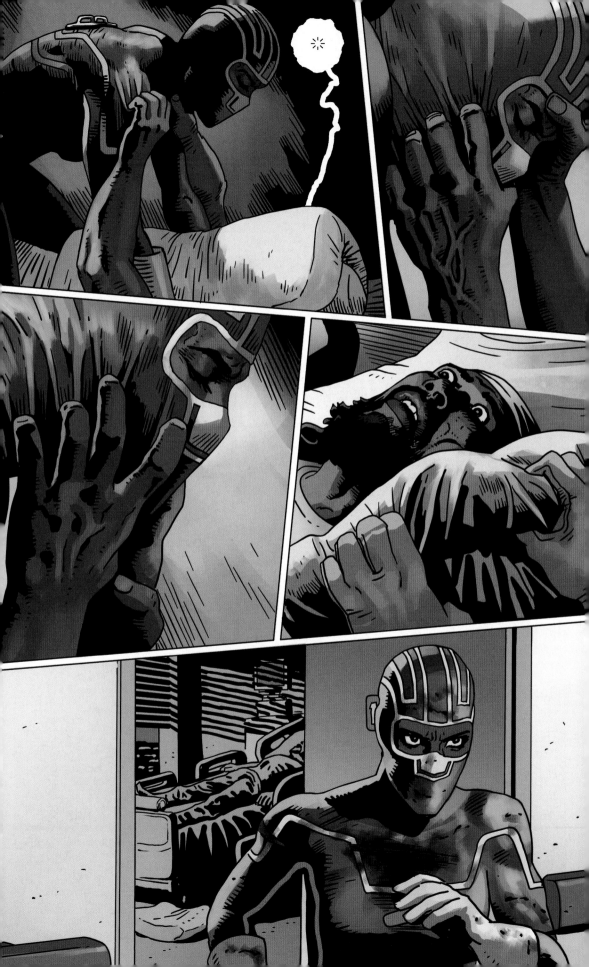

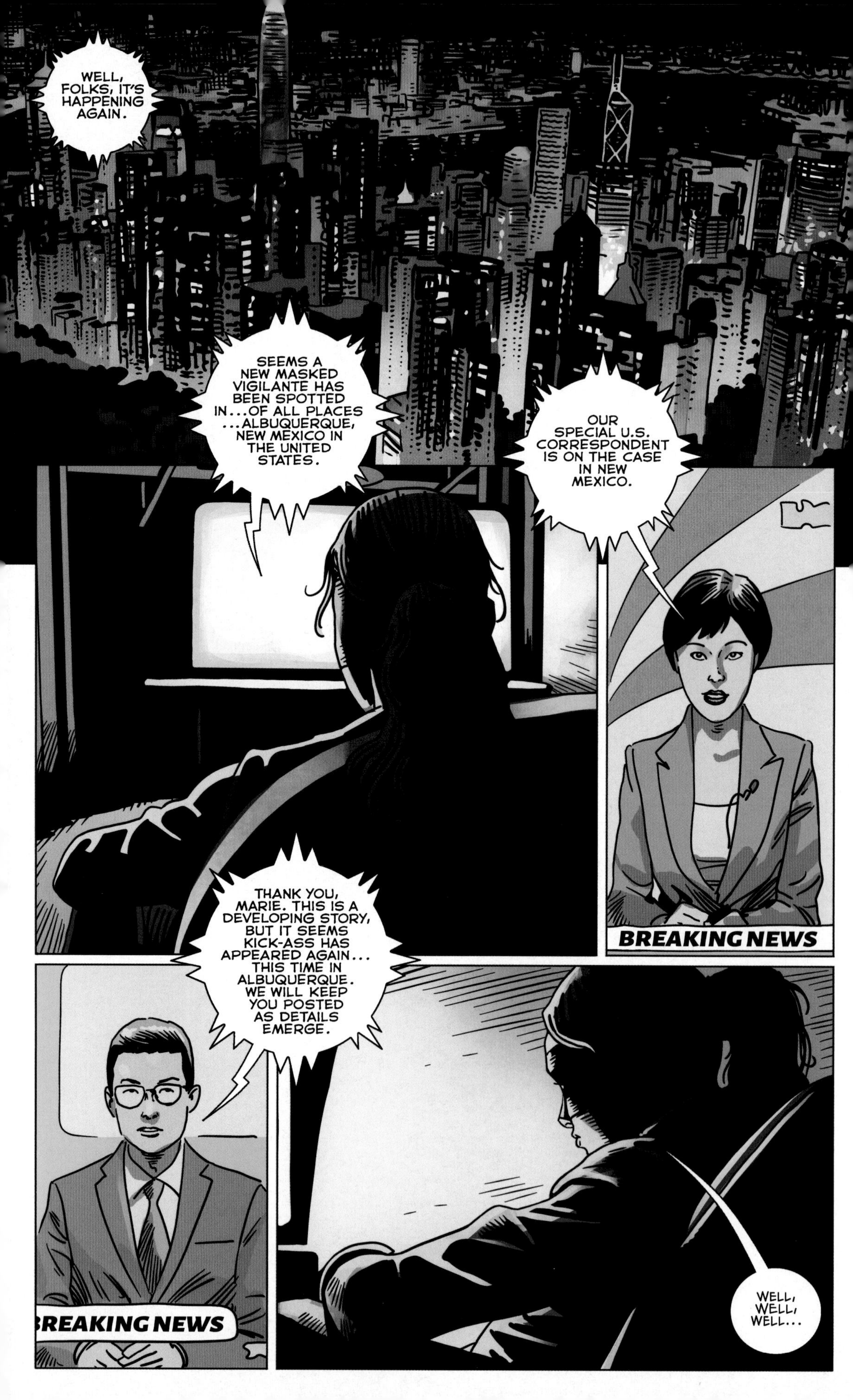
WELL, FOLKS, IT'S HAPPENING AGAIN.
SEEMS A NEW MASKED VIGILANTE HAS BEEN SPOTTED IN...OF ALL PLACES ...ALBUQUERQUE, NEW MEXICO IN THE UNITED STATES.
OUR SPECIAL U.S. CORRESPONDENT IS ON THE CASE IN NEW MEXICO.
BREAKING NEWS
THANK YOU, MARIE. THIS IS A DEVELOPING STORY, BUT IT SEEMS KICK-ASS HAS APPEARED AGAIN... THIS TIME IN ALBUQUERQUE. WE WILL KEEP YOU POSTED AS DETAILS EMERGE.
BREAKING NEWS
WELL, WELL, WELL...

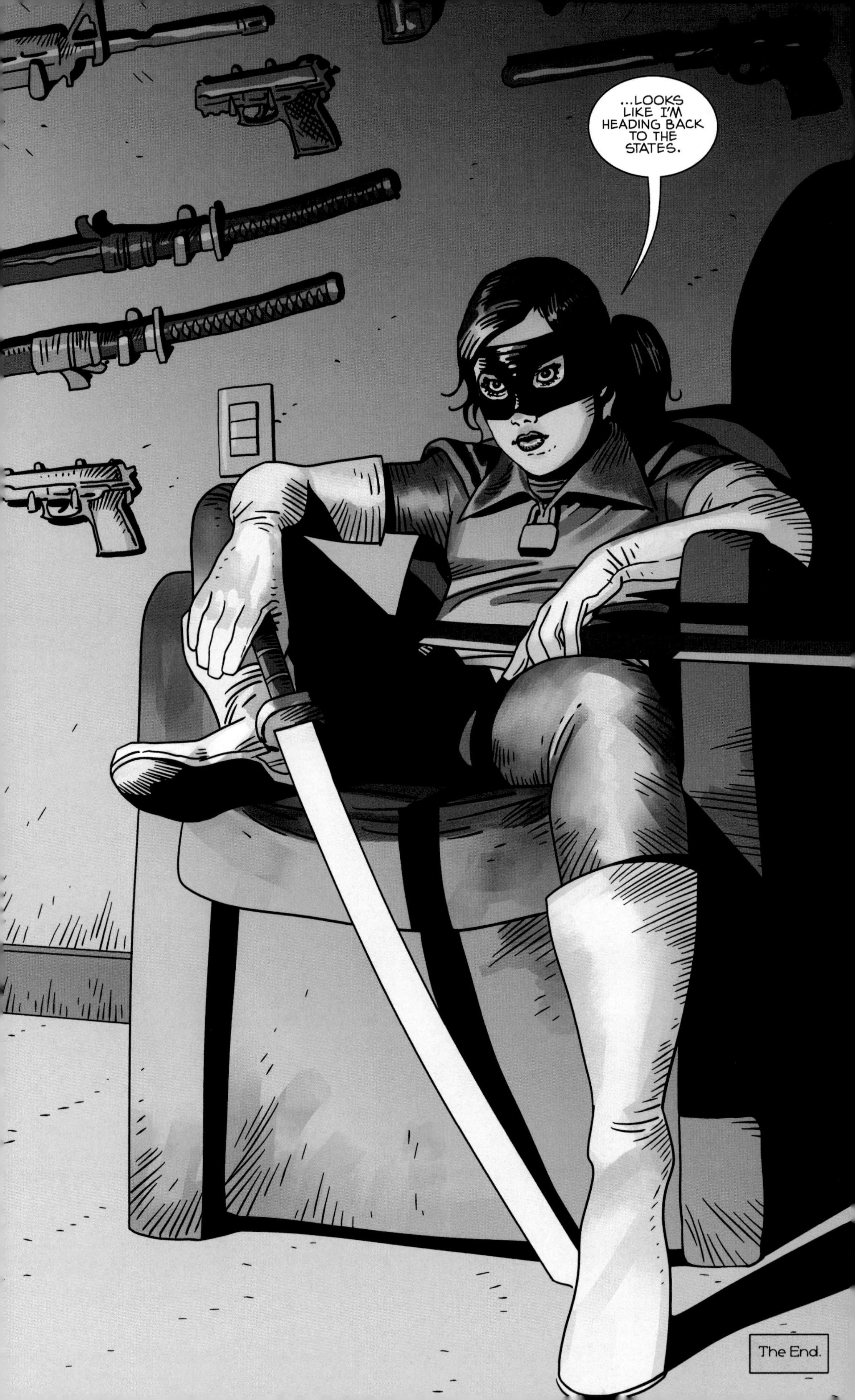
...LOOKS LIKE I'M HEADING BACK TO THE STATES.
The End.

KICK-ASS:
THE DAVE LIZEWSKI
YEARS
Vol 1-4

KICK-ASS:
THE NEW GIRL
Vol 1-3

MPLETE
HIT-GIRL
IES
HIT-GIRL IN COLOMBIA
MARK MILLAR • RICARDO LOPEZ ORTIZ
HIT-GIRL IN CANADA
JEFF LEMIRE • EDUARDO RISSO
HIT-GIRL IN ROME
RAFAEL ALBUQUERQUE • RAFAEL SCAVONE
HIT-GIRL IN HOLLYWOOD
KEVIN SMITH • PERNILLE ØRUM
HIT-GIRL IN HONG KONG
DANIEL WAY • GORAN PARLOV
HIT-GIRL
Vol 1-6
HIT-GIRL IN INDIA
PETER MILLIGAN • ALISON SAMPSON
ON SALE NOW

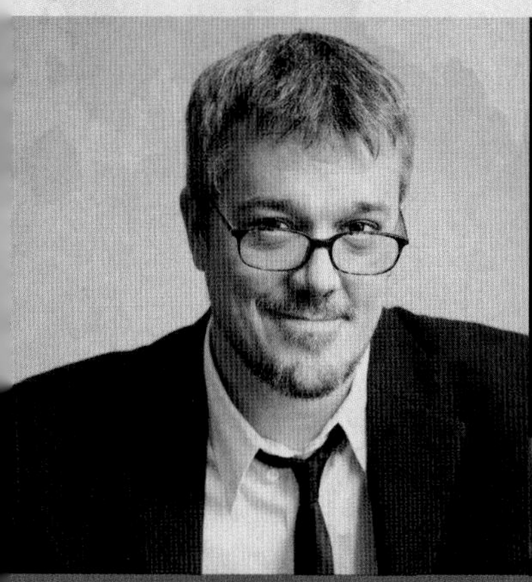

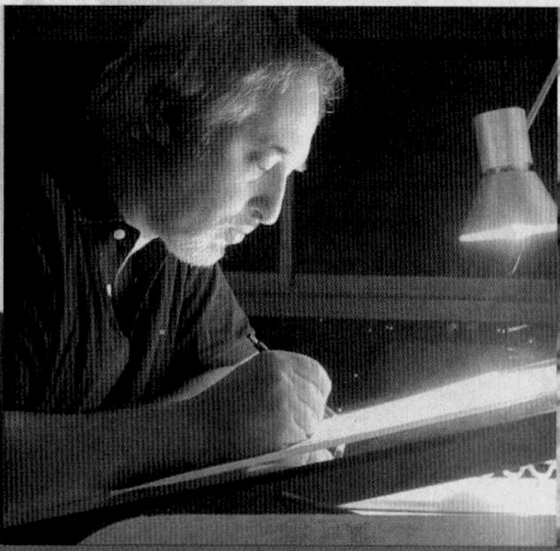

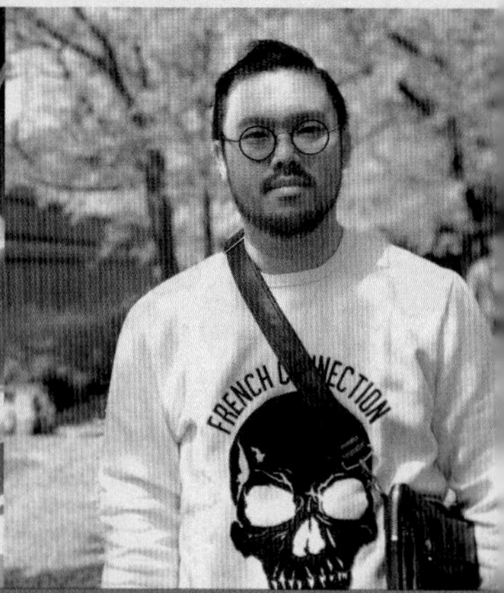

STEVE NILES

is best known for **30 DAYS OF NIGHT**, **CRIMINAL MACABRE**, **SIMON DARK**, **MYSTERY SOCIETY**, **FRANKENSTEIN ALIVE, ALIVE!**, **MONSTER & MADMAN**, **WINNEBAGO GRAVEYARD** and **BATMAN: GOTHAM COUNTY LINE.**

Niles currently works for comic publishers including Black Mask, IDW, Image and Dark Horse. Steve is currently writing **THE OCTOBER FACTION** for IDW.

30 DAYS OF NIGHT was released in 2007 as a major motion picture. Other comics by Niles, including **REMAINS**, **ALEISTER ARCANE**, and **FREAKS OF THE HEARTLAND**, have been optioned for film.

Steve lives in the desert near Los Angeles with his wife Monica and a bunch of animals.

MARCELO FRUSIN

is an Argentinian comic artist and illustrator who has published works in editorials across the US, Europe, and South America.

He is best known for his critically acclaimed run as the artist of **HELLBLAZER**, teaming with writers Warren Ellis, Brian Azzarello, and Mike Carey. With Azzarello, Frusin also illustrated and co-created the monthly western **LOVELESS**. He has also contributed to other Vertigo titles, such as **FLICH**, **WEIRD WESTERN TALES**, **WEIRD WAR TALES**, and **TRANSMETROPOLITAN.**

In addition to his work for DC Comics, he worked for Marvel illustrating specials of **X-MEN** and **WOLVERINE**. In Europe, he co-created the series **L'EXPEDITION** with the French writer Richard Marazano, published by Dargaud of France. He is currently drawing the next arc of **KICK-ASS** written by Steve Niles and published by Image Comics.

SUNNY GHO

studied Graphic Design at Trisakti University, Indonesia, before going on to work for companies such as Top Cow, Imaginary Friends Studios, and GLITCH.

He has colored an impressive array of comic book titles, including **MARVEL'S CIVIL WAR II**, **THE INDESTRUCTIBLE HULK**, and **THE AVENGERS**. For Mark Millar, he has colored **SUPERCROOKS**, **SUPERIOR**, **JUPITER'S LEGACY 2**, and **HIT-GIRL**.

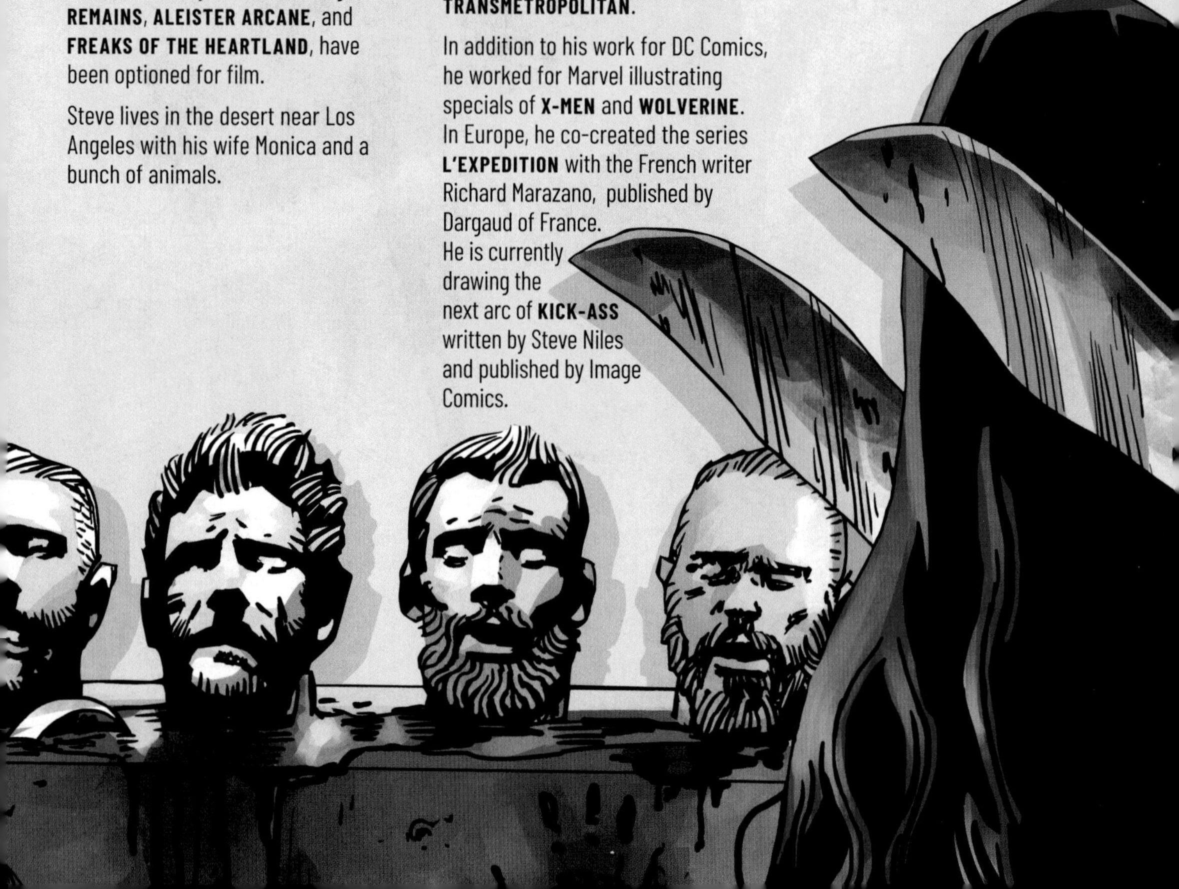

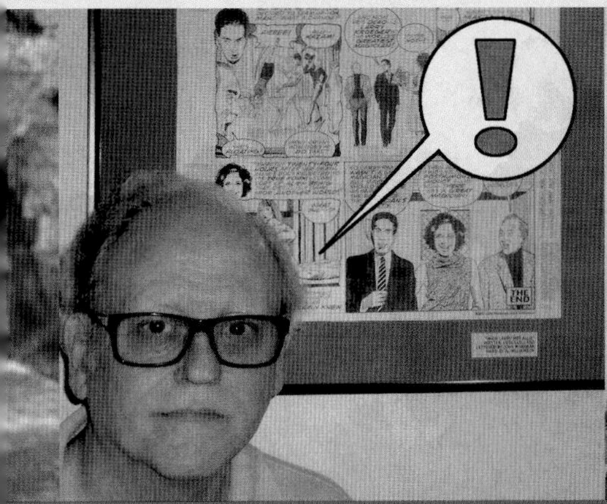

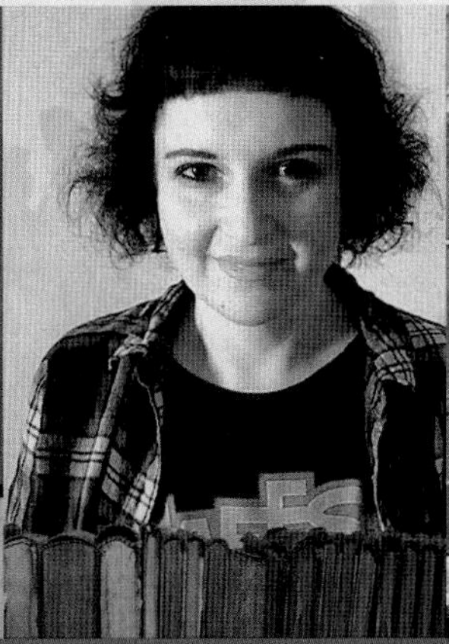

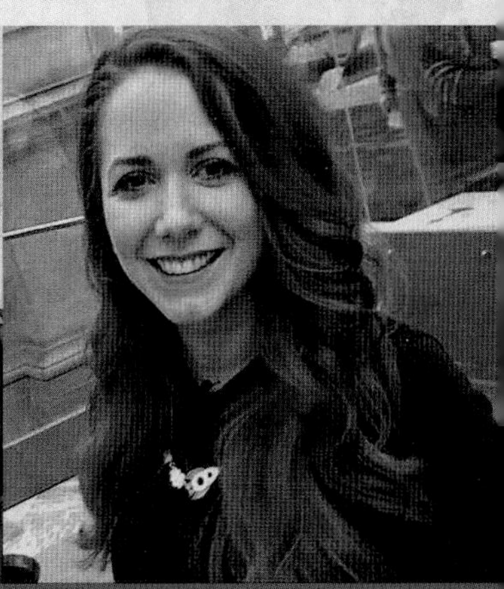

JOHN WORKMAN

managed to turn a love for the comics form into a career. During the past five decades, he has held the positions of editor, writer, art director, penciler, inker, colorist, letterer, production director, and book designer for various companies.

He created (with some help from Bhob Stewart and Bob Smith) the offbeat stories in **WILD THINGS** (with much of that material having first appeared in **STAR*REACH** and **HEAVY METAL**) and both wrote and drew the comics series **SINDY**, **FALLEN ANGELS** and **ROMA**. In 1991, he reflected on model Bettie Page in **BETTY BEING BAD** (Eros) and later produced the hardbounds **HEAVY METAL: 25 YEARS OF CLASSIC COVERS AND INNOCENT IMAGES: THE SEXY FANTASY FEMALES OF VIPER AND KISS**, as well as **THE ADVENTURES OF ROMA**, a reformatted graphic novel version of his earlier series.

He continues to write and draw – and to do a whole lot of lettering – for a number of comics companies on an international level.

MELINA MIKULIC

hasn't yet won an Eisner Award for Best Publication Design, for one simple reason: she's designed more than a thousand gorgeous comic books (including Fibra's editions of Moebius and Tezuka, and Marjane Satrapi's **PERSEPOLIS**) but all on the wrong continent. That is about to change.

She is a Master of Arts, and graduated from the Faculty of Design in Zagreb, Croatia, where she was born. As a graphic designer, she is primarily engaged in design for print, with a growing interest in illustration and interactive media. She now lives in Rijeka, where despite enjoying the Mediterranean climate, she rarely sees the sun, as she spends her time wandering through shadowy landscapes of fonts and letters.

RACHAEL FULTON

is editor of Netflix's Millarworld division, where she's currently producing **THE MAGIC ORDER**, **PRODIGY** and **SHARKEY THE BOUNTY HUNTER**.

She's also in charge of **KICK-ASS: THE NEW GIRL 1-3** and all volumes of **HIT-GIRL'S** world tour. Her past credits as editor include **EMPRESS**, **JUPITER'S LEGACY 2**, **REBORN**, and **KINGSMAN: THE RED DIAMOND**.

She is collections editor for the most recent editions of **KINGSMAN: THE SECRET SERVICE** and all volumes of **KICK-ASS: THE DAVE LIZEWSKI YEARS**.

She tweets about feminism, comics, and cats from the handle @Rachael_Fulton.

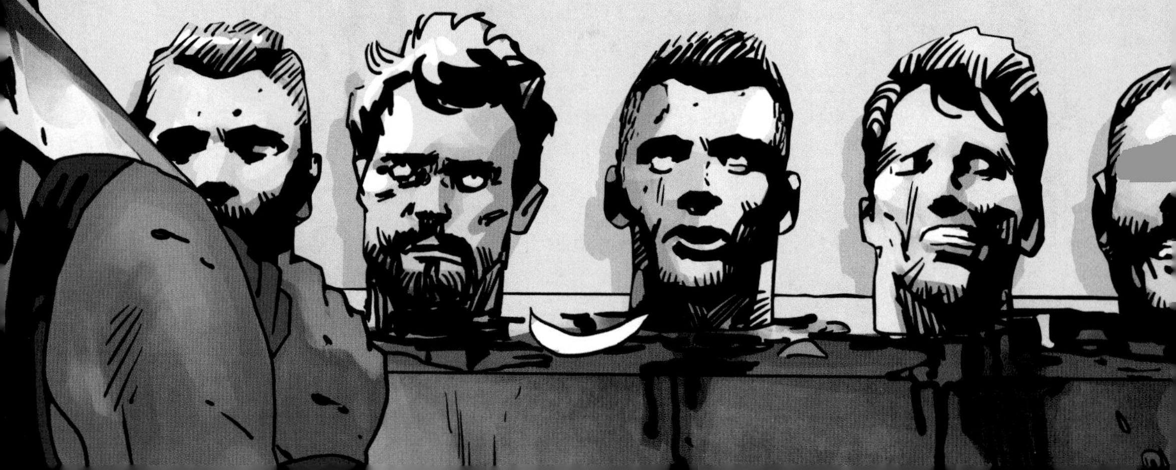

VARIANT COVERS

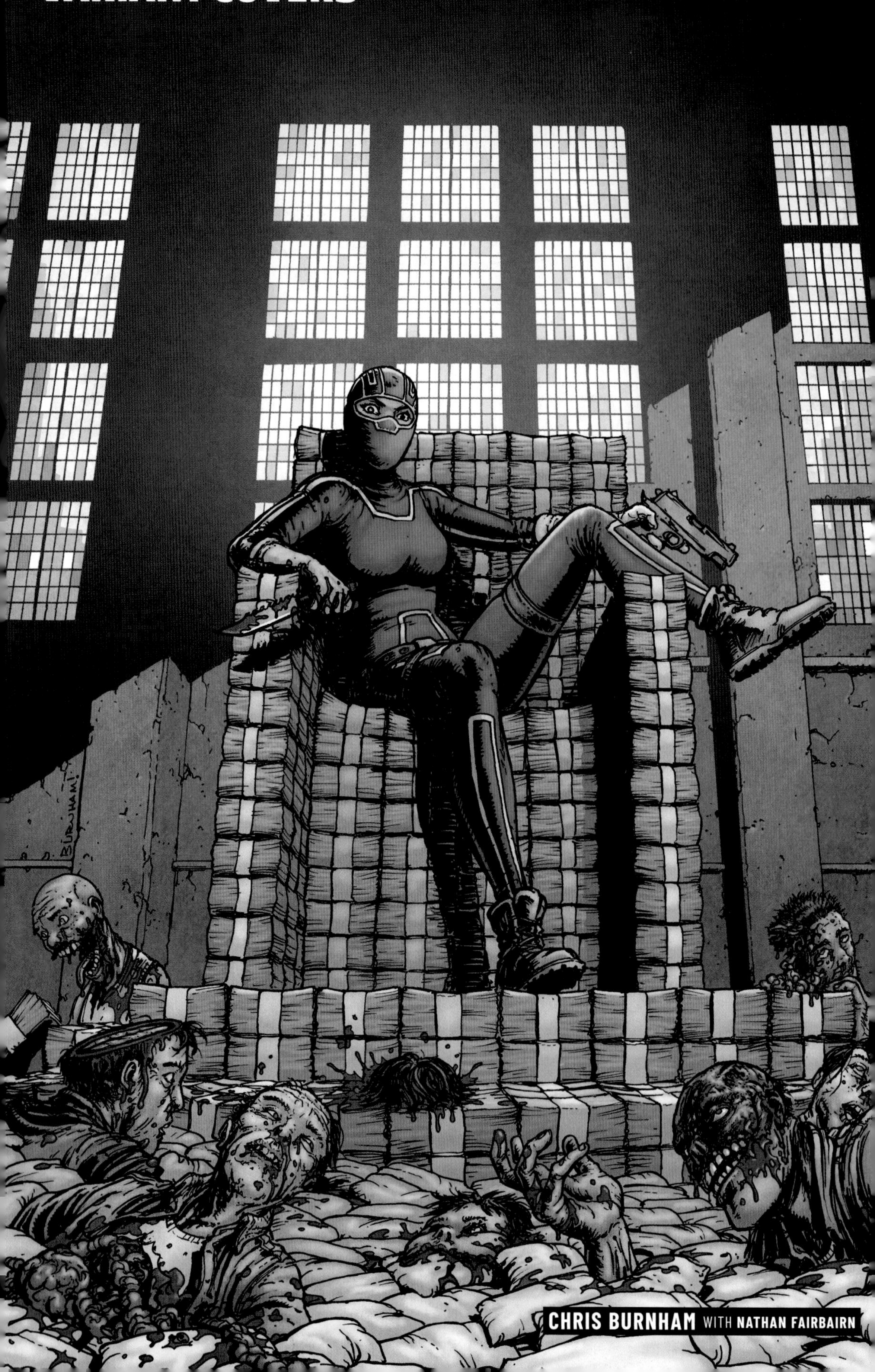
BURNHAM

CHRIS BURNHAM WITH **NATHAN FAIRBAIRN**

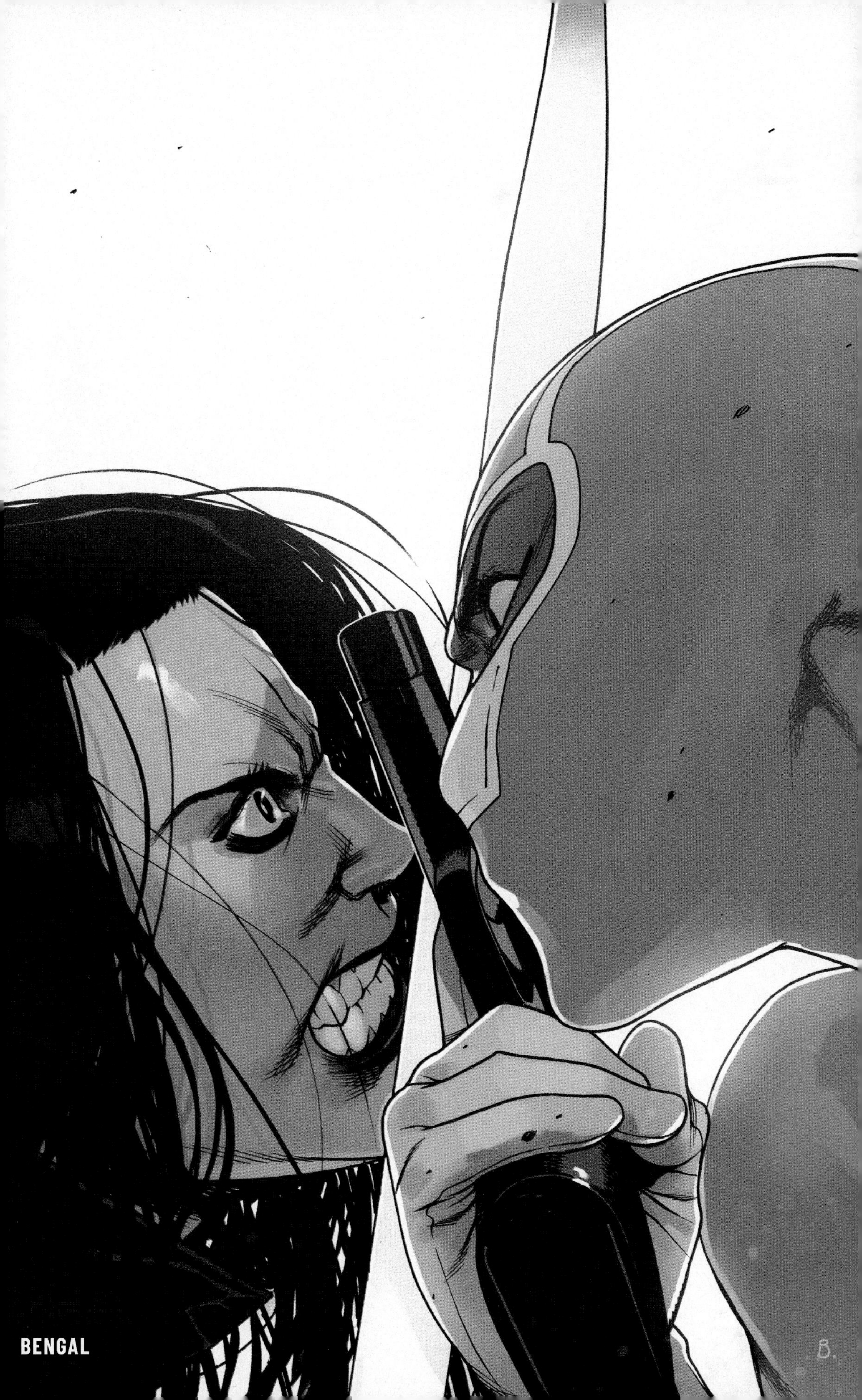

BENGAL

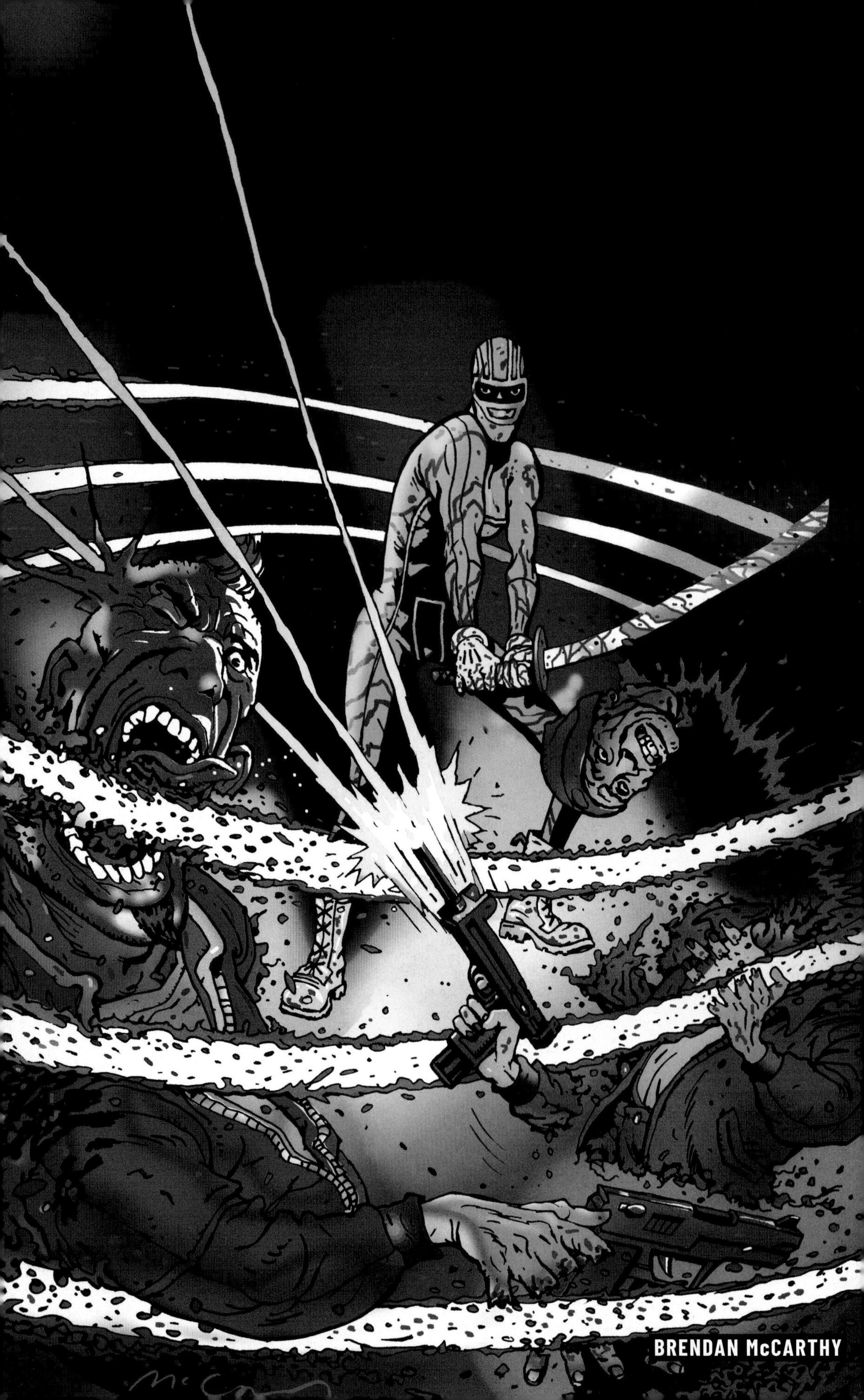
BRENDAN McCARTHY

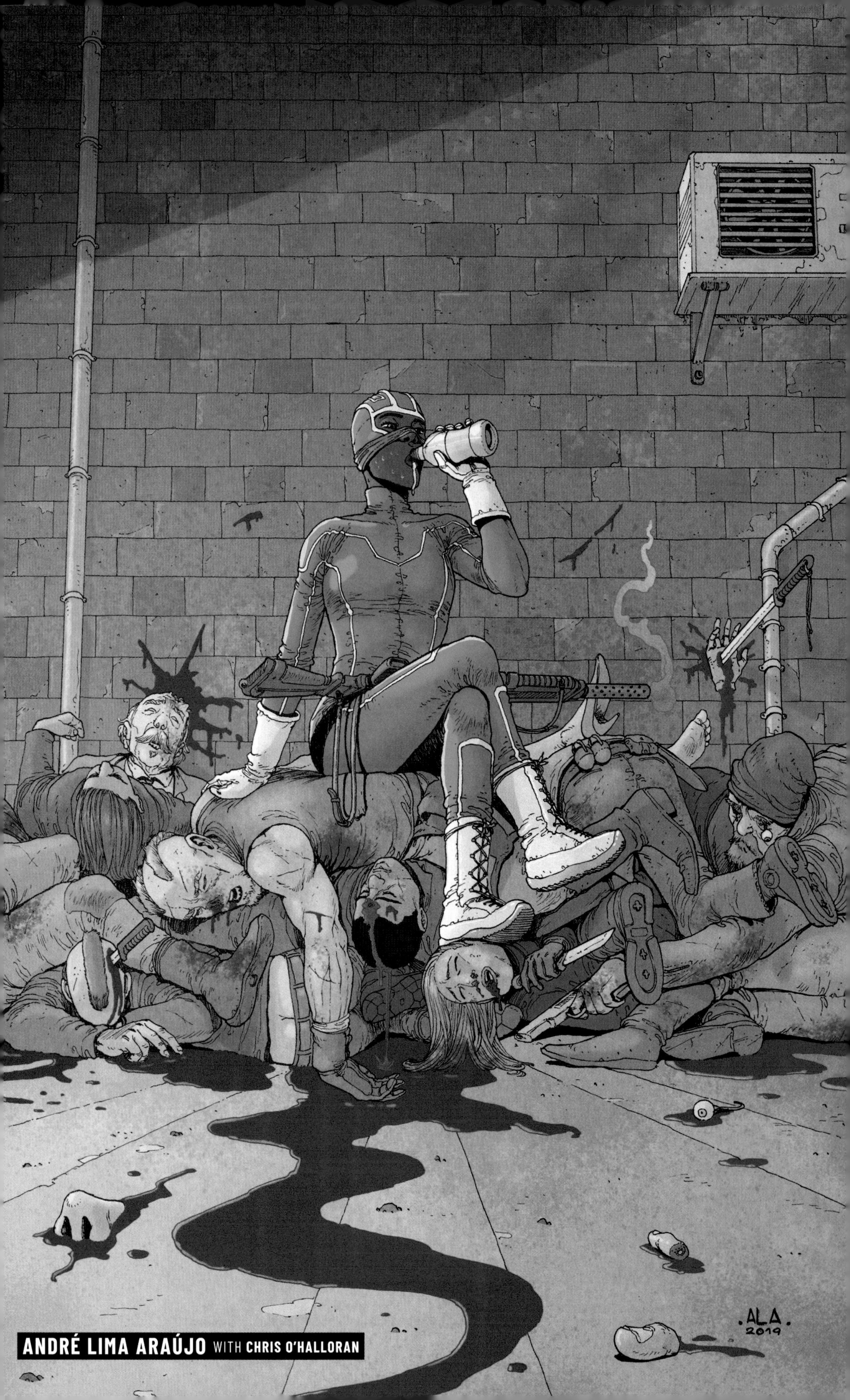
ALA
2019

ANDRÉ LIMA ARAÚJO WITH CHRIS O'HALLORAN

NET

FROM THE MIND OF

Huck
MARK MILLAR
RAFAEL ALBUQUERQUE
DAVE McCAIG

ART BY RAFAEL ALBUQUERQUE

THE MAGIC ORDER
MARK MILLAR
OLIVIER COIPEL
BOOK ONE

ART BY OLIVIER COIPEL

MARK MILLAR · GORAN PARLOV
STARLIGHT

ART BY GORAN PARLOV

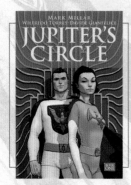

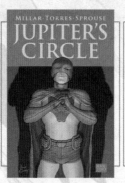

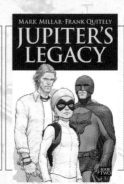

MARK MILLAR
WILFREDO TORRES · DAVIDE GIANFELICE
JUPITER'S CIRCLE
BOOK ONE

ART BY
WILFREDO TORRES

MILLAR · TORRES · SPROUSE
JUPITER'S CIRCLE

ART BY WILFREDO TORRES
& CHRIS SPROUSE

MARK MILLAR · FRANK QUITELY
JUPITER'S LEGACY
BOOK ONE

ART BY FRANK QUITELY

MARK MILLAR · FRANK QUITELY
JUPITER'S LEGACY
BOOK TWO

ART BY FRANK QUITELY

REBORN
BOOK ONE
MARK MILLAR GREG CAPULLO

ART BY GREG CAPULLO

Prodigy.
Mark Millar
Rafael Albuquerque
THE EVIL EARTH

ART BY RAFAEL ALBUQUERQUE

MARK MILLAR & LEINIL YU
SUPERIOR
FROM THE
WRITER OF
KICK-ASS

ART BY LEINIL YU

MARK MILLAR

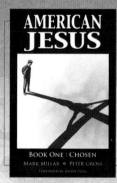

AMERICAN JESUS
BOOK ONE : CHOSEN
MARK MILLAR ❖ PETER GROSS
FOREWORD BY SIMON PEGG
ART BY PETER GROSS

MARK MILLAR · MATTEO SCALERA
SPACE BANDITS
ART BY MATTEO SCALERA

MARK MILLAR · SIMONE BIANCHI
SHARKEY
ART BY SIMONE BIANCHI

EMPRESS
BOOK ONE
MARK MILLAR
STUART IMMONEN
ART BY STUART IMMONEN

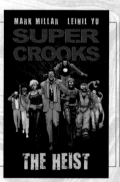

MARK MILLAR LEINIL YU
SUPER CROOKS
THE HEIST
ART BY LEINIL YU

MILLAR & McNIVEN'S
NEMESIS
ART BY STEVE MCNIVEN

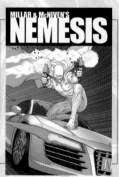

WANTED
MARK MILLAR · JG JONES · PAUL MOUNTS
ART BY JG JONES & PAUL MOUNTS

MILLAR MURPHY
CHRONONAUTS
ART BY SEAN MURPHY

MILLAR · CANETE
CHRONONAUTS
FUTURESHOCK
ART BY ERIC CANETE

MARK MILLAR DUNCAN FEGREDO
MPH
ART BY DUNCAN FEGREDO

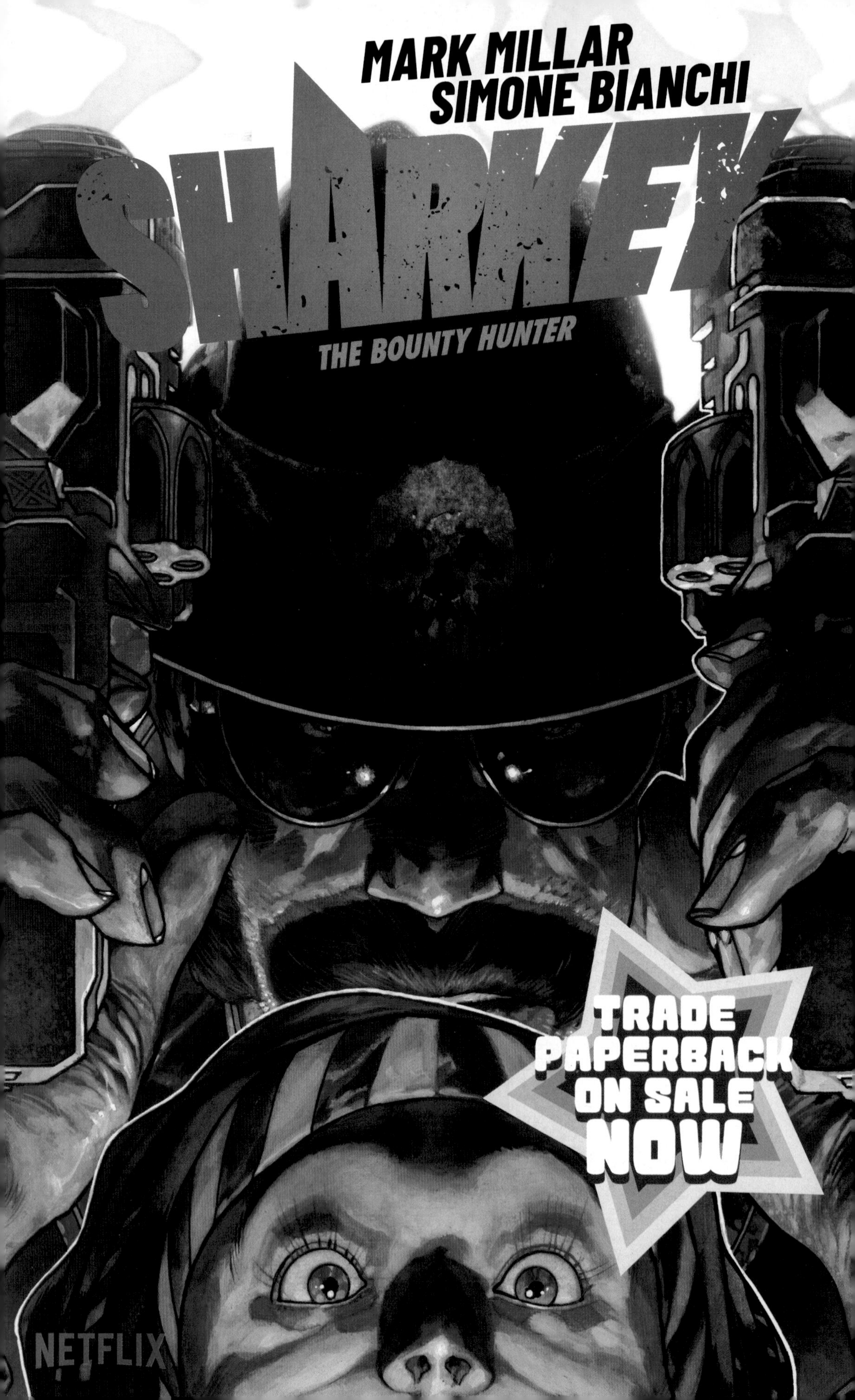
MARK MILLAR
SIMONE BIANCHI
SHARKEY
THE BOUNTY HUNTER
TRADE PAPERBACK ON SALE NOW
NETFLIX